TALK OF ANGELS

Other Books by Kate O'Brien

TALK OF ANGELS

A Novel

Kate O'Brien

with an Introduction by
Mary Gordon

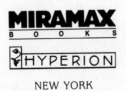

MIRAMAX
B O O K S

HYPERION

NEW YORK

First published in Great Britain by William Heinemann Ltd 1936, under the title *Mary Lavelle.*
Published by Virago Press Ltd 1984.
Copyright © 1936, Mary O'Neill
Introduction copyright © 1997, Mary Gordon

Library of Congress Cataloging-in-Publication Data

O'Brien, Kate, 1897–1974.
  [Mary Lavelle]
  Talk of angels / Kate O'Brien ; introduction by Mary Gordon.—
1st ed.
    p. cm.
  Previously published as: Mary Lavelle.
  ISBN 0-7868-6191-6
  I. Title.
PR6029.B65M3   1995
823'.912—dc20   95-17737
                                                    CIP

FIRST EDITION

10 9 8 7 6 5 4 3 2 1

CONTENTS

Amor, yo nunca penssé
aunque poderoso eras,
Que podrias tener maneras
Para trastornar la fe,
Fastagora que lo sé.

—*Canción.*—JUAN II.

KATE O'BRIEN'S *Talk of Angels*

There are affinities between the Spanish and the Irish, although the differences in climate, in landscape, and in self-
presentation obscure them to the imagination; we connect
the two countries with a shake of the head, a reluctant *aha*
tinged with disbelief. Both cultures adore the extreme and
the ideal, the dualistic, the choice that negates all other
choices. They worship the self-denying hero who, his spent
flesh still on fire, gives all. There is in the mind of both
peoples a strange and complicated pattern of simultaneous
feeding and starvation: the relationship between the auster-
ities of their Catholicism and their natural, and national,
vitality. They take life and their religion seriously, unlike
their Italian cousins who think life and death, heaven and
hell, are a bit of a joke. The Irish and the Spanish are full
of jokes, but the jokes have a sting to them, and they taste
of despair.

So it is not surprising, I suppose, to learn that upper-
class Spanish families were in the habit of hiring respectable
middle-class Irish girls to teach English to their children.
They would have understood that English is a necessary
tool for the harsh modern world, the world of commerce
and machinery, E.M. Forster's world of "telegrams and
anger." Yet they would have been reluctant to expose their
daughters to their old enemy: the Protestant English.

This is the situation of Kate O'Brien's Mary Lavelle. A
young girl from Mellick, in the West of Ireland (this is code
for O'Brien's native Limerick), engaged to a proper young
man who cannot yet afford to marry her, is advised by her

old Reverend Mother to take a job as a governess in Spain. While she is there she falls in love with both the country itself and the married son of the family. They become lovers and she returns to Ireland. In one way, this is the story of Mary Lavelle. But the richness of the novel, its packed prose, its aphoristic trenchancy, its acquisitive, relentless eye for detail, make it more than a "mere" love story. It is a novel, above all perhaps, of social observation and placement. And it is another piece of information leading to the completion of that endlessly fascinating puzzle: how does a young woman form a genuine and coherent self.

Mary Lavelle is, like many fictional heroines, a motherless girl. Her mother died in childbirth, and her father, a doctor, is a carelessly negligent parent who wounds by his indolent disregard. O'Brien gives us, in a few sharp strokes, an unforgettable picture of a type we may never have thought of, but, after her description, seem always to have known. "In 1912, when his wife died, having borne him eight children of which six survived her, Dr. Lavelle was already in his heart defeated, inefficient, and bored, yet having to fight to hold his work against doctors incalculably more competent than he.... His beauty was deceptive, for though it could promise either sexual or intellectual vitality ... Dr. Lavelle was possessed of neither. He simply had enough nervous energy to keep life jogging somehow in its monotonous track, and slowly to force his irritating young out of his way." (24)

For all that she seems an utterly conventional provincial Irish girl, Mary Lavelle, who knows herself most fully as a sister among brothers, is herself always uneasy and uneasily placed. She read the same books as her brothers, and dreamt the same dreams of wandering and adventure "until her heart was near bursting with her desire, her intention, to go everywhere one day, know everything, try everything, be committed to nothing. She would wander always, be a free lance always, belonging to no one place or family or person. That ... had been the only unshifting principle in a forever changing tissue of dreams. . . When she was twelve and thirteen her main idea had been to be free and lonely." (27) This desire for unattachment is the same as the mystic's; it is only in solitude that the soul can make its journey.

A year away from home, an opportunity to travel and see new places—all approved by Reverend Mother—the plan to be a governess to a Spanish family seems perfect. But, as her new employer, Don Pablo, the father of the family, notes, Mary possesses one quality that makes her unusual, and perhaps unsuited for the role of governess. She is astonishingly beautiful. When he meets her, this ironic, supremely self-controlled Catholic gentleman, this cynical anarchist, this admirer of Augustine and Unamuno and Racine, has his breath taken away by his first sight of the new "employee." "He had met beauty, mythical, innocent, and shameless. . . . Untouched, unaware, unflirta-tious, an unassuming governess girl, feeling homesick and uncertain ... quite unconscious that her brilliant beauty ravished the evening and rendered a skeptical and easily mannered elderly man, her respectable employer, unable to utter more than one or two banal sentences before he hurried away in fear of his own sudden, senile folly." (67) In *Talk of Angels (Mary Lavelle)*, the unknowing, tyrannical power of beauty is presented with an assiduousness that is almost relentless.

The reader learns of Mary's beauty through Don Pablo's observations, and through the ruminations of her fiancé, John, but Mary seems unaware of her own beauty, either as a possession, or an attribute, or as a marketable commodity. She understands, in a distant, distracted way, that john desires her, but since she is unable to return his desire, her understanding remains abstract. She's read a lot so she knows that a real woman is supposed to feel more when her lover kisses her than boredom and an eagerness for the kiss to be over. She feels a failure as a woman, incomplete.

Indeed, Mary's life in Ireland seems to have been a frozen half-life, of muffled perceptions and muffled sensation. It is not surprising that Spain serves as a thawing agent, the heat and the color warming the half-dead one to life. What is unusual in Kate O'Brien's treatment of this theme is the originality of her perceptions of Spain and her creation for Mary of a gradual and gradually expanding understanding.

Mary's first visions of Spain disappoint her. "Outside the station she had found a very showy street of offices and shops; some yellow trams; many beggars, many diseased and dirty people, some black-chinned workmen in black students' caps; an iron bridge, with beyond it apparently a busy square, some shabby trees, a shabby bandstand; a muddy river, clumsy-looking coal-boats; in the distance huddled heaps of slums, and the brown tower of a crumbling church; around the whole, red, sinister hills, deep-scarred and shadowy; above an undramatic pale blue sky." (73)

This is a characteristic O'Brien mode of description: the series of closely observed details piled, one on top of the other, like a litany, an incantation. In an astonishing series of long, loving descriptions of the Spanish countryside, O'Brien takes us through Mary's seduction by the land. But it is not only the land that takes her in. Her initial disappointment with Spain falls away as she makes connections both to the family she works for, and more importantly, to the other "misses," the other Irish women adrift in the city.

The description of the "misses" and their situation is the most engaging part of the novel. They call each other by their last names, and eagerly include the new, beautiful stranger. At first, Mary finds their roughness difficult to endure. "She found the crudity of the misses' intercourse surprising, their use of surnames *tout court*, their interest in the male sex, their prudery, their vindictive attitude towards their employers, and nonintelligent insolence towards the life that went on about them, their obvious poverty and social isolation, their distorted self-respect, their backhanded decency and *esprit de corps*. . ." (92)

What an astonishingly packed and efficient piece of prose this is! Once again, the sharpness of individual details creates an avalanche effect when they are joined together. The juxtaposition of qualities is surprising and masterful: interest in the male sex is coupled with prudery, nonintelligent insolence towards life around them is joined to backhanded decency and *esprit de corps*.

But O'Brien doesn't leave our understanding of the "misses" at the level of the personal or the psychological. Like a miniaturist Balzac, she places their situation in a rich social grounding. The most striking of the "misses," Agatha Conlon, bitterly describes their anomalous state: "That's what's up with all us misses. . . . We've never been graded. We come out here with the good old Irish small town notion that we're "ladies"—and then by degrees we're nothing. It turns us into what you see. . . . We came out in our green youth because our parents had no money to spend on us, and saw no likelihood of getting us husbands. We had qualifications for this job—in what other would you be given a comfortable existence merely because you are a Catholic and can speak English fluently, if badly? We're not even required to know how to teach. It's jam for the stupid." (204)

Of all the "misses," only Agatha Conlon has taken an interest in Spain. She has become an aficionado of the bull-fight and takes Mary along to one, to the horror of the other Irish women. Mary is mesmerized. "Slower than the crowd, she was out of step and lagging, still in the silence of the tragedy now finished with. She was absent-minded as its enactor seemed. Death, so strangely approached, so grotesquely given and taken, under the summer sky, for the amusement of nonentities, death made into an elaborate play, for money and cheers, and enacting in the course of the show a variety of cruelties and dangers; death asking for helpless victims as well as the hazards of courage; death and pain made comic, petty, and relentless for an after-noon's thrill." (116)

Somehow, the intensely formal drama of the bullfight frees Mary to know and to appreciate Spain. Her gentle charges, the three daughters of Don Pablo, involve her in the routines of their sheltered and cultivated lives. Pilar, almost ready to come out, is vain and obsessed with cloth-ing. Milagros is intellectual, her father's daughter. Nieves, the youngest, dreams of being an English boy. Mary's daily round, her place in the family, distant, but comfortable, her appreciation of the life of Spain, her visits to the cafe for the good-natured gossip of the other misses seem to be giving her the experience she wants. But then she meets Juanito.

The shock of desire is the final tap on the shell of Mary Lavelle's consciousness. Juanito, "one of the great men of Spain," has a perfect, rich and fashionable wife, and a little boy to whom he is devoted. But he and Mary meet, see each other, and all is lost. O'Brien grants sexual passion the same educative place as D.H. Lawrence does. Desiring each other, knowing their love to be impossible, Juanito and Mary nevertheless know and are fully known. Their Catholicism allows them the terms for understanding their situation. Divorce is impossible; a living martyrdom, shared although they must be forever separated, is a familiar text for these two raised on the lives of the saints, their flesh torn apart by wild beasts, their eyes wild from years of exile in the desert.

In loving Juanito and being loved by him, Mary grows from an unconscious girl to a woman capable of inhabiting the fullness of her life. She is even able to absorb, with compassion and a lack of revulsion, the declaration of lesbian love that is offered her by Agatha Conlon. She knows she can no longer take her place among the decorous trees of Mellick, under its cool, gray skies. She cannot be the wife of the young man with the terrier pup, who lost her by his inability to marry her without a nest egg, and through allowing her out of his sight. Yet Mary will become the "free lance," she knew herself meant to be as a child. Unattached, homeless, she finds her true vocation, like and not like one of the nuns who had the idea to send her to Spain.

Some very good books are immediately placeable as "of their time," and *Talk of Angels* is one of them. Or perhaps it seems older than its time. It is set in the Twenties, but it is a shock to see Mary smoking, so nineteenth century a heroine does she seem. Kate O'Brien was born in 1897, a full generation after the great modernists, but she seems to have taken nothing from them. The straight narrative line of *Talk of Angels*, its firm moral position, seem far removed from the linguistic experiments and psychological complications of Joyce, Proust, and Mann.

Talk of Angels has some of its roots in O'Brien's own biography. She was born in Limerick, her mother died when she was five, and she went on to convent school. Unlike Mary Lavelle, however, she went on to University College, Dublin, where her gifts were marked by the eminent Irish writer Austin Clarke. She worked for a year as a governess in Spain; it was that experience that began her life-long love affair with that country. She wrote two books about Spain, a travel book, *Farewell Spain* (1937) and a monograph on St. Theresa of Avila.

After Spain, she moved to London where she worked as a journalist for the Manchester *Guardian* and other newspapers. Her first nonjournalistic works were plays, but it was with her first novel, *Without My Cloak* (1931) that she began to win acclaim. *Talk of Angels* was her third novel. It was first published in 1936, at the beginning of the Spanish Civil War. Because we sense that we are reading of a way of life doomed to be lost, because we must think of Juanito as one of the heroic architects of the new Spain destined to be smothered by the dark blanket of Franco, the situation of Mary Lavelle takes on a real poignance. The dignity of the life, its richness, its imaginative and intellectual play will be, we know, squashed soon by the Fascist boot. The Hispano-Suizas will be driven, not by idealistic and elegant ladies and gentlemen, but by the children of torturers.

Another incident that roots *Mary Lavelle* firmly in its time is the fact that it was, when it was published, banned in Ireland. It is interesting to speculate whether it was the lesbian pass or the adulterous heterosexual love that was intolerable for the clerical censors. Perhaps it was the unavoidable Catholic consciousness that seemed to condone both these events that brought down the ecclesiastical axe. It is a typical Irish irony that the author of one book banned by the church should have written another about one of its greatest saints. But Kate O'Brien was comfortable with such extremes—she reveled in them.

Talk of Angels is remarkable for its mixture of qualities. It is aphoristic and rhapsodic, lyrical and spare, Romantic and Classical, untrammeled and restrained. It is also terrifically readable. But the pleasure of the readability needed be a source of guilt for those Jansenist minds schooled in the Irish mist or Spanish sun. It's not just a page-turner love story; undergirding it is a finely wrought, tough-minded prose that demands on its own strict terms, our attention and respect.

—Mary Gordon

PROLOGUE

The trunk of a 'Miss,' going over the Pyrenees, is no great matter.

It is a modest trunk as a rule, containing only the necessities of the simple. For that reason it does not seem to be merely luggage but achieves distinction, having according to the eyes that fall on it a comic, pathetic or reassuring aspect. For be it new or old it retains, like those persons in its place of origin who packed and labelled it, the air of never having wandered far from parish bounds—an appearance which subjectively is comic, pathetic or reassuring.

Such a trunk, exposed to Customs officers, keeps its self-respect. It offers to their examination the possessions of a girl setting out to earn her bread. On top, on the tray, they will find two summer hats and last year's winter one reblocked, and may lift the tissue-paper from a frilly afternoon frock and from two evening dresses, a new old and an old. Time, not the Customs officials, must reveal if a 'Miss' will need these, but it was probably her worldly aunt from Dublin who insisted on their going in. "The child looks sweet in her pink, and you never know…" When the tray is lifted the owner of the trunk, still anxiously at authority's disposition, yet hopes for a lessening of scrutiny. The officials are free to examine her face-powder, her lavender water, her talc. Clean handkerchiefs, darned stockings, new stockings. Petrol-smelling gloves. Frilly blouses, wollen jumpers. The silver brushes mother gave her on her sixteenth birthday. A workbox, a little manicure set. Nothing to be ashamed of. But chemises too, and nightdresses. The owner of the trunk grows fidgety as official hands plunge deep among these necessities until they reach her wrapped-up shoes, her handful of books, her odds and ends of parting presents. The trunk is shut then and the chalk squiggle imposed upon it. The girl and her equipment for the decent life may enter Spain.

As the men refasten the straps they do not think that a die has been cast. Nor does the owner, whose concern is with where she put her phrase-book, or with the problem of the porter's tip. Nevertheless, the strap-fastening and chalk-squiggling are gestures of fate, and she is afoot now, befriended by her trunk, on the errand of keeping alive.

A trivial errand from every perspective save that of the creature whose mission it is. From the angle of the mountains and history about Irun one is bound to disturb the far too easy and platitudinous derision of mountains and history. But on most mornings of the year the Pyrenees are shut from the human eye by their own rains, and fortunately the young are often indifferent or forgetful towards such facts of the world's past as may have been imparted to them. So neither altitudes nor ghosts can get in their hackneyed mockery as an unaware girl goes by them about her business. Her future is her treasure, small but proportioned to her, as history and mountains are not. Hers too, as they are not. That she is about to spend a meagre little of it, a time-marking year or two, under a strange sky, among voices and faces that will say nothing relevant to her, seems no more than a normal expediency, a something in parenthesis which hardly widens at all the unalarming distance between her and her reality, her personal dream, the place from which her own life will eventually flower. She does not know that youth is the future for ever becoming present and past; she does not know that what each man calls his own reality advances on him and shapes itself as much from without as from within, from accident as from preconception; she does not know that so long as heart and clock are moving a life cannot stay still.

There is a vast deal that a miss does not know. In 1922, for instance—the year of our story—she did not know any more than anyone else that nine years later a revolution would practically wipe out her obsolete and ill-defined profession. But she had no idea that it was obsolete, and had she thought so would not have greatly cared, for her choice of it as an expedient, however enforced-seeming, reveals her as an individualist, hand-to-mouth and inefficient, but capable of dream and unfit to march with earnestness in the column of female bread-winners, or indeed in any column at all. She becomes a miss because not her wits but her intuitional antennae tell her that it is an occupation which will let her personality be; she becomes one because she does not want to be anything but herself for long, because she is in love with a young man in Ireland maybe—all the English governesses in Spain are Irish—or is in love with love, or with indefiniteness, or with her home or her religion—because in short she has that within her which makes her politely unconcerned with the immediacies. She knows her eventual place, and will be content to fill it. Meantime she can be dutiful and responsible, docile to the just claims of employers. Pleased with new scenes too, and amused to smatter at a new language. An individualist who does not mind temporising. Someone poor maybe more or less befriended, someone with roots, someone modestly self-contained, she crosses the Pyrenees with her modest trunk.

THREE LETTERS

Casa Pilar,
Cabantes,
Altorno,
Spain.
12th June, 1922.

DEAREST FATHER,—

I hope that by now you have had my telegram and are not worrying about me any more. The children here, whose English is not bad, sent it for me over the telephone last night about an hour after I arrived. But I am still wondering if the people at the other end of the telephone managed to get an understandable message through. I hope they did, as this letter will not reach you for about four days.

I am very well. I slept like a dead thing last night and have almost forgotten how tired I was when I got here. The journey from Paris to Irun was uncomfortable and afterwards getting from there to Altorno was very complicated. No one seemed to understand a word of English or my very bad French.

It is very pleasant here and I shall be happy, I think. Everyone is being kind to me and the children get great fun out of acting as interpreters between me and everyone else.

Cabantes is only a little fishing village where a few rich people have recently taken a fad to live, finding Altorno

1

too noisy. The Casa Pilar is at the extreme end of the village, right on the little squat pier where the sardine-boats come in. The terrace of the house is only separated from the pier by a low, flat wall on which the children love to sit. They and their father are always talking with the fishermen and love watching the disputes that go on between them and the wild-looking sardine-women. The windows of my room look right over this little pier, and if I knew Spanish I am so near the boatmen even here on the second floor that I could hear all their conversation. It's lovely to have the sea so close to my windows. The house is very big, of yellowish stone and rather ugly. About a hundred years old, the children say, but their father only bought it when he was married in 1896. Everything is very luxurious. There are four bathrooms, I think, and I seem already to have seen seven or eight maids. The garden is big and has glorious dark trees all round it in a semi-circle. It is a quiet place to live in, and the view in all directions is lovely. The mountains away behind this house look craggy and red—the children say they are full of iron-mines—but across the bay and all around Cabantes is very leafy and flowery, and though foreign to me, of course, not a bit what I expected Spain to be.

I think I will find my work easy enough—except the English lesson every morning which I am worried about. I really don't know in the least how to teach. Otherwise, chaperoning the three while they have their other lessons, taking them for walks, escorting them to their friends' houses, and talking English all the time—that sort of thing ought to be easy enough. They had a 'miss' for two years until last June. They don't seem to have liked her much, but she taught them a fair amount of English. I like them, particularly the two younger ones. And I daresay I shall like their mother too when we can manage to understand each other. She is very pretty and seems kind. Certainly I am well looked after. I have meals by myself in a sort of breakfast room. They were apologetic about this, and said that it was because 'papa,' whom I have not yet seen, objects to having to talk to a stranger at every meal. I am greatly relieved about it. I dreaded the idea of having meals with them always. I believe misses usually have to.

I must write to Mother Liguori now, to thank her for getting me this job, and also I must write to John —so forgive me if I end up here. I will give more details of my life later on, when I know it better. My next letter home must be to Aunt Cissy, though. Tell her that she must excuse my not writing to her to-day, as really I haven't much time. Give her my love, of course, and to dear Hannah and the cats. And to Jenny and Sheila when you write. I will send them postcards one of these days. I hope that you and Aunt Cissy are keeping very well. I shall write as often as I can. Meantime be sure that I am perfectly well and happy and am almost certain to be quite content here.

With once again my best love to everyone,

Your loving daughter,
MARY.

Casa Pilar,
Cabantes,
Altorno,
Spain.
12*th June,* 1922.

DEAR MOTHER LIGUORI,—

I arrived here safely yesterday evening, and feel that I must write at once to tell you how nice everything seems and to thank you very much once again for finding the job for me and arranging everything. The three girls whom I am to have charge of met my train in Altorno with the car and we drove out here to Cabantes which is right on the sea—about ten miles from Altorno. The girls are very lively and I imagine I shall get on all right with them. They can speak some English, which is a relief, as no one else in the house or anywhere seems to speak anything but Spanish or Basque. I got into great muddles on the journey from the frontier, through not knowing Spanish. I must try to learn some quickly.

You will forgive the dullness and shortness of this letter, as I have not much time for writing to-day, and am still a bit tired from the journey. I hope that you are very well. I wish I knew something about how to teach English. These girls have to have an hour every morning of English grammar and composition. I am in a funk about that —but the rest of my duties seem easy enough.

I am very grateful to you about the job, and you know that I will do my best to be a success in it. I am very well looked after, and everyone in the house seems kind and friendly.

4

With every good wish and many thanks, dear Mother Liguori,

Your affectionate pupil,
MARY LAVELLE.

Casa Pilar,
Cabantes,
Altorno,
Spain.
12*th June,* 1922.

MY DEAREST JOHN,—

I have just had to write to Father and to Mother Liguori and my hand is getting tired—so I'm afraid you will only get a dull sort of letter. I'm sorry for that, because there are thousands of things I want to tell you. Still—how could I possibly tell them? You know I'm no better than you at writing things down. And, oh, that reminds me—have you written to me yet? Letters take at least four days from here to Ireland! Isn't that awful? Still, I'm hoping that you may have posted one the day after I left, and if you did I might with luck get it to-morrow. The postman comes twice a day, and always by the seafront. He comes in at a little iron gate from the pier, and every time this gate is opened a bell rings—just like a convent bell. When I'u in my room or the children's study I can hear it. I'm dying for news of you and Mellick and everyone. It seems much longer than five days since I left. And all the trains and boats and taxis I've been in since then! You must admit that for someone who had never travelled at all I undertook a pretty good journey once I started! All the time since

5

I left, in London and in Paris, and even yesterday at the frontier and in the little mountain-train coming here— though by then I was stupid with tiredness, I think—I was seeing things that I wanted to show you or tell you about. You'll never hear about them now though, because they are all jumbled in my head and I am so much occupied with things that are strange to me here that I cannot get back to the impressions of the journey. Anyway, it all went smoothly enough in spite of the language question, and I found people extraordinarily nice, even when we hadn't the least chance of understanding each other. (In Paris I discovered that my French, which was supposed to be good at school, is *worse* than useless!) Nothing nasty happened and no one was the least bit rude or sinister—so there was no need at all to be in the kind of fuss you got into, dearest. But lots of funny things cropped up, and there were muddles galore, and really it's no thanks to me, but only because of the kindness of several total strangers that I got to Altorno at all. I hope that Father or Aunt Cis telephoned you when they got my wire—they promised they would.

I wish I knew how to describe this place so as to make it seem real to you—but I never could. You see, it's entirely unlike everything you and I know, but it is not a bit like my idea of Spain—or yours, I imagine. And if I say that already after twenty-four hours I feel familiar with it, you'll say I'm mad. But I mean it. Perhaps it's the sea under my window that gives me the illusion— because now the tide is out, and the smell of seaweed is coming into the room exactly as if I were in Kilbeggan. I suppose that makes me feel less strange. The bay is lovely, and I have a grand view of it. It has two very long breakwaters, one jutting out from the extreme end of the sea-front, and the other from Torcal just opposite. Ships from everywhere—and fairly big ones, about as big as come into Mellick—sail past my windows up to Altorno. The children say that I will get to know all the flags of the world from watching the ships. But I prefer watching the goings-on on the little stubby fishermen's pier, right under my nose. The house is practically built on that pier, and the boatmen sit on our terrace wall by the hour. The ferries for Torcal start from there—it's amusing to see them load up, and the sardine boats come in here. When one is in a terrific bell rings, and the sardine-women come tearing up like demented creatures from the market-place. There are ructions then for about fifteen minutes!

There are mountains behind Cabantes—full of iron mines from which most of the rich people round here get their money. The children say that a great many Englishmen have jobs in these mines and foundries, engineers and so on—and that there is a large English colony in Altorno. But the mountains that I can see now across the water are only little hills. Torcal looks a pretty place—with white houses sloping down to the sea, and so does Playablanca, which is nearer here, and faces the breakwaters, and has a real strand. The only way to get from Cabantes to these places is in the little motor ferry boats I told you about. I went over this morning with the children to be shown the sights of Playablanca. These two places are very little more than summer resorts—especially Playablanca, which seems to

be nothing but new-looking villas; the children tell me
it is practically a dead place for ten months of the year.
It is very quiet now—August and September are its
season. All the houses are open then, they say, and the
strand is packed with children, and there are crowds of
yachts in the bay. The Yacht Club is built out on the
water. The king is a member of it, and he may be here
in September to race his yachts.

I like Cabantes much better than Playablanca. It seems
a very old little town with an arcaded market place, and
hilly streets going up to a brown church. It's a kind of
suburb of Altorno; electric trains go in there every half-
hour. The journey only takes about fifteen minutes, so
I shall go in on my first free afternoon. Coming from
the train last evening I thought it seemed a very lively
town—there was a lot of noise—but it looks poor and
wild and very crumbly and dirty—anyhow, the part we
passed through.

I can tell you very little about my life here, as I know
nothing of it yet. Serious lessons, from me and from the
other tutors, will go on until the end of this month and
then cease until October. But to-day the girls had a
holiday from all their classes—in my honour! They are
nice girls—Pilár, Nieves and Milagros—called after Our
Lady of the Pillar, of the Sorrows and of the Miracles. They
are seventeen, fifteen and fourteen. Pilár will be coming
out next year, she says—and she is very full of that
subject. She is dark, the darkest of the family, very
pretty, and laughs a lot. I like the other two better, I
think. Their mother is very pretty too. I have not seen
the children's father yet. Thank the Lord he won't have

a stranger at table with him every day, so I eat my meals alone. I'm delighted about this. The food is awfully nice, but you are expected to eat more than is humanly possible. There is wine on my table always, but I haven't had the courage to try it yet! Nice business if I got drunk! What would you say if you heard that of me?

My dearest—it is so difficult trying to tell you every-thing in a letter. My hand is awfully tired, but there are heaps of other things to say. About the house, which is very large and comfortable. I have an enormous room, with a huge white and gilt bed, very old-looking, but terribly comfortable. There are three long windows in my room, and they open on to a balcony and look over the bay towards Torcal. The sun is marvellous out there now and I can hear all sorts of sounds that are growing familiar already. But I must really go back to the study now—it is just across the landing, and the girls are probably waiting for me there—to go and play tennis, or something. They have a rather bad court. You'd like the garden, I think. At least, you'd say everything was ridiculously arranged perhaps, but you'd be interested in the curious trees, and the masses of flowers. Things flower twice a year here, they say. There are camellias and fuchsias, and roses everywhere—and simply torrents of wistaria! And you've never seen so many flowerpots—painted yellow and white and blue. They'd annoy you terribly, I think!

Oh, John—I must stop. You mustn't think that all this gabble means that I don't miss you. I wish I could tell you how I do! Hardly five minutes go by in which I don't think of you, or want to show you something

9

or talk to you. I get the most awful fits of loneliness for Mellick, and panic about everything. But I know these fits are very silly. It was the best thing to do, wasn't it—to come out here for a year or so, until we can get married? But there's no need to go over all that again. We thrashed it out so thoroughly. I'll be quite happy here, and I'll learn Spanish and get to know something about the world—or a bit of it. Which will be no harm, will it? I know you think me rather a fool—so perhaps foreign life—you could hardly call it foreign travel—will improve my mind for you. Dearest, I hope it will. You are so good and brainy, and have to work so hard for your pittance that it seems cruel to plan to marry you—and make things even harder the first minute they seem to improve. But I want to marry you—so what can I do, except promise to be a good wife? You deserve much more than that, but that is all I have to offer. Dearest boy, take care of yourself, and send me a lot of letters. Tell me all the news of Mellick. It's funny that, apart from missing you, I miss just being at home very much—although you know that with the way father has been going on lately I wasn't happy, and thought I was dying to be away from everything. But now the mere idea of Mellick makes me afraid of crying. Oh, John—I have never in my life written so long a letter, and I'm afraid you'll be saying by now that you hope I never will again!

Good-bye, dearest. Please write to me. Love from
MARY.

PS.—I don't like to put that snapshot of you on my table, as the girls are always hopping into my room. But I keep it in the drawer of my writing-table and often look at it. It's awfully like you, and looks very nice in the little leather frame.—M.

The writer of these three letters addressed them with care, the first to Dr. Thomas Lavelle, 25, Upper Mourne Street, Mellick, Irlanda, the second to Mother Liguori O'Dowd, Convent of the Heart of Mary, Mellick, Irlanda, and the third to John MacCurtain, Esq., 16, Marguerite Terrace, Ballyburnagh Road, Mellick, Irlanda. As she folded the many thin sheets of the last, she stroked the paper gently and smiled.

When she had written in this letter that already she felt familiar with her new surroundings, the statement rang curiously to her, but she had let it stand, knowing the phrase as true as she, unpractised in writing or thinking about herself, was likely to achieve. She did not re-examine it at present.

She looked about her receptively. Her room was, as she had said, enormous, and being furnished with pieces discarded as shabby by Doña Consuelo, victim, with most of her contemporaries of the middle-class, of *art nouveau*—it had an elegance dismissed from the rest of the house. Mary Lavelle viewed its white walls, baroque and immense gold bed, its chipped mirrors, and above all, the little gilded shrine from which Our Lady, in muslin dress and sapphire crown, smiled with lovely innocence—she viewed all this new setting with a pang of mingled homesickness and pleasure. And the sounds which came in through her open windows, already in twenty-four hours growing—as she had said—familiar, increased this mingling of emotion. For though she

heard them still with a foreigner's exasperated ear—the
boatmen's shouts, the strange, wild singing of some idle
boy—*cante hondo*, the children called it—the soft gossip
of women taking their ease on the pier—yet they had,
though incomprehensible, a summer evening orthodoxy,
an eternalness, so reassuring as to be very sad. She
smiled, nevertheless, against nostalgia—summer evenings in another place of white skies and grey waters,
of tall brown houses and shabby sycamore trees—
summer evenings where every sound had its immediate
meaning and a familiarity of twenty years—had they not
been sad too, and exasperating? Aunt Cissy was right,
very likely, about the folly of sitting in idleness, but
this room invited some assimilatory contemplation.
She smiled, counting its blessings. She had never been
ruler of so much space before, had never had three
windows and a balcony to call her own, had never slept
in a bed so vast and fairy-tale. She had been brought
up in unself-conscious habits and therefore was not so
much regretful as relieved that the mirrors' positions
made it impossible that she should see herself when
arranged for sleep—and yet this morning she had
wondered, lying there, how in fact one did appear in
such a cloudy resting-place. Now remembering that
absurd reflection, she laughed at herself self-consciously,
and opening her writing-table drawer, took out the
photograph of John MacCurtain in its little leather frame.
It was a brilliantly good snapshot. John with his pipe
and his terrier-pup, and his invincible, good smile. She
smiled back at him and his intense familiarity somewhat
neutralised her mood by exacting an orthodox reaction

of sentimentality. But she wished now that she had some of his courage. For at any minute she must return to her new charges in the study, and the girl was as shy as she was self-controlled. "Dearest," she said, and reluctantly put the photograph away.

THE CHILDREN

Pilár, Nieves and Milagros Areavaga waited for their governess in the study, discussing her in their own language with freedom and good nature. They were used to governesses. Their first years, until Pilár was ten, had been ruled by a Frenchwoman; after her there had been Fräulein until in 1919 their parents thought it time they learnt some English. So Miss Murphy, 'Miss Anita,' had taken charge, but a month ago had forsaken them for a household in Madrid, "needing a change, needing a little gaiety." This craving of Miss Murphy's had amused Pilár.

"I don't know what you're worrying about, Pilár," said Milagros now. Milagros, grey-eyed and fourteen, was remarkable for detachment. "When you're more used to her you'll see that she's exactly like a miss."

Nieves smiled. "How can you possibly think that?"

Milagros looked up from her needlework. "I saw the usual waterproof in her room," she said gently, "and the usual regrettable hat."

Pilár chuckled. "When a miss here in Altorno wants a new hat—you know, Milagros, *the* hat—what on earth does she do?"

"Climbs the steps to Allera and lights a candle, I imagine."

"Still, it's all very well for you and Nieves to take it so cheerfully—she's not very likely to be around

14

when you come out, but next year, really——"

"Does she shake *your* conceit, Pilár?" asked Milagros.

"A raving beauty for a chaperone—wouldn't you feel a fool?"

"I won't have a chaperone, perhaps."

"You'll have to when you come out."

"Perhaps I won't come out," said Milagros.

She could always amuse her two elder sisters, who laughed benevolently now.

"Will you stay up here embroidering always?" asked Nieves.

"Wouldn't be bad. Or I might be a nun."

"Oh no!" Nieves' thin face looked unhappy, but Pilár was bland.

"Good," she said. "Then we can shelve all our real praying on to you. But aren't we playing tennis to-day? Where is the Miss?"

"She's writing letters. Give her a chance," said Nieves.

"What does mother think of her, do you imagine?" Pilár was still worrying.

"Annoyed, very likely; but—well, a lot of money has been spent in fetching her here and perhaps her looking as she does won't matter much for the next twelve months——" Nieves shrugged in friendly imitation of their mother. "Father hasn't seen her yet," she added.

"He never will see her," said Milagros. The others looked interrogatory. "I don't think he has ever even seen us."

But Pilár was by way of being a cherished family beauty. "You go too far with your nonsense," she said severely.

"I wasn't criticising," said the fourteen-year-old.

"Oh no," said Pilár sarcastically. "You approve of father because you think he models himself on you." She moved towards a mirror on the wall and studied her complexion with gravity. She was the smallest of the three and was roundly and femininely made. Her frock of pale blue linen fitted and became her well. Her black hair gleamed and she had lively eyes of so light a brown that they were almost gold; they shone agreeably in a small, pretty face to which now, in her eighteenth year, she was allowed to apply cosmetics.

Nieves leant over the balcony. Thin and gawky in a 'middy' blouse and an old blue skirt, she looked an innocent fifteen-year-old. Her eyes were either grey or blue. There was a sweet and nervous beauty in her face. She liked the view from this balcony and took a great interest in the flags of the ships. Above all, she liked to see the English flag go by. Her chief day-dream was that she was an English boy at Eton. A Catholic, naturally, but at Eton. Catholics did go there.

Milagros scrutinised Pilár scrutinising her complexion.

"When Mother said you could paint your face, Pilár, did you know right off how to do it?"

Pilár smiled inattentively.

Milagros talked more to Pilár than to Nieves, because she was the better target for the kind of remark that occurred to the youngest sister. It was conceivable that Nieves might even die of pain if one made such jokes about her foibles as Pilár either ignored or giggled at. But Milagros admired Pilár really. There she was, complete, confident, cap-à-pie ready for everything. The

16

youngest sister did not analyse this temperamental condition—merely she felt it with pleasure. Her face, pale and bony like Nieves', was nearly always amiably composed. The grey of her eyes never gleamed blue as did Nieves'. Were it not for coltish awkwardness and for the schoolroom haphazardry of her clothes, she might have been mistaken for the eldest of the three girls. She suspected the day-dreams of Nieves, who looked indeed a shameless dreamer, but for the most part she let them be; she teased Pilár with accurate wit about the myths by which her idle hours were very probably fed; but no one scratched at her inner life, whatever it was. So the three grew in affectionate peace and detachment; they were well-behaved, intelligent children, happy and beloved, devoted to their parents.

When their Miss entered the study they all turned towards her with pleasant smiles and Milagros stood up and put away her needlework. Each of the three made an effort to switch her mind to the English idiom.

Their governess eyed them with caution.

"I'm sorry if I've kept you waiting. Shall we go to the garden now?"

They went down wide and polished flights of shallow stairs. Nieves carried the Miss's racket; Pilár, hanging on her right arm, carried her letters to give to the gardener; Milagros brought up the rear.

"We won't call you Miss Lavelle, if you don't mind," said Pilár. "We don't use names in that way in Spain. Miss Murphy was 'Miss Anita' here. What is your name, Miss?"

"Mary."

"Ah, Mary, Maria. So are we all Maria, of course. May we call you Miss Maria?"

They strolled through the garden to the tennis court. On the way Pilár, with a great deal of vigorous talk, gave Miss Maria's letters to the gardener to post. He was a smiling man with a gigantic black moustache.

"I shall never understand Spanish," said the governess as they left Jaime behind.

"Perhaps not," said Milagros, "but that was Basque. Pilár has a bad habit of speaking Basque to the servants."

"It's the only way of making sure they understand," said Pilár.

Nieves came out of a tool-shed with some rackets.

"Milagros is a snob about the way people speak," she said. "She thinks that her own Castilian is the purest in Altorno."

"Castilian? How do you mean?"

"Spanish of the educated, Miss Maria," said Milagros. "I beg of you don't learn any Spanish from Pilár."

The governess smiled at the juvenile pomposity.

This passage of English conversation, though conducted gallantly enough by the three Spaniards, was not unnaturally starred with grammatical and phonetic errors which, set down in narrative, would be tedious. But there was comedy in hearing all through it in these eager Spanish voices, the high, insidious singing of the Cork accent. Miss Anita must indeed have worn the green, and Mary Lavelle could only assume that she now brought to the Areavagas another kind of brogue. Poor Milagros, in love with purity!

They played tennis. Miss Anita had not been an

athlete. "She was about fifty, Miss Maria," said Pilár, "and rather like Jaime to look at—the same kind of moustache." She had not pretended to know even how to count in tennis. The new miss could do better than that. Nieves drank up the curious terms—'love, deuce, vantage'—an Etonian would know these things. Milagros lobbed with good-humoured indifference, but Pilár, whose figure was round enough to worry her, was all for energetic play. The four warmed up to the business, shouted and giggled, and when at last they dropped their rackets and Mary sank on to a wooden bench under a cherry tree, the children crowded to her, relaxed and friendly, wanting to gossip.

"Talk to us, Miss Maria; tell us about you."

Mary glanced backward over her own simple, folded life.

"Me? There's nothing to tell. My father is a doctor——"

"Oh? A good one?"

"I—I hope so. There are six of us. I'm the second——"

"How old?"

"Twenty-two. My mother died when I was ten.'

"Ah—who looked after you?"

"Father's sister, my aunt."

"What do you call your aunt?"

"Aunt Cissy."

They gurgled and had to have an explanation. Cecilia —Cissy. "Ugly name," said Nieves.

"I suppose she is an ugly woman?" said Milagros.

"No."

"Go on. Tell us more—about the others of the family. About where you live. Have you a—what is the English word?—Have you a—a sweetheart?"

Mary answered the questions except that about a sweetheart. Curiosity slackened by degrees; the effort to talk English could not be indefinitely sustained; Spanish phrases fell apologetically—small silences slipped between voice and voice.

"Just this time yesterday we met you at the station," said Nieves.

Pondering this, Mary looked about her. It seemed a longer time that she had known this view. While the children had been questioning her, looking at her with confidence, asking the English phrase for this and that, she had experienced a private shock—had realised with icy freshness that she was at last that unconsidered thing —grown-up. It had never struck her before that she had perhaps attained, or should attain to that condition. But here she was in a foreign land, in charge of something, a teacher, a giver, however diffident, of information, a paid employee, an adult. The news had sounded in her suddenly amid the talk, had clicked as if something moved in her breast to uncover the waiting fact. Acceptance had almost tied with it, and the girl had been unaware of any sadness, only felt, but vaguely, that something reeled away, that memory's recession stretched surprisingly. Mellick where she lived and had left her heart, where she would live again and die, was remote and cloudy in this minute—out of focus, as assuredly this actual view was also, since nothing could in twenty-four hours have grown as clear and intimate as it suggested itself to be. She considered it now, half resentfully. In the grassy foreground roses, camellias and geraniums overwhelmed the sight with flower, while to left and right the walled boundaries of the garden were loftily and darkly groved. The yellow stone block of the great villa cut off sight of the little pier and the open bay beyond the breakwaters, but straight in front, beyond the low terrace wall and the theatrical wrought-iron gate with its swaying bell, lay a part of that view that filled the girl's bedroom windows—Torcal's white villas, quiet water and idle yachts; the sands and roofs of Playablanca; a foreign funnel moving inwards to Altorno. Theatrical it might all be called—like the gate and the camellias, but that its colours were gentle and its mood unassuming. It truly did not excite resentment. But still it puzzled Mary—for it was not tame either, it induced the eyes, though without compelling them. It had no proclamation in it. In that it was—surprisingly—like Mellick.

The name sent her dreaming back again into what surely was reality. If it was seven o'clock at home now— but she supposed it wasn't yet—Father and Aunt Cissy would be sitting down to dinner in the breakfast-room at Upper Mourne Street. (The dining-room was rarely sat in save by the doctor's waiting patients.) The breakfast-room had a large window opening on to a little grassy back garden, very neat, with a stunted fig-tree in the middle. This room and the restricted view from its battered window-seat were for Mary enduring symbols of childhood. She could see the darning basket on the seat now, *The Irish Rosary*, the *Daily Sketch*. She could see the brilliant fall of evening light on the Turkey carpet, and the cats discreetly lurking at the sunny end, out of reach of the doctor's peevishness. She felt the silence of the room and Aunt Cissy's dumb uneasiness until a thump on the door would announce that Hannah was trying to open it while carrying a heavy tray. She would open it, as always, unassisted, and sweep in, as always, at the double, dishes rattling. Father at the sideboard putting soda water in his whisky glass. No Jenny or Sheila or Tom or Mary to snap at this evening. "Take your nose out of that book, sir!" "Think of sitting down to table with hands like those?" "Mooning again, Mary? Always this damnable moony look!" He was eliminating three small exasperations, though Jenny and Sheila would be home in August from their Belgian convent, poor kids, and would Tom ever persevere in his attempt to be a Jesuit? Heaven, what a row there would be if he did not! Well, Donal was gone for good, to his reportership in Leeds, and Jimmy was even further out of range existing no one knew how in California. These two brothers, the latter a year older than Mary, and Donal eighteen months her junior, had been her first, best playmates, and their shadows were often astir in her heart. Sometimes of late, sitting on the window-seat, she had wondered if either of them, far away, remembered the breakfast-room and the lively life they had led there when father was safe on his rounds. Disputes over claims in the new Sexton Blake, accusations about pages missing from *The Fifth Form at Saint Dominic's*. Well, here was she remembering too at last, in a foreign land, something which had seemed as much of self and as little to be remembered as one's right hand; here was

she, further from her roots than Donal, as far from them
for all intents as even Jimmy. And if there was a pang in
this reflection perhaps it was mainly of pleasure to be
sharing something once again with her lost brothers.
Ah, yes, the breakfast-room would be quiet to-night,
unless father, as sometimes arbitrarily he did, took
exception to Hannah's quite good cooking. Aunt Cissy
would make no scene against him, such as Tom or
Jimmy used to make, nor would she burst into tears as
Mary herself had occasionally been fool enough to do.
Aunt Cissy never answered Father—she echoed him.
She never stood up for anyone, never took anyone's part,
never uttered an opinion. She looked after the house
very well on a small allowance; she prayed a great deal
and confabulated with priests; she was a worry to the
children, but not a troublesome one when unsupported
by her brother; in his presence she was spineless and a
tell-tale. In her youth she had tried to be a nun and
failed, Heaven knows why; but the story gave her in
Mellick a romantic, 'apart' aura, and she was admired in
the town as a saintly and beautiful woman. Mary,
remembering her now, seeing her stand with grey,
bowed head to say grace, smiled at Milagros' assumption
that Aunt Cissy was an ugly woman. But she was a very
weak one, since assuredly though there was much to
resent in Dr. Lavelle, there was nothing to be afraid of.
He was no more than a lazy man who disliked his way of
life. He came of indolent 'squireen' stock, but as a third
son with no land to inherit had been put to a profession
for which he had no talent. In 1897, having scrambled
through his final examinations, he fell in love with the

pretty, eldest daughter of a respected physician in
Mellick. He persuaded her to marry him, and her father,
having no sons, was glad to leave his well-consolidated
practice to a handsome and promising-looking son-in-
law. But in 1912, when his wife died, having borne him
eight children of which six survived her, Dr. Lavelle was
already in his heart defeated, inefficient and bored, yet
having to fight to hold his work against doctors incalculably more competent than he. But in those earlier years
some of the convivial graces still stayed with him. He
was a man of great beauty, with a noble liveliness in his
face, above all in his caverned blue eyes, and all his
children had memories of him reading *Mr. Jorrocks* aloud,
or *Handy Andy*, or singing "Young Roger the rascal"
in a tremendous rollicking voice. In those days he liked
to sneak off to race meetings or to get a mount to a
Saturday meet. In those days everyone had a tolerant eye
for him, and when his wife left him with his family of
babies, Mellick had been profoundly sympathetic.
Indeed to this day, perhaps because grey-headed and
stooping he looked more interesting than ever, he still
had faithful patients and a certain number of well-
wishers in the town. But he was now an empty man; he
knew nothing and read nothing; tippled a bit, was over-
fond of his bed and was crankily unjust to his children
whom he seemed to resent and, without discrimination,
to dislike. For good or ill there was nothing more to
him than that. His beauty was deceptive, for though it
could promise either sexual or intellectual vitality,
according to the imagination that considered it, Dr.
Lavelle was possessed of neither. He simply had enough

nervous energy to keep life jogging somehow in its monotonous track, and slowly to force his irritating young out of his way.

The most irritating so far had been his eldest son Jimmy. Jimmy was eighteen and of school-leaving age in June 1917—what more opportune time for a father to dispose of a son? Dr. Lavelle decided to get him a commission in the Munsters. But Jimmy declined the offer and after the most alarming scene that his brothers and sisters had ever witnessed, he left his father's house, to which after that day he did not return. He wrote to Mary occasionally during the following years. He was with the I.R.A. They read that he was in jail. His father read aloud from the paper one morning that he was on hunger strike, and sneered so as to drive both Mary and Tom into a raging protest. Later, in 1919, Mary had met him sometimes by stealth, cycling to villages and farms near Mellick on errands for him or his flying column. No one at home in those days had known of her quite dangerous activities—she had often wondered what her father's reaction would have been were his house searched by Auxiliaries and his eldest daughter put in jail. But with the truce of 1920 all that had passed. Jim's flying column was no longer in the Vale of Honey, and his letters from Dublin were short and unhappy. Could Mary possibly get a pound out of Aunt Cissy for him? In November he wrote that he was going to America, working his passage, with a couple of chaps he had known in jail. Donal, from Yorkshire, had very decently borrowed ten pounds for him. He'd get a start somehow with that when he landed. He'd write. That was a year and eight months ago, and three postcards had turned up since then, the last from California. They did not suggest that he was happy.

Donal then—quite different. Small and sweet-natured, with a pose of literariness and detachment. As a school-boy wearisomely fond of saying: "A plague o' both your houses," and "a mad world, my masters." He had not waited for his father's ultimatum—"you take this excellent chance in the Bank of Ireland, sir, or out of my house you go!" He had found himself a job of the most miserable kind on a Dublin newspaper, and thence, after a year, had moved to a slightly less miserable one in Leeds. Mary had an idea that, in spite of something like starvation, he was not unhappy. His rare letters had jokes and quotations in them.

The loss of her two brothers made life with her father and Aunt Cissy seem empty. Mary had, or her father had in keeping for her, one hundred pounds of her own, bequeathed to her by her godmother, and though she repeatedly asked with diffidence for possession of this, her father withheld it, "against a rainy day," he said. Nor would he hear of its being expended on training for any form of employment. "Absolute waste," he said, "unless a girl is downright plain." So his daughter filled her time with household duties, and became skilful in them, made many of her own clothes and did a large part of the household mending, made cakes and ran errands. She cycled and played tennis, and went to small parties and dances. Except for fluctuating resentment of her father's peevishness and the cowardice of Aunt Cissy, she was not actively unhappy. She had a modest estimate of herself and had no very urgent desire to hurl a lance against the vague and mighty world. Jimmy and Donal, males and with better brains than hers, were finding the fight for individuality severe—but both had seen it to be necessary, and she did not. She realised the limitations of Mellick, and of her place in it, were she to be married or single—nothing glamorous or amazing. But no one had ever said that she was either of those things. As a child, reading the same books as Jimmy and Donal, she had dreamt as perhaps they had, on the breakfast-room window-seat, until her heart was near bursting with her desire, her intention, to go everywhere one day, know everything, try everything, be committed to nothing. She would wander always, be a free lance always, belong to no one place or family or person. That, curiously enough, had been the only unshifting principle in a for ever changing tissue of dreams, of which now she could remember little else. And that one clue surprised her. She had no idea of why when she was twelve and thirteen her main idea had been to be free and lonely. She had asked John recently if he thought it odd that a little girl should have had that notion of perpetual self-government—indeed it was only in recollecting her former self to please her lord that she actively realised this dominant intention of her childhood. John had smiled. "Do you think my having been so—so sure of myself then is likely to make me a bad wife?" she persisted. "Just you try being a bad wife," said John with tenderness.

Her father had been right not to waste Mary's hundred pounds in making her into a trained breadwinner. At her first dance, in January 1919, she had met John—or so he told her, for she had only vague recollections of the anxious parties of that winter. Her thoughts were too often away in the hills with Jim's flying column. But John would never forget his first sight of her. Her dress was of white tulle. She had granted him a dance, and without any effort of memory now he could always recall the feel of tulle against his hand. As they danced he planned his future. He was twenty-six and just demobilised from the Munster Fusiliers, a Major with a D.S.O. In September 1914, taking his uncle's and John Redmond's advice, he had gone off in private's uniform to the assistance of gallant little Belgium. He was a good soldier, had been wounded twice and had in general distinguished himself. The war had proved hateful to him, but he had made the best of it, and here he was, aged twenty-six, the nightmare through, back in his own town with his life to build, and on his arm as he waltzed a girl whose beauty passed all earthly rumour.

Mary did not remember that waltz, she said—and John rather liked the idea that she did not. His wooing had been careful, as at present he had not a position which would justify him in proposing marriage. His uncle, an eccentric and a miser, had taken him back, on demobilisation, into the subordinate clerkship in his shipping firm which had been abandoned at John Redmond's bidding. But at twenty-six when for eighteen months one has been accustomed to the pay and authority of a major, the £3 a week which seemed so splendid in 1913 when one was twenty had lost its magic. John had no intention of allowing the most beautiful girl ever created to live in penury. His salary must be enormously increased before he could make Mary his wife. He was the only heir of his uncle, but Jerome MacCurtain, who lived in disreputable lodgings and was popularly believed never to take off his clothes, disapproved of marriage, especially if contracted early in life. His nephew and his managing clerk had between them computed that he must be worth at least £50,000—so that admittedly John's prospects were good, though waiting about for more or less certain wealth and authority in a predicament of clerkly penuriousness and while having to suffer the unpredictable and sadistic whims of an ageing lunatic, was hard on a self-confident young man. Harder still for him, desperately in love and perhaps the most eligible bachelor in Mellick, with only one imminent death between him and his desire, to see his dream at large every day before the appraising eyes of other men and for a jot of honour to have to endanger the fulfilment of a fairy tale.

His wooing was careful too because he found the girl elusive and distraite and did not wish to imperil everything by frightening her. She was nineteen when he first danced with her. He could be patient. He was—but he was also watchful, and it seemed to him, as she approached her twenty-first birthday, as she passed it, that the pack of men whose eyes were always open for her comings and goings began to press in a fraction. It seemed to him too that some of her first elusiveness, 'awayness,' was departing, and that her eyes had recognition in them now for him, and for some others. He could bear no more. Uncle Jerome must surely die soon.

He put purpose and immediacy into his admiration. He won Aunt Cissy to his cause; he found Dr. Lavelle quite gracious and agreeable. In his hour he proposed to Mary —but though he had timed things well and was so much in love that feeling did in fact fill his tentative with poetry—she somehow wounded him. He would never tell her that as long as they lived—not now. But her eyes when he had wanted to see heaven in them for a second, had curiously failed him. Could she—but what could she be afraid of? She had asked for time, until the next evening. He had hated that. He wanted all or nothing, rapture or refusal. And he could swear she—well, that she did like him very much. However—that flaw, that reserve in her eyes, that begged and granted twenty-four hours—what were they all against the next night's gentle 'yes,' the bowed head, and the slim hand shaking as he held it to his lips? She was his. He would make her happy. He swore that glory to himself as he gathered her up.

When Dr. Lavelle heard that there could be no immediate marriage and that Uncle Jerome might stand in love's way for quite a while—at least until John might prevail on him to pay a real salary—he reduced his graciousness. Nevertheless he conceded that the engagement might stand, since he saw no inclination in Mary towards any other young man, and since also old Jerome MacCurtain really did look these days like a dying man.

Meantime he did not die. A year of engagement passed.

In the convention of Mary's upbringing a suitably affianced girl is a happy girl and Mary was therefore by her own conventional assumption happy. Moreover, though without particularly noticing this, she did sometimes undergo the sensation of happiness. There were occasional premonitions of emotion too—as when, loafing with John before the breakfast-room fire, they talked, he talked of the future, of married peace, of the house they would have and its garden, of the children who would grow and play there and of what those children would become, of growing old with her, of seeing their grandchildren. Her heart approved the goodness of this obvious plan and she perceived how well it became the good and spirited man who purposed it with her. She liked his face when he talked in this vein; there was penetrating sweetness in the way he would laugh over his unborn children. She felt both honoured and touched; she felt surprised too that a scheme which is or has been everyone's should seem at the personal proof so especial and exacting. In these moments of wordless and pure assent to him, sitting often out of reach of his eager, caressing hands but very sure of her intention to be everything to him that he most needed, she wondered why she had ever hesitated, even for a day, about being his wife. What more natural thing was there to be?

Sometimes when he kissed her her thoughts took a different direction of surmise. Kissing, she had understood from literature, hearsay and innuendo, was a pleasant privilege between two who loved, but until John came, hungrily compelling, no one had ever kissed her mouth. He kissed her now with masterful urgency as often as he might and Mary, glad to be orthodox in feeling and knowing intuitively that in love to give joy

31

you must take it, sought with expectancy for pleasure in
his kiss. But, to her chagrin, she did not find it. She
found in fact no more than a passing discomfort and
guilty sensation of relief as each kiss ended. Occasionally
too, in horror she caught herself being almost overcome
by a sense of the ludicrousness of kissing. But in the
main all she experienced was a mild physical discomfort
and, at the roots of her virgin spirit, an inadmissible
distaste. But no hint of these reactions escaped out of her
keeping; indeed she was so much ashamed of their
unnaturalness that they hardly ever moved into the
foreground of her thoughts.

The routine of life was not much disturbed by her
engagement. John came to see her every evening at a
quarter to eight. (Dr. Lavelle, who was not hospitable,
asked him to dinner only on Saturday nights.) He took
her to the pictures if that was their mood; sometimes
on fine evenings they walked by the river or towards the
westward hills, returning to drink cocoa together on the
breakfast-room window-seat or by the fire. But if by a
quarter past eleven the hall door had not slammed on his
retreat, Aunt Cissy would call cantankerously over the
banisters: "Is John *still* there, Mary?" And John,
giggling and mischievous, would mutter: "Damn Aunt
Cissy!" and snatch his Mary to his arms again. On
Sunday he sometimes borrowed the motor-cycle and
trailer of one of his friends and took her for a picnic.
They were happy in those outings. Both loved their
native county and John knew every field of it, it seemed,
with intimacy. He was observant of country ways, too,
of farm routine and seasonal changes or the dress and

habits of birds. Talking of these things with him, Mary was drawn into remembering summers of childhood spent on her grandfather's farm, and John, who was rustic born and bred, would remember childhood too, and looking about them over undulations and colours that their eyes had always known and the eyes of all their people before them, they would feel a great mingling of inherited sympathies and the tides of their peace would seem to overflow.

"It scares me to feel so happy," John would sometimes say then, and Mary would ask him why he should be scared. But he never answered that question. His intention was to be happy and he was not going to beat about for obstacles to put in his own way. The furthest he got in expressed anxiety was a puzzled stare at her and then: "I wonder if you *are* so crazily beautiful—or only just a lovely girl?" Mary, teasing him, would vote that she was crazily beautiful. "Which would you prefer, John?" "A lovely girl."

John was earning two hundred pounds a year and Mary sometimes pointed out that millions of people married and brought up large families on considerably smaller earnings. Also she reminded him that she had a hundred pounds, with which to buy a few tables and chairs. But though deeply tempted, he would not consent to marry her yet. She made him promise that when he had five pounds a week they would become man and wife, but even that idea, which enchanted, also worried him. He wanted a house with trees about it, he said; he wanted their love to begin where it might end. Meantime he lived in lodgings and saved what he could for his dream.

But he liked to bring her random presents—violets or a book of music or silk stockings—or, as one day, an old hand-mirror of thin, exhausted silver. "Look there, my love," he said, "and see why I'm so crazy."

Cherished by John, liked and half-envied by her friends, busy with girlish occupations, and sanguine for the most part before her father's peevishness, with her future life appointed as she herself had willed, nevertheless, when in casual talk her one-time history mistress, Mother Liguori, mentioned a post in Spain which needed filling and asked her if she knew of anyone who would like it, Mary suffered a brief thrill of pleasure as sharp and strange as it was unreasonable. She answered the nun's enquiry so vaguely that the latter marvelled to herself that the state of love could render shamelessly self-centred even this girl, distinguished for graciousness.

Mary's consciousness was at that moment confusingly turned upon herself. In an uneasy dream she left Mother Liguori and walked home. To go to Spain. To be alone for a little space, a tiny hiatus between her life's two accepted phases. To cease being a daughter without immediately becoming a wife. To be a free lance, to belong to no one place or family or person—to achieve that silly longing of childhood, only for one year, before she flung it with all other childish things upon the scrap-heap. Spain! She did not see how she could ever mention it to John. He would be shocked, would laugh, would tease her and tear the silly notion into shreds. It would become then one of their jokes—that brief idea she had had of vanishing to Spain. She smiled above her darning by the breakfast-room fire. She looked out into the dusk

at the barren fig-tree. Figs grew and ripened in Spain.
The word clanged on in her heart. But she knew that she
could never mention it to John. That night she did
mention it, and he and she had their first unadjustable
quarrel. For the first time he had to go home without a
kiss of peace, and Mary went to bed shaking, tearful,
ashamed of herself and profoundly excited.

It was the first real battle of her life, and she waged and
won it without ever knowing why she fought. Over a
period of a month it swung uncertainly and often during
that time she shook herself and said: "You're mad. What
is the matter? Why on earth do you plague him like this
about going to Spain?" She was unfairly armed against
John. For one thing, her father, understanding that there
would be no expense to him, and that the respectability
of the arrangement was vouched for by Mother Liguori,
favoured her enterprise. Another source of expense and
irritation would be out of his way. Mary gone, his home,
save for the summer vacation returns from abroad of his
younger daughters, would be empty and bearable
perhaps. And as Dr. Lavelle thought so thought Aunt
Cissy. The willingness of her guardians to let her go was
a good weapon for Mary. She had another that she did
not know about. She would never have made this
whimsical issue the cause of an ultimatum to John. She
would never have put a pistol to his head. She was his
betrothed who loved him, and therefore would only do
with her life whatever he and she agreed she should do.
But some unsuspected strength in her was ready to strain
long and hard to have his agreement to the fulfilment of
this impulse. John, however, though he believed in her

fundamental willingness to please him, could not yet be absolutely certain of it in every conceivable issue, and this dreamy obstinacy frightened him. Also he loved her tenderly, and had no heart to play the slave-master, or to imperil all their future trust for a bully's victory now. He thought her whim unlike her and unkind but he gave in to it at last, thinking he must.

So here she was, a four days' journey from him, and from all she was and again would be. Here she was, an unknown breadwinner in a foreign land. For no particular reason—merely because she had taken the idea into her head. She laughed softly and even somewhat cruelly at her own irresponsibility. Contemplation of it, making her feel guilty, also exhilarated her. She leant forward and smelt a rose Nieves had pulled. "Oh thank you," she said, as the child gave it to her.

A voice called from an upper window of the house. Doña Consuelo beckoned to the children from her room.

"If you will permit us, Miss Maria——?"

The three girls smiled politely and sauntered towards the villa, waving to their mother. "How like Pilár she is," thought Mary and, glad to be alone, stood up and carrying her rose in her hand, strolled past the house to the terrace by the little pier.

The air was cool and aromatic; the hour might have, for the most native to it, a pungent sadness, and Mary, inhaling it, knew suddenly that if she released her will, she could be sentimentally overwhelmed. She could weep now for a hundred trivial reasons and for no reason at all. She dropped her eyelids, still travel-tired, and felt a thin dew of tears against her lashes. She smiled and turned to thinking what this odd life might be like. She would be, she saw, neither master nor servant, neither running with the hare nor hunting with the hounds. She would eat alone, perform her duties without discussion, be circumspect and, she presumed, friendless in her private life. Her charges would be kind to her, in so far as she impinged upon them: Pilár, with condescension towards someone who, though presumably a lady, had actually to earn a living; Nieves in simple sweetness; Milagros remotely, or perhaps with good-natured malice. But to everyone she would be a foreign and more or less satisfactory machine. She would be unobserved, uncherished and, she hoped, unreproved. She had in fact put on a cap of invisibility, from under which, however, she could use her unlearned eyes with circumspection and in peace.

A ferry was being loaded for Torcal. It was the end of the day and a great number were passing into the little open boat for home. Clerkly old men, and laden peasant women, a cavalry officer, two ladies in beautiful organdie, two or three priests, many errand boys, many children and beggars. Tankards, baskets of fish, a dog, and an old man with a mule. Mary sat on the parapet, and watched the good-natured loading-up. It was difficult, it was amusing. She watched it and grew interested, smelling her sweet rose, forgetting awhile the homesickness that threatened her.

She heard deliberate steps on the flagstones near her. She glanced around, and saw an elderly-seeming man in black. Some visitor, or perhaps the children's father? She half-smiled politely. The elderly man, taking off his black felt hat, bowed a little and smiled at her. She smiled too.

"Our English miss?" The Spanish words were spoken with great distinctness.

Mary nodded.

"I am the father of your pupils." This was said in slow, uneasy English.

"You speak English?"

"No. Once yes, a little. But it is gone."

"Oh, it isn't," said Mary and hoped that their lame conversation might end now—with another smile. Don Pablo—she knew that was his name—seemed willing also to leave it at that, but glad on the other hand of an excuse to rest, leaning forward on his polished black stick. He gave Mary an impression of great weariness. Though neither tall nor fleshy he suggested that his frame was a bothersome load. He had broad, sagging shoulders and a heavy, greying head. His eyebrows bushed somewhat wildly over far-sunk, heavily lidded eyes. His nose was a broad, strong promontory and his long smile showed two rows of teeth so even and white as to be startling. His chin had a shadowy, unshaven look and his black clothes, untidied by cigarette ash, hung too loosely on him. Shadows and lines overdramatised his face in the evening light, so that Mary felt his foreignness with exaggeration, even remotely with alarm.

"You have come a long way, Miss. I trust you will be contented in our country."

"I am sure I shall."

He straightened himself.

"Do not sit too long here," he said in his careful, embarrassed English. "You will take a chill."

They smiled again politely and the man turned away and walked along the terrace into his house.

Mary was considerably disconcerted as she watched his retreat and reflected on their encounter. Had she behaved very badly, very casually? This man was her employer. Should she have made some foolish speech about her intention to be dutiful? Should she have stood up? What was the Spanish requirement? She grew hot as she wondered. Certainly he had shown no surprise at her behaviour; he had been kind. But she did not like him so far. Not because he was quite unlike her idea of a Spanish grandee—in twenty-four hours she had not yet seen anything Spanish that reminded her of Spain—but perhaps because he differed from anything which was familiar either to her knowledge or her imagination. As she watched him vanish through the great hall-door she reflected that she had already lost her first impression of his face which had seemed so formidable.

The ferry was gone now, and the pier was quiet again; a coal-boat bearing the Dutch flag moved out along the water; dusk was spreading rapidly from the hills. Mary shivered and rose to go into the house. She was light with a sense of unreality; she saw her surroundings fairly for a second, as from the inner side of a bubble. She was a little dizzy and paused on the threshold of the house, trying to get a sense of place. Some images of Mellick came, some forms, but darkly, merging together.

"I'm dead-tired still," she told herself, and went on through the hall and up the shallow stairs. "Complicated—that is the only word I can get for his face," she thought, "much too complicated."

DON PABLO

The Areavagas dined at half-past nine. Pilár explained to the new 'miss' that they did so because Papa insisted it was good for them to eat early. "He would really like us to eat at eight-thirty, like the common people, but of course Mama could not allow that! It's quite bad enough to be so little 'chic' as to dine at 9.30!"

On the evening of Miss Maria's first day with them the family came to the dining-room in good appetite, which was usual, and feeling talkative, which was perhaps only a little less usual. The 'miss' was safe in her own little dining-room and the children looked forward to talking her over with their parents, airing and receiving impressions.

While the maids went round among them with brown dishes of baked bread soup the five diners nibbled methodically from platters of olives and cold tunny-fish.

"Funny thing," said Nieves, "she doesn't mind a bit about eating her meals alone."

"Miss Anita hated it," said Milagros.

"Ah, but Miss Anita was fond of gaiety!" Pilár giggled and helped herself largely to bread soup.

"Pilár," said Doña Consuelo, "you know that bread soup isn't good for your figure! Did you weigh yourself to-day?"

"I'm starving, mother. To-morrow's the day, anyway."

"It always is," said Nieves.

"And might just as well be," said Milagros who held that in a year of weekly checkings at the chemist's Pilár's weight had not altered by a gramme. Pilár looked troubled now as she spooned her soup. She intended to be the most admired of Altorno's débutantes next year—but she liked good food.

The family sat, well spaced from each other, at a wide, long table, in a large and opulent room. It was a very ugly room; its walls were panelled in yellow oak and enlivened by Talavera pots and platters, also by some swords and bucklers in Toledo work. On a little shelf above the stove there was a model of The Cid's trunk. The table and sideboard were furnished with brilliant silverware, electric light blazed from up-to-date fittings and the summer night was shut out by curtains of red and gold brocade. Two maidservants moved noiselessly in felt slippers. They wore clean white cotton gloves. They were girls from the mountains and were believed to understand Castilian only when it was spoken very slowly and simply. The Areavagas said therefore what they pleased to each other in pure and rapid Spanish, eating the while with industry.

Milagros reproachfully indicated her empty glass to her father.

He sighed. "Really, Milagros, strong wine at this hour when one is fourteen——" he leant across and filled the glass smiling. "Your poise is certainly a triumph, child, considering your atrocious habits."

"I follow nature, papa."

"That's very liberal of you, my dear."

42

Doña Consuelo chuckled.

"Milagros darling, you say funny things." And she wondered in maternal amusement what sort of husband they would ever find for the queer child. But there was no anxiety in the frivolous thought. Doña Consuelo was happy on the whole about her family and inclined to believe that life would gratify her ambitions for it. Was not her son already cutting an easy path to glory? Alas, to do it he had to be far from them, in Madrid—but that was natural. He was endowed to serve his country in the capital and had already two years ago by his brilliantly satisfactory marriage shown that he could win whatever he desired there against all comers. Admittedly he carried more weapons than his personal beauty and intelligence. He was rich and bore a name much respected in the north and not without honour either in the *Ateneo*. Still, at twenty-three to marry the beautiful Luisa de Maraval and make the stiff old Condé, her father, seem to think that no alliance could so well become his distinguished daughter—that was augury indeed to Consuelo that her children would go far and in the right direction. She missed her son; since his marriage and especially since last Christmas when he became a father his visits to Cabantes were not as frequent as they used to be—but he still had an affectionate way of sweeping home whenever possible. He was the best and dearest of children. Now that he was so much away from her Doña Consuelo often wished more regretfully than ever that Pablo, her second child who had died twenty years ago when he was two, was living also, to be another rising star of Spain, an additional satisfaction to herself. But though two sons were always better than one, she could not whine to the good God. Juan was everything that a man and a Spaniard could be and if, as he developed, he seemed to seek his father's society and sympathy—no, no, not more than hers—but very much, well, that was the way of men. They had brains and from them created a world of argument, schemes, dreams and ideas where women need not enter, thank Heaven, and where feminine wisdom must be content to let them move in peace. In any case, who could grudge a son's devotion to so good and just a father as Pablo? Consuelo smiled now towards her husband and asked him if he did not think there was too much garlic in the rice?

"My palate is growing old and philosophic," he said. "You tell us, Pilár. You are less tainted than any of us by resignation."

Pilár did not always fathom her father's gentle jokes, and indeed he spoke them with benevolence so that she should not. For though, however he struggled against it, his habitual idiom was hispanically dry, he did not admire his own mild ironies, and was a tender-hearted father. So Pilár now took from his eyes a compliment in this exemption which he endowed on her and laughed contentedly under his favour.

"It's terribly overflavoured," she said. "It's delicious."

"Vulgarian!" said Milagros.

"I sometimes think that you're a bit of a vulgarian, Mila," said Nieves. "All this pretentiousness, you know——"

"There's something in what you say," Milagros assented.

"Children, children!" cried Consuelo, "what sort of creatures will your new miss think you?"

"Oh, mother, she likes us awfully," said Pilár.

"Anyhow," said Nieves, "it will be years before we can plague each other like this in English."

"Well, that's a mercy."

"Besides, she's a simpleton," said Milagros gently. "A quite exceptional simpleton."

Don Pablo turned respectfully to his youngest child.

"That is your considered opinion?" he asked with gravity.

Milagros loved such teasing.

"Yes," she pronounced, and beamed at him. "Yes, papa, I believe it is."

Nieves laughed sweetly.

"She just can't be, with that face. Wait until you see her, papa!"

"But it's the very face for a simpleton. Indeed," said Milagros, "if we are to believe that God is good, it is the only face."

"Your theology eludes me, child," said Don Pablo respectfully.

"She certainly is prettier than we require," Consuelo murmured, and a cloud of exasperation flitted over her calm brows. Pilár saw it with anxiety.

"But, mother," she said to reassure herself, "she won't be with us long."

Everyone looked a mild question.

"She has a sweetheart," said Pilár.

"One of Pilár's intuitions," Milagros confided wisely to her father.

"What do you bet then? When we were in her room before she'd finished unpacking, didn't you see that little framed photograph lying on her table?" Pilár's shrewd eyes queried her sisters', which had evidently not observed as much as hers. "It was of a very fine young man, I must say. Almost a gentleman, mother—really. But then you know she's—well she's really very like a lady!"

Consuelo seemed interested.

"My God, Pilár," said Nieves. "Anyone would think you were a Bourbon."

"That's not the way Bourbons talk," said Milagros.

"Oh, very likely it is," said Don Pablo.

"Anyway, she has brothers——" Nieves argued.

"Ah yes, but do you remember," Pilár asked her sisters, "that I dropped her letters in the hall on our way to the garden? Well—I did that on purpose. And one of them *was* addressed to a man with a different name from hers—some terrible name beginning with an M."

The detective paused in triumph. Milagros gave her a long laugh of appreciation but Nieves, the Etonian, had grown a little red.

"Oh, Pilár, you're a sneak," she murmured into her plate.

"But we asked her in the garden if she had a young man," Milagros prompted.

"And she dodged answering. Sure sign I'm right," Pilár smiled again at her mother, whose serene expression seemed now to tell her eldest daughter that, sweetheart or none, the too pretty miss would stay amongst them only as long as it suited the Areavagas to retain her.

46

Milagros mused on the hardihood or conceit of any sweetheart in letting Miss Maria stray so far. "Is it not true, papa, that in northern countries they think all our men are Don Juan Tenarios?"

"I believe they do regard you as an especially happy race of females, child."

Milagros gave him the pitying smile which he knew she enjoyed dispensing.

"When we were talking about Miss Maria to-day, papa," said Pilár, "Milagros said that anyway you'd never know what she looked like, because you'd never see her. And do you know why she said that?"

"How could I?"

"Because," she says, "you haven't yet even seen us!"

Don Pablo took in his three daughters in a gentle glance.

"Even Milagros nods," he said.

"No, I don't," said that Homer stoutly. "Some day I'll explain what I mean by that!"

"No doubt, no doubt," said her father. "Meantime, if my opinion matters in your argument about your miss, I think Nieves, who is the only diffident person in this family, is right."

"But how do you know, papa?" asked Pilár. "You haven't seen the miss."

"I've seen her and we've spoken."

"When?"

"On the terrace, two hours ago."

"What did you say?"

"Oh, nothing. Linguistic difficulties—and I was tired then."

"What do you think of her, Pablo?" His wife's voice was businesslike. They were paying good money for this miss, who really was not quite down to specification.

"I think, my dear, as I gather Nieves does, that she is very beautiful and that she is not a simpleton."

Pilár's brow clouded again and her mother's hinted at cloud. Don Pablo selected some green figs with care while Milagros scrutinised his face.

"You find that a little funny, papa?" she prodded softly.

"Well, my dear, now you say it, I do see the skirts of a joke."

"I wish I had a sense of humour," said Doña Consuelo.

Pablo Areavaga y Galdéz, now in his forty-ninth year, had married in his twenty-fourth, as lately his son had done. His marriage had been fortunate in that it was a love match and yet entirely satisfactory to his own family as well as to his bride's, the Parajos. Indeed to the latter the advantages of the union were marked, for in the last decade of the nineteenth century they were, though very wealthy, quite new and raw in their wealth and their tactful manœuvring for position in the governing class of Altorno was being watched then with some amusement by that formidable bourgeoisie. The amusement was good-natured, however. The Parajos were welcome, provided they tempered their ambition with respect for certain attributes and traditions which they would find in the ranks they entered. They had the master key. From being nobodies they had become in one generation, in twenty years, one of the largest owners in the great iron mines to the west of Altorno; they were solidly staked in

the city's great possession. It would have been silly to
deny their importance. Altorno's wealth, always growing
at that time, always deepening, inexhaustibly available,
it seemed, to the astute and watchful, was naturally, after
God, Altorno's god. Neophytes who conducted themselves with proper respect in the sanctuary were welcome,
though it was permissible for the faithful-born to smile at
small ritualistic errors. But it was certainly no error for a
Parajo daughter to marry an Areavaga. Indeed old
observers, applauding the perfect discretion of such a
move, saw no reason to smile, save approvingly, at the
perfect timing of the gesture. The marriage was exactly
the right thing, said the clubs and the cafés, and it was
understood that henceforward it would be necessary to
take Herónimo Parajo and Sons with seriousness. For
the Areavagas, as genealogies went in the industrial town,
were old in their wealth and power. Three generations of
culture and public service lay behind Consuelo Parajo's
bridegroom. As shipowners and ironfounders his family
had been among the earliest and most enduring builders
of Altorno's industrial greatness. Liberals always, they
had served their country well in the Carlist wars; had
twice declined with politeness to enter the nobility (this
surprising fact about them was Pilár's one grievance
against her paternal ancestors); had frequently been
Mayors of Altorno and in short throughout the nineteenth century were a leading family in the north of
Spain.

Pablo's father, Don Juan, had been a grave and
studious man. Before he took his place in business he
conformed with an Areavaga tradition and went to

Salamanca to read law. In due time he married into the lesser nobility. His wife was intelligent and even saintly and their family life austere and quiet. They lived in a huge cold house of dark stone which had been since 1800 the Areavaga mansion. They were scrupulous in observing the dignities and obligations of their position and though simple in personal tastes they were socially generous and practised both ceremony and charity. Don Juan saw always, however, that the circumstances out of which his duties and privileges arose were founded on false premises. He saw the evil plight of the industrial magnate, but neither his tradition nor his temperament would allow him to believe that the solution of it, if there was one, lay in the abolition of his class. He was a conscientious and enterprising employer whose experiments in the direction of social justice were observed with fear and discomfort by others of his caste and whose manipulation of private profits into housing and educational enterprises were viewed with pity as a dangerous expression of an admittedly legitimate individualism. He was, in fact, a rich man with a conscience—Christian, cultured, somewhat Jansenistic, but profoundly a Spaniard—that is, convinced to the last drop of his blood of the absolute dominion of personality over system. Given his dilemma and his intellect, he could never be either fanatical or smug and he went through life gravely and observantly, but in perpetual debate with it. Pablo, his eldest son, inherited his conscience, intellect and individualism, but took from his mother's saintliness a handful of poetic fire. Took too from somewhere further back in his genealogy a robust sense of the ridiculous and

an interest in his fellow-men which could forget the
rights and wrongs of their social state, and be content to
enjoy, love or deride them simply as presentations of
intractable life. He had more heart than his father, and
when he began his business life under the wing of Don
Juan he was received with favour in Altorno society. He
was not good-looking in the accepted sense and there was
perhaps something even Bohemian about his shaggy
head and perpetual cigarette-smoking; but he was full of
life, made good jokes and liked good talk, sailed and
swam well and was a good mountaineer. He read in all
directions without prejudice; was critical, gay and a
sharpshooter—in short, he was welcome in the clubs and
at any table of the Café del Teatro. He had been schooled
at the Escorial and afterwards at Salamanca, where,
somewhat to his father's disappointment, he had read not
law but modern history. Leaving the University he
travelled to France and England on a voyage of undefined intellectual exploration and after an absence
abroad of eighteen months returned to Altorno passionately glad to be in Spain again. He looked forward to
life, not fatuously, but with a true enthusiasm.

And life seemed eager to reward his faith. Very early
in his adjustment to its adult routine he met Consuelo
Parajo, and fell in love.

The malady, on which he had read and pondered much,
did not at first disappoint him. All that the natural man
desires of it it gave him and whatever a poet might exact
he could apply to it from within himself. His regret,
remembering the first years of marriage in which his two
sons were born, was that Consuelo his wife, though

happy, had not apprehended or drunk their happiness with a matched delight; for he had had at that time an answered, mended, explained, unravelled feeling which was, he still believed recalling it, a dramatically great and high sensation—whereas she had been steadily happy, in proportion to her girlish and human intention and understanding of happiness. A very different thing, as her young husband had seen with burning pity then. But for adjustment in the long years it had proved the better platform, and on its base of naturalness and non-exaggeration had salvaged both. There had been need of salvage—though not by her admission for Consuelo who never saw her life endangered by such an image. She, Pablo guessed, looking back good-humouredly from his middle age to the fourth, fifth, sixth and seventh years of her life with him, would have shrugged in unembittered recollection that they had been uncomfortable, and through his fault; she would remember too, having a head for dates, that they were the years between the births of dead Pablo and of Pilár; and would say, if pressed to defend them, that they were natural, normal years of difficulty, that she and Pablo had come through them very well, and look, had they not lived happily ever afterwards?

Pablo smiled sometimes as he played at surmise and listened to that unspoken, bright dismissal. He was no middle-aged fidget with a sexual grievance. He was a Spanish realist, a serious, domesticated man who loved his children and was honourably devoted to his wife. His life had been pleasant and in its setting and habits had nurtured the deep love he felt for his own region of Spain.

By now he knew the bay and the mountains with a long sweet tenderness which he liked to foster in his children; he knew all the characters and eccentrics too, and knew himself to be becoming nowadays an appreciated, respected one of them; at home he was a personality and very much the master of his house; he indulged in small tyrannies there which his wife most charmingly encouraged and to which his daughters deferred as to a law of nature; he adored his son Juanito and dreamt life over again ungrudgingly when he fell into thought of him. He was in fact in decent possession of his soul, but nevertheless he was undeceived and he knew what Consuelo did not, that when those years were over, first the years of incredible, self-indulgent rapture, and then the years of rage, when peace came, with Pilár stirring in her mother's womb—life's music ceased.

For by then he had learnt, among a million lessons, that the isolation of the self is not only inescapable, though in the youth of his love he had cried out against that, but that it is to some spirits essential; further he learnt that whereas it is invulnerable against passion, which indeed does not pause to assault it, it is resented by intimacy, and even tortured; he learnt that in that furtive shadow place of feeling where the one dies and the other insidiously stretches up to live—there the imperturbable loneliness of the heart becomes love's devil and mocker, no matter what capitulation love may win. In any case the battle will have been harsh and vulgar and Pablo might say that a man, having been its field, would do well to forget it, and above all to forget what the mind of his youth had been and what he had planned to do with his waiting years when in all seriousness he had harnessed life and love.

He had been an idealist, an everyday and matter-of-fact one, with simple, if somewhat anarchistic projects pressing on him for human justice and the betterment of his fellow-men. Nothing poetic or far-flung. He had been an impatient realist, a lover of life and a hater of its savageries. And he had one love that was stronger in him than any other he could feel—his love for his own country. He loved Spain with a quite simple mysticism, and all his energies when he was young burnt outward to be used by her. With less caution and more fire than his father he proposed to go further than Don Juan in industrial reform when, with his younger brothers, he would assume control of the family dower of wealth. But that would be a side-line, a mere gesture. Apart from it, and much more important, he would go into politics and he would write. In every practical way that he could discover he would work according to his spirit and conscience for his ailing country.

Love tripped him up while he was only discovering this ambition in himself and searching about nervously for mental equipment. Love for Consuelo. She was very pretty—light and quick as a bird and with ravishing music in her laugh. She swept him to infatuation, and though he told himself that he had other things to do than go wooing and though he grumbled about her being excessively wealthy, these grievances were only gnat-bites on summer joy—for he had lived chastely and this, love's first true visitation, was a mastery; he could tell himself too that he was marrying no rapacious and

arrogant aristocrat—for Consuelo's grandfather had
been a dockhand and did he not remember how as a little
boy he had bought water-melon from her mother's
mother in the market place? No, Consuelo and love
would be wings to his feet. Married to her he would be a
real man, fitter and wiser for the things he desired to
do.

He married the eldest daughter of the newly-rich
Parajo, and being a poet of sorts and a man of fire he flung
himself heart and soul awhile into a reckless oblivion of
love. Often in later life he wondered what he had learnt
in that wild place of passage, for though he knew that he
must have been in some sense remade there, curiously he
could remember no significant experience of it, and had
only an illusory memory of aloneness and silence, of
having been well and quiet and full of confidence. He
could find no clear picture of Consuelo in association
with these sensory memories, and could hardly hear the
echo of her charming laughter from that muffled year.
This absence of her hurt him, made him uncomfortable
in remembrance. It seemed a dangerously brutal thing to
recall a year of honeymoon only as a time of mysteriously
happy loneliness. But whatever the explanation of his
nuptial raptures and curious memories of them, it was
true that when after twelve months his father's death
recalled him to responsibility and general life, he had
learnt nothing that he could tabulate of Consuelo; she was
still a symbol, a gateway, and love between them was still
the ungoverned tempest, the irrational, impersonal force
of their wedding day.

The second year, saddened by mourning for Don Juan,

made busy by the complications of his intricate will, but glorified by Juanito's birth, shone more simply and humanly in Pablo's memory. For one thing, it had been externally a year of setbacks and perplexities. His father, guided by an exaggerated sense of family justice and by fear of Pablo's intemperate sense of social equity, had left his property to his three sons in a partnership well calculated to limit and hamper the authority of the eldest. At first the unravelling of the intricate testament, and then the realisation of its probable effect on his own intentions, as well as much bickering and uneasiness through all the ramifications of the family, had given Pablo food for disgust and weariness. But at home there had been Consuelo, waiting wide-eyed for their child— and then the child's coming and all the sweetness of paternity, and of his wife's restoration to girlhood and love. In that year, too, however, he had begun to understand that he took from passion a bliss, a health, an explanation of life which Consuelo would never find and he could never give her. This knowledge humiliated him, filled him with hesitations and with pity. She gave him herself, gave him his child, and remained as she had been. Learnt nothing, at least, that he could apprehend; felt nothing in his terms of feeling. He accepted that there were other criteria than his, admitted that she was a woman and that women are mysteries. He told himself that some fires are slow, some hidden; he realised that in any case each man can only feel according to his own nature and that against that there is no help from without, even though deep love minister. But anxiety began to gather round his heart. His wife became a person now instead of a symbol; he settled down to learn about her with an inexplicable panic in his heart for him and her. Soon he began to understand that he and she had married strangers, and it was then that he first turned to consider the value and inevitability of the spirit's solitary confinement.

High-sounding resignation, and perhaps the young man took some priggish pleasure in it. A woman's love apparently was, as all the generalisers said, a passive and receptive thing—conditions which made it as incomprehensible as it was necessary to him. If so it was, then it divided life into a man's activities and the place where he rested from them. As to the division which it might make for the woman—since somehow he could not believe that the whole of any human personality could go into the cherishing of lover and babes—well, that was the other side of the strangeness, and not to be worked out by him who had no clue. Let them proceed then, he and Consuelo, loving each other in close, unguessing union, but with time acquiring some knowledge of each other too, from longer, more respectful range, from their separated perches of meditation. So be it, said the young husband.

The older Pablo, looking back, could laugh at the well-meaning inhumanity. At that time, indeed until some months after the birth of their second son, he and Consuelo had had no real quarrel, no honestly drawn-out wrangle. Explosions of temper against trifles, hot, high moments about exciting nothings, had been all that they knew of anger in each other, sparks which seemed always to generate a renewal of passion in him, a

reciprocal voluptuousness in her. Their brief rage never
cooled into dispute or obstinacy. This fact, no more than
physical, kept them spiritually strangers. And so, im-
perceptibly and contentedly enough, Pablo undertook to
go his way in the unstormed region of his own ideas and
ambitions and to forget his pompous notion of marrying
love and life.

Thus the years of rage began, the years of hatred.
Soon he was to see that his "pompous notion" had only
been a silly young man's way of stating a truism, and that
in fact love and life cannot help but marry and stay
married with an exhausting violence of fidelity. Soon he
was to see that if a woman is passive and receptive in
passion, she can be compensatorily assertive in other
fields of expression. In short, once Consuelo got wind of
the way in which his patriotism took him, once she
suspected what bees were buzzing in his social conscience,
she would have none of such foolery. Admitted she had
married an intellectual, a Liberal; the Areavaga tradition,
she understood, could afford itself such flourishes, but
they had, in her philosophy, nothing to do with the real
business of life, which she would quite shamelessly have
declared to be the establishment, consolidation and
aggrandisement of one's own family. The Church, the
King and the Family made up the immovable rock upon
which the Parajos had managed to clamber in good time
for Consuelo to be born there, most native of its natives,
and it had never seriously occurred to her that there
might be any other camping-ground or look-out, at least
for such Spaniards as she, so carefully brought up, might
ever meet. Therefore to find in her own husband one

who sought the overthrow of the structure on to which all whom she loved and believed in had fought their way so courageously, was to have been cheated by him in his very first vows, she said. In short she would have none of his political ambitions or his intellectual associations. Their quarrel about how to live and what to live for became savage and for some years almost unceasing, since once it was acknowledged, it entered into every small daily issue. Both were generous, for instance about material things; both were shrewd also, with good heads for money, of which each possessed a great deal. But Consuelo, very feminine, and a member of the first really accepted generation of Parajos, was ostentatious and quite vulgar in expenditure, whereas Pablo was not interested in luxuries, and was attracted to simplification of life. When they married it had indeed been his idea to buy the Casa Pilár—he could not ask a radiant young wife to live in the old stone palacio of the Areavagas in the Callejon de los Sastres, already in the nineties becoming a slum. Besides he had been immensely attracted by the little fishing pier beside the terrace, and by the dark semi-circular grove of trees that girdled the big garden. Consuelo thought Cabantes a queer, remote, unfashionable place, but humoured his romantic notion gladly enough, and spent much money on furnishing according to the undisciplined, ugly notions then beginning to flourish amid the Spanish bourgeoisie—allowing into her bridal home almost nothing of the furniture from the old stone house in the slums. But Pablo furnished his library from them, and his own bedroom. And, as a sop to her own sense of thrift, his wife had allowed a few old things to find their way to some of the rooms on the top floor. But as Pablo cared nothing about décor and a good deal for the lapping sea, the trees and the gossiping fishermen about his wall, as Consuelo cared much for space and her own notions of splendour, and as both were seriously concerned for the health and well-being of their children, the Casa Pilár was a success and grew dear to them. And Consuelo, observing society follow them out, to build its villas at Torcal and Playablanca, watching armorial bearings go up on this new gate or that, and attending regattas at the Yacht Club to applaud the King's own yacht, often smilingly and half-wickedly congratulated her husband on his perspicacity in choosing his house.

But differences of opinion as to how and why to spend money were not their true quarrel. Pablo had no illusions as to racial troubles being assisted or increased by one man's austerity or self-indulgence. Consuelo was not criminally or vilely greedy, and he saw no harm in her fondness for French clothes or for Barcelona bric-à-brac. But she saw serious harm in his despair against the Spanish scene at the opening of the twentieth century. He belonged to the generation now remembered in Spain as that of '98—a generation so diversely gifted as to include Unamuno, Azorin and Benavente. Startled into attention to Spain's plight by the revelations of the disastrous Cuban war, and encouraged in rebelliousness by the period-vogue for Nietsche, this outcropping of talent had little in fact to unify it and was perhaps no more than a display of many greatly gifted and highly in-dividualised writers very busily at cross purposes, but the gifts and promises were great, and the beginnings seemed indeed like a profound renascence. Pablo smelt the air of his time and wanted to be where it blew freely. He wanted to enter political life and in its struggle work out, in writing and oratory, his difficult creed of anarchy and faith. He was a loather of institutions, but he believed in the human spirit; he regarded the existent Catholic Church with profound suspicion, but he accorded to its ideal and to much of its tradition an unwithholdable inbred devotion. Even at its worst it appeared to him to be the only learned religion, the only system of faith at once impassioned and controlled. And a system of faith was essential, he thought—indeed perhaps the only essential system. But as to secular government, to be acceptable at all, how it would have to be reconceived, in what terms of looseness and simplification! So that liberty, in its gravest and in its least sense, was indisputably everyone's and knowledge at every man's elbow who desired it. These things secured, there was little more that man's benevolent interference could or should be allowed to impose on man, he thought. He was in fact an anarchist—with a difference. As perhaps every Spaniard is whatever he is—with a difference. Certainly he was no Communist, but he was sick of the self-deceptiveness and inertia of Liberalism in Spain. His young idea was to seek the classification of himself in shooting off his impossible theories against immediate issues, and perhaps arrive eventually at a practicable code and a movement.

But Consuelo did not hesitate to remind him that he had married her before he started exposition of his ideals. He had gambled first on his personal life, had won what he wanted for it, and must stand by the consequences. She made him understand that if he now could not have other things to gratify his vanity, the fault was his, not hers. She had married one kind of man, and would not tolerate being fobbed off with another.

The battle was long, and was never really settled. Pablo, with all his own family taking the Parajo side against him, sold out his interest in the Areavaga possessions, established his affairs so that without greedy acquisition of more and more wealth his wife and family should be enabled to live in suitable bourgeois state, allowed the Parajos to manage Consuelo's wealth for her as she and they thought best and gave himself up to somewhat disheartened political writing, and to the expansion and improvement of the Areavaga Working Men's College, founded by his father. Also he took many lonely journeys about Spain, and spent some months of each year, between Pablo's death and Pilár's birth, in talk and meditation in Madrid, in the *Ateneo*. But he saw Consuelo's point, that he had cheated her, and he grew weary of estrangement from her—he never even thought of other women—grew weary of his own undeveloped theories too, and more and more addicted to a gentle life of escapist individualism. There was also his little son Juan, who ought to be brought up harmoniously, by the balanced love of father and mother. Perhaps Juan, Juanito, assisted to be himself, protected from the hard-set conventions and theories of his world, might be what his father was not—one of Spain's great men. Perhaps in paternity he would serve his dear country, who was failing her in himself. So he threw up the sponge, conceded domestic peace to Consuelo, stayed at home in his own region and fell a little bit in love with his wife again. But good-naturedly and without exaction now—indeed with a love she understood and appreciated much more than his first fire. Pilár, Nieves and Milagros were born of this mild renewal and Consuelo fell placidly in love with her husband. Nevertheless when after four years of marital union, he withdrew once more into celibacy and into the seclusion of his own room, never again to take her, or any woman, in love, she accepted his inclination contentedly, and their domestic life, founded on self-control and on their great love for their children, was a smooth and happy one. And Pablo, watching over the growth of his only son, and exercising passionately for him the detachment and patience of true love, sometimes gently teased his wife by saying to her: "You wouldn't have it from me, my dear, but believe me, your son is going to be one of Spain's great men." But she showed neither fear nor resentment of this joke, and indeed she liked the phrase 'one of Spain's great men,' so that it grew into a household word with which his sisters, growing up to adore him, liked to tease Juanito.

And now Juanito was in the battle. A lawyer and in politics in Madrid. A burning reformer, witty, courageous and humane, communistically inspired as his father had never been, but married to a Spanish aristocrat and unable to escape his personal faith in the Catholic Church. With his problem to work out, as his father had had, but tackling it more freely, and aided by the open, cynical willingness of his wife to let him ride at any old windmill. Withal he was only a boy, and married too young perhaps, his father sometimes thought uneasily. But he dismissed that thought as mere parental jealousy. Juanito was no more a womaniser than he had been himself, and had all the Areavaga inclination to marital fidelity. Therefore, since Luisa did not thwart or stampede his ambitions, contrary though they ran to her tradition, it was probable that the boy would be a lucky one, would eat his cake and have it, would be both happy in his private life and also 'one of Spain's great men.' If so, that was enough, and Pablo's own rather cowardly and bungled life might perhaps have been justified. But he would have liked to have lived to see something of such justification.

He peeled another fig.

"What's that sigh for, father?" said Milagros.

"For the deliciousness of life," he said with a sceptical smile. He was wary with this child, for he found her penetratively intelligent beyond her years. Once he had said to her when she was admiringly teasing Juanito that perhaps they were all wrong and that it was she who was to be 'one of Spain's great men.' "Ah well, there's room for more than one," she had said delightedly. Now he had certainly no intention of explaining his sigh to her, but the friendly inquiry made him almost sigh again. For besides desiring to see Juanito forge nobly into life, it would have been sweet to see these diverse and diverting little daughters some distance on their roads. But his last visit to Madrid, eight months ago, explained in some facile lie to Consuelo, had really been to consult a heart specialist. Nor had he gone too

soon—for after the journey from the north and before he
had seen the great man he had had an attack of sudden
hideous and choking pain while undressing in his hotel
bedroom which had not ended in death merely because of
the promptitude of an intelligent young doctor also
staying in the hotel. The specialist had had no difficulty
in diagnosing from that seizure, and Pablo knew now,
though he carried his capsules, his little pearls of hope,
from coat pocket to coat pocket, trying hard not to
forget them, that no man, however desirous of life, could
hope to survive or endure many seizures of angina
pectoris. Nobody knew why he moved slowly now, and
often looked strangely weary—he explained these things,
and his capsules, as precautions against slight asthma—
and beyond that he never discussed his health. The
doctor had warned him against all excesses—but there
were no excesses in his life, except in cigarette-smoking.
That habit he would not alter, even to lengthen life, nor
would he deviate from his customary manzanilla-drinking
with Cabantes' eccentrics, or in peaceful thought, in the
Café del Rio. He lived as he lived—his only excitements
being cerebral when, in rare indulgences, the old poetic
and patriotic longings came to trouble his nights, or the
buried dream of ideal love, not for any tangible woman,
but simply love as it had always in essence eluded him,
returning, made him restless and mockingly ashamed of
such traces of senility. The specialist had been puzzled to
find a cause in Pablo's smooth life for his disease—it did
not occur to him that a life deflected, reformed, reshaped
against the will, and in which only the mind is left to its
pointless, disappointed ranging, may be as much an

excess, a straining of nature, as any passion of greed or self-indulgence. It did not occur to the specialist that it may be as bad for one kind of man to live in tame normal patience as for another to live like Nero. In any case, amused at the doctor's bewilderment, Pablo had promised to do his bidding and avoid emotional excitement. And he had returned to his books, his sherry, his cigarettes and his pleasant family life in Cabantes, with awareness of them all much sharpened by knowledge of the disease that would take him from them sooner than he had wished to depart.

He had of course had no trouble in avoiding emotional excitement. Putting away the poets, and some of those shouters into battle who could still embitter and agitate him, he read Herodotus now and the Fathers of the Church, and sometimes Voltaire, and frequently, as all through his life, Don Quixote. He attended to the affairs of his Working Men's College and to his domestic concerns, and he sat on the terrace wall and talked to the fishermen, or in the Café del Rio where the waiter would sometimes sing a new flamenco for the customers. There was no emotional excitement.

Yet, this evening, strolling without premonition on to the terrace to see the ferry depart for Torcal he had encountered that against which he believed no man, however old or wise or tired, can be adequately armed. He had met beauty, mythical, innocent and shameless. As he thought now of what he saw he closed his eyes. A girl in a pale blue cotton dress and tennis shoes, a girl with very white skin and a faint rose-flush on her cheeks, fainter than that of the dead rose in her hand. Her hair, of

66

goldish brown, was curly and clung to her head like a
Greek boy's. Her blue eyes, boyish too, androgynous,
were wide and shy, but darkened by dark lashes and by
shadows of fatigue. Her mouth was a wide red bow. Her
carriage of head, neck and breast most virginal and pagan.
He had never seen before in the flesh—nor even in his
passion for Consuelo had he thought he saw—the old
eternal poetic myth of girlhood. But here it was.
Untouched, unaware, unflirtatious, courteous—an unassuming governess-girl, feeling homesick and uncertain
but with good manners accepting these conditions and
keeping them demurely to herself, looking about her with
interest on a new scene, and quite unconscious that her
brilliant beauty ravished the evening and rendered a
sceptical and easily mannered elderly man, her respectable
employer, unable to utter more than one or two banal
sentences before he hurried away in fear from his own
sudden, senile folly.

He smiled now at Milagros and poured out some
Madeira.

"No, child. I will not have you drink Madeira at this
hour."

He certainly had seen a joke in Pilár's innocent discussion of her dueña. Some nun in Ireland had selected
this girl to play watch-dog over others! Women could be
grotesquely amusing. Ronsard's girl they might as well
have sent—ah, those poets whom he had in his good sense
foresworn! He had perhaps another year to live. Well
then—he lifted his glass—he would live it as he should,
without senile corruption, without day-dreams of an
ageing man, to dishonour a faithful wife, his own self-

respect and virginal beauty waiting for her young poet. He would not be afraid of Medusa's face, since it was certainly not his business to play Perseus. He had been smitten by a vision in his garden, like any disgusting old satyr. But he was not a satyr—nor was he equal to the most suppressed emotional excitement. No harm in being able to appreciate, even at the eleventh hour, that which the poets persist in re-creating. No shame in saying 'yes' to it, that they are right, the flesh can, once in centuries, do imagination's trick. But there it ends. Ah, Consuelo—he smiled towards his wife, his heart much more flooded and troubled than he dared allow in his dumb soliloquy—ah, Consuelo, you know you can trust me, even with Ronsard's Helen in the house. There is no Ronsard left in me, if there was ever any. And I love you and my children, and to see beauty go clean and unscathed until love rends her—not old man's sensuality. Still it is something to have seen that face. To have all that youth dreamt, long ago and uncertainly, proved no more than right after all, in grotesque and mocking fashion.

He finished his Madeira, and with a sudden wordless gesture of weariness, one of his imperious mannerisms which no one in the house resented, he stood up dismissing his family, and went slowly and alone to his library.

SAN GERONIMO

It was cool under the plane-trees. Mary sat down near a statue of an old man in a frock-coat. Children played all about; nurses gossiped, suckled infants. A fountain trickled pleasantly. There was a church at the other side of the square. Mary could see its porch and open door across which figures moved perpetually; a friendly traffic, reminiscent of home. There was a break in the line of houses beside the church, so that, through an aisle of plane-trunks, masts and funnels rose into view from the valleyed river, and beyond them a wine-red hill-side. The sky, tender and temperate, was like Mellick's.

Mary had been a week in Spain and this was her first free afternoon, her first expedition of discovery in Altorno. It was four o'clock now and she need not return to the Casa Pilár until half-past nine. She felt a considerable sense of rest.

The week, by reason of its novelty, had seemed eventful, but had not been unpleasant. Now at the end of it she had the feeling that roughly she knew her routine—and her place. No Man's Land, she might have called the latter, though without any bitterness. For she liked, as she had expected to, its neutrality, its twilight. She was treated with kindliness by the Areavagas and her life was comfortable. The gentle servant-maids smiled benevolently on her; the children were companionable, taught her some Spanish phrases and gossiped amusingly;

and though she still approached her daily lesson in English grammar and composition with anxiety, she found the intelligence of her pupils a help in promoting its liveliness. Things were, in fact, going well; being a 'miss' seemed to be within her power. The hours of duty were long, but through many of them she had to be no more than passively present. From nine o'clock to ten on every weekday she gave the girls their English lesson; from ten to twelve she chaperoned whilst visiting professors instructed them in history, literature, mathematics, drawing, natural history and music. From twelve to half-past one they played tennis or walked in the garden, or Mary escorted the trio to the village on any errand they might have, or waited in a church while they said the Way of the Cross or went to confession. At half-past one she lunched, alone; she was left to her own devices in her room until about three o'clock, when they came shouting for her to set off on the serious exercise of the day, a long walk into the mountains, a scramble among the rocks of the wild shore, or a row across the bay to a cove beyond Torcal, where they had a bathing hut. (The girls were good swimmers and were pleased to find that their new 'miss' could also swim.) At half-past five they had to be home again, and they sat with Mary then in her little dining-room, drinking thick chocolate and sugar-water, and eating cakes. At this hour the second post usually came, bringing the 'miss' letters about which the children and the bearded postman at the window teased her. On three evenings of the week they were visited at six o'clock by a black-robed Augustinian father for instruction in Church history and Christian doctrine.

Afterwards the next day's lessons were prepared, with Mary's shakily given counsel. At eight o'clock the girls went downstairs to their mother in the salón, or to their father's library, and Mary might do as she pleased in her room until she dined at half-past nine. Sometimes before they went to bed the children came to her room again, or invited her to the salón, to gossip a little before saying good night.

It was a long day, and Mary was often sorry for her pupils, as they plodded dutifully to its end; but their parents, though extremely kind to them, believed in discipline and education, and it seemed that the girls themselves did also, so good-tempered and acceptant were they. Often too she wondered, who herself was young and in good health, how poor, elderly Miss Anita had stayed the daily course. By putting almost nothing of herself into it, she must suppose, since almost nothing of oneself was asked for. Indeed, that was the implication which underlay the whole arrangement—that a miss, though responsible for the safety and good behaviour of her charges, was in no true sense to assume authority over them or to impose or reveal personality; she was their tool, something paid for to be used by them for their benefit and, in reason, according to their whim. And, except when they expressly released her, she was to be amiably at their disposal all day and in so being would do well to keep herself and her possible moods and interests completely out of the picture. It surprised Mary that Doña Consuelo, who spoke no English and very bad French, had managed to convey that vague spiritual condition of employment from the very first day, merely by an attitude, merely by not seeming to see her employée very clearly. But from Pilár, who was naïve and had the philosophy of the bourgeoisie of Altorno at her finger-tips, Mary learnt quite specifically that a miss is a person of great responsibility but of no authority.

Mary could see now that, embraced for life, such a status might not be exhilarating, but for herself she welcomed the adventure in invisibility. From the cradle she had always been, without having to think of it, somewhat a person in her own obscure world. An eldest daughter, eldest sister; considered pretty, considered intelligent; successful at school and somewhat envied by schoolfellows for her natural graces; one of a family long respected in her native place; tentatively courted by more than one presentable young man, and loved by John MacCurtain. These simple facts were a part of her, yesterday, to-day and for ever; there was no ultimate escape from them, thank God, but it was interesting to hide awhile from even the most agreeable certainties, and where, if she had planned a thousand years, could she have found a more thorough shelter than in this curiously obliterating occupation?

She smiled now, thinking that after all one cannot be obliterated, but only hidden, disguised, and that it was pleasantly surprising to be Mary Lavelle, all clues and certainties thereto deep sealed within, and yet to sit unknown, unneeded, in the leafy square of a Spanish town. She anticipated no wild adventure; she wanted none. This was, to her simplicity, wild adventure. Six weeks ago she had hardly been aware of the town of Altorno; six weeks ago Spain was as far away as the mountains of the moon, and freedom from relationship to this one and that, freedom from being exactly what she circumstantially was and was glad to be, the most ridiculous and unnecessary of conceptions. Now because of a whim she had taken, because of a flippant obstinacy, here she was with a year of veiled leisure before her in which to "enlarge her mind," she had said to John, and "grow up," she had pleaded.

So far this afternoon had not shown her much which could conceivably accord with girlish previsions of Spain. Outside the station she had found a very showy street of offices and shops; some yellow trams; many beggars, many diseased and dirty people; some black-chinned workmen in black students' caps; an iron bridge, with beyond it apparently a busy square, some shabby trees, a shabby bandstand; a muddy river, clumsy-looking coal-boats; in the distance huddled heaps of slums, and the brown tower of a crumbling church; around the whole, red, sinister hills, deep-scarred and shadowy; above an undramatic pale blue sky.

She had gone westward from the bridge for her first stroll, along the street of pretentious shops. To her untravelled eyes these were very interesting, and indeed their displays and the motor-cars pulled up along the kerbs made it clear that wealth and self-indulgence had habitation in Altorno. The cosmetic shops enchanted Mary, and she gazed with respect at the young ladies who swept in and out of them. In Ireland in 1922 no respectable girl used lipstick or plucked her eyebrows. But Spanish girls—she had noticed this already and had observed Pilár's still discreet, sub-débutante self-embellishment with wonder—Spanish girls had a different idea. They left as little as possible of themselves to nature.

She had bought stamps from a woman in a tobacco kiosk, who wrapped them up in a piece of brown paper; had studied posters outside a primitive-looking cinema; had looked with respect on marble porticos of banks and clubs. Altorno was a rich, grand place—not beautiful like Dublin—where she had often visited the family of Uncle Tim, her mother's brother—but far more opulent. The hills, however, which met her eyes in every direction beyond the ornate buildings were not opulent at all. Their wine-red bareness and craggy edges were profoundly sober in effect—and yet she knew they were the fertile womb of limousines, French hats and platinum rings. Mary had walked on their slopes already, had seen the trucks descend the valleys with the raw wealth which founded this glossy splendour. She had seen some mining villages and thought them sadder and wilder than any poverty she knew in Ireland. It was an unlooked-for Spain. Busy, rich, common and progressive on the one hand—on the other, grave and pitiful. Where were the castanets and the flowers in the hair?

The stroll had brought her at last from the luxury streets to this peaceful square where she was glad to sit awhile. She liked the great façade of the church. She noted the immense and sweeping height of the porch, and the faded, sweet colour of the buff stone, so different from the bright grey banks and clubs. She noticed that ornaments were gently scrolled and wrought on its aged surface, and how the bell-tower, soaring up against the background of the mountains, seemed beautiful and patient as they, and almost as old.

A watering-cart, drawn by bullocks, passed her by; the plane leaves rustled dryly. She had seen many novelties in her week—these bullock-carts for instance, and men in blouses, and Andalusian wet-nurses; and tall-housed mining villages, and eucalyptus groves, and the yacht of the King of Spain, and lemon trees in cottage gardens; she had learnt to identify street cries and Hispano-Suizas, to buy tram-tickets and say thank you and 'I beg your pardon.' She had heard flamenco-singing, *cante hondo*. She had begun to drink wine at dinner, and to dip churros in her chocolate; she had studied her map and accepted the vastness and regionalism of Spain, and understood already that the north is not the south; already she had taken her place, felt attached, and might even smile at tourists. She had caught a hint of Spanish realism and Spanish vulgarity, a little of bourgeois routine. She felt a little at home. But, sitting here, in green shadow, while the Spanish afternoon dreamt and the strange sky gleamed with familiar homely tenderness —she felt an unexpected solemn movement in her heart; something like premonition took her, oppressing, puzzling. She felt not sadness but the inability to ward it off; not love but something like resignation to its possible pain; something like understanding of it. The heavy moment held, though she lifted common sense against it. It was as if what she looked on thus accidentally were ageing her, as if it were imposing knowledge. She was inert and puzzled; she felt as if she might never move again. She had noticed the gravity of

Spaniards and their power to sit still, to move slowly. She thought of that now, and tried to laugh at herself. "More Spanish than the Spanish themselves," she said, joking back to Irish history. But the weight stayed on her; her eyes remained stupidly fixed on the tall church and the plane-trees.

"So there you are!"

It was a ladylike, Co. Tipperary voice. A thin little woman in a chip-straw hat and a grey flannel suit stood beside her. Miss Harty.

She had met Miss Harty in Torcal three days before when her charges had stopped to speak with two girls in the charge of this other. Miss Harty, though unprepossessing, had been kind and curious. "So *you're* the new 'miss' at Areavagas'! I heard you were expected. How do they treat you? Is your room all right? Do you get bacon and eggs for breakfast?" Her questions were surprising, but she had told Mary that there were many misses in Altorno, and that—when was her afternoon off?—very well then, on Wednesday she must come to the café Aleman at tea-time and get acquainted. And Mary on her way in in the train now had wondered if she would ever summon courage to fulfil her solemn promise to Miss Harty. "Why aren't you going down to the café? Come on—I'll take you. Wednesday is a good day—there'll be plenty of us there. Come on—it's the other side of the bridge. What are you doing mooning about up here? I've just left my girls at a house near the park. Have to collect them at seven, the little brats! It's an awful life—you'll find that out! How're you getting on? You really ought to insist on a proper breakfast—

they treat you like dirt if you don't stand up for yourself, you know——" Miss Harty walked, as she spoke, with a fussy wobble. She galloped Mary back to the big street and past the luxury shops to the bridge. In the square at the other side where trams whirled and policemen blew whistles, it was necessary to move in a more Spanish fashion. Several narrow and ancient-seeming streets ran out of the square and Miss Harty cantered breathlessly into one of them. There she slowed up, and prinking in a shop window, did some readjusting to the chip-straw hat. "You never know who'll be seated in the Alemàn," she said to Mary. "There are a lot of English in Altorno." She paused outside the glass door of an old-fashioned cake-shop. "Here we are," she said, and made a somewhat flurried entry.

The shop was baroque, and smelt sweetly of rum and chocolate. The ornate counter was laden with cakes, and the mirrored walls had frosty patterns scrolled on them. Just inside the door a few marble-topped tables were surrounded now by English-seeming people. Further off the café extended in two large alcoves. Over the nearer archway Mary read the word 'Señoras' trailed in careless gold lettering through stucco leaves and cupids. It was under this word—into safety, she supposed—that Miss Harty led her, and to a marble table just beyond it at which some women were already seated.

"Hello, Harty. Sit down."

"Hello, Harty. How's the old heart?"

"Hello, Duggan. Hello, O'Toole. Let me introduce Miss Lavelle. The new miss at Areavagas'."

There were welcoming noises. One of the women slid

along the black leather seat against the wall, and beckoned Mary in. Mary thought as she sat beside her that she looked kind and mad. "I'm O'Toole," she said in a very agreeable Dublin voice.

Miss Harty sat down on the outer side of the table.

"Hello, Barker," she said to an elderly, fat woman. "I didn't notice you."

"Barker's slimming," said O'Toole.

"The Areavagas of Cabantes?" said Miss Barker to Mary. "Ah, quite a good house. Murphy was there, wasn't she?" Miss Barker had a Lancashire accent.

"Yes," said the sandy young woman, Miss Duggan. "Three girls. Murphy loathed it." Miss Duggan came from Kerry, Mary guessed.

Mary raised her brows.

"Poor old Murphy!" said O'Toole. "She's at the dangerous age! No, now, Harty—no use ogling out that way——" She winked grotesquely in the direction of the tables beyond the archway where the English people were grouped. "No use, my girl. He isn't there."

Harty giggled. "O'Toole, you're a caution."

The waitress came. Harty undertook to order Mary's tea. "Though I warn you you won't recognise it as tea." Her Spanish was slow and comic.

Tea was brought, and the absurd toast that the misses always insisted on and grumbled at. Miss Harty poured out Mary's tea. Mary was glad to have nothing to do; she felt paralysed under the staring of her companions.

"What brought *you* out here?" said Miss Barker.

"Oh, I wanted a job."

"Same old reason," said O'Toole. "What else would

bring anyone? Take off the hat, Harty, for God's sake, or else fix it straight on your head!"

Harty took it off. She was very freckled, and had small insistent eyes, like a bird's. O'Toole's own brimless hat was very smartly set on her head, and she wore an eye-veil. Her weather-beaten, lively face was almost as daringly made-up as a Spaniard's and the *décolletage* of her dress was very deep. Mary noticed that none of the other misses had on any make-up at all. They all wore shabby, decent English suits.

"I think I'll go and wash," said Harty.

"Take the shine off your nose, too, while you're there," advised O'Toole. Harty vanished through a door at the extreme end of the alcove.

"Well, what do you think of the club-house?" O'Toole asked Mary.

There were about six largish tables in this part of the café, the part reserved for ladies. At one table two Spanish women in deep mourning were gravely eating cakes. Scattered at the others were figures so suited and hatted that Mary assumed them to be members of her new profession. She realised that she was being well and cautiously observed by all these figures.

"It seems very nice," she said politely.

"We of the underworld make a home from home of it."

" 'Ssh, O'Toole," said Duggan.

"There seem to be a lot of misses."

"That's what I always say."

Mary laughed.

"See McMahon this morning?" Miss Barker asked Miss Duggan.

"Yes, in San Nicolas. She said to tell you she won't be here to-day. The children want her to drive to Zara with them."

"Ah! To see the miraculous shrine?"

"What is that?" Mary asked.

O'Toole winked at her.

"Saint Joseph has taken to lifting his eyebrows at the people of Zara, if you please."

Miss Duggan looked angry. "Be careful, O'Toole."

"But I'm only telling her what's happening. I expect he has cause to. I'm all for miracles, Duggan. God knows I could do with one or two."

Harty came back with a white nose, and the rest of her face as before.

Mary drank some tea.

"Don't be afraid of it," said O'Toole. "It isn't half as stimulating as it looks. There he is now, Harty. No, don't look round. It's a pity about your nose, but I've told you often enough how to do it."

Two English-looking men of indifferent age and appearance had sat down at a table beyond the alcove. Harty fluffed up the hair about her ears. Another miss came from the cloak-room and sat at the end of the table. She had an easier view of the two men than Harty. She stared at them until she caught the eye of one, and bowed to him. He bowed gloomily in response. She was young and plump.

"Well, Keogh—any news?"

The newcomer shrugged. While she talked she mainly kept her eye on the two indefinite men.

"Nothing much. Want a change of job? Callanan's

going home. Nervous breakdown. In an awful state. Not a bad place hers—only those two little boys—and 150 a month."

Duggan looked interested, but O'Toole shook her head.

"I get that now. I'll stay where I am as long as I can stick this hole. But I'm going back to Paris as soon as I can. The French—they're the people! God, I wish I'd stayed in Lyons!"

Everyone smiled. The glories of O'Toole's life in Lyons were an old story.

"Is it true," Miss Barker asked, "that Robinson is practically starving in Madrid?"

Keogh nodded gravely. "I was going to tell you. It's awful—sacking her at her age."

"Of course, she was quite useless lately," said Harty. "Could hardly walk a step."

"She ought to go home."

"She hasn't anywhere to go to."

"We'll have to collect, that's all. There must be about twenty of us in Altorno who know her——" Miss Barker began to count on her fingers.

"My God," said O'Toole, "I'm stony!"

"Oh, I'm not counting you," said Barker. "You hardly ever met her."

"I met her often. Poor old Robinson."

Misses came and went. Mary was repeatedly introduced. Everyone asked her about this or that condition of her job. Everyone told her it was an awful life. Everyone warned her to stand up for herself or she'd be treated like dirt. Everyone stared at her lingeringly. No one inquired what she thought of Spain.

"Take off your hat," said O'Toole. Mary obeyed. A fidgety silence fell on the table.

"Ee, but you're pretty, lass!" said old Miss Barker. Miss Keogh looked away again towards her two Englishmen and Miss Harty fluffed up her hair about her ears.

"Cheer up, girls," said O'Toole. "We have a decoy duck now, and no mistake. Maybe she's the very thing we needed."

Duggan and Barker smiled a little. One of the Englishmen was actually glancing at their table.

"Engineers," O'Toole stage-whispered to Mary. "There are a lot of them, English and Scotch, around. Jobs in the mines and foundries. Most of them are married though, and they're all very stuck up. We poor misses are not in their set. Oh dear me, no!"

Harty protested. "Some of them have been quite matey, O'Toole! And McFarlane *did* marry Miss Downey. Don't you remember?"

"Shall I ever forget? At what a cost! Poor Downey!"

"Do speak quietly," said Keogh.

"He's got his Harrow tie on to-day," said O'Toole. "Winchester yesterday, Eton on Sunday. A well-educated man."

"Jealousy badly becomes you," said Barker good-naturedly.

"They're deadly-looking," said Mary.

O'Toole gasped.

"My dear, good girl, they're men! Where is this you picked him up, Keogh?"

"I didn't pick him up."

"Mrs. Entwhistle introduced him to Keogh and me one Sunday at Playablanca," said Harty excitedly.

"Democratic of Mrs. Entwhistle!"

"As a matter of fact," said Keogh, "old Entwhistle isn't bad."

"No. She even goes the length of sometimes asking a miss to tea!"

"Well, a game of bridge and a buttered scone are mighty welcome," said Miss Barker. "I like Mrs. Entwhistle."

"I want another cake. Angeles!"

O'Toole went through a lively Anglo-hispanic pantomime with a waitress.

"You don't know much Spanish?" Mary asked her gently.

"Oh, I'm not so bad. I've only been in the country five years, you know. Harty's worse than me, and she's been here twelve."

Mary tried not to look amazed.

"Why don't you learn it?"

O'Toole shrugged.

"I hardly know one hundred words," said Miss Barker, "and I've worked all over Spain for nearly thirty years. We don't need to know it. All we're asked to do is talk English. But Duggan here studies it a bit, and Keogh speaks really well."

"Yes, you're good at it, Keogh. Not as good as Conlan, of course."

Keogh looked annoyed.

"How do you know? As a matter of fact, Doña

Rosario says she prefers my Spanish."

O'Toole smiled good-naturedly. "Well, I expect it's not as sarcastic as Conlan's. But anyone can see she talks like a native."

"Who is Conlan?" Mary asked.

"Oh, a lunatic. The worst-tempered woman in Spain —you'll meet her."

"Why does she speak Spanish so well?"

"God knows! She came out here from some village in County Wexford when she was twenty-one, and she's been here since. She's thirty-eight now. She detests the place."

Mary was irritated. "If so, why does she stay?"

"Because she'd hate the next place just as much. Conlan doesn't like anything here below. She's a bitter pill."

"She's a bit of a poser, I think," said Keogh.

"No, she's not," said Barker. "She's just not like the rest of us, that's all."

"*Deo gratias*," said Duggan. "One of her sort is quite enough."

O'Toole was laughing. "She's great sport. I don't care what she says, of course—I like the female, and she simply can't get me to take offence. It drives her wild."

"She sounds queer."

"Talk of angels——!"

A tall, thin woman crossed the café and entered the ladies' alcove. She stopped by the table and jerked her head in bored salutation to everyone. O'Toole beamed on her.

"Are your ears red? I'm describing you to the newcomer."

Miss Conlan's eyes skimmed over Mary while the latter was explained.

"Hardly likely to suit the Areavagas," she said then. Her speech was rapid and had Spanish inflections.

She was a very hungry-looking woman. She wore a shiny, threadbare navy blue suit and a white linen blouse demurely closed at the neck by a silver Tara brooch. Hatless, she was now engaged in folding up the small black mantilla she had taken from her head as she came in. Her straight brown hair was knotted untidily on the nape of her neck. She had a pale, fanatical face, nobly planned but faltering below the large eccentric nose to a too mobile, too bitter mouth. "What beautiful eyes!" Mary thought. They were deep blue and full of light, with black brows arching delicately.

Barker had to go, and Conlan took her place, opposite O'Toole. When Mary heard her ordering what she required from Angeles she felt both cheered and envious. The attitude of the misses to the country they worked in had been beginning to depress her.

Conlan drank her tea and ate nothing.

"Have a cake in God's name," said O'Toole, but the other woman did not even answer her. Some of the English people had departed now, but the two men who interested Keogh and Harty still sat on, smoking Gold Flakes.

"Were you at the football match, O'Toole?" Keogh asked. "I had to take my kids. The colony was there *en masse*. Nearly died laughing, of course."

"Roumania and Spain, wasn't it?"

"Yes. They never finished, I needn't tell you. The crowd objected to the referee. Nearly lynched him."

"The papers gave it to Roumania," said Conlan. "*El Debate* said they were the better team."

"Well, both teams looked mighty funny to me. I thought those two—they were sitting near us"—she nodded furtively in the direction of her two gentlemen—"I thought they'd split their sides. They left at half-time, and I didn't blame them."

"Who're you talking about now?" asked Conlan, but Mary suspected the cold mockery of her eyes.

Keogh did not answer the enquiry. Harty was agog about the match.

"Who else was there, Keogh?"

"Oh, the McVities—she looked frightful, I needn't tell you, and Mr. Harper and the Godleys and the Greenes, and practically the whole Consulate—and the vamp, of course——"

"Mrs. Mossiford?" O'Toole's eyes twinkled.

"Who else? Cradle-snatching again—his name is Bottom, I believe, and he's only just out from England——"

"What did you say his name was?" asked O'Toole.

"You heard." They both giggled and Duggan tried not to. Conlan looked at them as if puzzled.

"She's a cool one, that old Mossiford." O'Toole's voice sounded appreciative.

"She's going down the glen very fast though. She looked about ninety at the match. By the way, O'Toole," Keogh leant forward and spoke mysteriously.

"Did you hear what I heard about—about Corrigan?"
O'Toole hesitated.

"Well, I heard something."

"Keep it to yourself if you did," said Conlan.

"That she's in Barcelona—with him? And that there's some difficulty still about the German Consul marrying them there—if you call it marrying."

"I don't," said Conlan. "Shut up."

"Oh, go to another table, Conlan," said Keogh.

"I think I will."

O'Toole intervened.

"This happens every time you two meet," she said, "and I'm sick of it. I want to sit with you, Conlan, but I insist on my right to talk over the news with Keogh. Live and let live, woman!"

"Or live and let Corrigan live," Conlan amended.

"Ah, then you approve of Corrigan," said Keogh.

"What is there to approve of? I don't approve of spreading her news."

"She has pluck anyhow, the creature."

Conlan smiled derisively at O'Toole.

"Is Miss Lavelle your protégée?"

"Well, she came in here as Harty's."

Mary smiled.

"Must I be anyone's?"

Conlan raised an eyebrow.

"Don't trouble to be high-spirited," she said. "You'll find we're not embarrassingly friendly."

Mary bit her lip. She detested such elaborate acidity. It was harder to bear than her father's unstudied peevishness. O'Toole stroked her sleeve.

87

"We might be to you, alannah," she said. "You're a sight for sore eyes among the likes of us."

"Look your fill then," said Conlan. "You won't have her long to comfort your sore eyes."

"Why?" said Mary.

"What do you think you were hired for? To take the shine out of the delicious Pilár wherever you escort her?"

"Oh—that's silly—in any case, she's awfully young——"

"Rising eighteen. And Doña Consuelo is as shrewd a careerist as ever wore shoe-leather——"

Mary was exasperated and embarrassed.

"But I'm here to teach English. I'm not going into society——"

"You *bet* you're not!" said Keogh.

"Well then, there's no competition!"

"No one said there was. There'll be no proposals for you from the Spanish gentility—not if you're Helen of Troy herself. But," Conlan looked amusedly at Mary, "if you stand by, in entrance halls and on tennis courts, while Pilár makes her arrivals and departures—disguise yourself any way you like—you're not a good foil for the young lady."

"Oh, rot!"

"That's not what Doña Consuelo would say. She's a realist. She flew high and her daughters are to fly higher. When she stages them, there must be nothing around to suggest that they are not the most perfect creatures possible. You'll be going home soon."

"You're talking ridiculously."

"Beauty is at a discount in our job."

O'Toole preened herself livelily. "Don't overflatter us, Conlan darling!"

"Employers dislike it, and they're perfectly right. It's no good to you here. Corrigan was the only good-looking miss I ever saw in Spain until you turned up——"

"Thank you, Conlan," said the others.

"You're talking a lot of old-fashioned nonsense," said Mary angrily.

"That's because we're a lot of old-fashioned girls, dearie!" said O'Toole.

"Well, now you know what Conlan's like," said Duggan good-temperedly, as she got up to go.

"That's to say, you know the worst of us," said Keogh. She was absent-minded, because her two Englishmen had paid for their tea, and might go at any moment. She wanted to pass out, and perhaps speak to them, before they left. Apart from the inward thrill of that, there would be its display of worldly ease and social eminence to all her colleagues in the alcove. "I must be going," she said.

Harty adjusted her chip-straw hat and brushed some crumbs from her lap. She intended to leave with Keogh, who might have an audacity uncompassable by her. Keogh might stop and have a word with these two men. Then she, Harty, would also have to stop.

"I'm going your way, Keogh," she said, and was on her feet before there could be an argument.

O'Toole winked at Conlan, who paid no attention to her, and unfolded *El Debate*.

"Mind you don't trip over their big feet, girls; and for God's sake, Harty, straighten the hat!"

Mary watched the two depart. Keogh walked out with leisurely assurance. Harty bobbed behind her in a flurry. The Englishmen, busily lighting fresh cigarettes, jerked their heads. No words were exchanged and the two misses had no occasion to pause. They left the café.

"What could we do now?" Mary asked O'Toole.

"How do you mean—'do'? I'm off duty."

"Couldn't we have a walk or something?"

O'Toole groaned.

"Don't the Areavagas give you enough of it? They half-killed Murphy!"

Conlan looked up from her paper.

"Would you like a walk?" she inquired quite kindly.

"If she would, she isn't getting one," said O'Toole. "The two of you are sitting here with me for a while, and thank you."

"You'll lose your figure, O'Toole—your one asset, you tell me."

"Not while I stick it out with the Garcias, alannah."

Miss Conlan seemed much more bearable now, Mary thought.

"Shall we have more tea then?" she suggested.

Both women shook their heads.

"Can't afford such recklessness," said O'Toole.

"Oh—but I meant with me—as it's my first day——"
The invitation made her very shy. O'Toole beamed reassuringly.

"All right, alannah. That'll be lovely."

"Not for me, thank you," said Conlan.

Mary asked O'Toole to speak to Angeles, and listening, decided with amusement that she could have ordered what she required more easily herself. Conlan smiled, with her eyes on her paper.

"It's amazing," she said without looking up.

Mary and O'Toole drank their tea, and the latter launched on a rollicking story of her life. In France, in Lyons—ah, those were the days! "Frenchmen—believe me, alannah, they're the boys!" ("And her French is quite as good as her Spanish," Conlan threw in.) "Spaniards—they go to sleep standing up! They're nearly as bad, if you'll believe me, as those Englishmen of Keogh's." She dropped her voice, for the two men were still at their table. The narrations were exclamatory and shapeless, but her kind, over-painted face was amusing, and she was an absolute novelty to Mary, who coaxed her on to talk, and eat.

"Wouldn't you eat one of these, Miss Conlan?" she suddenly ventured.

Miss Conlan stared at her.

"No, thank you."

"Ah, Conlan—give the kid the pleasure of seeing you eat something!"

"How could that sight give her pleasure?"

"Well, it'd give it to me."

"Sorry to deny you a treat. What do you think of Altorno, Miss Lavelle?"

The very normal question made Mary shy.

"The town is rather ugly, I suppose," she began nervously—"it isn't a bit like what I'd expected——"

"Therefore you have written home that it isn't at all Spanish?"

"No," said Mary politely. "I don't know anything

91

about Spain, you see. So I couldn't write that."

"Do you want to know about Spain?"

"Yes."

"Then stop being a miss."

"Join the gipsies!" said O'Toole.

"But you know about Spain," Mary challenged Conlan.

"Oh, keep me out of it. I was never a 'smiling morn' like you."

Mary wondered if she would get used to these personal comments. She found the crudity of the misses' intercourse surprising; their rudeness to each other, their use of surnames *tout court*, their interest in the male sex, their prudery, their vindictive attitude towards their employers, and non-intelligent insolence towards the life that went on about them, their obvious poverty and social isolation, their distorted self-respect, their backhanded decency and *esprit de corps*—these distinctions of which this first afternoon's acquaintance gave her a considerable indication, made up a sad but novel picture. As a child she had with her brothers gone through a phase of Kipling-infatuation, and a line from that faraway reading came to her now as she sat in the Café Aleman: "from the legions of the lost ones, from the cohorts of the damned,"—she smiled to think how such an allusion, suggested by them, would amaze the misses of Altorno. But Conlan would accept it, probably.

These women came, undoubtedly, from impoverished wings of that not easily definable section of society, the Irish Catholic middle-class. Their backgrounds, within that classification, would differ. In Mary's own family, impoverished as she always remembered it and simple as its habit was, a tradition of formality and quietude prevailed. Her mother, aunts and grandmother had been restrained and low-voiced women; family life, in spite of her father's increasing irritability and meanness, had always retained a certain simple politeness which she and her brothers and sisters took to be the natural thing; good looks or their lack, or any other gift or defect of nature, were taken for granted by that politeness, and 'personal remarks' were very rarely tolerated; as for addressing acquaintances by their surnames only, as for abusing them to their faces by way of tea-table conversation, above all, as for allowing it to be thought that unmarried men could be a source of agitation to unmarried women—such things were simply not done in the world that Mary knew. She understood that codes of behaviour might vary, in her amorphous class, from house to house, but it appeared to her that the *sine qua non* of becoming a miss was not so much that one should be genteel by birth as that the veneer of gentility should have been sufficiently lacquered on by education in a good-class convent school. Mary, having been brought up in such a school, knew how its training enforced these rules of restraint and modesty which to Aunt Cissy, for instance, were absolutely a matter of course. Therefore, she argued, all misses must start out as more or less genteel, by Aunt Cissy's standards. However, it was a mercy that that lady was not present now to assess what they made of their gentility.

They had kept some of its essentials for better or worse. They were proud and self-reliant. (Mary noticed how each paid scrupulously for her own refreshment, and that O'Toole's acceptance of tea from her had been a graceful waiving of a rule, to please her; as for Conlan's inability to take bite or sup from anyone, that was a pitiful mania of independence into which such a temperament as hers might easily fall.) They kept their self-importance, merely to distort it, of course, in vain rages and protests against this or that insignificant detail of their position; still, misshapen thing, they kept it, and largely, madly lived on it. They kept a limping, penniless vanity and their racial power to jibe; they kept a most uncomfortable class-consciousness; above all, they kept their violent and terrible Irish purity.

As for the flowers of their training, the ladylike graces, the ground that they had fallen on was stony; these women were too lonely, unimportant and unamused to be graceful or gracious; they were too poor to be decorative, and their only social intercourse—with each other—slowly exasperating and starving them, they learnt, in jealousy and self-defence, to give each other no more than the roughest *camaraderie*. *Esprit de corps* was there, and showed itself, but bitterly and without sentiment, in times of trouble; there were antipathies and feuds; and, as between Miss Barker and Miss McMahon, a few friendships born of long association in loneliness. And O'Toole, funnily enough, liked knocking about with Conlan, who never said what she liked or didn't like.

Mary, sitting for the first time in her life among wage-earning women all considerably older than her, and seeking with little data to synthesise bewildered im-

pressions, did not realise that some reflections on her own
sex which these suggested to her were of a kind as new
to her as the experience that gave them shape.

"Take us round to your place, Conlan alannah, I'm
gasping for a cigarette."

"Come round if you like, but I've no cigarettes."

"Believe it or not, I'll buy some."

The three got up and left the Café Alemán, without
observing how the two Englishmen stared after them.

They crossed the big square again, went over the
bridge and up the street of grand shops. O'Toole loafed
enviously past these, her arm linked friendlily through
Mary's. Conlan, bareheaded, walked ahead of them with
an impatient step.

O'Toole was very dressy and had indeed, Mary
observed, an asset in her figure which, though she must
surely be forty, was really girlish-seeming and lovely.
In 1922 skirts had not yet ascended to the knee, but
O'Toole's dress of flowered foulard was as short as she
dared have it, because she knew her legs were beautiful.
Besides her legs and her eye-veil, she sported frills and
ear-rings and a strong, sweet smell of violets.

"I'd give an eye out of my head for that white fox,"
she said to Mary, halting before a shop-window.

"It'd be very little good to you then."

"Of course it's you should wear it—not an old throw-
out like me——"

"Don't be silly!"

"I can see you in it. Sailing into a theatre or somewhere, and a marvellous man at your side—a real man,
you know—none of these Spanish hop-o'-my-thumbs—

and that fur around your neck—oh, I can just see the whole thing!"

Mary smiled.

"I'd feel an awful fool in it," she said.

"I don't think! You're made for it. One of these days you'll have a husband adoring you, and giving you all sorts of gorgeous things!" They turned away from the furrier's window. Conlan was waiting impatiently at the corner of the block. "Were you ever in love yet?" said O'Toole to Mary.

"Oh—I don't know." She smiled affectionately to the ghost of John, but would not talk of him. "Were you?"

O'Toole gave a gust of laughter.

"God help us, child, what do you take me for? Was I ever in love? What else do you think has kept me alive in this rotten old world?"

"Why weren't you married, then?"

"Ah, that's a long story. That's several long stories."

"You bet it is," said Conlan, whom they had rejoined and who now led them down a side street.

"But I'm not dead yet," said O'Toole, almost wheedlingly, to Mary. "Hi, there!" she called then, and Conlan turned and paused. "I'm going in to Pepe for cigarettes and you must do the talking."

"You're running your credit too high with Pepe."

"I'll pay on the first. He doesn't mind."

"Let me get the cigarettes," said Mary.

"I will not; you've just given me tea."

"Oh, but, please——"

Conlan looked at her severely. "The sooner you learn the rules of our existence the better," she said. Mary

96

subsided. They went into a newspaper and cigar shop wedged between two tall houses. The proprietor, a bald, fat man with sad eyes and a slow, agreeable smile, received them courteously, and seemed to enjoy O'Toole's pidgin-Spanish salutations. Conlan did the real talking, and Pepe handed the *favoritos* to O'Toole with another slow, agreeable smile. The three misses went on their way.

"Pepe's got fat since his wife died," O'Toole remarked.

They turned into the square where Mary had sat by the statue in the early afternoon. They walked along the south side under the plane-trees and entered a dark, tiled hall, where a porter sat snoring.

"These are old-fashioned apartments," said Conlan. "You have to climb. The Gutierrez's are third left."

The apartment was large. The misses went down a long, carpeted corridor to Conlan's room.

"My kids are gone to their godmother's, I think," she said. "The place sounds peaceful."

Her room was immaculate and impersonal as a monk's. She opened a long, lace-screened window that overlooked the square. Mary, looking out, saw below her the fountain and children playing about the old gentleman in stone; saw, more veiled by the tops of plane-trees now, the church façade and tower; saw the rigid masts of ships and the wine-red mountain-side with evening light on it.

"Funny you should have this view," she said softly.

"Why 'funny'?" Conlan asked.

"What church is that?"

"San Geronimo."

"How old is it?"

"Sixteenth century. One of the few beauties of Altorno."

Conlan pushed forward a wobbly-looking wicker chair.

"Sit down," she said, but Mary walked out on to the balcony.

O'Toole lighted a *favorito*.

"You'll have to come in from there if you want to smoke," she said to Mary.

"In a minute."

Conlan sat on a straight-backed chair, took up an embroidery frame and began to stitch with care.

"Another altar cloth? God help us, alannah, you're mad." Then she looked towards the girl on the balcony and spoke softly: "Did you ever see such a pretty creature?"

Conlan looked at Mary too.

" 'Pretty' isn't quite the word," she said. She continued to look out of the window, neglecting her altar cloth.

"Shame to try to turn her into a 'miss,' " O'Toole went on. "Awful to think of her going the way of the rest of us."

Conlan smiled.

"Don't worry," she said.

Mary came back into the room.

"It isn't cheating if I smoke here, is it?" O'Toole looked amazed. "I told my children that I do smoke a little at home, but wouldn't in Spain if their parents disliked my doing so. They said their mother wouldn't mind very much my smoking in my room, but that Don Pablo thought it a bad habit!"

"Well, I never!" said O'Toole. "What business

98

is it of theirs what you do on the quiet?"

But Conlan's voice was kind as she replied:

"No, it wouldn't be cheating to smoke here if you want to. You don't seem to have the usual mania to assert yourself."

"Well, she'd better develop it. They give you hell in our job if you don't fight your corner," said O'Toole.

"But I really don't think that's true," Mary ventured.

Conlan smiled broadly at her.

"Hasn't Harty told you to insist on bacon and eggs for breakfast?"

"As a matter of fact she has."

O'Toole chuckled.

"Poor old Harty! That's the bat in her belfry! She's lost several jobs over it."

Mary's eyes widened.

"Does she get them in her present job?"

"She says so, but I'll take my oath she doesn't. Still— wouldn't it be nice to go home, and have that kind of breakfast once again? Wouldn't it, Conlan?"

Conlan took up her embroidery.

"I always loathed bacon and eggs."

Mary looked contemplatively at O'Toole.

"When will you go home?" she said.

"God knows. I haven't the fare. I'll never have it."

"But——"

"No 'but.' My brothers are married and have their own troubles. They don't want me. And if I got home I'd have no way of keeping myself. No, alannah, I'm here for the duration, I suppose, unless Romance comes my way, with a big R!"

Mary reflected gently that the R would have to be big. She lighted a *favorito*. O'Toole leant back contentedly and blew smoke-rings. Her beautiful legs were crossed. She had taken off her hat and eye-veil, and her red hair lay clammily against her tired, leathery forehead. She was singing softly: "Because God made thee mine I'll cherish thee—ee . . ." Conlan went on with her embroidery. The black tobacco made Mary cough a little. She looked about her nervously—at the picture of the Holy Family above the bedstead; at the *prie-dieu* and crucifix, the holy water font beside the door; the modest screen about the washstand. There were no photographs anywhere, no odds and ends from life. Above the writing table near the window a dozen books were stacked on a little shelf, all dressed in brown-paper covers, as nuns cover books.

"Do you read much?" she inquired timidly of Conlan.

"No."

"I love a good read," said O'Toole. "But of course you can never get hold of an English novel out here—Duggan has been promising me a loan of *If Winter Comes* for ages, but I'll never get it out of her."

"Where do you live in Ireland?" Conlan asked Mary.

"Mellick. Where do you?"

"County Wexford."

"Is that a nice county?"

"I've forgotten."

"How long have you been with these people?"

"Nearly three years. But I've been in Altorno for seven."

"Do you like it as well as other parts?"

"That mightn't be saying much. I loathed Andalucia.

Castile is the best of Spain."

O'Toole chimed in, abandoning her song.

"Have you really stuck the Gutierrez's for three years, alannah? How time flies! You ought to make a change."

"There aren't a lot of glorious jobs to choose among," said Conlan, "and I—like the view."

Mary turned back to it, leaning against the window pane. She had been diverted from her purposed discovery of Altorno; her feet had been set instead on the edge of a different field of exploration. Well, there would be time for both. These misses, her colleagues, were unexpected, admonitory figures, as full of morals and inferences as the church tower across the square. She felt solemn again, looking at that; felt the premonition and laying on of knowledge that the scene had brought her earlier in the day. But it fell more homelily now, as if evening eased it, or as if in an hour she had grown up somewhat. She relaxed against the window-pane. She was beginning to like the taste of the *favorito*. John would certainly forbid such strong tobacco. She smiled again to his ghost. She had no pang or longing, and was too young to reflect on their lack. It was good to be here and to observe this view. How tunefully O'Toole was singing!

A CORRIDA

IT seemed a long walk to the bullring, but when the ugly
building did become visible at the top of the road Mary
was not glad to see it. She had never felt so much
ashamed of herself as she was feeling now. She was
acutely frightened too and her confused emotional state
was inducing physical misery. The movements of her
heart were eccentric and painful and she felt a pressure
as of urgent tears behind her eyes. She stumbled and
jostled in walking.

Conlan went ahead of her, cutting their path through
the crowd, and spoke over her shoulder:

"Those two on the excited horses are in costumes of
the time of Philip III."

Far off Mary saw two riders in black velvet, but the
sight made her realise so much her predicament that she
feared she might be sick at once. Though that would be
a lucky thing. No one would expect her to go to the
bullfight then. And yet she was here of her own free
will; she had paid eight pesetas for a seat; she had invoked
the ordeal. "Oh God!" she prayed, "Oh God, forgive
me, please!"

They entered the huge building through a narrow
archway and found themselves in an unpleasant-smelling
corridor where ticket-holders, officials, vendors of this
and that rushed about in excitement. They hired two
cushions from a legless man, and mounted a flight of

stairs into sunshine again, into the open, crowded theatre. They found their seats—two sections of a wide concrete step, each with a number painted on it—placed their cushions on them and sat down. The crowd which surged about them, settling in, finding its seats, saluting its friends, was hilarious and good-tempered.

Mary, six weeks in Spain now, was finding that she liked Spanish people, individually and in crowds, liked the look of them. Not that she thought them excessively endowed with beauty. Indeed the townswomen, inclined to be dressy, were mostly rather comic, with pneumatic curves and lacquered, crimpy hair; and the men were often blue-chinned and fat. But the latter had—almost to a man, it seemed to Mary—a reserved gravity of eye that was arresting. It waited imperturbably behind even inane or hysterical liveliness and when a face fell into repose usurped it with a sobriety so profound that it held the attention as beauty might. Mary was startled sometimes to observe how persistently she had come to watch for this—among the fishermen on the pier at Cabantes, in football crowds, in the train for Altorno, in trams, at café tables—she sought and found repeated confirmation of an accidental yet desperate-seeming sadness. She thought, considering these new faces, of the looks of men she knew at home—of her father's beautiful features and the brown, lively forthright handsomeness of John. With either, the set of the face at any given minute proclaimed the mood, almost the thought—both had expressive, mobile faces. Indeed it occurred to Mary now that most Irishmen had such. But Spaniards wore masks. There was little guessing from a Spanish face the true humour of the soul behind it. If John was gay, if John was worried, if John was feeling especially enamoured, all that was in his face, and that was what his face consisted of. One had but to reckon with that, and when a change came, reckon with the change. But it seemed as if no Spaniard's mood could be taken to be the Spaniard of that minute. Always in laughter, salutation, or excitement, the observer would notice that the eyes were only waiting, their sadness withheld from this immediacy, but held. The moment of repose would give it back full dominance. It was a calm and sober sentinel. It kept the citadel quiet and untrodden.

She had learnt this at first from Don Pablo's face. He talked with the children on the terrace or if he met them as he came strolling from the Café del Rio. His daughters loved to encounter him. He spoke in Spanish with them as a rule, but slowly so that Mary might understand a little, and with explanatory asides sometimes in limping English. His face still struck the miss as complicated, but the sculptured sadness of its lines, the passionate isolated sadness of his black and narrow eyes, troubling her somewhat at first, seemed less oppressive as she grew observant of other faces. This darkness of philosophic grief in so many men could be no more than racial accident, and could not possibly spring from personal dissatisfaction, or from any conscious or ennobling discontent. Don Pablo, the miss had now decided, in so far as his face was disconcertingly still and sad, was thereby proved no more than Spanish. And he never had anything sad to say to his daughters—generally he was lightly informative, about the garden, or some phenomenon of the shore, had a story of some passing local fogey, or a joke, a political absurdity or what not, from the café or the morning papers. He teased the children gently, inquired as to the progress of Mary's Spanish, made her repeat some difficult word or phrase, and lighting a fresh cigarette, passed on unhurryingly, his sad eyes folded back in sadness. But Mary discounted now, as has been said, the complications of his face. For a mask must always complicate understanding; there was no help for that. If he wore one, perhaps it was no more than his black suit, a national uniform; and if she found it more interesting than other masks, that was perhaps because she could study it more often. In any case, she sometimes reminded herself with surprised amusement, the expressions of her employer's countenance were hardly her affair. Nevertheless, through liking him in their impersonal, accidental contacts; through liking the bearded, jolly postman who flourished her 'sweetheart's' letters at her; through liking Jaime the gardener and the fishermen on the pier; through liking the mountain-bred maidservants who waited on her with such gentleness; through liking, in varying degrees and for varying reasons, her three charges, and through, if not liking, at least respecting somewhat the serene, good-tempered Doña Consuelo, she had felt justified lately in her rather sweeping conviction that she liked Spanish people.

This liking was one reason why she sat at a bullfight, in a condition of shame and terror.

Although she did not observe the fact, she was growing up fast in this foreign soil, much faster than she or John, when they argued about the value of such growth, could possibly have anticipated. Left to herself anywhere, bereft of the family setting and the Irish back-cloth, bereft of the dominating authority of John, she might have put out unexpected shoots. But here where all was new and where duty, exacting only a minimum of personality, left her what she had never had enough of under Aunt Cissy's wing, time to observe and meditate; here where she was flung for sociability among a mixed company of tough and sad and battered fellow-country-women, all older than herself; here where, as it happened, the scene, the sky and the people were agreeable to her, she was racing very fast out of heedlessness. She was beginning to put two and two together with more method and detachment than John, for instance, might have thought quite necessary.

For in this very matter of the bullfight, he and she had agreed that, all things considered, she had better not distress herself by seeing one. She would certainly loathe it, and there was no point in the usual tourist's argument that one ought to see just one. She was tender-hearted to the point of folly about dogs and cats, and all helpless and dependent things. So, very glad that John approved her cowardice and lack of curiosity, she had gone to Spain with one great anxiety removed. She was not to be compelled to see a bullfight.

From the beginning she took some trouble to learn Spanish. It had been her intention to do so, but the illiterate insolence of most of the misses towards that language had been an added spur. As respite from a few dull classic novels which she bought at random, she formed the habit of skimming over the newspapers, guessing her way through this paragraph or that. Mainly she did this for the fun of showing off to the genuinely amazed O'Toole, and for the deeper satisfaction of taking a little wind sometimes out of Conlan's sails. But this superficial reading, making the immediate life of Spain more real to her, became attractive as Spain grew more attractive. She grew addicted to the newspapers. And in almost every one of them on almost every summer day she found news and pictures of bullfighters. A triumph here, a disaster there. Wounds, deaths and victories; disgrace and glory; music, ovations, the round of the ring; the ear and the tail and the hospital ward; and deaths again and alternatives and dedications. The everyday news of a Spanish summer. Strange and horrible.

Posters appeared about Altorno. The annual fair was coming, with its five great bullfights. Names which Mary knew from her newspaper-reading, names which no one in Spain could fail to know, were among the promised fighters. She heard them talked of in the train between Cabantes and Altorno; heard boatmen arguing their merits by the pier; saw knots of boys stand round the posters dreaming. Jaime, the gardener, showed her the hoard of duros he had saved with which to buy his tickets—Jaime, gentlest of men who cherished a miserable peacock and two bad-tempered dogs with a Franciscan sweetness. Mary was puzzled. Apparently all these easy, friendly, impervious people did really go to bullfights. The idea hurt her—and increased her curiosity about Spain. She wrote some of her bewilderment to John, and he wrote back, amused, and comforting her with the reassertion that whatever the Spaniards did, she at least was under no obligation to pretend to enjoy the butchery of bulls and horses. "To tell you the truth," said John, "it's a great relief to me to find that there still is something you dislike and resent in Spain. Your growing affection for the place alarms me sometimes, darling. Don't let any cad of an hidalgo try his fascinations anyhow. I miss you desperately—I could never tell you what it is like in this tomb of a town without you——"

She continued to read about bullfights and to worry about inconsistencies in the Spanish character. The children spoke of the coming fair, and asked her if she were going to a fight. She said no, and they did not seem surprised. Milagros said she would go with her cousins on Pronceda's day, at least—every day if possible. Nieves never went to a fight, could not bear the idea. Pilár was not going this year. "Next year, Miss Maria, when I'm out! Ah then—great fun. Very fashionable for débutantes to go—a kind of parade we make. But I cannot this year—it would spoil me, you see, for next time."

Mary was amused at that. Don Pablo never went to the fight, his daughters said. "He is like Nieves—he disapproves of it." But he made no rule for his children. "He says that it is Spanish, and so are we, and we must do as we choose about it. But still he gets angry with Milagros for liking it. I don't notice the fighting much, of course," Pilár ran on. "But it's fun to see everyone, and have everyone bowing to you, and turning their glasses on you—and you wear your newest clothes, and your name is in the paper and you're admired——"

"That's as may be," said Milagros.

"I'll never go," said Nieves.

Then in the Café Alemán on the Sunday before the fair, a number of misses, having escorted their charges to each other's houses, were killing time around the marble tables in the ladies' alcove, when Conlan said to Mary:

"Free on Wednesday?"

"Yes."

"Come to the bullfight?"

"Indeed she will not," said O'Toole protectively. "Don't mind her, alannah. What would you want at a disgusting thing like a bullfight?"

"The very idea," said Harty.

"What's coming over you, Conlan?" said Keogh. "You're almost sociable!"

But Mary, to her own astonishment, had said in an uneven voice:

"Yes, I think I'll go. I'd like to see one."

She was somewhat gratified by the flicker of surprise on Conlan's face. She knew that her willingness to take Spain as she found it, and to like her findings, roused some kind of irritation in this woman. So perhaps her decision was only a shoddy bravado, but she felt all the terror of the brave as she made it.

Conlan nodded.

"All right. I'll get the seats to-morrow."

The others protested, told Mary she'd only be sick, and she didn't know how lucky she was that she didn't have to go, as part of her job. But they soon wearied of the matter. The boringly recurrent bullfight meant nothing to them—just another aspect of the disgustingness of Spain. O'Toole alone looked troubled.

"You'll hate it, alannah. She ought to be ashamed of herself to suggest it to the likes of you. No, Harty—I don't think he'll be in this afternoon. I saw him walking towards the park—calling on Miss Phyllis Greene, I shouldn't wonder!"

"That frump?"

"Do you see that little sissy?" Keogh asked softly. "Just coming in now. That's Mossiford's new string, God help him. Rather nice, really . . ."

So here Mary was at the bullfight, because she liked Spaniards and sought to understand them.

Yet now as they surged about her in happy excitement, she hated them. Their jubilant air of holiday somehow increased instead of lessening her fear of what was to come, and she looked with venom on their bland expectancy. A fat, sallow man on her left smiled kindlily on her.

"English, señorita? Not like this. Horses make you faint. English ladies faint always."

Mary had never fainted in her life, but she thought it not unlikely that to-day she might uphold the English tradition. She felt miserable enough for any physical disaster. But she hardly smiled at the speaker. She would not imply that she was in convivial conspiracy with him against a few bulls and horses. And yet she saw the illogicality of her frostiness. She was here and had paid like the rest for her seat; she was as guilty and cowardly as anyone.

"It's twenty-five past four. The President ought to be in his box any minute now." Conlan indicated the silk-hung balcony above them whence the ceremonial would be controlled. In the boxes and balconies to left and right of the Presidential seat Mary saw the rank and fashion of Altorno, displaying and inspecting itself with fan and opera glass. A few exalted young women—this year's débutantes, Mary understood from Pilár's coaching—even wore the traditional shawls and high combs which had once been the only correct wear for ladies at the corrida, but now were regarded by many as unnecessary. Mary studied these archaic toilettes, and agreed with the judgment of those who had abandoned them. Far off in a balcony she thought she saw Milagros with her cousins, the Parajos.

"Pronceda is taking the first and fourth," said Conlan.

The President arrived; there was a burst of cheering; high in the theatre a military band struck up; the clock was almost on the stroke of the hour.

Mary sat absolutely still in her place. Her tier was ninth from the barrier, about midway in the huge, neatly graded audience. The theatre was packed. Opposite her in the sunny seats, the massed crowds looked oddly pink and white—'like hundreds and thousands,' she thought. The empty ring of sand seemed innocent and peaceful; the sky was very blue, and the mild air scarcely stirred. Then a tall door opened in the barrier and the men in seventeenth-century velvet cantered out. The ceremony began.

The procession came out with a glitter, saluted the President, and dispersed.

"The one nearest us is Pronceda," said Conlan. But Mary knew him from newspaper photographs. He was smaller than she had expected.

The men in velvet came forward again on their horses,

and one of them tried to catch the key which the President flung. He missed it, and the audience mocked delightedly.

Pronceda's first bull came into the arena with a tomboy charge, his stud ribbons fluttering from the hump of muscle on his neck. He was a great, blond creature with the bearing of courage, and the people applauded him. Mary looked away from him to the man who must presently destroy him. Pronceda stood at the barrier in talk with his sword-handler, eyeing the enemy. Two of his men, old and battered-looking fighters in shabby suits, were running the bull with comic and undignified speed. The matador took his fighting cape and walked to the centre of the ring. Black hat, black slippers, pink stockings, suit of pale blue and silver, he looked like a lovely toy. Mary wondered in panic why he strolled thus into the danger whence his men were very naturally scampering. He paused about ten yards from the briefly halted bull, paused and unfurled somewhat his magenta-and-yellow cape. The bull, a taker of challenges, rushed at it.

And so the attitudes began, the slow, proud movements.

But the horses came out to break them. Piteous, blindfolded skeletons like Rocinante, mounted by solid men in leggings of steel. There were no mattresses for the horses' bellies in 1922 and when Mary saw the bull get ready to charge the first of them she had to close her eyes, though despising herself for accepting such palliative while the trembling dumb creatures in the ring had none.

She looked at the second charge. "Take your punishment," she said to herself. "You chose to come here; the horses didn't."

She got punishment. The horse was lifted high; the picador, having used his lance stupidly, fell to the ground and the triumphant bull was lured off bravely, in a moment of deep anxiety, by El Niño de La Montaña, the second matador of the afternoon. Presently, to the command of trumpets, the horses left the ring, one of them in tatters. There was blood on the sand, blood on the bull's shoulders. He moved more cautiously now, but still with speed and self-confidence.

A tall youth in red and gold went out and challenged mischievously, banderillas in his hand. The bull charged with wild intention and went by under the boy's elbow, the two beribboned darts swinging now from the muscle of his neck. As neat as a conjuring trick. The applause was so violent that Pronceda, who had been going out with another pair, smiled to the people and handed them to his young apprentice, who this time ran to the bull, straight on the horn it seemed, and bending over it, tip-toe, planted his decorations and slipped along the flank like a ripple. To great applause he took a third pair from the barrier and once again displayed how unerring he could be in dancer's impudence before the bull. Pronceda smiled at him.

The trumpet sounded again. The bull was standing alone in wariness at the barrier. The sun was full upon him and made high lights on the streams of blood along his flank. The ribboned darts hung awkwardly. He drooped his head a little, but though baffled, was full of life. He knew his own wild strength, and liked the touch of the sun.

Pronceda took sword and muleta from his men, and

went and stood erect in the ring before the President's box. He lifted the sword and took off his hat. He was speaking but no one could hear him. He dedicated the bull, apparently, to a beaming citizen in a balcony. Then he gave his hat to the banderillero in red and gold, and walked across the ring out of the shadow to where the bull waited.

The last act seemed very slow and gentle. Very quiet. The thunderous noise, of counsel, enthusiasm and rapture, from the concrete seats, seemed no more than a faraway roof shutting in the two combatants in the lonely, still place of their drama. It was no more than a dimly suggested veil which blurred every issue but this mortal one. Within, in the ring, there was silence. The sun shone tenderly on Pronceda's hair, on his silver trappings, on the blond back of the bull. A small breeze flapped the muleta.

The matador drew his enemy to his breast, and past it, on the gentle lure; brought him back along his thigh as if for sheer love; let him go and drew him home again. He took the bull's blood on his coat, but never looked up out of his zone of silence to advertise the decoration. Again and again in classic passes he allowed the horn to skim him, then drawing back from the great, weary but still alert antagonist, he profiled and went over the horn, as gently as an angel might, to kill. The sword sank where the stud ribbons fluttered, in to the hilt, as bravely driven as if the dealer believed himself to have been dipped in Achilles' river. Pronceda, leaving it there, seemed hardly to be aware of his dangerous journey out and along the flank. He stood, his muleta almost furled,

very close to the bull's shoulder while it staggered to its
knees, and tried with savage nobility to rise again. But
this new bauble, this gleaming hilt among the ribbons,
darts and streams of blood, was the last honour. He
rolled over, dead, and the matador stood unsmiling at his
side.

Uproar claimed a hearing now indeed. The audience
rose, cheering and chanting its great pleasure. To the
sound of music, to thundering applause the brave bull
was borne out by mules and Pronceda went round the
ring, with the ear and tail of the enemy in his hand.
Straw hats were flung to him, and he flung them back;
leather wine-bottles, and he drank; fans, flowers and
walking-sticks—the red-and-gold banderillero laughed as
he picked them up. But Pronceda hardly smiled. He
looked small and lonely, and somewhat absent-minded.

Mary stood among the shouting Spaniards, not
knowing whether she shouted too or not. Had she been
searching for means to describe her state of emotion then,
she could have found no covering term, nor could she
indeed in many sentences have accomplished any record
of her immediate self. But that was not troubling her—
yet. She was—perhaps this is the easiest phrase—outside
herself. She was with Pronceda. Slower than the
crowd, she was out of step and lagging, still in the silence
of the tragedy now finished with. She was absent-
minded as its enactor seemed. Death, so strangely
approached, so grotesquely given and taken, under the
summer sky, for the amusement of nonentities, death
made into an elaborate play, for money and cheers, and
exacting in the course of the show a variety of cruelties

and dangers; death, asking for helpless victims as well as for the hazards of courage; death and pain, made comic, petty and relentless, for an afternoon's thrill. And staged in fancy dress, with brassy circus music, and played by an old rule of thumb, by puppet formula and timing. There it was, she had seen it, the tawdry bullfight, and all that she had known of herself was shocked, as she expected it to be, by its indefensibility, its utter, cynical cruelty. There was no escape from that and even now, in this moment of detachment from herself, this moment of queer dreaminess, its truth knocked and she admitted it. But meantime another, newer self stayed musing in the minutes just now spent; saw the bright cape swing and the man stand sculpted in his little dancing-shoes to let danger rip his silk; saw the innocent bull run towards the ribboned darts, receiving them in slow surprise, as a clumsy child might from a nimble, teasing one; saw the slim sword under the muleta, the matador's bent head, his quiet, balancing hand. Movement, and its refusal, made absolutely beautiful by a formula of fantastic peril; wildness become a pretty play; innocent ferocity fooled by a cunning little man in a fancy suit. For people to clap and while away an hour or two. A silly, shameful custom, of which Don Pablo very naturally disapproved. Burlesque, fantastic, savage, all that John had said—but more vivid with beauty and all beauty's anguish, more full of news of life's possible pain and senselessness and quixotry and barbarism and glory than anything ever before encountered by this girl; more real and exacting, more suggestive of wild and high exactions, more symbolic, more dramatic, a more personal and searching arrow to the heart than ever she had dreamed of. Here was madness, here was blunt brutality, here was money-making swagger—and all made into an eternal shape, a merciless beauty, by so brief a thing as attitude. Here—and Mary, to whose youth all knowledge was new, received this sudden piece of it as crippling pain—here was art in its least decent form, its least explainable or bearable. But art, unconcerned and lawless.

"I must try to remember," she muttered without clarity to herself. "I mustn't forget——"

Boys in red smocks were raking bloodstains out of the sand.

"It's a pity you saw that performance first," Conlan said.

"Why?"

"Because you couldn't possibly appreciate it, and it's unlikely that a bull will ever be killed so beautifully again in our lifetime."

Mary looked at Conlan. Her blue eyes were shining. The hungry, unbalanced face looked smooth and young. "You might take her for a boy just now," Mary thought.

Five more bulls were fought and killed, and Mary, partaking of the uneven miseries and bluffs and glories of the afternoon, understood a little Conlan's comment on the first performance. She was well initiated in one programme. She saw vulgarity and fake bravery and deliberate meanness towards the bull; again and again, with aching conscience, she saw the blindfold horses reined about for their ghastly minute; there was bad fighting, there were panics, and good manly strokes; slow bulls and brave; and once again, in the fourth fight—for this, even for the always great Pronceda, was apparently a day of days—a classic, cold encounter. She saw how the crowd, unfairly as she often thought, took good or bad or indifferent, as they judged, quite ruthlessly, and meted out reactions without a second thought. She saw disgrace when El Niño de La Montaña, a popular boy from the next province who had recently taken his alternative with brilliance in Madrid, and who now had done well if showily, with his first bull, could not kill his second, and had to hand his sword to Alarcón. Amid the laughs and hisses Mary trembled, watching his convulsed white face against the barrier. As the noise of mockery died she said in timid Spanish to the fat, yellow man beside her:

"Is it a terrible thing—not to kill your bull?"

He looked at her with surprise.

"Señorita," he said gravely, "the boy is dishonoured."

The stress on the deep verb was elegiac.

But the crowd forgot the mountain-boy as the sturdy Alarcón dispatched the sixth, a very gallant bull, with a great display of jolly courage. They gave him the ear—he was a sure and mannerly fighter—and to the sound of music he went round the ring. The bullfight was over.

The two Irish misses went silently through the shouting crowd down the long road from the bullring. Mary was too tired to think of how violently she had suffered coming up it. Too tired for anything but merely to walk and be silent. She had never before known this sensation, as of having been drained of all blood and power. She could hardly hear the tremendous din about her: the

lovely evening seemed remote, like an evening remembered. She paused automatically when the long walk
brought her to the bridge and the station for Cabantes.

Conlan raised her brows.

"Not coming to the café?"

Mary shook her head, and the other smiled. Her face
had gone back to middle age.

"Well, you didn't faint anyway," she said jerkily.

"No."

"I never in my life before asked anyone to go with me
to a fight."

"Do you go to many?"

"All I can."

"Why?"

"I like them."

"And yet you don't like Spain?"

"No. I wonder why the Church doesn't make it a sin
to go to the bullfight!"

Mary looked down the river towards the mountains.

"I think it is a sin," she said slowly.

Conlan laughed.

"Not for me, until the Church says so. You ought to
have some coffee."

She looked at Mary almost gently.

"No. Good night."

"There's another fight to-morrow. Could you be free?"

"No, no!"

Suffer all this to-morrow again? Oh, madness! In the
train and walking home along the peaceful waterfront she
carried still a sense of emptiness and unreality, a lightness
which saved her paradoxically from the physical sensation

of fatigue. She gave a penny to a beggarman whom she knew; she smiled at the children's boatman; she apprehended, with the dreamy casualness of a familiar, the summery sweetness of scene and hour. But a cloudy region of her mind was showing her other things: a boisterously running bull, a cape bunched up for a veronica, a blindfold horse, a drooped muleta, a matador's placating hand. Her head was full of the day's new images. She was glad to smell the seaweed and catch sight of the open windows of her room.

At the little monastic gate she met Don Pablo.

"Miss Maria! Your face is very white! Are you ill?"

"Why, no." She could think of no Spanish words. She moved her hands, and he noticed that they fell wearily, like her voice.

"But what is it?" His anxiety was polite but ruthless. She made an effort.

"I am a little tired. I have been to the bullfight——"

His face became very grave.

"Ah—of course. I am sorry you went. You did not like it?"

She looked, as if for help, he thought, into his eyes. He was startled by the childish searching, and was reminded oddly of his son, Juanito.

"Oh yes, I did," she said; "I mean—ah, it's impossible in Spanish—but Pronceda——"

"He fought well?"

She moved her hands again and let them fall in utter weariness.

"I could never say," she stumbled—"oh, I want to remember——"

"He is always like that, I believe," Don Pablo said. "He must be perhaps the greatest Spaniard now alive, and I for one would be glad to know him dead."

She smiled dreamily.

"Such courage can't live long," she said, as if reassuring him and her.

He thought with weariness that a man might look in contentment for ever upon her young, dishevelled head.

"Go to your room and rest," he said gently. "I'll tell them to give you some brandy."

She smiled in refusal and left him.

There was a letter in her room, from John. Taking it, she went and sat beside a window. But she did not open it. She smiled at the manly handwriting and thought of how the postman would have disliked being defrauded of his fun this afternoon. This perpetually recurring envelope delighted him. "That is right," he would say, handing it to her, "that is a fine young man. Always writing to you, always, always!" Over the bush of red camellias he would hand it to her, through the open window of her little dining-room, at breakfast or when she drank her afternoon chocolate, and then would pass on singing to the side-door of the house. One day she had heard him discourse to Don Pablo, sitting with him a moment on a garden seat, about how he teased the children's pretty miss because of her sweetheart's letters. The sun flashed on his glasses, and she could see Don Pablo smile at him.

"And all the same," said the postman, "if I were he, the sea wouldn't flow between us. What do you say?"

She had not caught Don Pablo's smiling answer. She

had been surprised then, she remembered—for it had been only her second week in Spain—to see the postman sit down for a chat with the master of the house.

She felt the love-letter in her hand now. It was very thick. That would have been a mighty joke for Estéban. But perhaps he wasn't here this afternoon. Perhaps he too was at the bullfight.

The bullfight! She closed her eyes. She must forget the bullfight, forget it forever. She was tired, tired. Someone came and put a tray with brandy on the writing table near her. She smiled, but was too tired to explain in Spanish that she did not want it. Alone again, she relaxed in her chair and the letter slid from her lap. She felt as if she had been on a long journey.

Sweetly the evening came up to her. That din on the pier was the loading of the half-past seven ferry for Torcal. No need to get up and look—she knew its routine by now and could see it behind her eyelids. She smiled. Old Chaco and his mule were there as usual, no doubt. And every passenger, however well-dressed, however preoccupied, was taking a part in getting the two squeezed in. A reasonable, realistic people, who in the midst of violent social wrongs and gluttonies, their own and their neighbours', yet hold each other's routine rights and day-to-day dilemmas most matter-of-factly in respect; a people who walk and talk together exactly as whim takes them, bootcleaner and yachtsman, waiter and marquis; yet each ever touchily self-conscious of his own especial social eminence; a people offering and accepting views on God and politics as naturally as they offer and accept cigarettes, and who refuse an alms they can well afford to a beggar whose condition they should never tolerate with "Forgive me, brother"; a people naïvely impressed by social gradings and material importance, yet quite unable to confuse those certainties with others, such as the value to each man of his ego, his pride, and his opinions; a people in fact whom no stupidity, no vulgarity, no ambition can ever render anything but simple in personal contacts—in that much, a hopelessly aristocratic people, and doomed, therefore, in a world which has outstripped the aristocratic principle. As wicked and greedy as democrats, communists, or what you will, but less likely than such cattle to escape the fruits of their many sins, because by a racial fluke—a tiny pinch of reasonableness, of detachment, in each mother's son— for ever destined to be persons, and unmanageable. So, though not a passenger, rich or poor, clean or dirty, but has his philosophic view on how transport between Cabantes and Torcal might be improved, the issue, while remaining very interesting to talk about, is clearly the practical concern of the ferry-owner—and meantime this small open boat is the vehicle whereby all who need to may reach Torcal. Therefore, though it takes some time each evening, and creates a bad smell in the boat and some danger and crowding, it is obvious that Chaco and his mule must be got on board. To that objective every passenger gladly lends advice and patience.

Mary smiled. To reflect thus, to generalise, was new to her, and she knew that she could never order such confused impressions so as to present them in decent form, to John for instance. "Darling," he'd say, "you've come back to me with your pretty head full of nonsense.

I must give you a good shake!" She could hear his deep, kind laugh. Ah! But if he laughed at her when she was as tired as this!

She opened the writing-table drawer, and took out the snapshot in the little leather frame. John at his best—his pipe in his hand, his terrier pup in the crook of his arm. That little smile—she could safely say she loved it. Safely say? How odd a phrase! For better or worse she loved this man, did she not? For better or worse. "I've been to the bullfight," she said suddenly, in a half-frightened voice, to the photograph. And then, as one might who, having begun on a difficult confession, does not know how to find courage to proceed, she looked away from the snapshot and despairingly around the room, at Our Lady, at the unopened letter on the floor, at the tall bottle of brandy.

"That's why I'm so tired! I was forgetting. I can't read his letter yet. I'm too tired—from the bullfight. It's queer that it should make me so tired. I must explain it to you, John." She looked at the photograph again and knit her brows.

Explain it? She thought of Mellick, the breakfast-room in her father's house, and John beside her on the window-seat; the cat on her lap, the barren fig-tree in the garden. "I will explain it to you, John." The bright cape swinging, the woeful horses, the darts and the silk suits, the running blood; the silly bugle music, the sun and the arc of shadow on the sand; the lovely sky; the utter graceful-ness and peace of courage; the driven bull, the shouting. John's baffled eyes and shaking head. "It stands for something that you can't defend, but that, in a way, doesn't need defending." But John would laugh at last, in the courageous manner he had and with which he swept off anything that threatened him or her. He would "give her a good shake," and forgive her her surprising crudity, and forget the whole thing. And that would be that, and she would never say any more. So she saw them now, in the breakfast room at home, herself and the man she desired to marry—saw them suddenly as if they were two people in a play, and she felt remote from them, and chilled and lonely. "Oh, darling," she said to the photograph, and repeated it hurriedly, as if its sound rang true against confusion, as if it snared a volatile reality. But as she bent to pick up her love-letter, she burst into a shattering storm of tears, and let it fall again unread.

A WALK WITH MILAGROS

AUGUST struck warmly on the little bay. Rumour of great heat in Madrid was soon confirmed by the opening of villas in Torcal and Playablanca. White sails raced over the water now, children's voices were loud on the sands and there were more Hispano-Suizas than ever in Altorno streets. Men lounged on the floating decks of the yacht club; boys wearing loin-cloths dived and tumbled at all hours in the sea; and in the mornings young ladies of fashion, in full-skirted bathing dresses, strolled with chaperones to the edge of the tide, and presently back again in a hurry to their tents. Ice-cream men were everywhere, and beggars too, and vendors of this and that; the 'Sporting' at Torcal offered dance-music all night to the elegant classes and municipal bands performed in the squares every evening. The season was here and many were hoping that the King might drop in to surprise it.

Pilár took a great deal of trouble with her appearance now, and Doña Consuelo even protested to some purpose against Nieves' casual dressing, but Milagros was good-humouredly allowed to go on being a hoyden. Lessons, save in English, music and drawing, were suspended; there were no more energetic expeditions into the mountains or along the rocks. The miss's afternoon duties consisted mainly in escorting the chic Pilár and her rather bored sisters to the villas or apartments of their friends, and killing time as well as she could until the time when they required to be shepherded home. This gave her a considerable amount of indefinite, dreamy leisure.

The weather, too induced dreaming. Mary wrote to John that she was growing "more moony than ever. What father would say now about 'that look on my face' I shudder to think!" And John wrote back: "Tell me what you moon about, my darling. Ever about married life? I'm moony too—and always looking for our house. I can't see it anywhere. I'd like it to be white and large and two hundred years old. And I'd like dark trees about it, cypresses and cedars; blue-green trees. But I suppose, in honour of Spain, we'll have to have a lot of nasty painted flower-pots with camellias in them—though I hate flower-pots and camellias. But I like Estéban, the postman. How do you pronounce him? He seems to be on my side. I wish he handed you my letters across a rose-tree though. I hate those old waxy camellias."

Mary, in fact, mooned not at all about married life. She wrote long letters to John, read his long letters with pleasure, smiled often at his photograph and prayed for him every night. But her imagination was engaged by the scenes and people about her. She walked among holiday crowds and out through the fishing hamlets that edged the bay; sat in squares at dusk to watch boys and girls dancing; explored the slums of Altorno, and poked about dark churches which, the guide-books told her, were 'romanico' or 'renacimiento' or both. Under portales of crumbling streets she fumbled nervously at bookstalls; she peered into shops where the work-people bought smocks and rope-soled shoes and salted codfish; she watched village boys playing 'pelota,' saw shifts of men leave the blazing foundries, sweating, sulky, exhausted; saw the wild swarming women and children they went home to, saw a shipload of weedy soldiers leave the dock discontentedly—for Morocco, she supposed. Once she saw an angry man-hunt over the hills, the civil guards very much in earnest about the capture of two miners who had absconded with the wages of the mine. Once too, over the same hills she saw a gipsy train melt westward, sad and grey, its mule-bells tinkling. She heard the Basque speech in the market place; amusedly once through the oration of a Basque nationalist she heard the names 'Arthur Griffiths' and 'Patrick Pearse.' She grew familiar with 'habanera' tunes, with flamenco. Sometimes watched children in the park play 'toro' and 'torero.' Frequently she turned up in the Café Aleman to taste the rough sociability of her colleagues; frequently she went to Conlan's room and, smoking *favoritos*, stared through plane-trees at the porch of San Geronimo.

Her imagination was engaged, as it would have been by any accidental escape from the accepted pattern of life as she knew it, but as that pattern was simple and northern and she young and untravelled, all these details of a strange people's routine impelled her to a confused, uneven excitement, and stimulated in her, perhaps too suddenly, potentialities of curiosity and response which life in Mellick had not so far troubled.

But the wound of the bullfight was in fact—though she tried to forget and ignore it—the gateway through which Spain had entered in and taken her. She did not know how much an afternoon in the bullring had changed her.

But, young and very conventional, to have learnt through the movements of one's own nerves the difference between shock and revulsion; young, virginal and virtuous to have learnt in one's own breast that emotion at its most crude can by relation to a little art enchant, overwhelm, and seem eternal—that is an awful lesson, most disconcerting to the gentle and orthodox. Mary, the tears that it had drawn from her shed, and her explanations feebly written to John—"I went to a bull-fight after all. It is terrible and inexcusable but it can be very beautiful too and one man did the most unforgettable things. You'll be surprised to hear that once it had started I quite forgot to be sick. But I was awfully tired afterwards——" her explanations written and rather irritably acknowledged by John—"I can't think why you went, you weakling—and really what could there be beautiful in a bullfight?"—tried to ignore the most disconcerting experience of her life. But she reckoned without the unalterable fact that she had undergone it, which is all that matters about any experience. So, willy nilly, because of a few broken sunlit images that would not leave her, she looked out on the Spanish scene with wider and more shadowed eyes than her lover in Mellick, dreaming of her, recollected.

Milagros talked with her—about the bullfight and other Spanish matters. Milagros was, to Mary's inexperience, an astonishing child. She was not what Aunt Cissy would call 'precocious,' meaning, without saying so, sexually over-ripe, but, on the contrary, cool beyond her years, and though completely and traditionally religious she liked to examine every phenomenon that came her way,

no matter how such might seem to others to threaten
faith or morals. Nothing appeared to threaten these in
her. Certainly the child was afraid of nothing, least of all
of her own curiosity.

She jibbed sometimes against Pilár's social programme, and elected to spend the afternoon with 'Miss
Maria.' So too did Nieves, but not as often or as success-
fully. Doña Consuelo thought it time that the latter
began to fight her shyness and cultivate social grace.
Also Nieves, who was very pretty and interested in sport
—a phase of the Anglophilism of the Spanish smart set of
that time—Nieves was very much liked by her young
friends and relations from Madrid. She was not easily
excused from gaiety, but no one cared how Milagros
chose to pass her time.

One afternoon she walked with Mary along the cliff
path of Torcal.

"Are you going to report Don Jorge to mother?" she
asked.

"I think I must." Mary sighed. "I wish Doña Consuelo
knew a little English or that we both knew more French.
It would make the matter less awkward."

Milagros chuckled.

"You're very dutiful. But of course you must do what
you think best."

Don Jorge was an elderly Andalucian priest who instructed the Areavaga girls in music. He had a very
handsome face, was indolent, suave and dirty-looking.
The nature of the subject he taught gave him a certain
liberty of movement in the study. The three girls took his
instructions in the theory and history of music sitting

together at their work-table, but for the executive part on the piano the two who were not to perform were encouraged to leave the room, so as not to unnerve the anxious third. The chaperone of course stayed where she was, in her chair near the window. Don Jorge made great show of temperament during the music-lesson, striding up and down, humming and counting the beat, bending over his pupil to explain, crowding alongside to assist, laughing and groaning and cocking his head. These activities seemed to be considerably intensified, Mary noticed, when it was Nieves' turn to occupy the stool. But in the very first week she discovered that she had to be deft herself in dodging unpredictable pats and pokes from the absent-minded musician, as he paused beside her in his ecstatic rounds of the room. The difficulty was to evade these unexpected caresses without allowing the child at the piano to suspect that anything untoward was afoot. But one day when she was still quite new to her duties, one day when Milagros was dashing with commendable courage through the Polonaise in A Major, Mary, off her guard for a minute—a Norwegian boat was swinging in between the breakwaters—felt a thick hand pad suddenly and greedily along her neck and shoulder, under her blouse. She sprang to her feet, fortunately making no noise loud enough to dominate the Polonaise. Don Jorge took one miserable look at her, then swung away to the piano, vociferously chanting, "Very good, my child, very firm. You're improving every day!" But Mary knew by his startled air that something in her face had given him a thorough fright and that henceforward she would be left in peace. So she was and for a time she thought he was less exuberantly avuncular with his pupils. She certainly kept a dueña's eye on him. But still, especially at Nieves' lesson, a kind of fever would engulf the man, rendering him sometimes, Mary thought, almost hysterical. Watching him, she occasionally felt a gleam of pity stir in her disgust, so quickly was she growing up, but the sight of him then, bending as close as he dared against the lovely, bored, untalented girl, his courteous victim, killed all patience in the disciplined Puritan from Mellick. She grew to loathe Don Jorge. And she had an idea that by now there was no love lost. The priest took what vengeance he could on her contempt by making quick, Andalucian jokes to the children which she could not possibly understand and which she guessed were some-times at her expense—so nervous did Pilár look, so miserable Nieves, so ironic Milagros. More often, however, she apprehended his witticisms to be of a more general unseemliness, but was maddened by her inability to understand his southern Spanish, and so protest, in accordance with her duty. The situation made her very uncomfortable.

This morning, however, as he departed he had said something, with a soft giggle, to Pilár, which had appeared for a moment to puzzle the girl. But then as she crossed the room her chaperone had seen understanding cross her face. Her cheeks had flushed, and her eyebrows had gone up in amazed comment.

Mary had at once made a speech to the three, ex-plaining her predicament in regard to Don Jorge's unsuitable sense of humour. The children admitted that

his jokes were often embarrassing, and that their parents
would be greatly shocked if they knew of the things he
said to them.

"Well then," said Mary, feeling a most unhappy prig,
"my duty is to your parents. I shall tell your mother that
I believe Don Jorge's witticisms to be unsuitable, but
that as I know little Spanish, she must please check my
impression with yours."

The children had looked solemn.

Now Milagros enlarged on the theme of pruriency.

"Mother will be very angry with Don Jorge," she said,
"but it's father who'll be really shocked. The Areavagas
are all Jansenists, you know—and a bit difficult." She
smiled. "I think the Irish must be Jansenistic too, Miss
Maria. But we get a strain of peasant common sense from
the Parajos—though mother and Pilár wouldn't like to
hear me say that! Still, it's the making of us, I think.
I'm often sorry for father that he's so correctly bred. His
mother was a terrific lady—and a kind of saint, they say.
That's an awful handicap, don't you think?"

Mary was preoccupied.

"I don't want to lose Don Jorge his job," she said.
"But I'm in a fix. I'm not here to judge if anybody's
right and wrong, but if I see something going on which
needs an authoritative decision, I truly am bound to
report it—don't you see?"

"Yes. I think you must—you being you. He doesn't
need jobs anyway. He's fearfully rich and mean. Lives in
filthy luxury in Altorno, I believe, and has no duties
except as chaplain to the Inmaculada Convent. They adore
him there." Milagros chuckled. "Personally, I find his

133

dreadful Spanish the most objectionable thing about him.
But apart from your duty as watchdog, Miss Maria,
which I quite see you must fulfil, do you really think very
much is gained, if an old man is prevented from making
his dirty jokes in one place, and is therefore released to
make them somewhere else?"

Mary smiled. The child's elaborate, hesitant English,
supplemented with Spanish at every fifth word, gave her
speculations a comic flourish.

"Nothing is gained for the world, I suppose," the
governess conceded, "but we'd be rid of a nuisance."

"His jokes are no nuisance to me, Miss Maria. When
you've read as much as I have—*La Celestina*, for instance——"

Mary had recently, in an account of Spanish literature,
come on a description of that work. She raised her
brows.

"You've read that, Milagros?"

"Yes. It's very brutal and characteristic. You should
try to read it a little, even if it shocks you. Father says it's
nearly as regrettable and characteristic as the bullfight, Miss Maria, but not as beautiful."

"He allows you to read it?"

"But of course. I read anything I choose. And yet
he'll be more shocked than it's possible to say at Don
Jorge's making nasty jokes. That's a curious thing about
father. But of course his private mania is respect for the
individual. That's why he'd never have succeeded in
politics. That's why no one but me reads his political
writings."

"Does he write?"

"Not lately. He used to write for Liberal journals. I'll show you some of his essays. But of course, though he calls them political writings, there are no politics in them. You see, he thinks exactly as I do, that any political organisation, no matter what, is most offensive. An insult to life, he says somewhere. Jansenist or not by tradition, he is intellectually an anarchist. So am I, of course. It's the only possible thing for an intelligent person to be. But unless you can have perfect anarchy, father would say, I think, that it's better to dodge organisation as much as possible—even at a terrible price."

"Would he say then that the present state of Spain is better than if there were a little order and justice?"

"He'd tell you, Miss Maria, that nothing could be worse than the present state of Spain, but he says that our condition is the inverted triumph of organisation, that is, deliberate and wily disorganisation, greedily and grossly applied. He often says that if a few hundred highly placed brutes and bullies would just drop off to sleep for fifty years, Spain might be saved. You see, I really think that a part of him believes that most people, let alone, are potentially good—especially Spaniards!" She smiled. "I don't agree with him there."

Mary thought how brainless and immature she must appear to this grave, eloquent and comic child.

"Then it's you who are the Jansenist, Milagros."

The child laughed.

"Not altogether," she said. "I've just got naïve common sense, like my favourite hero—Sancho Panza! Do hurry up with your Spanish, and read *Don Quixote*, Miss Maria. It'll transform you."

"I read stories from it in English when I was a kid, and I thought they were deadly."

"Stories from anything are deadly! But you know, Pilár *does* think it's a deadly book, and mother has never even tried to read it. Nieves likes it—but of course she's cracked on a thing from the English by a man called Malory—about King Arthur. That's Nieves' favourite book, she says. Incredible! Father and Juanito and I were once all reading *Don Quixote* at the same time, I remember—we all three read it very often—and we used to have great fun at dinner, talking like the barber and the curate and Sancho and everyone! It used to drive Pilár mad, but mother only laughed! But I really do believe it must be the most important book in the world."

Mary thought that her brother Donal, the most glib and conversationally gifted member of her family, would enjoy the chatter of this child. But absurd as she was, she had too good a mind for Donal and too soon would hurt his vanity. As for John—well, Mary knew what he would think of Milagros; indeed, in reply to an attempt at description of her he had written: "she sounds a nauseating little freak. Wants locking up in a reformatory, I'd say off-hand." Mary had been annoyed by that. There's such a thing as being idiotically off-hand, Mr. Lawgiver, she had thought, laying down the letter. And the annoyance had induced a timid meditation on whether or not small recurrent clashes of points of view on external matters were of little or great import between two who proposed to marry.

In girlhood, growing up in the companionship of her two brothers, Jim and Donal, Mary's sympathies—at the

disposal of either, for she loved them both—had always
in argumentative issue gone to Jim, the hesitater who
would not generalise, but who sought to display clever-
ness as little as he desired to be mistaken for that dreary
posturer, the plain, blunt man. Donal enjoyed the
flourishes of his own talk and to put a decorative cap on a
debate. John, Mary often thought, might have found the
deft Donal as maddening as Jim sometimes had done, but
not for the same reason. The latter, attracted by the idea
of plain truth, believed that a segment of it might
occasionally be arrived at, were a little trouble taken and
displays of personality barred, but John—his future wife
smiled uncertainly when this occurred to her—John
always knew without any trouble what the plain truth
was, and would have resented Donal's customary 'last
word,' because he knew the absolute rightness of his own
less literary and more manly summings-up. This foible of
her lover had always been clear to her, but she had
accepted it and the limitations it set on conversation—
with difficulty sometimes—as in the natural course of
things. She did not find it endearing in him. His power
over her came from his qualities of generosity and
honour and absolute kindliness, his curious and manly
sense of beauty, his disarming smile, his love of simple
things and of his native place, his power to weave dreams
of a dignified and fruitful married life. All these, the
flowers of good sense and good plain breeding, more than
made up, Mary always told herself, for any shortage of
that questionable thing, sensibility. John lived at ease
within the bounds of his own natural, lively and by no
means inhuman morality, and though good nature made

him tolerant of all that might lie outside that code, he wanted 'no truck with it,' as he would say, nor indeed with the ideas, accidents and histories through which his code had reached him. There it was, quite workable for the decent adult who wanted to enjoy, control and make valuable the life it postulated—and if now and then it happened not to work, no charity was quicker than John's to shield the failure with incurious and benevolent silence. But always what he called 'talk' and 'curiosity' were 'morbid,' and conversation with him, except about gardening, animals, topography, sport, or the office, was limited by his cheerful belief that the 'less said the better.' Mary, during a more or less tranquil year of engagement to him, had come to doubt the value, at least the entertainment value, of this motto, but had frequently told herself that there was no reason under heaven why an obscure and simple creature like herself should marry a man with no defect at all—if such a freak of nature could be found. She taught her heart to dwell with loyalty on all that she loved in her lover. Nevertheless when he kissed her and she half-simulated what she hoped was a correct response, she felt an irrational anxiety. "I'd know," she thought confusedly, "I'm sure I'd know if someone I loved didn't really love my kisses." And looking into his happy eyes, she would feel a little chill of unhappiness and pity. Perhaps his motto did occasionally lead him astray. Certainly since she had come to Spain he had sometimes in his letters tramped over her news and views with a heavier authority than she found patience for. Now and then she had had to put a letter aside half-read and wheedle herself into good-humoured affection for the writer before she could continue it. She was alarmed by her own brief exasperations, which she felt to be sharper than they had ever seemed in face-to-face tussles with John at home. Surely absence from him should have made her more tolerant since it made him more vulnerable? It did not occur to her that all these things of Spain that she chronicled for him and he dismissed impatiently were only unnecessary barriers between them in his eyes, whereas they were a part of everyday life to her now and by that insidiously endeared. And she was too young, and too orthodox in her respect for John, to have noticed that he was never more of a law-giver than when he was frightened.

Now, however, mild contemplation of the amusing Milagros having led her into uncomfortable thoughts of herself, she shivered a little and sought to escape them.

"Time we turned back, Mila, if Pilár wants to catch the eight o'clock ferry."

They went down the long hill into Torcal.

"Why will you never talk about the bullfight, Miss Maria? After *Don Quixote* it's my favourite topic."

"Well, I hope *Don Quixote* isn't so—baffling."

"Baffling—what does that mean?"

Mary explained. One advantage of conversation with Milagros was that though her need to dissertate compelled her to the use of many Spanish words and phrases, and to the misuse of many English ones, her thoroughness rarely allowed any expression in either language to escape misunderstood by her or her instructress. This foible was of value to Mary in her acquisition of Spanish, and was in general educative in exactitude.

"You think the corrida very terrible? Well, it is terrible. But we are not romantic. We are realists, and I think we are philosophically tragic. That is—we don't make a fuss or an illusion about tragedy, or think it very astounding, or better than comedy—simply, we are well acquainted with it, and we find it interesting and persistent and it doesn't make us squeal. Well, in the bullfight there is much accidental beauty, as it happens—you admit that?—but it is shockingly real. It is death and horror presented theatrically and really, both at once. But all the time the sun shines and we drink beer, and watch marvellous happenings. We are experts and have no illusions and we wait for success and failure in this and that detail. But we are spirits too and we cannot escape the thousand symbols, or the ache in our hearts. That is the bullfight—it is as symbolical and suggestive and heartrending as the greatest poetry, and it is also as brutal and shameless as the lowest human impulse. Nothing else can give you that in one movement. It is an immense thing—it must be faced."

"Perhaps by serious philosophers like you, Milagros."

Mary felt tired of the stumbling eloquence. Talk of the bullfight made her heart heavy.

"When the matador goes in to kill, we call it the moment of truth. Did you know that?"

"Oh, it's shoddy and wretched and cruel. Do let it be, Milagros!"

"With pleasure, Miss Maria."

They called for Pilár and Nieves at a very grand new villa full of gay people, and then hurried down to the ferry stage. Mary let the three girls talk together in their own language, and stood apart to await the complicated loading of the boat.

The scene wore its usual evening beauty, floating as it were in a mist of light. The water hardly lapped the pier. Yachts lay folded like sleeping birds and the hills beyond Cabantes seemed no more than a ridge of shadow above the radiant miradores of the town. The band was playing in Playablanca. A black-hulled ship steamed towards where Altorno lay, chimneys and campaniles wreathed in smoke as in a summer cloud.

Mary felt a movement of resentment against the inoffensive prettiness. "Postcardish," she told herself. Some troubled thought of her relationship with John evaded and yet bruised her. And Milagros' talk of the bullfight—so theatrical—had jarred her nerves. The moment of truth. How could truth lie, for any decent person, in mere parade of self, in the infliction of a deadly wound? And yet, examining her terms, she could find nothing in them to bar truth out—indeed, it sounded as if they might conceivably be necessary to its establishment. She felt guilty for having snapped at the courteous child, and that did not now improve her mood. Still, how the creature talked! Perhaps John was not altogether wrong. Ah! One would not be a miss for ever, Heaven be praised!

She got into the ferry and sat down. The children were a little separated from her by the crowd, and smiled in her direction. An old woman edged the corner of a basket of live hens on to her knees. The boat chugged off. Conversation was animated among its

141

serried passengers. Mary closed her eyes resentfully. She supposed she was homesick, so unaccountably heavy was her heart. She felt alien, dejected, out of tune. Almost as if she had been injured by this innocent place, as if it sought to wound her. She thought of Mellick and of how lovely it would be to hear voices that she understood. It might be raining now at home. She could hear the rain on sycamore leaves, could see a pale, watery break in the sky beyond the river. Aunt Cissy at the drawing-room window, catching the last light to read the *Mellick Sentinel*; Mourne Street wet and empty; a Benediction bell; a motor-horn; an eager step, like John's, along the flags. Images to connote a terrifying peace, a timelessness and changelessness most desolating in their personal call to her. A moment of truth indeed. Her truth was there where her own speech rang and her heart had formed its unpretentious habits. She had no Spaniard's need of a brutal and realistic manipulation of symbols; there was philosophic instruction and to spare in routine and decorum, in the simple and restrained ways of happiness and faith which she and John together understood. All this talk, all this dramatising was outside her need and reach, and only wearied her. John was generally right. 'The less said the better.' Her natural place was not in this ferry-boat of chatterboxes, this glittering foreign bay, this place of camellias and bitter wine and flamenco songs and bullfights—but in the rainy street of childhood where every sound and change of light was as natural as sleeping and waking, where she was known and where true love waited for her, where she had given her pledge of lifelong love.

The ferry bumped against Cabantes pier. The children, nearer the landing steps than Mary, sprang ashore, and she heard all three voices raised above the general landing din in cries of rapture and astonishment:

"Juanito! Juanito!"

JUANITO

THE famous brother must have arrived from Madrid. There had been talk of his doing so soon.

Mary had felt remiss at being separated from her charges in the ferry, but now was glad not to be with them for this first greeting. She glanced towards the delighted, girlish voices, but the crowd ascending the steps before her blocked her view. They would all be happy, she thought detachedly, to see their precious Juanito—Don Pablo happiest, she guessed. And the thought of his content, and the naturalness of this family emotion clouded her more than ever. It made her feel desolately lonely.

"Miss! Miss Maria! Come here, come quickly!"

The three girls were beckoning. She went obediently to where they stood with Don Pablo and—she smiled as she noticed it—the re-creation of his youth. For the tired man in black who leant on his stick and the upright young man in grey flannel were in outline most touchingly alike.

"This is our brother, Miss Maria! Juanito, this is Miss Maria! She can swim so well, Juanito—and she says she likes being in Spain!"

Juanito and Mary shook hands, and the man murmured something about being "very happy."

"His English is not as good as ours," Milagros said affectionately.

They crossed the pier to the little gate. Its bell clanged as Juanito held it open for his sisters and their miss. The talk as they all went up the path was apologetically in Spanish, but Mary caught its general drift. Yes, Luisa and the baby were with him—waiting to see them in the salón. They were on their way to Biarritz by car, to Luisa's people. They would stay here a day or two. "Biarritz, indeed!" The girls were indignant. "Oh, Juanito, you stay here!" But he smiled and shook his head. And Pilár admitted wistfully that Biarritz was really the place to go to nowadays.

The girls crossed the hall to the salón with a rush and loud exclamations. Mary went towards the staircase and ascended it. At the sixth step she glanced back. Juanito, near the salón door, was looking up at her before he followed his father into the room. The evening sun, pouring in at the landing window, lighted each very sweetly for the other, as with a fatal halo.

Their look was fleeting and decorous, a memory and unreal almost in the single beat of its exchange, but to both it gave an impression, an illusion of the gentle, mastering kind. These two were to know each other hereafter, and to arrive at their knowledge in reluctance, grief and protestation. Long pain lay ahead of the un-witting sympathy with which the eyes of each unprompted sought the aspect of the other, but for this once, if never again, they were innocent; in no vestige of their con-sciousness did query stir as to the end or centre of their story. Simply they looked for a mortal second.

Mary saw a light-limbed and heavy-shouldered young man, who wore his clothes and his dark hair untidily, as

did his father; who had, though in young health, his
father's pallor and tragically sculpted strong-set facial
bones. The searching sun showed eyes more innocently
opened than Don Pablo's and with more light and gold in
them. Young eyes, but meditative and poetic, set in a
questioning uplifted face.

He saw, but less defensively, that which two months
ago his father had beheld through half-closed, elderly,
reluctant eyes. A slender girl, in tennis shoes and cotton
dress, a girl with lightly curled short locks, with slender
neck and sweetly springing virgin breasts; Greek-headed,
with grave features and white skin. Now that she turned
back from the light to look at him the blueness of her
eyes which had already startled him, was veiled, but he
noticed that they were blue-shadowed, and that for all her
grace and youth, for all the unconscious arrogance of
fatal beauty, she was a little weary in this moment, a little
lonely and off guard. His nerves leapt to this perception
—for it was the most poisonous of weapons, to look as
this girl looked, and yet be vulnerable.

The reciprocal glance was over, as has been said, in the
beat of a second, and Mary vanished round the bend of
the stairs, but as Juanito entered the salón, his thought
climbed after her involuntarily a step or two. She moved,
a stranger and of no special consequence, through the
house in which he had been born and which was crowded
for him with the ghosts and memories of a singularly
happy boyhood. There was disturbance, which he did
not apprehend, in that reflection, as if her breaking in
among the shadows of his growth meant some inevitable
victory for her. But she moved unassumingly among

them, no more than a homesick girl, hankering no doubt for some faraway, unimaginable house where her childhood mourned for her, turning towards it now in heart perhaps, since she was weary, as his heart turned in weariness always to this house. She climbed the staircase with her unguessable foreign dreams, unaware of the flocks of his she brushed against. That made her seem more than ever touching. His imagination turned uneasily from her beauty to her loneliness. As he crossed the salón to complete the family group his eyes were a little closed, like his father's.

After dinner that night Mary settled down to write a long letter to John. It was somewhat overdue, and she hoped for that reason to make it as kind and entertaining as possible, though she feared she was not in entertaining mood. The strain of absence was telling on both her and John, and to her alarm they were sometimes surprisingly irritable with each other in their letters. She knew she felt irritable—and volatile—to-night, but as there was no reason at all for such a mood, she was resolute to master it, and write at length and tenderly to her betrothed, who, this morning's letter told her, was not feeling well.

"My dearest one—forgive me for not having written in the last three days. It is rather hot here now, even at night, and I've had a lazy fit. But I think of you an awful lot, and I was terribly grateful for to-day's dear long letter. I hope there's another to-morrow! The time they take is maddening—oh, I wish we weren't so far away from each other. But I mustn't think along these lines to-night or I might burst into tears! To tell you the truth I've been in a peevish state all day—I think it's acute homesickness. Or perhaps a touch of the sun. I was quite snappy with poor old Milagros this afternoon—it's weighing on my conscience. However, no one is in the mood to notice my ill-temper, fortunately, as the son of the house—I told you about Juanito, the brilliant lawyer and político in Madrid?—has arrived suddenly, and they are all enchanted. He seems nice, very like his father. His wife and baby are here too, but I haven't met them yet.

"Oh, John—what are you doing to-night? I'm so bored with myself. I wish you and I were going to a movie or a dance. The band is playing like mad in Playablanca, and I'm sure there are swarms of people dancing under the trees. It's lovely the way they dance all night in these shadowy squares. This band is very strong on last year's tunes. Do you remember that silly one about 'keep looking for the blue bird'? Well, that's what they're playing now. Something about April showers. I wonder what words the Spaniards put to it?

"I'm distressed to hear this morning that you're having toothache, and such an awful time with the dentist. I can't imagine why—your teeth look so marvellous. Don't let him take out any of them—it would be sheer idiocy. You poor, poor boy. Please let me know how it goes on, and if you are managing to sleep better. It's very dreadful for you. I wish I could send you some sound, womanly advice on how to cure yourself, but even if I could it might sound a bit absurd coming from me! What a dreadful wife I'll make—even toothache makes me feel a green incompetent. Dear heart, do get your doctor to give you something to make you sleep. How callous

148

I am, when I come to think of it, wishing we were dancing to-night, when for all I know you may be in misery. That's the worst of being so far away—I simply can't keep in step. Moods run away with me, and seem to have no relation to real concerns. Am I being dreadfully unsympathetic? Please forgive me if you think so—I'm very troubled about you. I wish you were here. I think I could almost persuade you to like Spain a little if you saw it. Anyhow, you couldn't help liking this lovely warm night and the silly music coming over the bay——"

There was a knock at the door. Nieves came in.

"Miss Maria, Juanito's brought us some flamenco records, and Milagros says you like flamenco music, so mother wondered if you'd like to come downstairs?"

Mary thought, in a crisis of shyness, that there was nothing she would like less. But Nieves looked very eager. The children were hurt, she noticed, when she resisted their occasional attempts to brighten up her evenings. But if this invitation came from Doña Consuelo it was probably a polite form of command, and had some particular purpose in it. The miss put her letter away and brushed her hair. As she did so she remembered Pilár's saying once that the Conde de Maraval had been in the diplomatic service, and that Luisa, Juanito's wife, having spent a large part of childhood at the embassy in London, spoke beautiful English, and was in general an authority on English standards and customs. Very likely then Doña Consuelo sought a ruling from her daughter-in-law on the English speech and general attributes of the new governess. The victim winced. She would have given a great deal to find strength to excuse herself.

"Come on, Miss Maria—do come."

She descended with Nieves, telling herself as she went that John was right when he called her a weakling.

There was a great deal of high-spirited fun going on in the salón, which made it easy to enter and cross to where Doña Consuelo sat with her son's wife in the mirador. The miss was presented to Luisa, who smiled and spoke to her in very fluent English, and made her sit beside her on the window-seat.

Luisa was a fair-haired Castilian. Her eyes were green-gold and her skin had a gold bloom on its pallor. She was slender, and wore a dress of a dead gold colour. Her hands reminded Mary of the hands of angels in Italian primitive nativities. She was dramatic and enchanting to behold, so happily did she harmonise mondaine with eternal beauty.

It was Mary's first encounter with a woman absolutely mistress of her world, one who possessing tradition and sophistication has the wealth and wit to make this accident flower in personality. The untutored girl from Ireland saw in one glance the flawless outward glory of such extravagant endowment, but she felt too with a thrill of simple admiration its mighty inner power.

"How brave of him to marry her," was her first clear thought. There was no felinity in this; it was nothing more indeed than the comment of a provincial, startled at meeting a creature so unusual as almost to seem a different species. But this astonishment was singularly sensitive, for Luisa was far too highly civilised to make a parade of

civilisation. Her grooming, dress and manner were of a
simplicity so perfect that they should have deceived as
naïve a person as Mary, and had she not been by accident
herself of formidable beauty, perhaps she would at first
have missed the true ring of steel. But Greek, however
unsuspecting and untried, usually knows Greek.

Mary—perhaps merely because she was very young—
had no sense of competitiveness against other women.
On her own ground she usually was, whether she
thought of it or not, the most beautiful of her sex in any
random assembly, which probably means that she could
at least compete on any ground. But though sometimes
secretly pleased and even startled by glimpses of her own
reflection, she was trained in unselfconsciousness, and
in the belief that though comeliness is an agreeable and
assessable thing, beauty is at the mercy of capricious
opinion. She knew that John held her to be as lovely as
the evening star, and she was grateful for his fantastic
faith, but—this worried her sometimes—it did not move
her. Had it wavered, she would probably have been
surprised and hurt, but while it lived it was a tender
joke—no more. Nothing in her trembled to his sweet
illusion, though lately she was faintly and uneasily
aware that some nerve in her waited to be thus disturbed.

Now, however, though she had a brief thought of what
a hopelessly rustic creature she was in her cheap cotton
dress, made in Mellick, her main sensation was a lively
mixture of astonishment, curiosity and delight, as she
studied this perfect flower of the great world. And she
continued to marvel innocently at the audacity of Juan
Areavaga y Parajo in marrying such a miracle. For he

seemed simple to her, boyish, young and untidy, a human being like her brothers and herself, a rather dreamy person like Nieves, like Don Pablo.

Luisa was very charming, very easy to talk to. She had never been in Ireland, but had heard much of its beauty and of the great charm of its people, had read the poetry of Mr. Yeats, had seen the Irish Players. She admired the Irish-Spanish hero, de Valera, thought the civil war in Ireland tragic but inevitable, and the Treaty compromise a grave mistake.

Mary hesitated. She felt uninformed and uneasy about this new outburst of fighting.

"Do you then sympathise with the nationalist ambitions of the Catalans and the Basques?" she asked Luisa.

The other raised her brows.

"You take an interest in our intricate affairs?" she said with surprise. "Your question is difficult. The Kings of Castile have been kings of all the Spains for a very long time. Myself I cling to the long tradition, but Juanito says my clinging is of no importance!" She laughed very prettily. "He says that some form of federated autonomies will have to be conceded. And Juanito belongs to the future. He is assuredly, as his family say, 'one of Spain's great men.'"

She smiled down the long room to where her husband was amusing himself with his three young sisters and the presents he had brought them.

"Listen, listen, Miss Maria!" cried Milagros. "You are going to hear Pepito Paco, the greatest of all flamenco singers." She waved a record and put it on the gramophone.

"El Chico de Triana," said Juanito.

The great wild "Ay!" superbly held against the passionate, low urge of the guitar. Then the zigzag, savage singing and the coaxing, sudden "Olé." Music that tore the air and seemed to burn it.

"There it is, Miss Maria—there you have us at our most appalling." Milagros beamed at Mary.

Luisa smiled.

"Do you really like it, Miss Maria?"

"Not in the ordinary sense of liking. It reminds me of our traditional singers at home. But they make just a miserable drizzle of a sound compared to this. That's why I think this much better—it is so much more crazy."

Luisa looked at her thoughtfully.

"How beautifully you speak," she said after a pause. "So purely, and yet with that strange, faint nuance that simply is not in the English voice."

Mary was embarrassed.

"But that's a defect," she said shyly. "I feel very uneasy in case I pass it on to these children."

"Uneasy? You should have heard the English of their Miss Anita! Some mountain patois, I suppose!"

Everyone laughed reminiscently about Miss Anita.

Don Pablo sat at the shadowy end of the room and listened with pleasure to the flamenco. To have his son under his roof again was a happiness so violent that he realised sadly he must support it with as much physical inaction as might pass unnoticed. The shock of Juanito's arrival in the afternoon had warned him very clearly that deep pleasure, always held in some suspicion by his spirit, was a crude and incontrovertible physical menace now. Not that he feared to die—he would have said and meant. But life which had naturally, and not ungently, put out one by one the lamps by which he had walked—his patriot ambitions, his passion for his wife, and then the dear, companionate dependence of his son—had now, ironically and even comically, lighted another among his shadows. He supposed that so long as he saw the joke he might be permitted to wish to linger awhile in the cold glow of this perilous pseudo-consolation. And even were the secret follies of his unforeseen dilemma something more than his self-respect could always bear or smile at, there were still such hours as this of seeing Juanito again, there were still flowery summer nights and flamenco music, there were the whims and antics of his young daughters—a man of philosophy might still be excused for wanting to live awhile in cautiousness. Contemplation was left, and he had the habit of it. He turned it now on the two young women on the window-seat.

Admirable creature, Luisa. Catching tags of her easy talk he smiled. When he had first met that shy, foreign girl on the terrace of his own house he had been unable to think of anything cordial to say to her, and yet he thought it probable that he was better informed than Luisa as to her Irish background! Descent from courtiers was a very potent asset, and Luisa, even in the hypothetical new Spain of which Juanito dreamt and which would be distasteful to her, would make a brilliant wife for a man of ambitious intention. Everyone was grist to her mill—even this quiet bird of passage. It was likely that the Irish girl, who came from a small provincial town, had never met anyone like Luisa before. Don Pablo smiled. Two such made indeed a remarkable meeting.

"Have some turrón, papa?"

He took a piece. The room was littered with sweet-meats from Madrid.

"Oh, Pilár, do think of your figure, darling!" Doña Consuelo wrung her hands imploringly.

"I am thinking of it, mother! It's spoiling my whole evening!"

"But Pilár, my sweet, your figure's perfect!" Luisa beamed at her. "Anyhow turrón isn't really half as dangerous as potatoes—because it doesn't turn up so often!"

"But Luisa, I adore potatoes!"

"Well then, you mustn't, naughty! No woman in her senses should adore potatoes."

Nieves and Juanito were muddling busily with a box of contraptions which Juanito said was a wireless set.

"Everyone's rigging them up in Madrid, mother. You really must let me erect this for you here."

"By all means, my son, if you know how to," said Doña Consuelo with gentle irony, for the young man was handling coils and wires and head-phones with an incompetence which in him was novel and amusing. Mary looked interested. She had helped John to install a set in the breakfast-room at home.

"I believe you actually understand these absurdities, Miss Maria," said Milagros, and dragged her over to the puzzle. Mary bent with Nieves over the sheaves of printed instructions.

"You won't be able to do much to-night, I think,"

she said shyly; "there's the aerial and the earth, you know."

Nobody's knowledge of English was equal to such technicalities, but Don Pablo sighed contentedly.

"Thank God! Life as I know it is granted a reprieve."

But Juanito was eager about his novelty and looked crestfallen.

"I feared that," he said.

"I was certain of it," said Nieves.

"A lot of mouse-traps," said Milagros, waving a contemptuous hand at the apparatus.

"That's what I think, Mila," said her father with a chuckle.

They started the gramophone again. A woman's voice singing a tango tune. It moved slowly, and the room became quiet for it. Mary sat down on a stool beside the untidy box of wireless apparatus. She had heard this tune before and had seen tango danced to it under the plane-trees of the Plaza San Martín. She remembered the grave, neat steps of the dancers. There had been a boy in blue overalls who danced with a girl in black. Mary could have watched them for hours and now, reminded of them, tried to escape from self-consciousness by recalling details of their grave and lovely dance.

Self-consciousness! She supposed that that was the word for her present discomfort. She had spent evenings in this salón before, with the children and their parents, and though she had felt shy and foreign then, and handicapped by the English-Spanish struggle of the talk, she had retained always her saving sense of invisibility and even unreality. That all about her was an interlude, and irrelevant impression. To-night that blessed feeling would not come. Instead there was a sense that eyes were on her, and a restless inclination to use her own, to look about and fidget. It must be that the grand and lovely creature, Doña Luisa, induced so odd a nervousness—and yet, when over there with her on the window-seat she had not felt it quite so much. But that was no more than the spell of the other woman's good manners. She talked so well and simply that at close range she made one forget oneself and one's deficiencies, no doubt. But telescoped and without the distraction of words—no, no, that was not all. She looked across at Luisa now. The beautiful creature, bending forward, was whispering some joke to Doña Consuelo, and Mary, looking at her steadily, realised with a sinking heart—she could not imagine why —that her fear, her excitement did not come from there. And yet, what else was there that was new and alive in the atmosphere? She knew the children now, and understood their kindness and casual unkindness. She understood—for her own purposes—their mother. Don Pablo's friendliness was becoming as natural to her as her prayers, as thoughts of John or home. As for this brother, he was so clearly the brother of the house, the son, so naturally one of them, and so boyish with his sweets and his wireless. Ah, God, what could there be to alarm her there? And yet her eyes swept the big, ugly, cluttered room with an indecorous restlessness. She wanted to escape, to be at home. She wanted to be where she was mistress of herself, and not paid to sit demurely through the sociable whims of others, not paid to sit and suffer unexaminable tensions. She wanted to be in her own house, to be able to raise her eyes to her own moods and say what came to her lips. "John!" she found herself thinking for the first time in her life, "John, why weren't we married months ago?"

The tango tune drawled on. Guitar and saxophone, and vulgar, brooding female voice.

Juanito leant against the wall and listened, half-closing his eyes. To come home was always heaven to him. From Salamanca, from Paris, even from his honeymoon, and nowadays from his beautiful apartment in Madrid, to come back to Cabantes, to play the fool with his sisters in this big ugly room that Luisa, naturally enough, thought so comical, was his idea of being happy. He had been very lucky in his life so far and was sensitively and superstitiously aware of that. His parents had wreathed boyhood with peace. They had kept him at home until he was eighteen, letting him share tutors, games and fads with cousins and friends and outside of such mildly conventional arrangements, trusting him to feed his mind in his father's library, and in conversation with whomsoever he encountered. The two parental loves, his mother's, natural as sunlight and tender and possessive without inhibition, and his father's, cerebral, unexacting, stimulant and proud, had balanced each other happily. He had gone out from their shelter timidly enough, but nourished for manhood. Transitory mistakes and griefs of later growing had taken their thrust at him and had taught him those many things, bitter, sweet, shocking or practical, which no parentage or cherishing can avert, but always, whatever the kick, lesson or triumph, there was this place to come back to—cradle with his mother's love to quiet him; academy with his father's brain for measuring-stick; or hermitage if he liked, with all that his spirit had first known for theme of meditation. He had come back with various excitements, various perplexities—and then one night had come home in great anxiety, heavy with passion for Luisa de Maraval. On that occasion he had spoken with urgent clarity to his father. Generally they had managed to understand each other through euphemisms and generalities, but now all trouble had one name, the pronunciation of which was a curious kind of anæsthesia by stimulation.

His father had failed Juanito in that conversation. Looking back the young man saw that Pablo, being what he was, could not possibly have risen to the exactions of the hour. He himself was twenty-three, very suddenly in love and alarmed by the difficult implications of possible marriage with a creature like Luisa. In a feverish state. Probably what he had craved was sentimental backing up and justification. "Go ahead, my son, if you love her. It is grand to be young and in love—I was your age when I met your mother . . ." He had never in his life heard his father talk in such strain, but he yearned to be pushed over his own precipice, and was in such a crisis that bathos, even on Pablo's lips, would not have startled him.

But there was another line which his father might have taken. He knew his son's political faith. Juanito saw Spain as the field in which the eventual inevitable battle would be fought against centralisation and the slave-state. This was long-sighted of him, for he considered that before the tussle could begin the slave-state would

have to be established and to function. In fact he believed
it his political duty to help to found something which he
must rely on his grandsons to overthrow. In argument
he often took analogies from physiology to clarify his
belief—but, in fact, he didn't care a snap for analogists.
He simply saw that Spain's aching need was for the
ruthless establishment in every cranny of the peninsula
of justice, order, health and knowledge. Knowledge
above all. And the only relatively quick way to such a
goal was by an antiseptic scouring out of all precedented
establishments, and the enforcing of the main principles
and practices of Communism. But the Communistic
theory, he would say, could be no more than a means to
the truly vital creature—never, never, in any bearable
world, an end. Desperate diseases need desperate
remedies, and Spain was desperately ill. But she had
traditionally a deep, conserved vitality, a patience and a
racial sense of time's vastness which could be used for
the imposition of an immense yet transitory and experi-
mental process. The character of his race preserved,
Juanito believed, in colossal measure, the qualities of its
colossal defects. He could catalogue them minutely, and
examine them with penetration, but for the ultimate
putting away of the Communism he hoped to see established, and for the retention of its so necessary residue
of good, his main hope lay with two or three: Spanish
insensibility to Time-spirit, which gave compensatory
long-sightedness; the secretiveness and pride of the
Spaniard which made him, in his own defence, respectful
of the secret and unknowable ego of his every fellow-man;
the superstitious religiosity which would keep Spain for

ever familiar with the principles and parables of Christianity. Communism would come to Spain, he hoped, as purge and disinfectant, but religion would not go, he thought, though a long period of impotence and martyrdom might very well be waiting for it. No harm in that, however, he said, to his mother's real alarm. No harm, but on the contrary, much good fruit, very likely, both for Church and State. "But, Juanito, you go to Mass!" Doña Consuelo would say, "and you're such a good Catholic boy!" And he would laugh at her affectionately, so that she told herself, looking at his gay, non-fanatical face, that all his talk was no more than the youthful, topsy-turvy nonsense Pablo used to dispense in their early married life. Communism would come, Juanito dreamt, within fifty years, and within a hundred, if Spanish individualism could at all be trusted, it would be gone, leaving knowledge, the only true good, behind it.

His father would shudder tolerantly at this dream. "No end can justify the risky imposition of citizen-servility," he said. "You're a dangerous Jesuit, Juanito; God give you sense!"

But Juanito said that his faith was in the Spanish character. "Bread by all means, father! Bread for every-one as soon as possible, bread for belly and heart and brain—but in the end—your great-grandchildren will see —not bread alone. *Pan y toros!*" And if any Red in a Salamanca café answered to that that Communism would not take away the people's bullfights, Juanito would laugh and dismiss him for a literal ass.

He had vigorous intelligence, was a serious student of

law and constitutional history, and was swift in applying knowledge to the illumination of life as it flowed. He was too Spanish to be any kind of Utopian, but too sure of life's essential value to each man, irrespective of that life's conditions, to wax morbid over impertinent theories of hell upon earth. He had no use for Spain's reigning house, and would be glad to see it marched across the Pyrenees once more; he detested militarism and antiquated imperialism, though, touch of the conquistador, he believed in adventurous development of the earth's resources. To mention the Moroccan war to him was to invoke the eloquence of honest fury. He was, in fact, when he began to practise law in Madrid in the autumn of 1919, when he began also to write for liberal publications, and to debate in the *Ateneo* and wherever disinterestedness might raise its voice, a truly promising and serious young man.

"My trouble is," he wrote to his father in those days, "that I am my own political party. My notions have a few non-committal friends, and flocks of enemies. I haven't even, like Louis XVI, one soldier. I must take a wife to remedy that."

And the next thing was that he was in love with Luisa, the perfect flower of all he proposed to sweep away. But so intelligent, so used to the dialectics of philosophers and statesmen, and even of reformers, by chance so cultivated and sceptical and twentieth-century, and so bored by the flâneurs and athletes of fashionable Madrid that she beckoned the admiration of the original, boyish and—so her brothers said—very promising and dangerous creature six months her junior, whose grey gold eyes blazed on her with such an innocent and eager passion.

Eager, he was, and perhaps innocent. But he saw the traps for his mind in what his desire now prompted. And he had read and thought and talked of women, and knew how the best of them might chop up a man's intrinsic hopes to warm the domestic fire. He fled to his father with a thousand questions—and Don Pablo had no answers.

Perhaps the boy, in the darkest place of his heart, desired to be pulled back authoritatively from his alluring precipice. Perhaps he desired an angry argument—the first between him and his father—or to be affectionately counselled as to his own youth and hot blood, the difficult individuality of his ambitions, the danger of trying to adapt these to all that a de Maraval represented. Perhaps he hoped to be advised to wait a year, to go away, to travel in England or Russia or Argentina, and see if twelve months' absence made any difference to his love.

Don Pablo said none of these things. He sat by the library fire, lighting cigarette from cigarette, and listened in helplessness to his son.

Juanito described Luisa to him and recounted all that he knew of her. His father thought that no one with a vestige of faith in life could hear the vibrations of his voice unmoved, or without pleasure. But that acknowledgment made to his own heart, he knew himself impotent.

The dilemma was an old one and crusted with platitudes. Life's apparent pattern was repetitive, and only its inner accidents could make it precious or painful.

There was no answer in the single experience of any man, nor did general reference cut much ice. Love might, like Shakespeare's Cleopatra, help to gird the warrior, or also, like that heroine, play billiards and unman him. Juanito, turning away from his Luisa, could shelve his personal question for a time. In her arms, or another's, it would be answered, but the answer was simply not to be predicted. Pablo desired his son to have the life of useful activity and mental strife which he was fitted for, wanted him to go out in the open, where he belonged, and take the cuts, blows, shocks and delights that were the due of Unamuno's 'Man of Flesh and Bone.' At forty-six he would not be what he himself was, a desiccated looker-on, a somewhat ashamed contemplative, an ineffectual ironist. Indeed, the idea of Juanito thus distorted made him smile incredulously—but at twenty-three he, too, had been voluble and vigorous—and had suddenly found himself where Juanito now had come, inflamed as he was, and in the same natural agony.

Still he had no answer. Memory of his years of passion with Consuelo exacted from him a loyalty as meticulous as did that of those intentions and ambitions which she had manœuvred out of his reach. Men were conceited and ponderous about their purpose in life, but love, though it cooled more easily than ambition, gave as a rule more immediate satisfactions. Gave children too, he thought, eyeing his distracted son. And did anyone imagine that this impetuous Juanito, single-handed, could have his idealistic will with Spain? Would any sane man urge him forward on such a quixotic sally? But since he was going forward, and must certainly in

some measure fall short of his immense intentions—
might not love, or its memory and its growing fruit, be
the best provision against winter?

Don Pablo did not know. For himself, and he could
count his blessings, he found middle age lonely and cold.
More so than ever now this son was straining off from
him. For himself, the compromises he had made had not
availed. But no one was to know that, least of all
Juanito. And perhaps the latter would eat his cake and
have it. That ought to be possible. The boy was worthy
even of such exaggerated luck. And in any case perhaps
it was the nature of middle age to be lonely and cold.
Who could say? Perhaps all that satisfied, or at least
inspired in human life were the years of youth's con-
flicting fires? Perhaps the personal battle was itself the
goal, its outcome of no matter.

"I see, my son. I see your dilemma. You must work
it out. Neither I nor your mother would see anything
against your marrying above your station."

Juanito had stared. It seemed no time for irony.

He did work it out, in marriage with Luisa. And now
he was twenty-five and the well-pleased father of a son.
And if he suspected his keen-witted wife of being more
amused by his 'original notions' and proud of his
brilliance than sympathetic to his seriousness—well,
perhaps it would be rather maddening to be completely
understood by a wife. Luisa was loyally helpful in many
ways, even while she mocked at theories which, she
quite frankly told him, she tolerated because she knew
them to be impossible of realisation; she arranged their
life as much as possible to please him and without

involving him in the vulgarities and extravagances of Madrid's smart set; she was gracious to his queer collection of friends, and a tolerant, light-hearted companion to him; she loved him and she gave him sensual peace.

So here he was, a lucky and spoilt young man, at home again where he loved to be, and without a cloud in his sky.

Yet as he leant against the door and listened to the tango, he felt somewhat tired, a little heavy. Through half-closed eyes he considered the children's governess. Smiling inwardly, he thought how right his mother was, that indeed it was ludicrous for any girls to have such a dueña. The whole dueña business was absurd, of course, and would have to go in this generation. Then what would all these stupid, genteel Irishwomen do for work? Not that this particular one need worry much about bed or board. No doubt some stalwart suitor in Ireland was slaving away in an agony of eagerness to provide her with the best he could manage of both. Milagros had made some joke at dinner about Estéban counting up the love-letters. Curious really that she should be here at all! She was most strangely lovely. He would tease Pilár about her, just a little. Sweet, vain Pilár! Such chaperonage really was hard luck.

Juanito was being dishonest and superficial in these reflections. Keeping them vulgar deliberately, so as to ward off an under-strength which he dared not apprehend in them. He was afraid of something. Ever since his eyes had met this girl's when she turned towards him from the staircase two hours ago, he had been, in profound surreptitiousness from himself, afraid. And therefore it

166

was not quite true to say of him to-night that there was no cloud in his sky. There was one, not as big as a man's hand, but he did not ask himself to perceive it. For this very fact, this not choosing to see, this vulgar superficiality of comment, was itself the cloud.

It grew as he ignored it, and as the time ran on he forgot to feed himself flippant commentary. He slipped past his own guard into real observation.

She sat erect, her hands clasped loosely over her crossed knees, her slender body outlined as flowingly as if she were a figure in a dream. The curly edge of her neutral-coloured hair made an angelic nimbus, but there was nothing Christian in the face it framed. Those features came unflawed—oh, impossible marvel!—from Greece's most exacting and fastidious time. A virgin, pagan face. The face of untaken Aphrodite. Beauty as little to be known or held as the rakish Cyprian's, as unlikely to be satisfied or satisfactory in the bread-and-butter world. A myth from a long outmoded heaven—and yet, there she sat, as girlish as you please, and rather shy, in her cotton dress. An employée in his father's house. A good girl from Ireland, with proudly held shoulders and a look of loneliness. While beauty unfurled from her as from a rose.

Absurd, unfair and comical. Juanito felt something shudder in him, and almost heard himself laugh. Tricks of encounter, tricks of thought—what was there to be afraid of in them? A fulfilled man was master of himself, and a few flowery meditations on a lovely face were no more important than a reading of poetry. All in the day's work. This girl had not risen from sea-foam. She was made in the common human shape, and like Luisa, like his sisters, would go her natural way of uneven happiness and unhappiness, to satisfy a man, bear his children and die. There she was, more beautiful than was necessary, but pitifully human. Look how shy and lonely she could seem, like any other! Bracing himself thus, he continued to look at her through half-shut eyes, but the cloud spread as he ignored it, and his mood remained heavy.

Don Pablo also looked at his children's governess, but he was growing used to that weary pastime. He supposed that the easy modern attitude of crossed knees and hands clasped over them, must really be an ancient pose, so well it showed the turn of wrist and ankle, the long, sweet line of thigh. Pilár's protectress—he smiled—was so beautiful to-night as to seem again Medusa, or a flame-sworded angel at the gate of Paradise. Exaggeratedly armoured for her duty. He wondered what his daughter-in-law made in her secret heart of an encounter that must indeed be novel to her. She, conscious of her own intricate beauty, knew its history too, and its dependence on the training and suggestions of that history—knew the lights and shadows that best beautified it and the legend that gave it potency and bloom. She knew it, in fact, for an exacting, and, in a sense, exotic attribute. But here was simplicity, unschooled, defeating it at its own sophisticated game. Here was innocence calling up all the tricked-up poets' images of which it knew so little, and leaving them winded and ridiculous. Don Pablo smiled benevolently upon the subtle and alert Luisa. He could understand how clubmen and experienced sensualists might debate between the two, the daughter of Spanish aristocrats and the provincial doctor's child. But for himself he could only smile with good nature on the defeated. Luisa had Madrid in her hand, and one of Spain's best young men for husband; her photographs were welcomed in any sophisticated magazine in any part of the world; if Juanito's revolution ever came, his exquisite, aristocratic wife, playing her part of aristocratic revolutionary, might for a while be a figure of world interest. In any case, exquisite and virtuous, she was marked out always for victory. Save only here. This girl who took nothing from Spain but her wages, and who would vanish soon into the decent, obscure, unphotographed society she came from, this nonentity who had no notion at all of the nonsensical things that he and, perhaps in another way Luisa were thinking—this girl exploded his daughter-in-law as thoroughly as Quixote the wine-skins. Amusing and moving truth—like many of Cervantes'. Poor Luisa! And what a pity in a way that absolute beauty must be, to be itself, all that Luisa was not, and this harmless destroyer of her was! Innocent, ignorant, untouchably young. But therein, in transience, since all these qualities must pass if loveliness is not to be disfigured into imbecility, is beauty's essence. Intricate as a seashell or a windflower and simple as either, it must, like both, for beauty's sake, lose life and lustre. Luisa would be able to call quits with this rival at last, as anyone would, in the graveyard.

Don Pablo, the philosopher, was not often so distracted from his son, especially nowadays when the latter's dear comings were rare and hurried. *"Mignonne,"* he murmured, not hearing the crude tango tune,

"*Mignonne, allons voir si la rose——*" But then, afraid that senile meditation took him perhaps too foolishly far, he looked away from his daughter's governess, and turned his eyes, for discipline, upon his son. And Juanito, he saw, was looking, gravely, sadly, where his own eyes also had rested.

THE POETRY LESSON

Luisa and her baby stayed at Cabantes only two nights. Juanito said that he would remain a few days longer. His father's accentuated look of weariness made him reluctant to hurry away, he said, and in any case he felt just now in particular need of the refreshment of Cabantes. Luisa understood but, as she told him with good-humoured tenderness, two days was her maximum of endurance of the comfortable Casa Pilár. "It's curious, don't you think, *chiquito* that the two most attractive rooms in this house are the schoolroom and that room where I believe they put the 'miss'?"

Juanito smiled but even to help Luisa's nerves would never have suggested to his mother that there was anything wrong with the Casa Pilár. In any case, tables and chairs did not matter passionately to him, and a disloyal, unencouraged part of him considered that there was something almost vile in æsthetic shuddering. Sometimes in Madrid, in his beautiful apartment, all dead blue, white and crystal, which overlooked the whispering acacias of the Recoletos, he thought with an uneasy, unmentionable sense of present degradation of the big, ugly drawing-room at Cabantes, and the smoky quiet harmoniousness of his father's library. But there it was. Décor was Luisa's foible, just as she might say that certain boring, one-track theorists were his. She knew at least how to live and let live, and though for a man of honour that could be a dangerous accomplishment, obviously a husband must practise it in minor things.

Mary, at breakfast in her dining-room on the second morning of Luisa's visit, saw the daughter-in-law's departure distantly and out of one eye, while she read her letters. She had not known that Juanito was in fact staying longer, and reflected that the children would be pleased. There was a great deal of hubbub round the car—all the family chattering gaily, servants chattering too as they stowed away baggage. The brilliantly dressed Andalucian nurse emerged from the house with the baby, who was kissed by grandparents and aunts before the foster-mother mounted with him into the car. Yesterday under the cherry-tree Mary had seen the child sucking from the great, heavy breast of the peasant girl in fancy dress. The sight, which was one to which she was accustomed in Altorno's parks, troubled her, but Milagros insisted that fosterage was one of Spain's most justifiable traditions. "Look at us, Miss Maria! Are we any the worse?" Anyway, this baby ought to become an attractive person, foster-mother or no, she thought dreamily. Then as he saw Juanito bend into the car, presumably to kiss his wife and child, she turned her full attention to her letters.

Ten minutes later all that she could see of the garden was empty, save for Doña Consuelo, who plucked some roses from an overweighted tree. Mary braced herself and went out to her. In scrupulously prepared and very simple Spanish she made her diffident report upon Don Jorge. Doña Consuelo looked startled and serious, and made her repeat what she had said. Mary did so, feeling miserable. She was thanked then very warmly, and even patted on the shoulder. The unpleasant duty over, the 'miss' withdrew. At eleven o'clock, when the Andalucian priest was expected as usual, Doña Consuelo entered the study and announced without explanation that Don Jorge was not coming, and that until a new music professor was arranged for the children were to practise the piano under Miss Maria's supervision.

The three girls fluttered with interest.

"Is Don Jorge ill, Mama?" Milagros asked with a twinkle.

"No, Milagros. Your father has this morning telephoned to tell him we do not require his services in future."

The girls laughed softly and their mother retired.

"Oho!" said Nieves. "Father must be in a fine rage!"

"What did I tell you, miss?" Milagros hopped about the room in amusement. "We weren't even consulted! Papa just lost his temper and went to the telephone. Oh, I wish I'd seen him! He's really the simplest man!"

"No music for awhile, thank God!"

"But Pilár," said Mary, "you have to practise."

Later when the girls and Mary were playing tennis Juanito and Don Pablo, who had been strolling in the long dark grove that encircled the garden, stood to watch, and the young man asked if he might play. None of his sisters would abandon her right to be in the game with him, but Mary, a little dispirited over the Don Jorge episode, was very glad to give up her place in the set. She sat on a bench nearby to watch, and Don Pablo came and sat beside her.

He spoke Spanish always to her now, as simply and slowly as he could, and in short sentences. His face was old and heavy this morning, Mary thought, and his mouth more bitterly curved than usual.

"I apologise from my heart, Miss Maria, for the coarseness of Don Jorge, and I thank you for reporting it."

Mary murmured an uneasy protest, but he went on. "I expect that his behaviour was more objectionable than you allowed my wife to understand, because I think it likely that a young lady of your age and inexperience would hesitate considerably before making a complaint. It was lax of us to employ the man, but he has some talent for music, and musicians are few in Altorno."

"Please, Don Pablo—I beg of you! The whole thing makes me feel unhappy and unkind——"

Tears of embarrassment came to her eyes. She was wishing she had never taken on this absurd job with its absurd dilemmas. He turned and looked at her, the bitter solemnity of his face relaxing into gentleness.

"That is very nearly the worst part of the man's offence," he said. "That he should place you in so uncomfortable a quandary. I believe I am more angry for the insult to you—for you are after all a sort of guest in Spain—than for the cruel cheapening of my daughters."

He looked away towards them on the tennis court, and suddenly smiled philosophically and waved a hand as if to dismiss the memory of the Andalucian music-master. "Their hearts are light," he said gently.

Juanito seemed light-hearted too. He played tennis well, though Mary thought that John could probably beat him in two straight sets. But he was far too good for his sisters, and now all three were jovially lined up together in an unconventionally concerted effort to defeat him. He looked towards Mary.

"Do you allow this dishonest arrangement, Miss Maria?" Mary nodded a rather shy, amused acceptance.

"Nieves would prefer the game as it is played," Don Pablo mused affectionately; "she has high, English standards. But even she will waive a point for the fun of amusing Juanito. They love him very much."

Mary said nothing. It was natural that young girls should love an only brother, but she thought that this Juanito was the sort of person who would always be given love. She had heard a great deal about him before he came home, and at first meeting had been, in a relieved way, disappointed. She had somehow, though no one had described him as an Adonis, expected great beauty, and she found instead an irregular, erratic face; she had foreseen some of the dandy airs and masculine smartness of Madrid which now enlivened Playablanca, but this boy was as untidy as his father and indeed the shadow on his chin to-day would have disgusted John. She had thought he would be profoundly occupied with his own affairs, and even somewhat pompous as became a young man set for fame, but he seemed to be more than content to loaf about with his parents, gossip with his sisters, put on the gramophone, and eat turrón. And yet, simple and unexacting as he was, the house was alive in an unprece- dented way now that he inhabited it. There was, as it were, an easier hum of friendliness throughout it. Mary was quite prepared to believe that Juanito was an intel- lectual and a man of serious intentions, but it seemed to her that his greatest gift and his most potent would always be his power to make things go, his fluidity, his exaggerated but absolutely true simplicity. Anyone as disarming and unaffected as he would always seem, in a world of pricks, hesitations and anxieties, a kind of miracle. Affection must always be at the command of such a temperament, she thought, and she wondered now, as he dashed about the tennis court, why on earth on that first evening in the salón she had had some curious moments of thinking him subtle, broody, even—God forgive her!—personally discomfiting. She had certainly got him all wrong. She saw that now. Probably his resemblance to his father—and his possible fatigue after travel—had misled her. Don Pablo must have always had a very different temperament from his son, much more recessive, much less simple. She looked at him now as he sat beside her smoking, his eyes half closed. Impossible, she thought, ever to tell what he was thinking.

That was well perhaps. He looked now at his sweating, laughing son, seeking to decide once and for all whether the expression he had seen on his face during the playing of a vulgar tango the other night was abstracted, and irrelevant from the girl on whom his eyes happened to be fixed, whether it was no more than the signal of a transitory mood of dreamy appreciation of her such as any man with life in him must feel, or whether in fact it was the mask of someone freshly wounded by desire?

Knowing his son well, and watching him in the last twenty-four hours with a care which by its acuteness offended his own spirit, Don Pablo had almost come to the belief that the graven weary look on his face that

176

night had been in fact induced by some remote irrelevancy of thought. Juanito was in love with his wife, and would be for many years yet. He was safe. Odd as it might seem, he was safe even against this girl. And something childish about him now as he played this very foolish tennis game with his sisters seemed absolutely to endorse his safety.

Don Pablo smiled and lighted another cigarette.

"And this is the man, Miss Maria, who would have us believe that he knows of several ways to save Spain!"

The next morning while he drank his chocolate some piece of philatelic news in his morning paper reminded Juanito of his old, forgotten stamp collection in the schoolroom. He rose to his feet—he was alone in the dining-room—then paused and stared out of the window. How we fool ourselves! he thought. How we seek for the rope that is going to hang us! She would be there, giving the children their English lesson. And what if she was? Was he not meeting her twenty times each day? Had he not stayed here for the sake of such futile meetings? Why strain at a gnat while you swallow the camel? He stared into the passionately enflowered garden.

His mother came in, pulling off her mantilla. She had been to Mass.

He smiled affectionately, and kissed her.

"Good morning, my son," she said. "You look a little tired. Did you sleep well?"

"Oh yes, I always sleep well at home."

A maid brought Doña Consuelo's chocolate, and with another pat on her son's cheek she turned to the table and sat down. Juanito gathered up his paper and left the room.

English verse was being dealt with that morning in the schoolroom. The children had a liking for poetry, and Milagros had a formidable appetite for it. Mary was not learned in literature, but she had been shocked to discover that 'Miss Anita' had found for these pupils no better English food than the 'Inchcape Rock' and 'I stood on the bridge at midnight.' She herself read and examined with them now such poems in her own Oxford Book of English Verse as she happened to like best or was sure she understood sufficiently to analyse with them. As there was only her copy of this anthology in the house, the children transcribed the poems they liked and memorised them. Meantime, urgently instructed by the three, especially by Milagros, Don Pablo had written to London for various volumes of English prose and verse—Jane Austen's novels (they were all three enchanted with *Emma*, which they were reading in Miss Maria's copy), the Temple Shakespeare, the *Songs of Innocence*, *Tales of Mystery and Imagination*, and for Milagros, to save her the otherwise certain labour of copying out the whole volume, an Oxford Book like Miss Maria's.

To-day, as a surprise for her teacher, Milagros had copied and learnt a poem of her own choosing. She was eager to show how accurately she could declaim it.

"Let me do my surprise poem now, Miss Maria, or I may forget it!"

Juanito came in, tiptoeing and apologetic.

"You're just in time!" said Milagros. "I've learnt a

lovely poem—I chose it myself in Miss Maria's book!"

The young man smiled at Mary, who, though she disliked an audience at her randomly conducted class, felt at ease with him now, and did not very much mind his unlooked-for intrusion.

"May I hear her say her poem, Miss Maria?"

He, like his father, spoke Spanish to her always, slowly and clearly. She answered in English with a clarity which she tried to make as courteous as his.

"She'll be offended if you don't."

Milagros cleared her throat.

"It's a sixteenth-century pastoral poem," she announced pedantically.

"But Mila, unless you let me have the text to read, I'll never understand."

She handed him her neat copy of the poem. Then, closing her eyes, the child repeated the English lines with a careful foreign thoughtfulness.

> "Come live with me and be my love
> And we will all the pleasures prove——"

Mary was surprised. Milagros usually liked to wrestle with a Shakespearean sonnet, or with Wordsworth, or the difficult Lycidas, but her voice had a childish contentment in it now as she threaded her way with care through the shepherd's clear list of delights. The room was full of sunshine; the far-off noises from the bay made a happy under-music for the verses.

> ". . . By shallow rivers to whose falls
> Melodious birds sing madrigals.
> And I will make thee beds of roses . . ."

179

Mary looked up indolently towards Juanito, wondering what he made of his little sister's chanting. He stood against a bookshelf at the other side of the work-table. The sheet of paper was in his hand, but his eyes were not following the lines. They were upon her, and half-closed, more grave than she had ever seen them, grave and unhappy as his father's. There was something helpless in his look so that she could not, even in self-defence, turn from it. She took its danger and felt it, could almost have had the courage to name it to her thudding heart, for an illuminated second. Then she looked away. "He's very young," she thought wearily. "He's very beautiful."

The poem drew to its end.

". . . Then live with me and be my love."

Milagros sat with her eyes shut for a second hypnotised by her own echoes. Juanito, with the sheet of paper still in his hand, left the room.

"I don't care much for that one, Mila," said Pilár good-naturedly.

"But Juanito? Oh, where's Juanito?"

"He looked awfully bored," said Nieves. "Really, you know, Mila, it's a bit much to expect him to like English poetry."

Milagros was very much hurt.

"It's a lovely poem," she stormed, "and the point of it is that a *baby* could understand it! Oh, it's not like Juanito to be so rude to me!"

The rest of the English lesson went badly.

But orthodoxy is not intimidated by enigmatic glances and passing moments of discomfort. The well-trained

Irish Catholic, being as Milagros surmised somewhat
Jansenistically instructed, is easily made to understand
that human nature, left to itself, can be not merely incredibly sinful but incredibly foolish. Mary Lavelle,
although in her twenty-third year, would in fact have
found it hard, up to now, to have unearthed from
memories of herself any thought or action which an
impartial judge could have stamped as exemplary of
extreme human wickedness or imbecility. Not because
she was heroically pursuant of virtue, but because her
life was sheltered and her nature innocent; also no doubt
in part because the man who had won her heart, as the
saying is, had not, as yet at least, disturbed her senses.
But in spite of this accidental personal immunity from the
more severe tests on human frailty, Mary knew by hearsay
—from confessors, from school retreats, from missions,
from the exhortations of the catechism—that she was a
sinner, a weak thing of flesh. She remembered that when
she first learnt to read and found her prayer book a useful
field of exercise for the new accomplishment, she had
frequently entreated God, in a long and resounding
orison, to deliver her from her concupiscence. But to this
day she was uncertain how to pronounce that word, and
was glad that there never seemed occasion to utter it.
She knew, however, in theory, a reasonable sufficiency
about the tricky sixth commandment, and she was no
fool.

Now, therefore, she shook herself. She sat by her
window after dinner in her wobbly wicker chair and,
watching the stars thicken beyond Torcal, she examined
her novel and ridiculous state of mind. She could see

181

that the terrace below was flooded with light from the salon; she could hear the children's gramophone music clashing against the band from Playablanca. Their brother was giving them a dancing lesson, no doubt. He had said that he would do so. With something remotely like pain she turned her thoughts away from their probable antics.

She was having an attack of being a fool, she told herself. Perhaps it was her turn. She had seen other girls make fools of themselves in season and had heard the rubbish they could talk about any rude or unlicensed ogler. She had seen some of the 'misses' almost swoon, God help them! if any wretched English consulate clerk or engineer chanced to look their way in the Aleman. She had always felt superior to such goings-on, and blessedly uncomprehending of them. Well, those days were over for her, apparently. But what in fact had happened?

Three days ago, meeting Juanito, she had liked him, finding him simple and gentle as his father, whom she liked with complete simplicity, as one might a good priest or any good friend. Thinking over this son of Don Pablo as she walked upstairs from their first encounter, she had inadvertently looked back, to check her impression of the physical resemblance between the two men, and had been startled and, she supposed, pleased also, to find that he was looking up at her. But that look—so grave and gentle—although it had lingered in her mind as she went on upstairs to her room, had been easy enough to forget. Though she remembered it now. Still, she could almost swear that she had shaken it from her mind long before Nieves came with the invitation to hear flamenco music. Her only sensation then, she was sure, had been misery over the ordeal of meeting the distinguished daughter-in-law. Curiously, that had not proved an ordeal, but all the time that she was in the salon there had hung upon her nevertheless, as from some other source, a heavy sense of ordeal. There had been eyes on her troublingly; not the formidable Luisa's, there had been an exaggerated sense of gaucherie in herself, and even of unreality; she had not known what to do with the silly wireless parts, or how to face the movements of getting from a standing to a sitting posture. There was a tango tune and its obviousness and the impersonal memory it brought of the dancers in the Plaza San Martín had blurred discomfort and had made her even feel a little happy. But she had gone up to bed with a new uneasiness for company, and when she said her prayers had found it necessary to pray with a double energy for John, for his well-being and happiness.

The next day she was herself again, and very much embarrassed to remember her disgusting mood of the night before. She had kept detached from the family life as much as possible, and had finished her interrupted love-letter to John. On the morning of his wife's departure she had cautiously allowed herself to notice that Juanito looked young and agreeable standing in the sunshine by the car and she could not swear that pleasure had not menaced her deepest heart as she realised that he was not in fact going away. But cold consideration of him as he played tennis with his sisters had completely reassured her. He was an innocent boy and no adventuring ogler, and she must have been in some mad, inexplicable state herself on the evening of his arrival to imagine that his eyes rested on her with any particular attention, any more appeal than one might imagine, say, upon occasion in his father's eyes. It was the Spanish look, the Spanish mask which was a masculine uniform, as she well knew, and meant nothing personal in or from the wearer. She must have been ill or crazy to have thought she felt pain or response or pleasure in reaction to looks which were perfectly innocent and without significance.

But then this morning—that silly business of Milagros' poem?

Mary paused. She stood up and moved out on to the balcony. The night was brimful of beauty. She took a breath of it. Come live with me and be my love and we will all the pleasures prove—ah, what had happened this morning? Nothing, nothing. No more at the worst than that a silly cocksure young Spaniard who perhaps thought her pretty, had been vulgar enough to take advantage of his little sister's innocent whim to stand and make tragic eyes at a governess. Ah, but tragic eyes. Yes, they were tragic, set in his young, white face. Why they were so there was no guessing or why he stared so helplessly at her, but belittlement of him was going to be of no avail. He wasn't cocksure, he wasn't vulgar. She knew nothing of him, but she knew that. Whatever this brief folly was that she was going through, it was her own and she must work it out and strangle it alone. He might have his foolish fancies too, but he was a man and no doubt more used to these absurd temptations, less alarmed by them. Perhaps in moods he liked her a little, but she—she straightened up against the balcony and looked out coldly towards Torcal—she had, for some unsearchable reason, inevitably and instantaneously liked him.

She stayed very still, considering that. The gramophone music came up to her—the band was temporarily silent. She could see Doña Consuelo's shadow reflected on the terrace from the window. And his passing shadow, with Nieves' as they danced. She drew back and leant against the window-sash. Yes, she liked him, but what of that? John had told her that he, having seen her across a room, was in love then and for ever, but that that sort of thing never happened to a girl. Thank God! It certainly hadn't happened to her—nothing such as John described. She was probably out of sorts, overlonely. She must go to the Alemán, look up Conlan and O'Toole. Being a miss was perhaps a rather depressing kind of job. She would have to be careful.

She was careful. For the next day or two she encouraged the children to go revelling here and there with their brother, and to shake off her society, having his escort. She pleaded headaches and too much sun and this and that. They, eager to gallivant with him, did not struggle against her laxity. She managed to avoid more than the briefest contacts with Juanito. She was very well pleased with her own mood of detachment.

On the third day the children, whom she had not seen since noon, came in to drink afternoon chocolate with her in a disgruntled mood. Juanito was going to Biarritz that evening. Fernando somebody-or-other

wanted his sports car driven over, and Luisa had telephoned that she was bored. "Well, that's nice in a wife,"
said Milagros.

Mary finished her chocolate.

"You children won't want me then," she said. "Would
it matter if I went out, now it's cool?"

No, of course it wouldn't matter. Nieves looked at
her gently.

"You look awfully tired all of a sudden, Miss Maria,"
she said.

Mary went out and, without purpose, took the train
to Altorno. She had a wild pain in her heart that terrified
her. Luisa was bored, and the boredom was about to be
ended. Oh, it was astonishing how unaccountable and
disgusting one could be! An innocent sentence could
ulcerate the day. Five days could change the perfectly
well-known, the simple valley of oneself, into a place of
circus and buffoonery, where nothing kept its stance or
features for two consecutive seconds. A minute, a day,
a look, a verse of poetry, and peace could be in tatters,
one could be reeling off like this without intention into a
boring town, simply because it would be impossible to sit
quiet in one's room and hear the happy departure to his
wife and child of a perfect stranger. Come live with me
and be my love. God, help me! Oh help me, help me,
please. Teach me how to pray. Teach me how to love
John as I should. Oh help me, God.

She did not go to the Aleman. O'Toole might be there
at this hour, or Keogh, but she felt unequal to either.
Conlan would be at home. She thought of going to the
Gutierrez appartement, but she decided not to. Conlan

would probably be engaged with her children, and anyhow her eyes, so blind and fanatical, could sometimes search with savagery. If only she were kinder, or anyhow not so mad. Ah, where to go to forget this irrational, humiliating pain?

She bought an evening paper and went into a cake-shop in the Alameda San Tomás. She pulled off her hat, drank coffee and read about a bullfight in Valencia. There were some English engineers in the room. They spoke loudly, smiling in her direction. They offered each other Gold Flakes and out-of-date *Daily Mails*. I must tell Harty about this place, she thought.

She calmed down. Pronceda had had a mediocre day apparently, but it had been a triumph for a man called 'El Sastrito,' of whom she had heard Conlan talk. He had, she gathered, a quick and dancing style, a more traditional manner than Pronceda's. She recalled the latter's sober movements; he had seemed in a tragic dream as he went round the ring.

The cake shop grew quiet at last, the paper boring. He was on his way to Biarritz now, and she presumed that she had suffered the last attack of her humiliating malady. She might as well go home. It was nearly eight o'clock. She paid her bill and walked out.

She did not take the train, however. She turned into the racketing mazes of old Altorno. In Spain the clocks are not put on in summer and at this hour the town, shut in by its obliterated hills and velvety, dim-starred sky, was fiercely illumined and shadowed, through plane-trees, archways and shop windows, by torrents of white electric light. It was the noisiest of Spanish hours, the pleasure hour before supper, when girls paraded, five and six together, singing, when every café chair was filled and every beggar, shoeblack and seller of lottery tickets was crying out his trade. Tram-bells clanged excitedly, motor-horns sounded and policemen blew their whistles; evening papers were yelled on every corner, young men guffawed at the girls and tried to sing flamenco; the bands were tuning up in all the squares.

Mary walked through the familiar commotion, carrying her hat in her hand. She liked the Spanish females' way of going bareheaded and though she knew it was not correct for a miss, she sometimes risked it, taking a cue from Conlan. She heard men tell her at every other step how beautiful she was; she was used by now to this inoffensive pleasantry, and smiled her fleeting thanks. To-night she walked quickly and took in with eager appetite the violent noise, the violent light and shadow. They seemed to hold herself away from her, to give her time to breathe while a recent pain ebbed off. She would be all right in an hour or so, if she forgot about herself. She hurried through the narrowing streets and came out into the Plaza San Martín, where the bandstand seemed about to burst with noise and light, and where, under the clipped, close-tented plane-trees, workboys in overalls danced, very gravely and beautifully, with their red-mouthed girls.

She paused here. She loved the Plaza San Martín. She stood very still under a plane-tree on the corner. She had stood here before to watch this lovely dancing—nowhere, she believed, could everyday dancing be made to seem so noble as by the common people of Spain. Often standing there she had wondered what it would be like to be one of them, to dance to that raucous music, over the uneven earth, in and out of the shadowing trees. Young men had asked her often to be their partner, but she, under two traditions, that of a young lady of Mellick and of a 'miss,' had always had to refuse. But her refusals had been taken as friendlily and shyly as she tendered them. She had sometimes wondered lightly what John would say if she had to confess to him that she had taken to dancing with overalled men in the slum squares of Altorno. To-night she did not think of John. She leant against the tree, and looked at the figures moving in beauty through the violent depths of light. She knew the tune they were dancing to: 'I met my love in Avalon . . .'

Juanito found her under the tree. There was a white, hard light streaming in on her obliquely.

"I looked everywhere," he said. "I tried the Alemán. Then I remembered Milagros said you often watched the dancing here. I walked all round the square, and was just giving up when I saw you."

He spoke hurriedly, so that she barely caught the meaning.

"Will you dance with me?" he said.

They danced. 'I met my love in Avalon.' The band thundered it.

"I'm going to Biarritz," he said. "I'm on my way. The car is there by the river."

"I know."

"I had to see you again. I had to find you."

"Ah, I'm glad."

"You too?"

She looked into his eyes, but could not answer. They

went on dancing. Life was fantastic. One minute you were afraid to breathe for pain, the next you were dancing in the Plaza San Martín.

"I have the poem," he said. "I'm trying to learn it."

She thought of the bullfight suddenly, of how it ravished her memory. This too she would need to remember.

She looked with precision at his young, smooth neck, so near her, and at his silky hair and blue silk collar. As if memorising, she moved her fingers gently within the cool strong shell of his. His hand felt familiar; so did his arm about her. She thought that these things would be easy to remember. She ventured to look into his eyes, which were fixed upon her face, half-closed and very grave. As grave as his father's. I shall see him every time I look at Don Pablo, she thought contentedly.

"How do you say your name—Ma-ry?"

Ah, the sweet stumbling accent!

"Just that way—as you said it."

They went on dancing, in and out of shadow.

"When the music stops, that is good-bye," Mary said.

"I know. But I had to say it."

"It's all there is to say."

The music stopped. They walked out of the square.

"Good-bye."

He did not answer. He stood and looked at her as if that was all that there was left to do in life. She drank his look for a wild second, and gave him all that there might be in hers. Then she ran up a narrow street, as if the ground burnt her.

CANDLES AT ALLERA

WHEN Mary went to the Café Alemán on her next free afternoon, there was a group of familiars at the corner table in the ladies' alcove. With the exception of O'Toole, they greeted her coldly.

"Come here, alannah, till I make room for you! You're as hard to find these times as a ten-pound note."

Mary slid in beside O'Toole on the black leather seat.

"Hello!" said Duggan.

"Hello!" said Keogh.

"Hello!" said Harty. "How're you finding the job? Treating you like dirt, I suppose?"

"I thought perhaps you'd left Spain," said Conlan.

Mary smiled and ordered chocolate from Angeles.

"You're learning Spanish," said Keogh with condescension. "What's the idea?"

"What do you want with chocolate?" said Harty. "You should insist on tea in the afternoon. You really should, you know."

"How are you, alannah? What's your news?" Mary had no news.

"Nice hat, O'Toole," she said.

"Do you really like it, alannah?"

It was a shady hat with a wreath of little roses. O'Toole looked raddled and gay under it.

"It's idiotic," said Conlan.

"Where did you get it?" said Keogh.

Hats are only worn in Spain by the women of the wealthy classes, and by them for more or less formal occasions. Hat shops are extremely rare in provincial cities. Hats are displayed to the rich at seasonal manne-quin parades held by Madrid or Paris designers in the best hotels of wealthy towns, or they are made by little obscure milliners. The misses did not, as Milagros thought, obtain their English velours and panamas by the miraculous intervention of Our Lady of Allera; if any one of them went on leave she might be commis-sioned to bring back a hat for a friend, or sometimes a sister at home would send a head-covering through the post, or if all fruit failed, the miss carried on with an aged hat. Or if she was Conlan, she wore the hat she originally brought to Spain until it fell to pieces, and then she went hatless or in mantilla, out of no compliment to the country she lived in, but through necessity. But *esprit de corps* was offended by such behaviour. A suitable hat should be obtained and worn by every normal miss. But not such hats as those in which O'Toole made a guy of herself.

"Where would I get it but from a milliner?" said O'Toole. "And it's paid for, what's more."

Mary smiled at her.

"You're looking very lively," she said. "What's up?"

O'Toole's eyes looked perceptibly disingenuous for a second.

"Nothing in the world, alannah. You're a bit white in the gills. Feeling the heat?"

Mary nodded.

"You're a cute shot, Miss Lavelle," said Keogh. "You'll get on in life, I shouldn't wonder."

Mary looked puzzled.

"Only my fun," Keogh went on. "You've been seen in the Pastelería Ruiz in the Alameda lately. That's the new place, Harty my lamb, that the colony are suddenly so keen on!"

Harty got fussed.

"Where is it, Keogh? How do you know they're keen on it?"

"Barker says Entwhistle told her. It was you who saw Miss Lavelle there, wasn't it, Duggan?"

"I saw you coming out of it," said Duggan to Mary.

"Is it called Ruiz? I was in there one night last week," said Mary, and as she remembered that night last week her voice grew soft and a veil seemed to drop about her.

"Good for you," said Keogh with detached acidity, "but"—and her eyes were brighter now as she looked towards the outer café—"some people still seem to prefer this place."

Two Englishmen, the two whom Entwhistle had introduced to Keogh and Harty, were settling down at their usual little marble table, and making a certain amount of manly noise.

Harty's handbag slid to the floor. She dived for it and came up in a fuss.

"For God's sake, Harty, straighten the poor old hat," said O'Toole.

Conlan read a Madrid newspaper. Misses came and went to other tables, joking and nodding as they passed. O'Toole ate a baba rhum with enjoyment, and Keogh looked out towards the Englishmen, determined to catch the eye of either and bow to him. Mary recalled the first afternoon she had sat here, learning the customs of what O'Toole called 'the clubhouse.' Only ten weeks ago! It seemed longer than that. Oh heavens, how much longer!

She pulled herself together.

"Tell me what you've been up to lately, O'Toole? Did you go to any of the bullfights?"

"No, alannah. I can't stomach a bullfight. Not but what I was invited to them all—and to barrera seats, if you please."

"Aha!" said Keogh, absent-mindedly contemptuous. "Some of your gentlemen friends from Lyons in town?"

"No, indeed," said O'Toole, delighted with herself. "I live in the present, Keogh."

"Who invited you?" Mary coaxed her teasingly.

"That'd be telling, alannah."

"You're a good liar, God bless you," said Keogh.

"Better than you think, when it suits me," said O'Toole good-humouredly.

Conlan put down her paper.

"You're overeating," she said to O'Toole. "Come for a walk up to Allera."

"What's the time?"

"Are you in a hurry?"

"Go on," said Keogh. "Light a candle for the intention of the gentleman with the barrera seats."

"I might do that."

"May I come?" Mary asked Conlan.

"There's nothing to stop you."

The three paid their bills and left the café.

They went up out of Altorno, by broken and weathered flights of steps, to the miraculous shrine of Our Lady. It was a hot day, and they rested frequently on crumbling wooden seats and on grass banks.

"It's a filthy old town, Altorno," said O'Toole.

"That's true," said Mary, in tired, unwary dreaminess.

The river, twisting under mine-gashed hills, past furnaces, churches and coalyards to where Torcal and Cabantes waited, and at their elbows the sea; the smoke, the foundry flames, the yellow trams; the convents with grilled windows; sinking roofs of slums, the old brown campaniles and leafy plazas—Mary looked down with gentle eyes——

"I believe you like the hole," said O'Toole.

They climbed past outpost wineshops and deserted villa gardens, black with cypress, bright with tangled fuchsia. They passed a cemetery with broken gates, a forgotten tram-line and a tramcar smothered in wistaria. They came at last, in heat and silence, to the church on the hilltop where Our Lady vouchsafed miracles. A number of women sat about the plaza near the porch selling long wax candles, a peseta each.

"Our Lady of Allera refuses no request," said O'Toole.

"Ah, but that can't be true!" said Mary.

"No Christian request," said Conlan.

Each bought a candle and they entered the church. Mary did not know what intercession to lay before Our Lady. She followed Conlan and O'Toole to where, under a blaze of votive lights, a lovely pink-cheeked Virgin soared, as if dancing, in an alcove, amid a flock of little angels who swung on gilded wires. Baroque and happy, with rings on her fingers and a rakish coronet on her head. A lovely, inattentive creature before whom to lay a prayer.

Mary lighted her candle and fixed it on a brass spike.

"For John," she said, "whatever happens. Oh Queen of Heaven, for John!" And kneeling on the cool, flagged floor she prayed with deep anxiety for the man in Ireland to whom she was promised in marriage.

"Come on now! None of your transports," said O'Toole in a stage whisper to Conlan.

They came out at a side-door and through a battered Romanesque cloister into another shabby plaza cooled by plane-trees and where stone benches on its northern edge invited contemplation of the city below. Two nuns walked up and down saying their rosary; in a distant corner children played pelota against the blank wall of a house.

"Let's sit awhile," said Mary.

The shade was delicious where they sat, the view untidy and worth contemplating.

"Do you know what, alannah?" said O'Toole to Mary.

"What?"

"Well, excuse me if I'm wrong, but for the very first time this afternoon something has struck me about you that never struck me before!"

"What?"

"That you're in love—God help you!"

Mary said nothing. The silence became uncomfortable.

"Have I put my foot in it?" O'Toole asked gently.

"No, you haven't. I *am* engaged to be married."

"Ah!" O'Toole seemed greatly relieved. "Sure, that's it, of course. But how in the name of God didn't I notice the symptoms until to-day?"

"What are the symptoms?"

"Oh, I don't know. But I never before felt sadness in you. Not that that's such a great sign really!"

"I'm glad. What are the signs?"

"Ah, don't ask me, alannah. I'm getting old."

"I've never heard you admit a plain truth before," said Conlan. "Are you in love yourself by any chance?"

Mary shuddered inwardly at the wisdom revealed in this sequence of thought.

"Ah nonsense," said O'Toole. "Being in love is a children's game—for this baby and her like." She patted Mary's knee. "But believe me, alannah, there's nothing to be sad about in having a nice man say he's fond of you."

Conlan raised her brows.

"You're talking like a matron," she said. "Upon my soul, you are almost talking sense. What's happened to you?"

Mary said nothing.

"What's he like, alannah?"

"What's who like?"

"Come off it. The best beloved. What's he like? Why didn't you tell me about him sooner? Why did you come all this way away from him?"

"Oh—he's very nice. He's twenty-eight."

"Go on. Why aren't you married?"

"He's poor, and won't marry me until he's better off."

"Fool!" said Conlan.

"He'll be rich some day. He'll own his uncle's shipping business. He lives at home in Mellick. His name is John MacCurtain."

"And why are you here?"

"I thought I'd better see a little life. I'm a green sort of creature, and he was through the war and knows the world. I thought I might as well quicken up my wits for him."

"He must be an ass," said Conlan.

"He's nothing of the kind."

"Sure he isn't, alannah. He's a hell of a lucky devil, that's what he is!"

A shadow fell across the three. Mary looked up and saw Don Jorge, the handsome Andalucian priest, smiling on her with great friendliness.

"My little friend, Miss Maria—is it not?"

He twanged the Spanish words carefully for her.

Mary bowed and made no attempt to speak. O'Toole eyed him with amusement, Conlan read her paper. He continued to stand and smile.

"A good view—as views go in this dull region of Spain! And you come with your friends to beseech some girlish favour of Our Lady of Allera?" He smiled understandingly. "Very nice. Very nice. How are my little friends, my charming little musicians?"

"They are well, thank you, Don Jorge."

"Give them my greetings—if that is permissible. But——" he smiled tolerantly—"I doubt it. The good Don Pablo—oh well, no doubt he is right. In the south a little pleasantry—oh well, good-bye, Miss Maria."

He moved off, then turned back with another smile.

"You do not, of course—it would not be possible for a young lady of your class, I think—you do not dance sometimes in the Plaza San Martín?" He paused in good-humoured enquiry.

"No, Don Jorge."

"Ah, of course not. But I saw—if I may say so—a very beautiful and I think foreign girl dancing there one night last week—and she, well I assure you, Miss Maria, she might have been your double!"

Mary raised her brows.

"Curious," she said. "Good afternoon, Don Jorge."

He bowed and walked slowly away. O'Toole was chuckling now.

"What was he saying to you, alannah? He's the old fellow who teaches music, isn't he? A rather dirty old bounder, I believe."

"That's putting it mildly," said Conlan. "I wonder Don Pablo ever let him near his daughters. I gather from your conversation he got the sack for his charming manners."

"Yes," said Mary. "Actually I played tell-tale on him —I still feel pretty awful about it."

"Rot!" said Conlan. "What else was there to do?"

"He seems a sneery old boy," said O'Toole. "I didn't like the cunning look in his eyes. He hasn't any hold over you, alannah, has he?" She giggled delightedly at that absurd idea.

"How could he?"

"You weren't dancing in the Plaza San Martín?" said Conlan quietly.

"What's that?" said O'Toole. "Oh, please tell me what he was saying."

"That he saw my double dancing in the Plaza San Martín!"

"He was drinking, alannah, and got you on his brain! Your double would take a bit of finding."

"That's a fact," said Conlan.

"Wish we could smoke," said Mary, to change the subject.

"Impossible out of doors. There'd be a riot, alannah."

"It's lovely here—is that long pink building the Carmelite Convent?"

"Yes," said Conlan. "I go to seven o'clock Mass up there most mornings."

"Do you still do that, you idiot?"

"All that way up before breakfast?"

"I like it. Even Altorno looks bearable at that time of day."

"But with San Geronimo across your square?"

"Always crowded. I hate swarms. Only a few old women go to the Carmelites, and then there are just the nuns behind the grill. You can pray in a place like that."

Mary wondered, looking at the starved and dreamy face, what Conlan saw in human life to pray for.

"Ah, Conlan alannah, you're cracked."

"Not far off it perhaps," Conlan agreed.

"Well girls," O'Toole said after a pause. "What about climbing down again?"

"What's the hurry?"

"I'm in none," said Mary.

O'Toole looked a little uneasy perhaps. She glanced at her watch. Conlan smiled at her faintly.

"What's the matter, O'Toole?"

"Oh, nothing really. Just—I've one or two things to do this evening."

"Well, so far as I know, no one is stopping you from doing them."

"That's a fact." She stood up, very elaborately at her ease. "Neither of you coming down with me?"

They shook their heads, and Mary could have sworn that a light of relief went over O'Toole's features.

"Off with you, O'Toole," she said gently. "Have a good time!"

O'Toole giggled.

"Who said anything about a good time, alannah? Ah well, ta-ta, to the pair of you. Be nice to the infant, Conlan!"

They waved her off and she crossed the plaza quickly, her beautiful legs and hips making her seem no more than a girl as she receded.

Conlan frowned.

"She's up to something, that one."

"Why shouldn't she be?"

"It seems as if you and she are two of a kind."

Mary did not ask for an explanation.

"Perhaps we are," she said. "I like her awfully."

"I've noticed that," Conlan answered curtly.

Silence fell. The two sat at extreme ends of the bench and leant in idleness against the trunks of plane-trees. Mary set herself to examine, as if for a memory test, the hazy, winding river, the bridges, squares and other identifiable landmarks of the town. She looked for the Plaza San Martín, with a certain caution, but nevertheless refusing to ignore it. Then, having taken her fence, as it were, she hurried her eyes away from it, and searched like a busy child for the Cabantes station, the Jesuit church, the park. Because that was the thing to do, she was discovering, to live outwardly, to read all kinds of informative things, to talk and listen, to notice details; in fact to keep the mind fussed and a little tired. That was the way to smother panic—just to keep piling irrelevancies over it with steady industry—bury it in a good-sized rubbish-heap.

Don Jorge, of course, had for the moment set back her simple plan somewhat. He had taken a shrewd kick at her ambuscade and indeed given her such a fright as she had no intention of examining. That too must be buried, smothered with its cause. By living outwardly for long enough and with determination, all would be restored. A bad dream would vanish. A memory, a sensation which already sometimes seemed so unreal and fantastic that perhaps it was indeed only a dream, would be rubbed away, lost, misshapen by the persistent loading up and tossing about over its face of every kind of rag, bone and bottle from the rest of life. She was becoming quite expert at living outwardly, and could even sit up in bed laboriously reading *Pepita Jiménez* and looking up all the words until she was so sleepy that no fear, however watchful, could prevail against darkness. She was quite wily. The exercise of self-evasion did create a fundamental sense of strain—a vague feeling of exhaustion, as if one were getting thin too fast, or, as O'Toole said, "feeling the heat." But she supposed that practice would make it easier, and that after a while there would cease to be any need to fly from real thoughts. One great source of refuge at least there was, into which she released herself now, although with a suspicion that it was not an entirely honest palliative to take—her letters to John. These now were longer than before, more carefully written, more descriptive, more amusing, and affectionate. They helped her very much. She must try to memorise this view, for instance, this lovely Spanish evening atmosphere, so as to give him a fairly true impression of Altorno and the miraculous shrine. It was a good place to have come up to. If only that wretched Don Jorge had not passed by! If he had in fact recognised Juanito—oh, let it be, let it be! Smother it—stifle it. If one had field-glasses up here one could almost identify people on the Puente Cristina, or in the Café del Teatro.

"So you're engaged?" said Conlan.

"Yes."

"God knows one might have guessed." Her voice was harsh.

"Does it matter?"

"When is he going to have enough money to marry you?"

"In a year or two."

"How long will you stay out here?"

"A year at most."

Mary looked about her somewhat wildly, in fact, as she said that.

"What's up?" said Conlan.

"Nothing. Why?"

"You look queer. As if you might faint."

Mary tried to laugh. "I didn't even faint at the bull-fight," she said.

203

"I didn't really expect you to."

But the bullfight was not a safe train of thought. It created uneasiness; suggested that life is perverse and tragic. Better not talk of the bullfight.

"What do you think O'Toole is up to?"

"Nothing probably. She's a bit of a playboy. She gets fits of pretending there's a mystery in her life!"

"Why shouldn't there be one—sometime?"

"Now?"

"But—well, surely some of those engineers and people must be fairly old?"

"If they were as old as Methuselah they don't have to marry a nobody! O'Toole's not in their set!"

"Oh, set be hanged! Whose set *is* she in?"

"No one's. That's what's up with all us misses—don't you see? We've never been graded. We come out here with the good old Irish small-town notion that we're 'ladies'—and then by degrees we discover we're—nothing. It turns us into—what you see."

"Absurd!"

"No. If we had any brains or education it *would* be—but then we wouldn't be here. We came out in our green youth because our parents had no money to spend on us, and saw no likelihood of getting us husbands. We had qualifications for this job—in what other would you be given a comfortable existence merely because you are a Catholic and can speak English fluently, if badly? We're not even required to know how to teach. It's jam for the stupid."

"You're very hard on your profession."

"Profession?" Conlan paused a second. "In spite of

Harty's determination to prove us martyrs, the trouble is that we're in clover. We're a lot of incompetents and we know it. And the comfort we live in with these people—pace Harty!—demoralises us. We know we'd never get it anywhere else for so little effort, and that it's unheard of in our home towns. Well, we get used to it and although the wages are small and make it impossible to save for old age—they're far more than we're worth, and they pay for tea and bickering in the Alemán."

"But what happens in the end?"

"In Spain one leaves that sort of inquiry till to-morrow! One miss actually married a member of the colony. She lives in Birmingham now. Another, Corrigan—you've heard of her—got mixed up with a German a few months ago, and disappeared with him. Two that I've known have become nuns, and about three have gone home to Ireland in the end. But most of us have no one to go home to, and no way to keep ourselves alive, if we did that. You see, this job makes you incapable of earning a living in other work. We just settle down, most of us, and die here. The sensible ones attach themselves to one family and make themselves pseudo-useful to it for two or even three generations and then—well, they're an institution."

"Like Barker."

"Like Barker. She's been with the Menandre Colomas for thirty-five years. By the time she'd chaperoned all the kids of her first lot the children of the elder brothers were wanting a miss, and so on. She's been passed on within the family to all their households. They adore her now."

"She's a nice old thing."

"She's not bad. But here's a funny thing. The Colomas are one of the most highly civilised families in Europe—extremely well-bred as these things are reckoned —and they *all* speak English with absolute fluency in a powerful Blackpool accent!"

"Naturally!"

"Barker's one of the best of us. She's kind and reliable and fond of her comfort. If you're like that and that's all you're like, ours is a good life. The houses are usually full of servants; you don't have to do a hand's turn for yourself, and whatever Harty may say, no one treats you like dirt. No. If they did, it wouldn't be so dreary. But— oh my God!—you drink Valdepeñas and eat turrón and walnuts, you're moved from place to place in an Hispano-Suiza, you sleep ten hours a night. And you say your prayers and keep your place and at last you die, carefully tended. And you're given a nice funeral. And if there's anyone left who remembers you in Ireland they get a kind letter about you, and your personal effects."

"Well—what more do you expect?"

"Nothing more."

"At any rate, the turrón and walnuts side of the life can't matter much to you!"

"It doesn't. I'm the other extreme of the 'miss' variety."

"You certainly are. But in-between types—Keogh, for instance?"

"Keogh wants to be married, but she's been here nine years and could never go home and learn shorthand now. She likes her comfort."

"At any rate she had enough politeness to learn Spanish."

"Politeness?" Conlan laughed. "Perhaps she thought that if she couldn't land an Englishman she might work a dago. But there are no husbands here. She knows that really. She'll weather through her man-mania and settle down like Barker."

"Do you ever feel—about this man-question—as—as Keogh does?"

Conlan looked at Mary as if she might strike her.

"I? Feel as Keogh does?"

"I beg your pardon."

There was silence awhile. The pelota-playing children had grown tired and were sitting on the parapet nearby. They giggled and whispered 'miss' as if the word were a mighty joke. Mary smiled at them and they crept nearer.

"You have brains," she said presently to Conlan, "and you loathe comfort as much as you loathe Spain. Why did you stay here?"

"It isn't Spain I loathe—it's life. Anywhere."

"Why?"

"My evil nature. I'm at cross purposes with it."

"Always?"

"Yes. I might have sweetened a bit if I'd gone in there, for instance——" she pointed towards the long, pink convent with grilled windows.

"You might. Why didn't you?"

"I thought of it sometimes. But, as you may have noticed, I'm not saintly. I'm just religious."

"When you were a kid did you loathe life?"

"Oh, I suppose not. I can't remember. There was nothing very terrible. We were poor and my father was a martinet, but my mother was nice. She died just before I came to Spain. Father's dead now and my sister is married at home. Two of my brothers died in the war, and the youngest is in New Zealand."

"What was it like at home?"

"Kildalgan? A deadly little town—very pretty. Woods, I remember, and streams. My father was a bank manager and I suppose he had a fair salary, but we seemed to be very poor."

"You ought to go back to see your sister."

"Her? Good God! She married a frightful man who kept a public-house. He was twenty years older than her too. There was a most awful family rumpus."

The children were directly in front of Mary now, grinning and telling her that she was "guapa." She wished she had a few sweets to give them; she didn't like to pay for their flattery with pennies.

"County Wexford was nice, I think," Conlan went on. "Flat, you know, with trees and mill-wheels. When I first came out I used to think a lot about going back."

"Where did you come to first?"

"To a big barrack of a house on this side of the Sierra de Gredos, near Avila. I spent my first entire year there. The whole winter and the whole summer. Nearly five thousand feet up! I remember I thought I might die! After the softness and the rain at home and all the muddy woods! Ah, but Castile is good. It's the best of Spain. Castile and the bullfight—those are two things it's no use arguing about. You either like them or you don't."

"Why do you like the bullfight?"

"Why do you?"

"I haven't said I did."

Conlan smiled.

"I like courage anyway. I haven't any myself—no one has who remains a miss for life. And I like brutality better than sentiment. I like the look of the thing, and all the rules and ceremonies. And I'm a fair judge of it by now. Death interests me too—going so near it. I do quite frankly admire good matadors."

Mary pondered this speech with some admiration. Then noticing a look of serenity on the other woman's face, she tried a mild joke.

"Have you ever had 'a crush' on one?"

It was taken quite amiably.

"No. I've never had a crush on any living creature."

Mary felt a pang of envy. She was a little tired now, though glad to get Conlan talking. The more talk the better these days—anything rather than the lonely hazards of silence.

"Are you in love with him?" Conlan asked.

"With—with whom?"

"The man you're engaged to."

"Why—yes."

"You're certainly in love with someone."

Mary looked away northward over the view, now high-lit and theatricalised by the descending sun. She resented such breach of reserve as this insinuation, such breach of the peace. She had, as if in revenge against it, a sudden savage desire to be rid of her companion and alone with a craze that was drowning her, to be alone and surrendered, to let her silly scheme of living outwardly go to the devil awhile. Biarritz, she said to herself—and struck a wild blow thus at her own defences—that's where he is, in

Biarritz with his wife and baby. Oh God! Oh God!
And a tune rang through her as harshly as if played by a
band at a bullfight—'I met my love in Avalon.' She let her
eyes stare down on the green roof of San Martín. Did I
dream it? she begged herself, oh, did I dream it? Anyhow what do I know of him? Is he one-half so good a
man as John?

But this was idiocy. This was certainly 'having a
crush.' Steady, steady! This other woman could be as
sensitive as she was crude. Mary turned to look at her
and the eyes of the two met in a strange long glance.

"How beautiful the creature can seem!" Mary thought,
and the irrelevant reflection calmed her.

"What's your name?" she said, stumbling back from
anguish.

"How do you mean? I'm called Conlan."

"Your Christian name?"

"Oh, a vile one, Agatha."

"Agatha. I hate the surname habit. May I call you
Agatha?"

A very faint flush rejuvenated most tragically the
starved, thin face.

"What is your name?"

"Mary."

"Ah!"

They fell into an awkward silence now. The children
grew cheeky around Mary, and she gave them a penny
each. They were delighted.

"You're mad to start that; come home."

They stood up and crossed the plaza. All the way down
the flights of steps they said nothing, though they paused

now and then to consider the view. Outside the Cabantes station Mary paused.

"Come and have a cigarette in my room," said Agatha off-handedly.

"No, thanks; I'm very tired."

"Sorry."

The voice was savage in its offended dryness.

"Oh, please don't be so touchy!" said Mary wildly, and turned to descend the station steps. But Agatha caught her arm.

"Listen," she said quietly, "listen and believe me. It's insanity for you to dance in the Plaza San Martín."

Mary ran down the steps to her train.

IN THE CALLE MAYOR

As far as Burgos, where beyond lacy, yellowing trees the towers of the cathedral rose with a deprecatory and juvenile-seeming grace, and even to Valladolid which revealed to the passing travellers only a sugar refinery and a bullring, the children talked to Mary in a high-spirited, merry race for her attention. They were all in communicative mood. Milagros and Nieves, both admirers of the Cid, through whose country they were now passing, but differing in their conceptions of his personality, argued fiercely together as they gave their miss the history of eleventh-century Castile. And Pilár kept breaking in with prophecies of their doings in Madrid, which delighted, even while they side-tracked, the historians.

An expedition to Madrid was as much after the children's hearts as it was unexpected. It was now almost two years since they had seen the capital, and a few days ago Tia Cristina, their father's eldest sister, had written inviting them to visit her there in order to buy some winter clothes. Such a suggestion was irresistible to Pilár, and her younger sisters were very willing to put up with a few hours in dressmakers' salons for the sake of some days in Madrid.

"Mademoiselle," Aunt Cristina had written, "will be delighted to be at the children's entire disposal. It will be like old times for her, she says, when our own girls were at home. You know, my dear Consuelo, how perfect is her dress sense, and that she will take them to exactly the right modistes and milliners . . ."

So at first it had appeared that Miss Maria need not go to Madrid. But Milagros announced that she would not go without her.

"You know how it was last time, Mama! There'll be no one to take me anywhere unless I tag along the whole time with Mademoiselle! And I'm simply not going to spend all day and night watching dressmakers stick pins in Pilár! Please let me have Miss Maria! There's the Prado and bullfights and bookshops—I really must have *some* personal freedom!"

Don Pablo smiled.

"I sympathise, Mila. By all means take Miss Maria." And to Mary he said: "Don't let her exploit you. Shake her off and see some of the sights. Take a semi-holiday. Doña Consuelo and I have both observed that you are looking a little tired. In any case, Mila," he turned back to the excited child, "you are on your honour to go to a certain number of dressmakers, and I understand from your mother that to get you reclothed is now a matter of positive urgency."

So they set off from Altorno on a brilliant morning. The four had the railway carriage to themselves. Juliana, the children's maid, a strong, elderly Basque, sat in the next compartment, in charge of the luggage, and, in general, of the comfort of the party. As the day lengthened even Milagros grew disinclined to talk. Lunch, wine and the Castilian sun made her dreamy.

"We ought to cross the Douro soon," she said.

Afternoon light lay over the plain. It was the third week of September and about some farmsteads peasants were still winnowing crops of rye and wheat. Men in suits of black cotton straightened themselves to see the train go by, and sometimes a boy waved his wide straw hat. The land was blond, unbrokenly; its fairness stretched without pause or hurry to meet a sky so far away and luminous as to be only in the most aerial meaning blue. There were undulations, there were valleys; but within this spaciousness the breaks they made were like sighs which alleviate meditation; hamlets were so buff of roof and wall as almost to be imperceptible in the great wash of gold; roads made lonely curves across the quiet and bridges of pale stone spanned shallow rivers. Here a shepherd called his goats for evening milking; there a bell rang for a village funeral.

Mary remembered what Agatha had said. "Castile is good." Since crossing the Ebro in the morning she had looked out on the landscape through which she travelled with a cautiously growing amazement which now flowered into absolute pleasure. Goodness like this, which waited on no preconception, bore no relation to any customarily applauded excellence and yet was older-seeming, gentler, simpler and more obvious than any human scene before encountered; goodness like this—immediately appealing, pastoral, austere and tender—was not what she had looked for.

In the brief weeks of her acquaintance with Spain she had fallen day by day—she saw that now—a little more and a little more in love with it. This love had, timidly, fed curiosity, and curiosity, humoured somewhat, had

refuelled love. It meant that much of her wages were
spent at the bookshops and market bookstalls of Altorno.
So that already she had gathered up, to await a personal
test, a fair collection of other men's impressions of Spain.
In skimming them, predispositions encouraged prejudice. Thus the white-skinned Western Christian in her
could not bear the suggestion that Africa began beyond
the Pyrenees, and all writers who, either in condescension
or admiration, stressed Moorish Spain and made little of
its Christianity, were held at arm's length. She could not
possibly judge such judgments, but her hope turned from
them. If Arab philosophy and Arab fiddle-faddle art
were truly dominant in the peninsula, then great, good
and stimulating to others as such a residue might be, it
could never have her heart; she would have made a
mistake in her twelve weeks on the northern coast—that
was all. And Ford and Washington Irving and Gautier
and even the cheerful, stolid Borrow, whom to her
surprise she liked, must be allowed to have their various,
improbable Spains; she would bury hers. But she had in
fact small hope of such escape. Already, like Isabella the
Catholic, her desire had built a city of Santa Fé. The
Moor would fall. She could not lose her Spain. Yet she
had been afraid to see Castile. Here if anywhere she would
find the Spanish heart—so her intuitions insisted. But
Conlan, snappy and unbalanced, Conlan coming in
peevishness from her Irish woodlands to a wintry
plateau four thousand feet above the sea and who might
by her nature easily mistake the over-emphatic and the
savage for the true—Conlan said "Castile is good." And
Mary's heart had sunk a little. Still, Conlan had compared

it with the bullfight. Nevertheless that admiration was suspect and savage in anyone. Mary had never dared to analyse it in herself. Meantime in confusion of heart, and half hoping she would never have a chance to see it, she had waited for Castile; it was to be the test of her whole relationship with Spain. And here it was, to left and right of her, as gentle as Heaven.

The absolute rightness, absolute goodness of it made her feel recklessly light-hearted—as if she had cast a die and won. She laughed a little to herself as she gazed on fold after fold of the fair-haired land. Arab indeed! Though it had this much suggestion of the east, that, pure as it was of all school Bible vulgarities, innocent of palm-trees and ornamental wells and lazy ankletted women, it might be taken, for its poverty, beauty and heroic, gentle intransigence as a possible setting for the miracles and discourses of the New Testament. Which proved it Christian surely, Castile, the greatest of the Spains?

"What are you laughing at, Miss Maria?" Nieves asked her.

"Oh, all this! I like it."

"Do you really, Miss Maria?" Pilár looked out reflectively. "It's very poor country really, and the climate is savage. Of course it doesn't always look as colourless as now—summer and the harvest have drained it to nothing."

"I like that look. I thought, you know, it might be a kind of desert——"

"Oh no!" said Milagros. "All sorts of things are farmed all over it. They have to work like blacks though, the peasants."

"They look like that," said Mary.

Milagros glanced at a group of them in a field below.

"Yes. Desperate ascetics! That old man looks as strange and mad as if he'd been painted by El Greco! Ah, but you should see Castile in winter, Miss Maria. It really might frighten you, I think!"

"Do you remember that drive two years ago, when it was snowing in Avila?" Nieves spoke dreamily.

"Yes. Ah, Miss Maria, you should see Avila in the snow!"

"I'd like to," Mary said.

"You keep on smiling! I believe you're very happy to-day?"

"I believe I am."

Juliana, who had produced lunch from a basket—as Doña Consuelo did not approve of dining-car food for her daughters—came into the carriage now with a merienda, or late afternoon refreshment. Everyone was hungry. Juliana took her own food in the young ladies' company, and the conversation switched into Basque, for the old woman, a strong Basque nationalist, had much to say that amused the children in expression of her horror of the strange, pale country they were travelling through. Milagros translated now and then for Mary, but she was well content to half follow the talk through its gay pantomime, or not to follow.

They passed Medina del Campo. Shadows were long across the fields now and a breeze moved through lonely poplars and acacias. Mary was sorry that darkness must come and this journey end.

She had been very happy all day, as Milagros said—but

217

there was no reason for that. Indeed, would she but examine the superstitious delight she took in her sudden infatuation with Castile, she must see that it could only be the omen of trouble. The more she liked of Spain henceforward, the worse her silly plight. But like the drunkard who will take the pledge to-morrow, she went on tippling at her mania in various self-deceiving ways, whilst uneasily assuring herself that nothing could be easier than to give it up. For one thing—she often told herself this—she might go home. There was nothing to prevent her doing that. The Areavagas would be polite and regretful, but Doña Consuelo really would, it was obvious, prefer a different type of miss. Her father might be annoyed, but John would be delighted, would stand by her. Probably he would consent to get married at once. Yes, it would be perfectly easy to go home. It would settle everything. If the worst came to the worst— she did not examine her own meaning here—she could do that.

Meantime there was this visit to Madrid which, in the normal way interesting and affording, if nothing else, this lovely panorama of Castile, could to her secret heart only mean pain. But not fatal pain; the kind she was in need of and which would cure, more quickly than any amount of self-control and reasoning, her absurd, persistent condition of schoolgirl malaise. For that was all that was the matter with her. Although she was contentedly engaged to be married and in a day or two would be twenty-three, she had contracted a school-girl crush for a practically unknown man, as a sixteen-year-old might with greater cause for Owen Nares or

Michael Collins. That was the humiliating all of it—and was it not astonishing how such foolishness could hurt? But it would be over in no time. Madrid, and the probability and danger it held of seeing him again and seeing how totally she had misunderstood him and what a wicked idiot she had been, Madrid would give the final twist and put her right.

It would not be so bad a twist either. Because an unwise young married man meets you in a public square and dances with you for three minutes, you are not thereafter seriously in love. Good God! let's hope not. Since that was absolutely all, since there had been no word or sight of him in four full weeks, since even his customary halt at Cabantes on his return from Biarritz had not been made this time, he and Luisa going directly from France to Madrid instead and telephoning their apologies and explanations to his irate sisters! Since that was all and it was nothing, and she had still some sanity left, the whole absurdity must blow over any minute. It was induced by loneliness and the somewhat exhausting heat —and a rather impetuous foolish liking she had taken to all things Spanish. The heat was almost ended now, she would get her liking for Spain into perspective, and if loneliness did not decrease, she would go home. She had in fact an answer for everything. Meantime if going to Madrid in her present shaky state was somewhat like going to the dentist, it offered rewards too as to a brave child, and how blessed to be rid of the nagging tooth!

None of these fidgety and optimistic reflections explained however her mood of simple happiness as the train raced southwards in the dusk—nor were they at

present struggling to overtop it. She watched the
landscape until darkness wrenched its last suggestion
from her, and then she turned and tried to follow
Juliana's grave, Basque reading of the children's fortunes
in their hands.

They were delighted with the lusty news she gave them
of two, three husbands, ten, twelve babies. They translated hastily for Mary. Nieves was to have a dark and
jealous man and travel far. Pilár would be a millionairess
and twice widowed. Milagros—this raised a good laugh
—would marry a matador.

"Tell the miss! Tell the miss, Juliana!"

Juliana told the miss. She would marry and have six
sons and live in a wood. She would be a very old woman
and always beautiful. She would be lucky in love, very
lucky—and if she wasn't who could expect to be?

"I think all those fortunes sound absolutely true," said
Milagros.

The journey was a very happy one.

Pilár had explained to Mary that the fact that Tia
Cristina lived in an old-fashioned apartment at the
extreme west end of the now unfashionable Calle Mayor,
overlooking the site of the proposed but unbuilt cathedral
and literally within a stone's throw of the King's palace—
"not that Tia Cristina would ever want to throw a stone
at it," said Milagros—Pilár had explained that this
inconvenient foible was a very great proof of the
importance and paradoxical fashionableness of Tia
Cristina. For just because smart Madrid was now moving
east, beyond the Cibeles and the Prado, it showed how

'chic' Tia Cristina was that she still lived, like the King, in quite the wrong quarter.

Mary, when she woke the first morning and looked out of her westward window, approved Tia Cristina's conservatism. She had slept badly. The noise of the night had been astounding; the excitement of the journey, the wine drunk at supper, the strange bed, the thrill of being in the centre of Spain—there were plenty of explanations of her restlessness, but at seven o'clock she stood at her open window and felt as ready for the lovely, golden, noisy day without as if she had slept for ten unbroken hours. And before nine o'clock she was out in the stream of it alone. Milagros had put up a strong fight to go with her, but Mademoiselle, privately instructed no doubt by Doña Consuelo, was resolute at breakfast that dressmaking schemes for all three girls should be put in motion at once, so that a requisite number of things should be arrangeable within the span of their stay. Mademoiselle was a Parisian version of Barker, with only this difference: that a lifetime in a Spanish household had so hispanicised her that she now spoke French inaccurately and save in her really serious understanding of clothes—for others, that is, her own being ludicrous—retained nothing, one would say, almost even no visual memory, of Paris. She was an insidiously authoritative little old woman, and was, like Barker, very securely nested, for by now, after thirty-five years of her undefined usefulness and companionship, Tia Cristina, a rich and selfish widow, could not have faced life without her. Mary, pondering her at breakfast without either sympathy or spleen, was light-heartedly conscious of the

Frenchwoman's surprised dislike of her. But she was mercilessly glad to yield up the protesting Milagros to her, and to be free to go as she pleased for this first sunny morning.

She came back to the Calle Mayor for lunch at half-past one, having accomplished much sight-seeing. She was hot and exhausted; very glad of the ice-cold beer which she was given. In Tia Cristina's house she ate with the family, and now that she could follow Spanish conversation and was used to her charges, now especially that she preferred talk to silence, she found the arrangement temporarily agreeable.

"What do you think of Madrid, Miss Maria?"

"I love it."

She said it shamefacedly. The acknowledgment made her feel guilty for her own good reasons, but apart from them it struck her that her unfailing reaction to all Spanish phenomena of immediate liking must be monotonous to others and make her appear a fatuous ass. Nevertheless, there it was. As useless to deny her liking for Madrid as that she had two eyes in her head. It was architecturally common; it was noisy and hot; it had a smug, prosperous glitter over it which she suspected a more experienced traveller would call provincial—but it sparkled with sunshine and fountains and the most natural good manners under Heaven; the streets were wide, the acacias green and sibilant; the shoeblacks all told her gently that she was *guapa*, and the sky—ah, useless ever to try to wreathe Madrid's sky in words! Looking up at it once during the morning—she was sitting on the stone parapet in the King's courtyard, and had been considering his western view with envy, the foreground of dark, descending woods, the little dried-up Manzanares, the blond and leafless undulations of Castile and far away, in diamond clarity, the white peaks of the Gredos—looking up from this out of the hot September morning, considering the temperate trans-parence of its blue, its inexplicable fairy sparkle, the sweet vague movement of its gauze of cloud, it had struck her that here, without doubt, was the sky as it should be, here was the ideal roof for an ideal world, here was Heaven's formula.

She knew, had anyone asked her, that in Madrid she was more than two thousand feet above the level of the sea. But she knew nothing of blood-pressure, or that she was by chance so constituted that altitude exhilarated her, renewed courage, emphasised youth and created a great sense of well-being. Such knowledge could not, however, have altered the fact that Madrid delighted her. She hurried about, the most eager of tourists, between nine and half-past one. She walked under the shabby portales of the Plaza Mayor and knew from her reading of Ford that Charles I, when Prince of Wales, had seen a great bull-fight there, at which, unexpectedly, a young woman had played matador. She admired the equestrian statue of the seventeenth-century king. She walked round the battered and noisy Puerta del Sol, remembering the 2nd May and Joseph Bonaparte, 'Bottle Joe,' and Borrow's story of the Insurrection of La Granja. She strolled down the Alcala and into the Paseo del Prado, looking for Gautier's blue-eyed Manolas, and smiling at the soft compliments of every other man. She hesitated on the steps of the Prado

Museum, but postponed its ordeal for a more collected hour. She bought postcards and wrote them, while sipping horchata on the terrace of a café in Pi y Margall—mischievously sent John a picture of Pronceda profiling to kill. She walked homeward, map in hand, down the curving Calle del Carmen and across the clattering Puerta, and so, past all the nineteenth-century small-town shops of Calle Mayor, to Tia Cristina's apartment and the view from her windows of the Gredos—almost as good a view as the King's. Yes, she loved Madrid. There was no help for it. This business of getting Spain into perspective would have to be postponed another day or two.

It was postponed rather more indefinitely than that. So was that salutary last twist which was to end the schoolgirl ache in her heart. She did not see Juanito, though on the second evening she heard his voice. She had come in, hot and gay, from an expedition with Milagros. The windows of her room were open to those cool airs from the mountains which are the evening benediction of Madrid. She pulled off her clothes, put on her dressing-gown and lighted a *favorito*. She sat in peace. Tia Cristina's apartment was on the fifth floor and was not overlooked; indeed only a few downward-straggling houses and a vaguely hinted suburb across the river carried the town further than this airy corner. Mary liked exceedingly the way the dreaming, golden plain lapped almost to her feet as she sat at ease in a window of the capital. All the noises which a noisy, cheerful people can make when gathered together for urban life were clashing against each other in the nearby streets, and yet clearly and friendlily in sight lay the peace of stubble fields and browsing goats, even the snowy quiet of mountains.

She sat and smoked. The children were dining to-night with Juanito and Luisa in the Paseo de Recoletos. They were getting ready now, and were excited, as they had never seen Luisa's apartment but only the photo-graphs of it which had appeared some months before in the Spanish edition of *Vogue*. Pilár did not know how to make herself elegant enough for so chic a setting, and was being helped to dress by the delighted Mademoiselle.

Mary switched her thoughts with deliberation to the evening ahead of her. She must dine, she supposed, with Doña Cristina and Mademoiselle. Depressing prospect. But as the meal would not be served until half-past ten, and as it was now not long after eight, perhaps she might go out—to a cinema, or to walk by the lake in the Retiro. Or perhaps she had better not. The two old ladies might be scandalised. Better stay in, write letters, and cause no trouble. She moved unhappily in her chair. She was really afraid of solitude nowadays, especially when it came swift on the heels of exhilaration. She wished she could go out again. How absurd a life!

There was a knock on her door.

"It's me, Miss Maria—Mila! May I come in?"

She came in before Mary could answer, dressed for her party, and in a gay fuss.

"We're just off; Juanito's come to fetch us. Ah, you can't come out to say good evening to him? I told him you would!" She called back along the corridor, speaking Spanish. "She can't appear, Juanito! She's undressed!"

His voice sounded grave and shy in the distance.

"Never mind, Mila," he said. "Another time."

Milagros smiled again at Mary.

"Good night, Miss Maria! Have a good rest. We've a lot to get through to-morrow!"

"Good night, Mila—enjoy yourself."

Mary stayed in her room and wrote letters. Later she dressed and dined politely with Doña Cristina and Mademoiselle.

The next morning she went with the three girls to the Prado Museum. They had visited it at intervals since babyhood and were familiar with reproductions of its contents. They were partisans of this and that and dragged their miss about from one old favourite to another. Pilár had always liked Murillo but this time found him boring. She took a sudden fancy to Titian's "Venus and the Lute-Player," studying both versions with excitement; she became infatuated with Goya's decorative cartoons of Spanish life. Nieves liked Velasquez' little infantas. Milagros admired his dwarfs, and Goya's portraits of the Bourbons. They were in some confusion about El Greco, but Nieves liked The Day of Pentecost. All three liked "The Surrender of Breda"; all three adored "Las Meniñas." They bought a great many postcards at the desk, and went back to the Calle Mayor in Tia Cristina's limousine.

Mary was really exhausted, for the first time since coming to Madrid. She had never been in a great picture gallery before. Strolls round the Dublin gallery with Uncle Tim, her mother's eccentric brother, were her only experience of looking at paintings, and now the children's

226

familiarity with names and dates, and even their blithe
and comic willingness to decide that this was a "rotten"
painting or that a "glorious" impressed her heavily with
a sense of her own ignorance and slowness.

She returned to the gallery alone the next morning, in
great diffidence. She spent three hours there and walked
back dreamily along the Carrera San Geronimo to the
Calle Mayor. Her mind was hung with broken memories
of paintings; she was tired and in so far as she considered
herself felt irate against the smallness, impotence and
ignorance of one tiny, silly, self-conscious human life.
But she was inhaling too an air that was strange to her,
blown in from abstract life, remote, impersonal, held in
perspective as genius orders it. She was awestruck and
tremulous, but not defeated now, or too much bothered
by her own ignorance. For as to that she had reflected,
standing before Rubens' "Three Graces," that she could
no more have written *Kubla Khan* or explained how it
was written than have painted this picture. Nor kill a bull
as Pronceda did, or analyse his way of doing it. Yet it
would not occur to her that she had no right to read a
poem, or no possible chance of understanding it. "But
these are so big!" she had answered herself in panic.
"And there are so many of them. And I'm getting old
already—I'm very old beside Milagros! Perhaps if I had
looked at paintings one by one day after day since babyhood as I've read poems—ah, but then I'd be smug and
sleepy about them as we grow about poems we believe
we know. There's something to be said," she sighed,
"for sudden, exhausting encounter. There's really something in being half-choked and stupefied. Ah, but if I

were younger, if there were time! And this is only *one* of the world's galleries!" She hurried awhile on that thought as if she heard 'time's wingèd chariot.' But meditation held her up again, and so did pleasure and bewilderment, and frequently sheer fatigue. But she was in the main at peace, as she wandered, her white face lifted dreamily, from flower to flower of these immense fresh fields. And going home she held her mood delicately, unwilling to lose her dim, shy perception of life as the artist apprehends it. But as the lift carried her up to Doña Cristina's apartment she thought of Mellick and that in a year or so she would be married and settled there—and her eyes filled with tears.

The exhilarating days skimmed on. With or without Milagros Mary saw most of what was said to be interesting in the capital. She bought books, and souvenirs which she hoped would please John and Aunt Cissy and her little sisters. She went as often as she could to the Prado Museum. Once again she went with Milagros who, patriotic as any Spaniard, was shocked to discover her miss disposed to believe Rubens a more exciting painter than Goya. She kept Miss Maria a long time in the little octagonal room, explaining the savage greatness of the greatest of all satirists in paint, discoursing too with detachment on what she called the emotional conflict between 'La Maja Vestida' and 'La Maja Desnuda' until she gathered a crowd of vastly amused listeners and had to be hurried away by her dueña.

The two sat afterwards under the acacia trees in the Paseo, and drank lemonade while a shoeblack whitened Miss Maria's white shoes.

Milagros talked.

"I hope no relative sees me here," she said. "Not that they would mind at all if you *looked* like my miss. But unless they've met you, how are they to know? And I don't think Tia Cristina would think I ought to sit in the Paseo with you. You're too beautiful. Well, you saw just now—in the Museum. If you were a real miss no one would have cared what I was saying about 'La Maja.' But *you* standing in front of the Maja—well, that just naturally makes a crowd!"

Mary laughed at her and paid the shoeblack, who smiled with worship as he withdrew.

"You see," Milagros went on—"you see that shoe-black. God help him! Men always adore you, don't they? Why, father would, quite innocently, die for you, I think, and so, I suspect, would Juanito!"

"You talk rubbish, Mila."

"Oh no. That's not rubbish. Do you know, miss, the first night you were in our house I said at dinner that you were a simpleton, a perfectly beautiful simpleton, and Nieves said you weren't. And father said Nieves was right. I was annoyed at the time. I think now that they're right, but somehow I think that I really *was* right when you came. Was I, Miss Maria? Do you think Spain is having a marked effect on you?"

"What do you think?"

"Well, honestly I think it is. I—I think it's changing you in some absolutely visible way—and yet, why on earth should it?"

"Why on earth?"

"Much better if it didn't. Really it would be much

easier for you if I were right—if you stayed a simpleton. I—I get quite uneasy about you sometimes, Miss Maria!"

They laughed immensely at that and finished their lemonade.

The next morning the day's pursuits were being disputed in Doña Cristina's dining-room when Luisa was admitted on a friendly call.

"Hullo, children! Hullo, Miss Maria. They tell me you are in love with Madrid. Most diplomatic stranger!"

She looked beautiful and urban in dark blue with tiny white ruffles. Whilst she joined in the game of what to do or what not to do with the fresh day, the telephone rang. It was Don Pablo speaking from Cabantes. Pilár spoke to him, the other two dancing around her, waiting their turn.

"Miss Maria, father says that really it's you he wants! There's a telegram for you and he wonders whether he should open it and read it to you in his best English accent, he says!"

Mary smiled.

"If he likes," she said, feeling embarrassed, "but really it's unlikely to be important."

Everyone looked surprised.

"Well—to-day's my birthday—it's probably only good wishes!"

"Ah, your birthday!" the children shouted.

Luisa smiled.

"And those particular wishes are not to be read aloud! Tell your father, Pilár, that his curiosity is not to be fed! He is to send on the telegram, unopened!"

So it was done. Mary thought with a heavy heart of John, wording his message of love. She had expected to be back in Cabantes yesterday—he had begged to know exactly where she would be on that day—but Tia Cristina had made the children stay some further days. Mary felt sad as she thought of that tenderly planned telegram missing its aim.

"That settles the day!" said Milagros. "It's Miss Maria's birthday, and I'm taking her to the bullfight."

Everyone laughed.

"Convenient for Mila!"

Luisa thought that on her birthday Miss Maria should have real English tea. Therefore, she said, after the bull-fight she and Milagros must come and meet the others for a merienda in the Paseo de Recoletos. There were only two places in Madrid where one got English tea, she said —at the British Embassy and in her apartment. With acclamation from everyone except Mary, this plan was agreed upon.

The bullfight was superb. Sanchez, Quintin and Villaroja—Villaroja, the great Mexican, awkward-seeming as a heron but quick as a hare, and braver than any of the hundred bulls whose horns had torn him. Unlike Pronceda, whose art suggested that death, on the seam of his coat all through the fight, was really as remote as the North Star, Villaroja seemed to offer himself, gnarled and stooping, as danger's unmistakable butt, the corrida's starving harlequin. But loping on to the horn and past it and back again with perilous looseness, and driving in at last with a straight sword and an open offering of himself, he fought as nobly as a saint that afternoon. The crowd gave him every honour in their power and even Milagros was bereft of comment.

Mary was glad of the child's silence as they walked together to the Recoletos. She was glad too of the profound exaction of the fight. Nothing could hurt her for the moment; she had been drained for to-day of every dreg of feeling. She was numb and empty now. If he was there, it could hardly matter. If he seemed to remember, she would have no strength to be troubled, or if he seemed to forget. And if he wasn't there, even that could not hurt this mood of translation and weariness. Her eyes shone still in wild, tired reverie of the corrida, and her curls clung damply, as if sculpted, to her forehead.

He was there. Luisa's drawing-room had three big windows and he stood in the furthest of them, his eyes on the doorway, as Milagros and Mary came in. The room was much more beautiful than rumour and Vogue's photographs had suggested, so easily beautiful indeed, so deprecatory and gracious in its harnessing of baroque and First Empire to each other and to the sunlight, flowers and gaiety of immediate and happy human life, that, like Luisa's own well-disciplined sophistication, it ought to have deceived the naïveté of a girl who never before had set foot in a room which was the conscious expression of an isolated æsthetic sense. But Mary was not deceived. Curiously, as her nerves acknowledged the atmosphere of unforced beauty and therewith the passionate intelligence of Luisa which could go so far as to strain nothing, not even by the shadow of a hair her own pure taste, who could give this young man of generous ideals a room to share with her which, while being a flawless setting for herself, need yet seem no more to him or another than such unvulgar and reasonable beauty as all men might with justice hope to reach, curiously as she applauded this exaggeration of wifely skill, a thought repeated itself from the Cabantes meeting: How brave of him to marry such a miracle! For life, as livable, still seemed to this child an affair of give and take, and love a matter of truth and for better or worse, and all the exquisite hoodwinking which seemed the unceasing pastime of intelligence in feeling was frightening to her—vaguely, though truly, as she sensed it.

Pilár and Nieves were there, and Luisa, lovely in a cloudy blue dress, was having great fun explaining to them all the silver paraphernalia of English tea. Mary was greeted very gaily, and asked if everything on the tray was as it should be. To the children's great delight the ritual began then with the silver spirit kettle. Juanito, in his usual untidy flannels, came and sat near the round tea-table, having smiled at Mary.

"I must watch this funny business," he said in his stumbling English.

Yes, she knew she had been mistaken. This was the cheerful boy of tennis-playing and turrón. Not a cloud, not a memory in his face. Happy and at home. Thank God to know. Thank God to be so tired that there was no reaction—hardly even relief. It was just a fact, checked up and made certain.

As it was her birthday she would drink it in the really English way, with cream and sugar? But first you warmed the pot, didn't you? Oh yes—Mary agreed.

"Why, Miss Maria," said Pilár, "you're so Spanish already that you've forgotten how to make tea?" Milagros

233

said that the ceremony looked amazing, but that the bullfight had been terribly moving, and might she please have
chocolate?

Luisa rang a bell.

"You're a hopeless old villager, Mila," said Juanito.
"You're a drag on my career! How was the bullfight for
you, Miss Maria? Did you like Villaroja?"

He looked across the table to Mary with simple
friendliness in his gold eyes. She tried to memorise the
expression. To-morrow if pain returned she would need
an exact record of the innocent look.

"He fought very beautifully," she said. "I suppose it
was perfect really. But——"

"But what?" Milagros seemed about to be shocked.
Mary turned to her with relief. It was always easy to talk
one's mind to Milagros.

"Well—Pronceda seemed to fight his bull as if they
were alone, as perfectly as he could, and you could take it
or leave it. This man appealed a little—like a clown."

"That's true about Villarojas," said Juanito.

"What a purist you are, Miss Maria," said Luisa.

"I suppose you're right," said Milagros. "I wish I'd
said it first!"

Everyone laughed. Tea began with a great deal of fun
and cautious sipping.

"Two more days!" said Nieves dolefully.

"Do you mean that?" Juanito looked surprised.

"Yes," said Milagros. "There's to-morrow and the
day after, and then we go. Tia Cristina will have more
than done her duty then in her own opinion!"

"Still, there are two full days," said Pilár. "And Tio

234

Manolo is taking us to the new 'zarzuela' on the day after
to-morrow. It's the first night!"

"And first he's taking us to dinner at a really rakish
place, he says, on the Paseo de Rosales!" Milagros looked
delighted. "Only we're not to tell Tia Cristina!"

"Will you be sorry to leave Madrid, Miss Maria?"
Again that innocent look in the gold eyes. She answered
it a little wearily.

"Yes," she said. "I've liked it very much."

"Milagros hasn't given you much peace, though, Miss
Maria," said Nieves, "and father said you were to have a
semi-holiday."

"Yes," said Pilár. "That's really on my mind. You
must let Miss Maria have at least one day to herself,
Mila."

"Oh—but I'm not much of a nuisance, am I, Miss
Maria?"

Luisa laughed.

"Of course you are, you egoist! You take to-morrow
off, Miss Maria, from breakfast to midnight."

"Oh no, she can't do that! I want her for a lot of
things to-morrow! I'm free then. The day after Mademoiselle has nailed us down about shoes and underwear
and God knows what!"

Mary smiled at her.

"I had been wondering, Mila, if I could have the day
after to-morrow——"

"But of course!" said Pilár. "What are you going to
do, Miss Maria?"

"There's a train that goes to Toledo in the morning——"

"Ah yes, Toledo." Luisa agreed that she must see Toledo.

"I'd love to go with you," said Milagros wistfully.

"Well, you're not going," said Pilár. "It's Miss Maria's private holiday. And anyhow, don't you want to go to the zarzuela with Tio Manolo?"

"I think zarzuelas are idiotic," said Milagros. "A real blot on the Spanish tradition."

"You're a tiresome prig," said Juanito. "Miss Maria, do have one of these lovely little honey cakes!"

"There's an awful lot to see in Toledo," said Nieves.

They began to enumerate. The cathedral, and the hospital and the Alcazar and El Greco's house, and the gates and the walls and the Burial of Count Orgaz——

Mary said that she had an uncle in Dublin who believed that that picture was probably the greatest in the world. "He's never seen it, of course."

There was a great laugh.

"Still, your uncle in Dublin must have more sense than you, Miss Maria," said Milagros. "The way you go on about that old Rubens——"

"Ah, but Mila," Juanito looked interested. "Rubens is an absolute painter. Just what a painter should be! Now Greco—that overrated, hysterical——"

Luisa held up her hands.

"Juanito, not so soon again!" she said gaily, and then in explanation to Mary: "We rather know Juanito's views on El Greco, you see."

He coaxed Mary once more with the honey cakes.

"Your uncle is wrong, Miss Maria. Believe me. Still, if you go to Toledo the day after to-morrow, you certainly must see the Count Orgaz."

So the birthday party went, with nibbling and gramophone tunes and brother-and-sister joking, in the lovely
blue-and-white room overlooking the Recoletos. Mary
took her part in it with a good grace, if with a faint
weariness which the bullfight had induced. She told
herself that she was glad to be there and that now her real
business in Madrid was done.

A HERMITAGE

THE Plaza Zocodover is a small sunny triangle. Toledo
slides down from it in narrow, noisy twists.

Mary sat there in a café at eleven o'clock, with a day of
sightseeing ahead, and screwed herself to bear it. Guides
and touts were buzzing round her since she had left the
station and taken the bus for the theatrical ascent over the
bridge to the crest of the city. They worried her still like
flies, like itch, as she sat and drank horchata. Were
she well, were she happy, she would have disliked this
hot, fantastic town, she thought. But she had been in
desperate need of pretext to get out of Madrid and be
alone for even one day. So she had stuck to her holiday
plan, though caring nothing now for expeditions. She
could bear no more of Spain. She must close her
sensibilities, and grope her way home as decently as
possible. It was well enough to talk, for purposes of self-
control, of schoolgirl 'crushes,' well enough to say that
that pain is welcome which burns out pain—but is love,
however foolish, necessarily schoolgirl folly, and is pain
identifiable from pain? Was she in fact, for all her bluff,
grown-up and in a woman's dilemma? Was she un-
suitably, illicitly in love?

Ah—let the day take her—with its burden of Gothic
and 'mudéjar' and 'plateresco.' Let its heat and olive-
trees and tortured terecos—take, weary and stupefy her!
All she wanted now was to be wearied and hammered by

Spain, until the word became synonymous with exhaustion, and, at home at last in quiet Mellick, the merciful mists of tradition and common-sense would descend on a nightmare interlude.

This Toledo! She would see it—or know the reason why. She would be active and unpausing, and to-night so tired that really she would sleep. To-morrow then she would travel once more across the Castilian plain that had so gently fooled her. Back in the north, out of reach of his innocent, cold, forgetful eyes, she would make her plans and excuses, and go home.

In Mellick, with her hand in John's, her misery would cease. But if it did not, she could only tell him of it, and ask his help. While she was here alone in this hot, foreign place, all she could do to help herself and temporise was fidget, look and see and keep going, and never pause to let the pursuing tides of adult, vulgar, unexplainable wretchedness overtake her frightened heart. Oh, see the sights, she cried to herself. Keep fussing and moving—and get away as quickly as you can: You've read of heart-break, and sick, hopeless passion, but you've held on well enough so far to the idea that you could not—whatever you felt—feel fatal, novelist's love. Don't dare admit the hellish idea now. You green young fool—don't dare look inward at your preposterous, inglorious distress. Look round you, outward. At this fantastic yellow town above the Tagus, this meeting-place of Moor and monk—look out and be instructed. Keep going until you go home.

In Mellick there were blessed mists and rain, and the old rules were absolute; there goodness held its ground,

and faith and promise were synonymous with love; there
peace would be rediscovered and knowledge of herself;
there she would have her old bearings and steer by them
honestly and happily. Ah God, to be back there, back in
her own quiet heart, in coldness and tenderness. Soon,
soon . . . the sooner the better. She had not known
that life and travel and experiment could maim one thus.
She had had enough. But it would end. And until it did
—well, here were novelties, for instance: a Moorish
palace, a Gothic cathedral, the Burial of Count Orgaz.
She knew enough already to know the span thus covered.
Wide enough to hide in for a day—and to give exhaustion.

"Oh, go away, please! Leave me alone—I don't want
any of you!"

The touts and beggars laughed at her foreign Spanish
and pressed still more about her. She buried her face in
the guide-book, but they continued to compliment her on
her beauty and beg her patronage for the day. She
thought of Milagros and longed for her. Milagros, her
dueña. She thought of Conlan. She would be sobering
company to-day—would keep the inner and the outer
world at equal distance, and give sanity a chance.

"I'm too tired for this place. I don't like it. I wish I'd
gone to Avila!"

She put her hands across her eyes and gave herself up
to a moment of darkness. The noise of the admiring
touts fell away; there was a sudden cooling silence
over her; she felt as if she sat in shadow. She opened
her eyes and found that so she did. Juanito stood
above her, having scattered the crowd.

She stared at him, helpless against pleasure.

"You?"

"May I sit down?"

He pushed away the horchata, and ordered beer.

"Shall I apologise? Shall I explain?"

"No. Not yet. Not yet."

"You knew I'd come?"

She looked at him in amazement.

"How could I know?"

"The children said it all for me at tea the day before yesterday. You must have known what I was thinking!"

"It never crossed my mind."

"Oh!—But have you forgotten then—the night we danced?"

"I—forgotten?"

"Mary—may I have to-day?"

She stared at him still, but almost surreptitiously now, as a miser at his treasure. They were to be together for a day. That was his idea. Oh, he was mad, he was incomprehensible! Oh, Heaven, Heaven!

She could make no answer, though she tried to. She gave him a little smile. Then she sipped her beer. She held the big, frosted glass in both hands and looked out over it in peace on the untidy, triangular plaza. She was completely anæsthetised. The hot and frightening pain, the fidgetiness, the prickling fatigue induced by two nights' broken sleep—all were gone; resentment against Toledo's Moorish gates and chattering guides had vanished too. Pleasure flooded her, welling up coolly from her surprised and grateful heart. She sat very still and deliberated lazily on Juanito.

He watched her. He had no idea of the wild happiness he had brought, but he rejoiced nevertheless in the little smile that flickered dreamily across her face.

He was an honest man, and here at the outset of his life honesty was being tripped up. He had suffered since the day on which he first saw Mary, resented the wasteful accident of desire for her, and had fought it with realistic honesty for his own sake. But some trickster within had decided he must attend Luisa's tea-party. To test his self-command, he said, and show himself how dreams and absence can inflate a nothing. And she had come into the room, looking somewhat whiter, somewhat thinner than in Cabantes, with bluish shadows stressing the innocent, blue gravity of her eyes, and with silky curls clinging thickly, as if sculptured, above her deep and snowy forehead.

The tea-party was very nearly unbearable. But she was there and every faculty must therefore be held as steady as might be, the better to appraise her. But by the end of the merienda, when dusk filled the windows and Luisa's crystal lamps sprang into light, he was bemused and beaten, almost drowned in the clear sea of beauty. He was infatuated and had no idea how to manage his disaster. For the present all he could think of was how to see her, how to learn her better. So with an almost drunken cunning he had planned, even while he praised the honey-cakes and wounded her with the blind-seeming forgetfulness of his eyes, to find her there to-day. That was all he had been able to think of or foresee. And here she was, smiling as happily as a little boy as she drank her beer.

Life would be long, no doubt, and Juanito believed already that the least, or least to be held to of its satisfactions, would be those which sprang from the appeal of another face, another life. Yet now, looking at Mary's contentedly-drinking mouth, at her down-drooped eyelids and the long, uneven fringe of her lashes, measuring the androgenous, speckless beauty of her head and throat and bony, vigorous hands—he felt a load of durable and fanatical loneliness descend on him, distorting the whole shape of his future. He took it with a desperate sense of peace.

Meantime, there was to-day. Mary turned to him, smiling.

"There's a lot to be seen in this town."

"Speak Spanish," he said, teasingly, in Spanish.

She repeated her sentence in his language.

"That's lovely. Speak Spanish all day."

"I couldn't possibly."

"I'll make you."

"There's an awful lot to be seen."

"What?"

She laughed.

"Where shall I begin? The Cathedral?"

"No."

"The Burial of Count Orgaz?"

"No, no."

He called the waiter and paid for the beer. He put his hand lightly on her arm and they walked away from the café. They crossed the plaza and halted beside a black sports car.

"There isn't a thing to be seen in Toledo," he said.

She looked about her and laughed.

"I expect you're right. But I'd better buy a paper-knife or something!"

"You're a good conspirator."

She went into a souvenir shop and he followed her. They bought postcards and a large reproduction of the Count Orgaz. "For your uncle in Dublin," Juanito said. Mary looked at miniature swords in leather shields and thought of John, but did not buy one. They drove through a Moorish gate and over the muddy Tagus.

They travelled slowly towards the south. The car was hooded and cool. They went past olive groves and desolate farms, and up at last by a narrow, stony track to a hill-top on which tall rocks made embrasures of shadow and pale, bleached lichen was clean and springy to the touch. There was a little broken chapel of stone among the rocks.

"The Hermitage of the Holy Angels," said Juanito.

Mary looked back at the golden town below her on a far-away hill, the theatrical, legendary place, walled and turreted by Moors, divinely spired by Christian passion, and gently circled for ever by the yellow Tagus, in whose waters even from here she could see women at the eternal business of beating linen. She was content with this perfect view of it.

"Will you smoke?" said Juanito.

As he lighted her cigarette their eyes met and held each other in gravity.

"I have much to say to you," he said.

They stood and leant their shoulders against a shadowing rock.

"Yes," said Mary, "I suppose we have things to say."

"You don't seem afraid of me at all?"

"Afraid of you?" She looked at him in wonder.

"And yet I'm showing up as a bad character."

"So am I."

"Ah, Mary! I'm a Spaniard. You know nothing about me except that I've been married two years and have a son. I'm a Catholic, and I pass for a serious citizen. My parents are exceptionally good to me, and believe in me, and that I have honourable standards. So does my wife. You are a foreigner here, and a very young girl. You are employed to teach my sisters and you're not rich, I imagine. So, if I ingratiate myself with you, and force myself on your attention and carry you off up here into this lonely mountain—there is no excuse for me, and you ought to be afraid."

There was no smile on his face. But Mary smiled.

"We're two of a kind," she said. "I'm Irish; you know nothing about me, except that I'm employed and trusted by your parents and sisters. I am a Catholic like you. I am engaged to a man who believes in me completely. So, if I ingratiate myself—oh, Juanito, let me talk English!"

He would not smile.

"There is no excuse," he said. "And the explanation is only the common one of any cad. I am infatuated with you."

"Infatuated!" She repeated the word gently. "Yes. That's the explanation. I'm infatuated too."

He moved away, catching his breath sharply. She stretched a hand as if to pull him back, then let it fall.

"We have to-day," she said. "That is all we'll ever have."

"You can't isolate a day."

"Can't you?"

"You'd have to be a brute—a sort of animal—to do it."

Mary made no answer. She was standing erect against the lichened rock. She looked across the pallid landscape towards Toledo.

"What am I to do?" he asked.

"You planned this escapade. I didn't. What did you want from it, Juanito?"

He would not attempt to answer so complicated a question. He was too proud and true to deny the flame of common desire, or to protest the impossibility for him to tempt her to assuage it. Nor could he make any half-true yet silly-sounding speech about merely wanting to be with her, merely wanting to explain. What was there to explain? He had seen her, and thereafter was increasingly in trouble, out of soundings. There was no redress, no decent way of alleviation, and a strong man would have let it go at that. But he went with every thought of her, from strength to folly, from despair to resolution, from weariness to savage longing. He had had no justification in coming to Toledo—but neither had he had a plan. He was in pain, that was all—in confusion. And out of such a disorder could not bring himself to plead. That much of the lawyer and the man of sense remained in him. And as he looked at her now and accepted his own helplessness, he saw hers too—saw again, as in first seeing her, the awful strength of her vulnerability. She was a young girl with a troubled heart. It was intolerable. He could think of nothing whatever to say.

She spoke, looking down at Toledo.

"I think we're lucky, in a way," she said, in slow, deliberate English. "We have an illusion about each other—which people often have. But we will never have a chance to lose it."

"Don't you believe in love?"

"I did, I think—until I knew it."

She smiled at him, brilliantly and slowly.

"What do you mean?"

"I've never been in love, Juanito—until now. So I used to think it a lovely, suitable thing, that would grow in its time. I thought I'd like the feeling and be able to manage it and make—people—happy through it. Just now I don't think it's like that."

"What do you think?"

"That it's a perfectly unreasonable illusion—and must be borne as that. It's of no use. It's not suitable or manageable. It blurs things, puts everything out of focus. It's not a thing to live with. It's a dream."

"A dream?"

"Yes. That's why we're lucky. It can only stay like that for us. We'll never be given the chance to mix it with reality. Why, look where we have to come even to talk of it!"

She jerked her head in indication of the rocks and golden hills.

He stood at her side and considered her. She still leant against the towering rock. Her shoulders were squared to it, and her hands hidden in the pockets of her linen jacket. Her feet, in rope-soled shoes, pressed up and down gently, tight together, against the springy lichen. Her short, unsettled curls stirred softly. The dark blue, careless clothes and composed, braced attitude of meditation gave her for the moment the non-voluptuous, introverted air of a boy.

Then she surprised Juanito. Leaning over, without moving her feet, without taking her hands from her pockets, she kissed him, tenderly and honestly, on his mouth, and with a little sigh leant back again, straightening her shoulders contentedly against the rock.

"There's no excuse for tragedy," she said.

His face had become transfigured. All the heavy, manly look of doubt and lust was gone; his features were swept pure by startled happiness. His golden eyes were wide and radiant. He did not move.

"You—you kissed me?"

Then she saw the beauty and astonishment of his face to be almost overwhelming, so that she had to grow flippant to manage pleasure. "*Sí, señor*," she said. "*Dispense me!*"

"But—what did you mean?"

"Dear love, I meant what I did."

"You kissed me," he repeated stupidly.

She laughed again.

"There's a poem in English," she said, "which doesn't fit the case at all——" and contemplating with delight his aspect of youth and well-being, she murmured to herself: "Say I'm weary, say I'm sad . . ." Weariness and sadness waited no doubt—for him and her in appointed times. But not within this accidental day. Not if she could help it.

"Show me the Hermitage of the Holy Angels," she said, and took his arm.

They scrambled down a slope of lichen to the broken gate of the little chapel. It was a small, forgotten jewel of romanesque, and its stone was bleached fairer than the lichen. Time had crumbled its gentle decorations, and obliterated the memorial lettering of tombstones; its only furniture was, on its southern wall, a low relief of gay, exulting angels. Their wings were chipped; their heaven-directed trumpets almost worn away. Sunlight poured in on them through glassless windows and through a hole in the roof. A solitary magpie hopped about the floor.

Mary looked at the angels with great pleasure.

"Have you ever seen them before?" she asked Juanito.

"No, I've never been here; but father told me about the place once, and I've always meant to find it. He says these angels are one of the most beautiful things in Spain."

"He knows them?"

"Yes."

Mary leant, half in the sun, against the porch. Her eyes were still upon the angels. "Northern, and twelfth century. Really Christian. The Spain I like."

"And yet your face is pagan."

"I don't like that. But so long as you don't think it's Arab——"

"The first night I saw you I thought of Aphrodite——"

"Ah! Venus? A heavy creature—a Rubens woman."

"Then she isn't you."

He picked her up and carried her from the door of the Hermitage. "I will carry you back to Toledo," he said.

"Don't. I like it here."

"Didn't you like Toledo?"

"I wouldn't have liked anywhere this morning. Put me down, Juanito."

He put her down.

"Just before you turned up," she went on, "I was wishing I'd gone to Avila. What a muddle that would have been!"

He laughed.

"No muddle. I'd have been there."

She looked inquiring.

"I rang up the children at nine o'clock, and managed to make sure of your movements."

She gasped a little.

"You know, you're a terrible hypocrite!" she said. "Playing the agonised guilty creature one minute, and the next revealing deep powers of deceit."

"But I'm not 'playing' anything. Both things are perfectly true, and I'm letting you see both!"

She shook her head at him amusedly. He held out his cigarette-case.

"I've a very good mind to kiss you again."

"Ah!"

Their mood paused, dangerously.

"But no," she said. "Give me time to think. I haven't worked things out as cunningly as you." To take sting from this she put her hand through his arm. "I'm so happy, Juanito," she said gravely, "and all about

250

nothing! I'm happy, happy, happy!"

"I'm not," he said, his radiant eyes belying him. "I—I can't play comedy."

"You must. Just for to-day, Juanito. Only this one day."

"I'm counting every second of it. I've never known seconds go so fast."

"Nonsense. It's early yet." She looked about her amusedly and in particular at the broken Hermitage. "When does the restaurant open?"

His smile was really nervous and apologetic now.

"Any time you like," he said and pointed to the car.

"You brought lunch?"

He nodded shamefacedly. She broke into a long, sweet laugh.

"But you're disgraceful! You're a hardened villain! Are you always doing things like this?"

"What do you think?"

"Dear love," she said.

They ate in the car; there was delicious food, and Moselle packed in ice.

"I shall begin to talk now," said Juanito contentedly.

"Do."

"Do you understand Spanish as well as you seem to?"

"When you and your father speak it, I understand almost everything. You're so polite," she said gently. "But I'll stop you if I miss your points. Only you must allow me to answer you mostly in English—or even in French."

"But your Spanish is better than your French."

"It sounds better, but I know more French grammar."

"I like you to talk Spanish," he said obstinately.

"You always seem to be crying for the moon."

"Do you like cold omelette?"

"Very much. Go on. Talk."

He did not obey her at once. She watched his white, mobile face and felt how true it was that he could not play comedy. And yet, there had been times in her brief knowledge of him—his wife's tea party, for instance— when his impersonation of indifference had caused her bitter suffering. Still, that was not comedy, she believed, but a true effort after virtue, or perhaps a performance of comedy within and for himself. She thought of the kiss she had given him and wondered on what immediate prick of impulse she had acted. All she knew was that, the untimely swift decision taken, the gesture itself was as deliberate as any she had ever made. She had thought of John as her lips touched Juanito's and had even recollected cruelly the distaste with which she suffered his hungry mouth. It occurred to her now that whatever she might do or not do in future she could never be more purely faithless to John than she had been in the second of that kiss. This realisation was simultaneously cold and regretful. But it had reassurance in it too. Faith drives out faith, and she had already, in her gaiety of to-day, a notion that she had cast her lot. Not with Juanito, whose fate was shaped already, in Spain and Spain's future, and with his wife and child. But merely because of him, of what he made clear about the remarkably distinct and sweet sensation which underlies the relationship of love. For the purchase of this accidental knowledge, for this brief hint at a theory which she might never test, she was beginning to suspect that she might have to sell the orthodox order of her own life, and the present happiness of another. At least already she had been deliberately faithless to those things; she was risking loneliness for herself, and almost certainly undertaking to cause pain and humiliation elsewhere. She had read in her time of all those regrets and griefs and misunderstandings which are, in fiction, the certain flowers of love—but John, whenever she debated them, had denied and scorned their reality. She had been reluctantly glad of his solid faith, and would be glad now to go on in it, but it had happened to her that it was gone. Whatever was to be the end of this dear escapade—and it had, after all, only this day's steadily shrinking span—she knew now about regrets and griefs and faithlessness. Knew them all quite clearly in herself, and would have to reckon with them.

Juanito poured more wine into her glass.

"You've called me 'dear love' twice to-day," he said, and his voice shook. "If I were to call you anything like that—oh, Mary, I couldn't bear it! What do you mean by it?"

"What I say. I've fallen in love with you, Juanito. I fell in love that first night."

"I fell in love with you. There was no help for that. But why should you like me?"

He turned his white face to her with an entreaty in it that was almost angry.

"I don't know. I just liked you."

"What are we to do?"

"Nothing. Nothing at all. That's the beauty of it, dear love. There isn't a thing we can do. We've simply

got to get over it. And every old fogey in the world says
that in fact people do get over it. We've got to-day,
Juanito, thanks to your quick wits!" She smiled at him.

But he went on, his face full of discomfort.

"If I were free——"

She laid her hand on his.

"Do you really think it necessary to say that sort of
thing to me?"

"Ah yes, it is necessary——"

"No, Juanito. Stop hurting yourself. Or, if it must
be said, let me say it." She paused. "If you were an
American, say, and your wife had a little lost her interest
in you, and divorce was part of the code and religion you
were brought up in, and would not displace your ambitions and ideals, and make you into a kind of exile without
occupation—then you and I might have a clumsy sort
of future to discuss. But as it is, we haven't. We're
Catholics, and you're a Spanish patriot and 'one of
Spain's great men,' and you have a wife and son to whom
you are devoted, and your wife is devoted to you. So
you see, our 'infatuation' is simply an uncomplicated pain
which we must get over. We are not going to maim and
maul each other, Juanito, in the name of love."

"No. We can't do that. But what are we to do?"

"We have to-day. To-morrow I go back to the North,
and as soon as I can I'll go home to Ireland."

He drew a long, slow breath.

"Then what will happen? When you get to Ireland?"

Mary bit her lip and stared through the windscreen.
She was trying to remember what life was like at home.

"When I get to Ireland? Ah!"

"That man—that John?"

"Please, Juanito! I didn't ask you to talk about—Luisa——"

"I'm sorry. Oh, I'm sorry."

They sipped their wine in silence. Mary thought of John and Mellick; she began to fidget with her souvenir postcards.

"Explain them to me," she said unsteadily. "I'm terrified of Milagros' questions."

Juanito thrust the lunch-basket outside the car, and settled in its shade to describe Toledo. He was a good guide, and Mary learnt a great deal of the city's history and tradition from his quick descriptions; understood exactly where the famous 'Burial' was hung in the silly little church of Saint Thomas, and began to believe that she had truly walked herself through the twisted streets to El Greco's house on the outskirts, and had sat in his flowered patio. She studied the postcards carefully; details of the Cathedral and the Hospital, old doorways, beautiful rejas—she would feel vile to-morrow, talking to Milagros. His little sister, the kindly, eager little girl. Well, she would be going home soon—away from this beginning of lies. That was well. She would be unhappy now with his three sisters. Away from them it would be better; in Mellick there would be only John to deceive—or hurt. Only John. She couldn't see the postcards suddenly. Her eyes were filled with tears. She heard Juanito's voice, but not his meaning. A tear splashed on the postcard he was holding, on his hand.

"Oh! Oh!" She covered her face, and the cards slid

to the floor. Juanito took her in his arms. "I can't bear it! Oh, Juanito, I can't bear it!"

He held her and laid his mouth against her hair.

"Dear love," he said, taking her phrase. "Oh, Mary, little love! Oh dear, dear love!"

The gates were down at last. The fever, courage and joking, the bluff of 'we have to-day.' Their peace, the little they were to know, their knowledge of each other, came now to them, not as Mary had played for it, in comedy, in the gallantry of a graceful hail and farewell, but in their tears—as so often peace is granted. Clinging to each other now, unable to let go, and without heat or passion, but rather as two bereaved, they found the comfort of grief. Crying out each that they could not bear the wound the other had inflicted, they drank the sweet charity of mutual compunction. Afraid together they gave each other heart. Clamouring together against the brevity and bitterness of this day, they read in each other's eyes that it was honey-sweet. So in tears, shame and cowardice they came truly home at last to each other's hearts, losing sight of beauty and physical delight, and piercing, by the accident of one tear dropped on Juanito's hand, to the inexplicable core of sweet rightness for each other which underlay and drove their immediate superficial illusion. So, wet cheek against wet cheek, and quiet and miserable as children, they gave each other everything in their reciprocal acceptance of denial, and too broken-hearted for desire they saw almost dully the full, great curve of their unattainable love.

It was one kind of consummation. At least as it ebbed it left them deeply tired, deeply and naturally content with the temporary refuge of each other's breasts, and as instinctively sure in tenderness as the most surrendered lovers.

"Oh, love—why am I crying? Why did I make you cry?" Mary stroked Juanito's wet, stained face. "I wanted to-day to be perfect."

"It is perfect."

But his whisper shook and broke. He kissed her. Desire flamed slowly in them then, to match their mood of grief, and adding to the knowledge which that had brought its contradictory mood.

Mary, precariously at peace in this deep embrace, looked towards its logical end, which she knew now her love desired and half intended. And she saw that for Juanito's sake, not for hers, they should forbear. Were there such a thing as loving without exacting love, were it possible to save a lover from the afterwards built up already by himself, she would be Juanito's now contentedly, and disappear to-morrow to reckon alone with the repercussions in her of her own decision. Without cheapening her integrity and in particular without belittling her insult to John's love, she yet could see that time would make manageable to her and would keep her own the consequences on her side of her surrender now. The central sin against Catholic teaching would be her affair and Heaven's; the offence against John was hard and shoddy-seeming, but the most monstrous conceit could not claim that one jilt could for ever maim a handsome and self-confident man of twenty-nine. No, she could reckon even with John. For herself—ah, all that she would gain and lose by this one day would be her

secret for ever. In direct relation to herself, she had no
fear whatever of the gamble. Richer or poorer thereafter,
what need it matter? She could earn a living, and the
world was wide. She would have had the brief, dear love
of 'one of Spain's great men.'

She sighed and ran her hand appraisingly through his
silky, floppy hair.

"I love you," he said. "I love you."

Yes, there was the rub. He would insist he loved her.
But he knew he loved other things too, was in fact made
up of other things—whereas she was a pure and senseless
accident. All that she was not was his being, and what she
loved. Should she take him now, and then disappear
without leaving traces, she would injure his peace of
mind and his self-respect most savagely. She would
leave him, dear, traditional romantic, sweet good boy,
to brood on her youth and lost virginity and virtue, her
Catholic honour and honourable upbringing, her purity
and beauty, her disturbed desires, her broken engagement, her risk of childbearing; she would make it impossible for him, moreover, to be at peace with the wife
and child he had cheapened; she would shake his belief
in himself, and for a time at least, an important span of
time in his rapidly flowering life, she would expose him
to great danger from his own hidden regrets. Should she
take him and face the music, ask him to face it?—ah,
senseless! What could she give him, in disgrace and
exile, to replace his work and patriotism, his wife and
baby, and the admiring love of his parents and sisters?
Should she take him, and stay in Spain? Find some occupation in Madrid, and be his mistress in secret while he

wanted her? She paused on that, the only possible solution, but a mean one. It wasn't the kind of thing to enrich Juanito and make him happy. It wasn't the kind of thing that she herself could bear, even for his sake.

Yet here he was, his heart against her, his murmuring love a cradle for her too clear thoughts. She curled to him with deliberate pleasure, and smiled at the illogicality and comedy of their predicament. He put his hand under her chin and lifted her face towards him dreamily, as if uncertain whether to kiss her or smile.

"What is it?" he asked.

"I'm thinking how dishonourable we are," she said.

"Do you think I don't see that too?"

"My darling, your trouble is that you see everything, feel everything. Ah, if only you were a little coarse, Juanito, a little stupid!"

"Would you like me better then?"

"There's no possible way of liking you better," she said, and kissed him wildly. Then with suddenness she pushed him from her. "Let's get out and walk."

They went by the tall stones and down the slope past the little Hermitage to a stretch where the lichen flowed more smoothly and was less broken by rocks. They went hand in hand with slow steps.

"In the Spain of which I'll be Premier," said Juanito, "there'll be divorce."

"And you a pillar of the Church?"

"The Church will have no pillars then. I'll be a Catholic."

"Will they have you for Premier in that case?"

"We'll see. My plan of government would take a good

deal of expounding. I'm after a Communism very different
from Lenin's. I want it understood as what it is, pure
Utilitarianism, plain, materialistic justice. With no
spiritual attack or message. The spiritual basis of life
must be left alone, unless you can isolate it and know
what you are attacking—and how can politicians do that?
I believe, you see, that every single human situation
differs from every other and that therefore the only
possible spiritual rule of thumb is the Christian, the
Catholic, which in the end provides for that principle,
and can, when it works honestly, get moderate results.
Which is all that any intelligent man can hope for.
Utopias are unpleasant, slavish dreams. All that politicians can give is fundamental health and the roots of
knowledge. It is for parents and theologians to inject
the civic virtues if they can, and the artists to give whatever answer they can to human aspiration. But the real
issues will always be unmanageable. There is no such
thing as legislation for happiness. You see what I mean,
my darling—there'll be divorce in a future Spain, and I
daresay the courts will be fairly busy—but—supposing
you and I—and Luisa—were living in Moscow now, or
in London—would we be any clearer in our minds?"

"We might be tougher people."

"Then we wouldn't be you and me and Luisa—and,
after all, we might crop up anywhere."

"Well, we mightn't be Catholics."

"That's true. But we might be decent people anywhere—to whom external arrangements are no use. That's
why father says the fewer laws the better—save strictly
utilitarian ones. He says we must learn to live by the

spirit and on our own thought—and that laws brutalise us. And yet he can sometimes be almost as Jansenistic as my grandfather."

"I never can decide whether he has very little faith in life or very much."

"He doesn't know, I imagine. He's a dreamer anyway."

"What would he say to us—if we weren't you and me?"

"Ah, there you see! That 'if' would alter everything for him. But he believes in self-control. He might even condescend to say that it gives the best results!"

They leant over an embankment and looked about them. The colour of New Castile was tawnier and less appealing, Mary thought, than the lovely land north of the Guadarramas, and olive farms scattered over it made dark and sultry stripes. But the sky was flawless, too lucent to be blue and with an almost frosty sparkle in its brilliance; up here indeed the air tasted of the exquisiteness of heaven. For miles around it seemed that the world hardly breathed; Toledo lay and sparkled like a dead, fairy tale city, a decorated sleeping beauty; here and there a sunburnt village was outlined against a hill. Motor horns sounded rarely, as from another sphere; magpies strutted on the lichen and an old white goat cropped gently among the rocks.

"A good place for a hermitage," said Mary.

Juanito smiled.

"I was thinking a good place for love."

She took his outstretched hand.

"We must stop thinking about love, my darling."

"I was repeating my poem to myself," he said.

"I know it off. The one Milagros learnt."

"Ah, Milagros!"

"I got the book—the Oxford Book."

"Well, did you read the one that follows it—the answer?"

"I learnt it too—for discipline."

"I read it the other day—for the same reason. . . . 'Thy gowns, thy shoes . . .' Do you remember? ' . . . soon break, soon wither—soon forgotten, In folly ripe, in reason rotten.' "

"Ah, sweet!"

"Don't look like that! I believe in 'thy gowns, thy shoes, thy beds of roses'! But since I can't have them— oh, Juanito—one has to do something to stiffen up!"

"Is there no way for you and me?"

"No way on earth."

"I truly have to do without you?"

"That cuts both ways."

"No, no. I'm a man like a million others, just someone you happened to like—God alone knows why! But you —oh, I've never dared to praise your beauty, because there simply is no way! You are the sort of accident there's no believing in! You have a face that would feed and fill the heart for ever and ever, do you hear? You're a dream, a trick, and when you're gone I won't be able to believe in you! I'll simply never be able to remember your face! No one could remember it, Mary!"

"Oh, but you must remember! Please, please remember me!"

"How can I? I'm an ordinary man, a politician—I simply can't get you stamped on my mind! You're too

various, too strange—I'll never see you clearly when
you're gone!"

"Ah, that is cruel of you! Don't say that!"

"Stay with me!"

"How?"

"I don't know. There'll be a way! We stole to-day,
didn't we? We can steal more days—Mary!"

"You know we can't!"

"Is there any morality in taking to-day and piously
refusing to-morrow?"

She laughed.

"No more than there is in kissing you, and then
pushing you away! I know I'm a hypocrite, Juanito—I
know perfectly well that every time I look at you now I'm
as unfaithful to—John as if—as if I were your lover."

"Ah, love—could you be that?"

He had her in his arms now and each could feel the
thundering of the other's heart.

"What do you take me for? What do you think I mean
when I say I love you?"

Their mouths met again.

But curiously in this kiss, most wildly urgent, they took
and gave within their passion that passion's vital, fatal
creator and destroyer—their hopeless understanding of
each other.

Juanito stroked her curly head and spoke to her, his
mouth still hovering on hers.

"It's no use, no use."

"Dear love, I told you that."

"I love you far too much. It would be hell."

"It would be hell."

"Oh, Mary, oh my love—if you could know!"

"I'll always know. But remember me. Promise you'll remember!"

"I don't see how I can. The more you love a face the more it dodges you."

"No. I'll remember every flicker of yours."

They moved on over the lichen, and came to a rock against which they sat on the springy ground.

"I'm tired," said Mary. "Oh, I'm tired."

He gathered her against him.

"Rest. Shut your eyes," he said.

She did not shut her eyes, but they sat very still. Evening stole mistily on Toledo, and laid long swathes of shadow between the hills. The quiet deepened, and they, a part of it, were quiet too, almost forgetting their grief. Their day was slipping from them in tremendous beauty, but they felt small and tired—comforted to be together still, unequal to the heroics of farewell.

"I wish we could go to sleep here," Mary said.

"I wish we could."

She closed her eyes. Her head lay across Juanito's heart in an innocent, baby attitude, and the posture of sleep stressed the delicate young shadows of weariness about her eyes. He studied the pure textures of her face, and reflected that men can walk out to be hanged on April mornings with apparent composure because their fleshy dullness mercifully is unequal to the onslaught of personal knowledge. Imagination bursting the solid shell is madness, but he was tough, he thought with shame. She is in my arms, tired out with the uselessness of feeling, he thought. That's all I have given her. Weariness. And to-morrow she'll be gone. To-morrow I'll go mad trying to remember this dear face. He looked down at her in anguish. The shadows grew long and the cold breeze crept round the hill. Mary shivered and opened her eyes.

"I must go back to Madrid," she said.

They went towards the car, past the little chapel.

"The Holy Angels," Mary said, but she did not go in to look at them again. When they got to the car they found that they had left a door open and most of her postcards were blown about the hill.

"I'm glad. I don't want them."

But one lay face downwards on the step of the car. Juanito picked it up.

"It's of the Holy Angels," he said. "I didn't know they were ever photographed."

"Ah!" It was a very good picture of the low relief, with 'Ermita de Los Santos Ángeles' printed in the margin. "I'll keep that one. I'll keep it always."

They looked at the postcard gravely together.

"Will you really keep it always?" Juanito asked her. "Until you die?"

"Until I die."

He took his pen and wrote on the back of the card: '*Recuerdo de hoy*. Juanito.'

'Souvenir of to-day.' She would remember. She got into the car, holding her postcard gently.

They drove home to Madrid, slowly and saying little. They left Toledo behind them with only a glance. In Aranjuez, leafy and forgotten, they halted and drank coffee in the dusk. To each the other's face seemed pitifully weary now. They went on to Madrid, still inert and without anything to say. As lights and houses began to accumulate ahead, Mary slipped her hand along Juanito's arm for a second or two.

"Thank you," she said. "It was a lovely day."

"What am I to do?"

"Ah, love!"

"This isn't good-bye," he said.

"Juanito, you know it is."

"It isn't," he said. "It isn't good-bye."

She said no more. Madrid was roaring all about them. It occurred to her that to drive her thus in his own car to Tía Cristina's house was very indiscreet. She said so, and he only turned and gave her a half-smile. He pulled up outside his aunt's apartment house, got out and walked with her to the lift. He seemed quite unaware of his indiscretion. She held her postcard carefully in her hand.

"Thank you, Juanito," she said.

He smiled at her, the innocent baffling smile that had so often wounded her.

"*Hasta luego*," he said, and smiled again through the glass door of the lift.

Mary dined politely with Doña Cristina and Mademoiselle, who required very little conversation of her. The children were out at their *zarzuela*.

ROMANCE

Four days after her return from Madrid, Mary had a free afternoon and went into Altorno. She looked forward to a few hours of the rattling society of her colleagues.

Life at Cabantes was hard to manage now. The children talked incessantly of Madrid, and Milagros, who loved Toledo, grumbled still good-naturedly about not having been allowed to accompany Miss Maria there; her questions about this and that celebrated sight were hard to answer. Don Pablo too seemed interested in Mary's sight-seeing, and she was sometimes disconcerted to find him looking at her with what she imagined to be a more penetrative and questioning glance than formerly, though always his eyes were very gentle. Estéban, the postman, was a real trouble. He was exuberantly glad to hand her love-letters again across the camellia-bush, and made a great deal of noise about the dislike he had felt for having such precious communications forwarded to Madrid. He also told her, and told whomsoever he met in the garden or at the side door, that she was looking tired and sad, that Madrid had done her no good, and that she must not pine. The sweetheart in Ireland loved her still—look if he did not! She must preserve her beauty for him; the good Basque air would give her back her roses! Estéban's eyes shone very kindly behind his spectacles, and Mary found his cheerfulness almost insupportable. Less supportable were the letters he brought. The loving, discursive and now and then faintly worried letters from John. Escape to her room, from Milagros and Don Pablo and Estéban, meant imprisonment with them, and with the miserable problem of reply. And escape from them, even in sleep, led only, so it seemed, into the tormenting, ghostly peace of Juanito's arms. *Recuerdo de hoy.* She was remembering.

On Wednesday she hurried to the Café Alemán. She longed for O'Toole's benevolent "alannahs," for the sad pantomime of Keogh and Harty and the engineers, for Barker's "Ee, lass!" for the touchy, uncertain friendliness of Agatha Conlan. Nobody in the café would give a rap about Toledo; none of them would joke her about John.

There was much animation in the ladies' alcove, and in particular round the table usually occupied by Mary's set. As she crossed the café she saw Keogh in her usual place. Harty, Duggan and Barker were there too, and Miss McMahon. Two or three less familiar colleagues, Miss Kennedy, Miss Burke, and an old one called, Mary believed, Miss Doolin, were standing by the table. But she could not see O'Toole or Agatha, and, unwilling to face such a throng, was steering for another corner when Keogh and Harty called to her in some excitement. Barker made room for her quite eagerly on the leather seat against the wall.

"Come on," said Keogh. "What do *you* think of the situation?"

Mary looked blankly at all the enlivened faces. "What situation?"

"Bluffer," said Duggan.

"You know all about it, I'll take my oath," said Keogh.

"About what?"

"But Lavelle's been in Madrid, of course," said Harty.

Mary nodded.

"Please tell me—what's up?"

Barker told her.

"O'Toole's got married."

"O'Toole? Oh, I—but——?"

"To a dago," said McMahon.

"A fat little dago with a huxter-shop," said Keogh.

Mary was smiling broadly. "Oh, but she might have told me! What a ruffian the woman is!"

"I can't understand it," said Harty.

"Disgusting!" said Miss Burke.

Keogh shrugged. "She's a low type—always was!"

"What do you mean—'low type'?"

"Keep your hair on, lass," said Barker to Mary.

"But what's disgusting? I don't understand you! What's the harm in O'Toole's getting married?"

"To a little shopkeeper?" Miss Kennedy looked quite ill as she asked this question. Keogh, able to concentrate on the business, as the other tables were still empty, and as it was really an interesting scandal, looked at Mary and spoke as if to a mentally deficient child.

"I don't know anything about you, Lavelle, but we misses are most of us ladies——"

Mary laughed in Keogh's face. "Ladies be hanged!" she said. "Where *is* this sneak of an O'Toole?"

"On her honeymoon, I suppose," said Harty, getting the giggles.

"Ee, what a honeymoon!" said Barker mildly.

"She's a bounder," said Keogh, "making mud of us all like this!"

"Corrigan's little episode was not half as much of a slur," said Miss Kennedy.

"Will no one tell me whom she's married?"

"A newspaper-seller that she used to buy cigarettes from."

"Pepe? You mean to tell me she's married Pepe?"

"Is that his name? All I know is he sits outside his emporium in shirt-sleeves every evening!" said Keogh.

"How she could?" Miss Kennedy shuddered.

"It's marvellous!" said Mary. "That nice man, Pepe! But of course—we're all fools! It's—it's been obvious all the summer that he adores her! Oh, I think it's awfully nice!"

"Are you in your right mind?" Keogh enquired.

"What's up with you all?" said Mary. "Are you jealous, or what?"

"Jealous?" They screamed the word.

"If it gets round the colony——" said Keogh uneasily.

"And it certainly will," said Miss Kennedy.

"We're looked down on quite enough as it is," said Harty, who had no tact. They all glared at her.

"Who looks down on us?" Keogh enquired.

"Still, this is a fearful thing for a miss to have done," said Miss Burke.

"Common, over-sexed creature," said Keogh. "Change of life perhaps."

Mary sprang up.

"Keogh, you're a rotten beast!"

Barker took her by the arm.

"Ee, lass, drink your tea!"

"Not with Keogh! Put it there, Angeles, please!" She pointed to another table. Keogh looked unperturbed; most of the other misses were amused. Mary trembled with rage. "Where's Agatha?" she asked, and seeing their surprise: "Where's Conlan?"

"God knows!"

"I had a row with *her* about this wedding yesterday," said Keogh.

"Sit down, Miss Lavelle," said Miss McMahon. "You know perfectly well O'Toole shouldn't have lowered herself to marry a man like that."

"I won't sit down." Mary pushed her way out from the crowded table. "O'Toole is one of the nicest, kindest women I've ever known, and as far as I know Pepe, he's an angel. I'm delighted at this news, and I think you're a pack of fools."

She strode to the other end of the alcove.

"Ta-ta!" said Keogh, and everyone smiled.

Mary read a paper and drank her tea. She was half sorry now that she had lost her temper over such a pitiful absurdity as the misses' social code, but otherwise was happier than she had been for days. Her pleasure for O'Toole was profound and true and drowned awhile all personal trouble. Great news. But O'Toole might have told her. She must find Agatha after tea. She hoped O'Toole wasn't still on a honeymoon. She longed to see her and wish her happiness. Pepe, nice man. Oh, good luck, to marry a Spaniard and stay in Spain! Her thoughts ran away with her a little here; she slipped a fraction off guard.

At the other table her colleagues giggled and chattered, relaxed now and even amused, having expressed their social horror. They were in fact, so far as Mary could gather, letting themselves go somewhat on the esoteric subject of marriage—made temporarily less inhibited by O'Toole's very deplorable audacity. Barker and McMahon, both rather waggish when roused, were telling spinsterish stories—about pyjamas, one seemed to be, and another about a man who wanted his bride's nightdress to be nine yards long. And then Barker told very sibilantly in good Lancashire vein about the girl who remarked to her husband as she lay in bed and watched him undress on their wedding night, that she saw nothing novel or surprising in marriage, to which he replied: "You wait till I get this sock off!"

Keogh looked uneasy.

"Sh!" she said.

Some Englishmen had arrived at the other tables. But Barker was immensely encouraged by the wild laughter of her colleagues.

Mary felt it to be fortunate that Agatha was not around. How much better to be mad after Agatha's fashion, she thought, than in the way of these unhappy others! And she looked with embarrassment at the flushed and giggling faces of the outraged, ladylike misses.

She paid for her tea and left the café.

She went over the bridge and along the Gran Via, then down the Calle Pelayo, in which Pepe lived and had his little shop. She went into it. He was there behind the counter in his shirt-sleeves, fat and gentle, gently smiling.

272

"Oh, Pepe! Is it true? Is it really true?"

She stretched her hands to him, and he seized them, his gentle smile becoming a beam.

"Yes, yes," he said, "if you'll believe it, it's true! Oh, I'm so happy, I'm so proud!"

"You must both be terribly happy. Where is she?"

Pepe lifted the counter-flap, and led Mary in through a little passage.

"O'Toole!" she called as she went, "O'Toole, where are you?"

She heard the familiar, gracious laugh, and in a sunny room, full of saucepans and flowering geraniums and singing-birds in cages, she found the disgraced O'Toole. Her battered face was as absurdly made up as ever, and her eyes were full of joy. Mary hugged her and gave her a shake.

"You're a sneak! You're disgusting! When did you do it?"

"On Saturday morning, alannah. God help me for a maniac!"

"I've only just this minute heard!"

"How could I tell you? You were in Madrid!"

Pepe looked on with his happy smile. Mary turned to him.

"She'll really have to learn Spanish properly now, Pepe!"

"Yes," said Pepe, "that's what I say. To speak like you, like Miss Conlan——"

"Oh, she'll never speak like Miss Conlan—but you'll really have to improve, O'Toole!"

"I don't see why, alannah!" She glanced at Pepe.

"You hypocrite! You know you like my funny Spanish! It makes him die laughing sometimes, alannah! It's quite an asset!"

Mary shook her head and laughed. It was lovely to see O'Toole so happy.

"No good for the shop," she said. "You'll muddle things. Won't she, Pepe?"

"Oh, he minds the shop! I have to mind the stew, and the canaries! Sit down, alannah—I'm simply delighted to see you!"

"Oh, but I wish I'd been at the wedding!"

"I wish you were. But he wouldn't wait: he wanted to take me to see his old mother in Pamplona for her fiesta last Saturday night! We were back on Sunday! That was our honeymoon!"

"How happy you look!"

O'Toole's face softened. So did her voice.

"Yes, I'm happy," she said, and laid her hand shyly for a second on Pepe's sleeve. He had a bottle under each arm and was preparing to celebrate Mary's visit.

"Will the shop be all right?" she asked.

"The customers shout when they want me," he said.

"Conlan came to the wedding," said O'Toole. "Disgusted and disapproving, I needn't tell you—but Pepe likes her, if you please!"

"Oh yes, I have liked Miss Conlan for many years," said Pepe.

"Where is she to-day?"

"On duty, I think. She was in here last night. I hear there's ructions in the clubhouse over my little surprise?" O'Toole spoke English now.

"Yes, they're all jealous, poor devils."

O'Toole put her arm round Mary. "You're a nice kid," she said.

The three drew their chairs up to the plush-covered table near the window. The sun streamed in; all the caged birds were singing. Their glasses were filled with a very fine manzanilla. Mary lifted hers.

"You'll be happy always," she said to the two in Spanish. "That's a certainty."

"Oh, alannah!" Tears sprang to O'Toole's happy eyes.

"Rosita, my dearest," said Pepe.

"Did you know my name was Rosie, alannah?"

They ate anchovies and shrimps, and lighted *favoritos*.

"Pepe," said Mary. "Did she ever pay her bill?"

"Every penny!" said O'Toole indignantly. "What are you insinuating?"

There was a shout from the shop and Pepe darted along the passage.

"How long have you known you were going to do this?" Mary asked O'Toole.

"About four weeks, alannah. I'm nearly as surprised as yourself. I suppose it is a queer thing to do? A Spaniard, after all—and I'm not used to—to cooking and canaries and what not!"

"It isn't queer at all. It's so natural that I'm amazed now I didn't see it coming! After all, he always used to beam at you when we came into the shop! And he's awfully nice."

O'Toole smiled very gently.

"He's no Adonis, of course. But then I'm not Venus, am I?"

Mary thought of Juanito carrying her over the lichen.

"I must give you a wedding present," she said hurriedly. "What would you like?"

"You'll do nothing of the sort, and thank you! There isn't a thing lacking here, as you can see!" O'Toole waved a mocking hand round the gaily overcrowded room.

"Another pair of canaries?" Mary suggested.

Pepe came back and sat down near his wife.

"It used to be lonely in here behind the shop," he said gently, and poured more wine into the glasses.

Mary looked about her. The room was kitchen and parlour. It had a porcelain stove at one end where saucepans bubbled. There was a dresser full of shining pots and dishes, and the gay, flowered wallpaper was almost hidden by portraits of Pepe's family and the shining cages of birds. Geraniums cascaded flowers and scent. Among the framed photographs Mary noticed some of matadors, and on a peg on the central wall hung a matador's hat and processional cape.

O'Toole saw where her eyes rested.

"Yes, alannah, believe it or not—this blackguard was a matador once! And I actually have a stepson who is a matador!"

"Oh!" said Mary. "Oh, Pepe! May I—may I just look at the lovely cape?"

"Indeed, of course, Miss Maria!" Pepe hurried with her to the peg on which it hung. Mary stroked the silk gently.

"You were a matador?" she said in wonder.

"Yes—and I was a good matador. I come from Pamplona, you see! Then, when I got fat I was a picador, but my late dear wife, she did not like it——"

"And your late dear wife was right!" said O'Toole. "Neither does the present holder!"

"But, Rosita, I am so no longer!" he smiled at her.

"No, but your son is, my stepson! That nice boy there—look, alannah——." She pointed to a photograph near where Mary stood. "I haven't met Hilario yet, but I've had a lovely letter from him. It's a crime that child being a matador! I'm going to put a stop to it, so I am!"

"Oh no!" said Mary. And to Pepe she said: "His face is like yours. He's very young?"

"Yes, Miss Maria. Only sixteen. A *novillero* still, but he has the gift. He will be a great matador. You'll see—some day you will hear of Hilario Valdez!"

"It's barbarous!" said O'Toole. "That pet of a boy! I won't allow it! I mean that, Pepe!"

Pepe and Mary both smiled at her.

"She will learn to understand the corrida," he said optimistically to Mary. "It is absurd, this being sick and so on."

O'Toole chuckled.

"You wait and see how absurd it is, my boyo!"

"But here is Miss Maria, who feels how just it is, the bullfight—and Miss Conlan—she understands it like a matador!"

O'Toole beamed at him.

"It's as plain as the nose on your face, Pepe, that

you should have married Miss Conlan," she said.

He shook his head.

"Brave indeed would be the man——" he murmured.

"What do you think Conlan would have said to his proposal, alannah?"

Pepe mused over his glass.

"I was quite brave enough," he said. "I was a very audacious, impertinent man, to propose marriage to an educated foreign miss—a lady——"

"Lady yourself!" said O'Toole.

"When did you propose, Pepe?"

"One afternoon six weeks ago, Miss Maria, when she came to pay her bill. I screwed up my audacity. And she said——"

"I said, in my best Castilian, alannah, that I was knocked cold! And that we must get acquainted first. So we went for a few strolls on the Alameda in the evenings, and here we are."

Husband and wife looked at each other with simple, kindly satisfaction.

"If I may say so, Miss Maria," said Pepe, "it has been for me a very great romance."

Mary remembered how O'Toole had said something, the first day she met her, about Romance with a big R.

A saucepan boiled over on the stove. O'Toole dashed for it.

"These confounded all-day stews that this fellow likes," she grumbled gaily. "I've no idea how to do them! He'll die of indigestion, God help him!"

There was another shout from the shop and Pepe skipped along the passage. O'Toole strolled back from the stove and leant against the window sash in a bower of geraniums. She looked very graceful. Good sherry, the emotion induced by Mary's good wishes and her tussle with the stew had seamed her careful, exaggerated make-up, but her eyes were more benevolent than ever and her air of peace was almost beautiful. She pulled a geranium leaf and biting at it looked affectionately down at Mary.

"And how are you, alannah? You look a bit thin, or something."

"Oh—I'm all right. That day we went up to Allera, were you engaged to Pepe?"

"No, I was thinking him over. We were walking out!"

"I suppose we must call you Rosita now?"

"Sure! I must say it's nicer than Rosie!"

"Doña Rosita O'Toole y Valdez!"

"Sounds very grand! Funny thing, my father was a man with social ambitions—quite a snob, if you'll believe me! He was a barrister in Dublin and spent most of his life trying to get grandees to have a drink with him. I wonder would he turn in his grave if he saw me now—living in two rooms behind a newspaper stand!"

Mary smiled.

"I suppose he *would* be surprised. But it seems a very nice life." She looked almost wistfully about the big, bright room.

"It's a nice life. And do you know, alannah, already I'm getting as daft as Pepe about these damn canaries!" She smiled up at the nearest cage. "Still I wish I were younger!"

"Why?"

"I'd like to have babies. A few babies would drive Pepe mad with delight."

"A few matadors?"

"Not on your life! A few nice, steady little tobacconists. But I'll never have the luck!"

"Why?"

"Well, between you and me and this bird-cage, I'm forty-two. And my hips are very narrow," she added with a little vain smile.

"They certainly are. You have a marvel of a figure."

"There's nothing wrong with your own. But you're not telling me what's up with you?"

"I don't think there's anything up with me. Do I look as if there were?"

"You do, somehow. God knows you look lovely, lovelier than ever, if that's possible. But—I don't know! Is it the heart?"

"Ah—you're in a romantic mood——"

"Is that chap at home causing any worry?"

"None at all."

O'Toole pulled another geranium leaf.

"Well, believe an old married woman—love is the life."

Mary looked up and her eyes were full of tears.

"I believe you," she said, and then she sprang to her feet.

"But, alannah!" O'Toole's arms were round her. "What's the matter? I never meant a thing! No, no. Don't run off crying! Please, oh please, alannah!"

They were in the passage.

280

"I'll come back another time. Let me go, now—there's an angel!"

She kissed O'Toole. "I'm delighted about you and Pepe," she said, and fled through the shop while husband and wife stared after her in affectionate distress.

She hurried down the street and into the Plaza San Geronimo, drying her eyes. She sat on a seat near the statue and gradually composed herself. Although it was dusk a few children played around her. There was a star or two in the dark blue sky behind the roof of San Geronimo, and when the baize door within the porch of the church swung open now and then she could see candles lighted for Benediction.

She had often sat here, or in Agatha's window just above, since that first afternoon when the beauty of façade and plane-trees had first caught her eye. She had brought various moods here, gaiety with O'Toole, or argumentative friendliness with Agatha, and sometimes before she had gone to Madrid, forlornness and perplexity. And always the place had given her again, whether or not she resisted it, something of the emotion and foreboding of that first day. But now, San Geronimo calmed her. She dried her eyes and looked about her without agitation. Then she began to smile at herself. What a scene-maker she was becoming! First a public row with Keogh in the café, and then with O'Toole a fit of weeps! "Ah, Juanito!" she said, "look how you've turned me into an idiot!"

"Hello!"

Agatha Conlan stood before her, mantilla and rosary beads in her hands.

"Hullo! Been praying?"

"Yes. I said one for you. When did you get back?"

"On Saturday. Didn't you get any of my postcards?"

"I got them. Thanks very much."

"Sit down. It wouldn't have killed you to write."

Agatha sat down.

"Heard about O'Toole?"

"Yes, I've just been with her."

"Absurd—at their age."

"I think it's grand."

Agatha smiled. Her profile looked noble in the dusk.

"I knew you'd say that. Anyway they're embarrassingly pleased with themselves."

"They're sweet—not a bit embarrassing."

"Come up and smoke?"

"Oh, let's sit here. I feel so tired."

Agatha looked at Mary sharply, said nothing for a moment.

"How was Madrid?"

"It was—I liked it."

"See anything of Castile?"

"From the train—and I was in Toledo one day. Castile is lovely."

"I'd like to see the Gredos again."

They fell into silence. Mary thought of the view across the Manzanares from Doña Cristina's apartment, thought of Juanito's shy, grave voice: "Never mind, Mila, another time."

When Agatha spoke again her voice was curiously nervous.

"If you liked Castile—you did, didn't you?"

"Oh yes—I liked it. Why?"

"Nothing. I just thought we might save up and go to Avila sometime. Mad notion—but I haven't had a holiday in years——"

Something shuddered in Mary.

"I won't be here," she said.

"Ah well, in that case——" Agatha's voice was normal and hard.

They were silent again awhile. It was quite dark now; the children played no longer round the statue.

"I thought you—liked Spain?"

"I must go home."

"I see."

"I haven't said anything yet. I'll speak to Doña Consuelo to-morrow."

"To-morrow?"

"Yes."

"You mean you're going at once?"

"In a week or two, if they can let me."

"That's—surprising."

"I suppose so. I'm—I'm awfully tired. I must go home."

"Well, you know your own business best."

An old woman came begging. Mary gave her a few coppers.

"Jealous of O'Toole's bliss, I suppose?" Conlan's voice was savage. "Want to catch up on her?"

Mary looked at her in surprise, but the dusk revealed nothing more than the noble, bitter profile; she looked back at the stars above San Geronimo.

"It'd be nice to be as happy as O'Toole," she said.

"But that's not why I'm going home."

"Why then?"

"I've told you. I'm tired. I'm tired of Spain."

"You're very fickle."

Mary said nothing to that. Far off in the Alameda a band was playing "The Blue Danube."

"I ought to be going back to Cabantes."

"Do you really mean that you're leaving Spain in a week or two?"

"If I can arrange it."

"They'll find you changed at home."

"In what way?"

"You've grown self-centred."

"Ah! Perhaps I have. This life is too lonely. I'll improve when I get away from it. It would be nice if we could go to the movies now."

Agatha laughed.

"It's been a funny summer," she said.

"How do you mean?"

"Well, O'Toole's affair. And then—your turning up."

"What's funny in that?"

"Nothing, really." The voice was crazily nervous again. "Do you remember the day at Allera?"

Mary nodded.

"I told you a lie that day. You asked me if I'd ever had a crush—on a matador, of all people!" She laughed. "And I said I'd never had a crush on a living creature. That would have been true up to the first day I saw you. It's not true any more." There was a long pause. "I wasn't going to say anything. I had just made up my mind, while you were in Madrid, to try being nice to a

human being for a change, that's all. I didn't write; I was
thinking about you too much to write. I thought it quite
funny that O'Toole's romance, and my absurd infatuation—began more or less together. But now that
you're going in a week——" she laughed again.

"Agatha—please!"

"Are you shocked? I like you the way a man would,
you see. I never can see you without—without wanting
to touch you. I could look at your face for ever. Every
time O'Toole calls you 'alannah' I want to murder her.
It's a sin to feel like that."

"Oh, everything's a sin!"

"I knew it was wrong; but lately I've been told
explicitly about it in confession. It's a very ancient and
terrible vice. Good God!" She laughed again softly,
almost tenderly.

"I'm sorry, Agatha. Oh, I'm sorry."

Mary stretched her hand out timidly, but the other did
not touch it.

"I shouldn't have said this at all. To-morrow, I'll go
half-mad when I remember. But the cool way you said
you're going in a week! Must you do that?"

"I must."

"I—I won't be able to bear it."

Mary watched the baize door swing and swing again
in the porch of San Geronimo and caught each time the
gleam of candles. People going in incessantly to pray, as
Agatha did so often, as she did, as Juanito too, perhaps.
Seeking strength against the perversions of their hearts
and escape from fantastic longings. Seeking mercy,
explanation and forgiveness because they are so vicious

as to love each other, seeking wearisome strength, in the midst of life, to forgo the essence of their own. Oh bitter, unforeseen exactions! What an astonishing need there was, as life explained itself, of this incessant in and out to altars, this perpetual placation and entreaty. Heart after heart was found to be in pain, or like poor John's, about to receive its charge. Oh, Lord have pity! Help us to have pity on each other, to make some sense sometime out of this tangle of our longings!

"I'm sorry. Oh, I'm sorry, Agatha!"

"Don't cry!"

Mary buried her face in her hands.

"I can't help it. I'm always crying lately. I'm going crazy!" She sobbed so that her shoulders shook. Agatha stretched out her hand and stroked the curly head.

"Don't cry," she said. "It'll all be over soon, whatever it is. You're young. It'll be all right. Don't cry."

But Mary was too tired to stop at once. Agatha withdrew her awkward hand. Crowds came out of San Geronimo where Benediction was over; the band in the distant Alameda swung from waltz to waltz; a cold breeze rustled the dead leaves about the statue.

Mary straightened up at last.

"I must get back to Cabantes," she said. "Oh Agatha, forgive me for behaving like this."

"Forget it. Forget the rot I talked."

"It wasn't rot."

They looked at each other and tried to smile. But they were weary. They stood up and walked in silence along the square. They stopped at the corner and Mary looked at her watch.

"I must run for my train," she said. "Don't you come any further."

"Good night then."

"Good night."

They looked at each other uneasily and parted. As Mary ran up the Calle Pelayo she caught a glimpse of Pepe behind the counter in his shirt-sleeves, gently gossiping with a customer. And she thought of the geraniums, the canaries and the matador's cape.

GOOD-BYE TO THE CAFÉ ALEMÁN

MARY's trunk stood open in the middle of her bedroom. It had been carried in from the box-room an hour ago, very well dusted and neatly lined with white paper. She had already arranged some books in the bottom of it. All the furniture in the room was laden with her clothes and personal possessions. She was leaving Spain the next morning.

Departure had been easy to arrange. The Areavagas were surprised and regretful, but Don Pablo had said, fixing her with his gentle, searching eyes, that she must of course do exactly as she desired. And Doña Consuelo had added very graciously that whereas of course she was far too young and beautiful to be a dueña, yet the children had grown so much attached to her and were so happy in her company that they had hoped she would stay among them at least a year. Mary apologised for the trouble which her change of plan was causing and was most kindly reassured. It was arranged then that she should leave Spain on October 15th. She would have been a little more than four months away. Twelve had been the minimum of her intention.

She had written to her father and to John, to announce her return. It was to be temporary, she wrote, to placate the one and warn the other. She was going to find another job, but not in Spain. She would explain things when she got home. Meantime no one was to worry.

She was sorry to be so restless and unsatisfactory, but she was perfectly well and would soon find another job, now that she was somewhat used to the world. Aunt Cissy's acceptance of the news, from Mary's father, had been querulous and half-hearted. John's replies—they came in flocks—were a terrifying mixture of delight and un-easiness. But she did not read them attentively—she did not dare to. In her further letters to him she stuck with brutal, weary courage to laconic statement of external facts, and to a promise of verbal explanation of her strangeness. She was far too tired to be either more or less subtle with him.

Now she was packing her trunk. The children, most sweetly and disarmingly distressed at her going, had laden her with presents and souvenirs. Each of them had entreated her to stay even a little longer—just until Christmas. Juanito would be here and they would give her a lovely time. Could she not possibly bear them a little longer? Why, why must she go? She made up desperate stories—about her father's health and her homesickness. They were not convinced. Estéban stuck to it that the whole thing was the sweetheart's doing—and was the man not right? Could anyone blame him? They would miss '*la guapa irlandesa*,' and the letter-bag would be a good deal lighter—but the young man at home was showing sound sense. No use in their grumbling! Don Pablo listened sometimes to this exposition of the matter, and Mary saw him smile at Estéban as if in agreement.

Pilár and Nieves were fretful, but they grew resigned. Milagros, however, after a first storm, was mulish in distress, and would not mention Miss Maria's going. She bought her an old, illustrated *Don Quixote* and marked her own favourite passages. She bought her a little matador doll. She learnt poem after poem from the Oxford Book in a kind of frenzy of desire to please. But every time the approaching departure was mentioned she turned her head away and bit her lip.

Mary would be glad to be in the train to-morrow, out of reach of all these dear and emotional people. This packing—ah, it was a weary business. How had she best pack the flamenco records—Nieves' present? Or Pilár's little baroque shrine, a reproduction of Our Lady of Allera? Turrón too, and a leather drinking bottle and some Talavera dishes and a lovely, flowery jug for wine? And all the presents and souvenirs she had collected, in her first pleasure in Spain, for John and the others at home? The books she had bought too; her bulky Spanish dictionary? Yes, she was going away more laden than she had come.

She sat at her writing-table now, near the open window, and sorted the contents of its drawer. It was a sweet, blowy afternoon, with a sky full of movement and with racing curls of foam on the grey water. There was animation on the pier as a boat had just come in with a catch of tunny fish. Mary tried not to think of how far she would be from that happy, familiar noise by to-morrow afternoon, and the afternoon after that and after that. Oh Heaven! What were all these papers? Letters from Aunt Cissy, letters from John, letters from Sheila, from Tom, from father, letters from John, letters from John. Here in its usual corner, in its leather frame, the little snapshot of John. She picked it up. John smiling, with his fox-terrier pup on his arm. She stared at the photograph in despair. What was she to do? What on earth was she to do about this honourable, decent, tender-hearted man? What a stranger he seemed now! Had she truly ever kissed him, ever rested in his arms? She let the photograph fall back into the drawer. No—in all her life she had only kissed Juanito. She had never rested against any other heart but his.

She opened the blotter on her table. In a pocket of this, by itself, away from every other personal possession she kept the postcard of the Holy Angels. She took it out now and looked at it, at the gay windswept figures, the frayed wings and crumbled trumpets. She did not yet know how she would bear it safely home. In her suitcase it would be hard to get at. She could not bury it safely in her trunk and so be parted from it for the four days of her journey. It might fall out of her handbag, or get bent or damaged. Already, she noticed, her perpetual handling had frayed it just a little.

She turned it over. '*Recuerdo de hoy*. Juanito.' Ah, but if I could forget? Cruel one, let me forget! Did he know that she was going to-morrow? Surely he must. His mother wrote him frequent letters full of family gossip, and would certainly have mentioned the imminent departure of the miss. Yes, assuredly he knew—and gave no sign. That was well. That was the best way. There was nothing he could do to prevent her going, and she was grateful to him now for making it easy by acceptance. But she thought of how once before, having danced with her on the Plaza San Martín, he had disappeared into a silence and neutrality that had seemed almost unendurable, and had emerged from it with complete audacity, without a doubt of her having understood, sweeter, dearer than she had remembered. He exacted an exaggerated faith, but he repaid it. He had said it was *not* good-bye, had said '*hasta luego*.' Ah, but it *was* good-bye! She had meant it so, and so it was. Much better that he was being proved wrong. Good-bye, Juanito. Thank Heaven that, whatever her future was to be, she would never see him again.

The door opened and she turned round to see Milagros on the threshold, looking timid and desolate.

"Come in, Mila," she said, and laying her postcard down, crossed the room towards the hesitating child. A gale blew about her. "Come in. Shut the door."

Milagros came in. She looked at the trunk and then at Mary.

"I—I don't want to see you packing, Miss Maria," she said in a wretched voice, "but I—I'd like to give you these, if you'll take them."

She laid on Mary's bed the collection of reproductions she had bought for herself with such gaiety in the Prado Museum.

Mary could say nothing. She stared in misery at the child. Milagros burst into tears then, and flung her arms round her.

"Oh, don't go! Don't go, I entreat you! It's been so happy since you came! Oh, stay! You're lovely to look at, and you're so kind and such fun! Oh, Miss Maria! We'll do anything for you if you'll stay! I beg of you! Oh, please!"

Mary held her and stroked her hair. It was grotesque, all the pain this journey must cost, here and at its other end. What madness had ever prompted her to come to Spain?

"Mila! Mila darling! I'd have had to go some time—you know that. And when you come to study in England—you are going to, aren't you?—well then, we'll meet again, and we'll have marvellous times! You know we will. This is only temporary, Mila. In a year or two we'll have great times together in London. I promise you. Hush, pet, don't cry!"

But Mila broke away, shaking her head, and with her handkerchief to her eyes. Pointing blindly again to the postcards she rushed from the room. Mary stood and looked at a few of them: Las Meniñas, La Maja Desnuda, The Day of Pentecost. She gathered up the bundle and crossed with them to her table. She looked for her other postcard there—her greatest earthly treasure. It was not where she had laid it down. It was not anywhere in the blotter or in the open drawer. She searched the chair, the floor, the open trunk, the balcony—and standing there in the gentle breeze remembered the draught that had swept the room as she crossed it to Milagros.

She stood dumbfounded. It was gone then, gone on the wind. Her one sweet treasure. All that she had of him or ever would have. She looked despairingly down on the wide stone terrace. There was nobody there and nothing. The flagstones and parapet were empty of it. So apparently was the pier. But where had it gone? The wind was surely not strong enough to carry it out to sea? She could search the terrace and pier—ah, but if she was asked what she looked for? No, it was gone. She could not tell her loss. Well, if it was ever found and puzzled over, there was nothing about it to—to incriminate him. It might be any boyish souvenir of his, blown randomly out of his house, where so many were stored. It was gone—the one thing she had intended to keep for all her life. Oh, God was hard on her—with perfect justice. Still her eyes searched the wide stretch of the pier. She would have one look when she went down—never mind what the world thought she was looking for. The postcard. Was even that too much for her to be allowed to keep?

The convent bell rang a quarter to four. She had promised Agatha she would be in the Alemán at half-past three. True indeed, she had grown self-centred! Agatha, poor Agatha. She must hurry. She must leave her packing till to-night. She would be glad to have it to do. It would make her tired.

She pulled on hat and coat and went downstairs. Before she ran to the station she searched for her postcard boldly on the empty terrace and among the coiled ropes and fish-baskets on the pier. She looked down at the choppy water too. The fishermen, lounging now, the tunny fish disposed of, smiled and asked her what she searched. A little picture, she told them with audacity, but trying also to seem indifferent. They helped her to look, but smiled at her hoping to find such a thing on a windy open pier. Obviously it was lost. She ran towards the station to keep some part of her appointment with Agatha.

She found the latter at their usual table, reading a newspaper.

"I thought you'd forgotten," she said without emotion. Mary apologised.

The place was very quiet. It was not a day when many of the misses were free, and in any case just at present, since the quarrelling over O'Toole's marriage, Keogh and her friends were patronising the Pasteleria Ruiz, in imitation of the English colony.

"Every two years or so the misses break away from the Alemán," Agatha said. "But they always come back. I like it best when it's out of fashion, like this."

Mary was silent. She felt lifeless. She brooded on the loss of her postcard, trying to rationalise all the confused miseries of departure into the pain caused by that small, sentimental accident. But Agatha was also in the forefront of her mind. She felt discomfort and guilt about her, and a deep sense of regret at this parting. She felt that there were certain things which it was obligatory for her to say, yet did not know how to say them. It was about a fortnight now since their conversation in the square of San Geronimo, and though they had met at least four times since then neither had referred to Agatha's confession of that night. But curiously enough, although she had, as she had expected, suffered very deep misery in the day or two which followed that conversation, her relationship with Mary had not suffered or been made painful. Instead, a certain relaxation, even an affectionate, unspoken peace had entered it. For Mary had not been frightened or repulsed. Perhaps Juanito was right in calling her a pagan and her face Aphrodite's; certainly, now that feeling consumed her for him, her understanding of feeling in others, as, for instance, in O'Toole and Pepe, was immediate and natural. So, though no word more of emotion was said between them, her voice and manner with Agatha had automatically become easier and more sisterly, not so much because Agatha fantastically and perversely loved *her* but because, like her, she was fantastically and perversely in love. Agatha felt this unuttered sympathy, and it made her reaction from her own confession less savage, easier to bear. It also made her sense of loss much deeper, and this afternoon's meeting of farewell a pain almost insupportable.

"You're really going to-morrow?"

"Yes. I'm really going."

Agatha had never asked her why she had taken this decision, or what was the cause of her tears when they talked in the Plaza San Geronimo. She knew that Mary was not going home to marry, but merely to escape from Spain. Something had happened in these four months which she could not support. That was all that Agatha knew and she could understand it. She asked no teasing questions.

"Have you said good-bye to Pepe and O'Toole?"

"Yes. I was in there last evening. O'Toole says she'll see me at the train to-morrow."

"She's dejected over your going."

"You and she—you've been so good to me, both of you."

"Ah—please!"

"Agatha—I've thought very much about what you said that night—about being fond of me."

"Well—did it disgust you?"

"Please don't say that. You take one kind of im-

296

possible fancy, I take another." There was a pause. Agatha sipped some tea carefully. Mary looked at the strained, fanatic's profile and felt great affection for this woman she was probably talking to for the last time.

"I hate to have made you unhappy," she said. "But it'll pass soon—won't it?"

"I hope not."

"But——"

"It can't be such a ghastly crime to—to think about you. She turned and smiled at Mary and said quite pleadingly: "Have you got a photograph—a snapshot?"

"I—I'm afraid not."

"Oh, but at home you must have. Will you send me one?"

"If you'd really like——"

"Oh, thank you. Don't forget."

Mary looked about the ladies' alcove, and out past the Englishmen's tables at the frostily decorated mirrors.

"I feel as if I'd known this place a long time," she said.

"Don't ever come back," said Conlan. "Don't ever come looking for me in the Alemán again."

"Why?"

"I'm going to settle into old age now."

"What of that?"

"Well, Keogh always says that I'll be the sort of muttering hag children throw stones at!"

Mary reached for Agatha's hand, which was not given to her.

"And suppose you are, could I throw stones?"

"No. But don't come back. If you're going now, stay away. Truly, I beg you. You've—upset me very much. I'll pull myself together somehow when you're gone, and become the sort of bitter pill I am. Only, stay away."

"Will you never leave Spain?"

"Never. I can always get work. Although people don't like me, they know I teach English better than the others."

"Will you ever write?"

"I don't think so. I'll write to thank you for the snapshot."

"Why have you—liked me so much?"

"Ah!" Agatha smiled slowly, and looked out across the empty, quiet café. "I'll never forget my first sight of you. You were sitting where you're sitting now —in a crowd of misses. And you had no hat on, any more than you have now. I had never known anything about attraction to other people or about the sensation of pleasure human beauty can give. If you had turned out to be a conceited mean little bore of a girl—you would have had to be tolerated—because of that first second. In gratitude. But—you were nice as well. So I fell into what my confessor calls the sin of Sodom."

"They have queer names for things," said Mary.

"They know their business. And hard cases make bad laws."

"Will you come in here much? I'll be trying to imagine your life."

"I come in most days, as you know. But you

have to forget Spain—not remember."

"That's true."

Mary looked at her watch.

"Are you in a hurry?"

"I'm afraid I'm in a bit of one." Mary spoke guiltily now. She was in fact in no hurry at all, but she had an odd desire to keep some part of this last evening to herself. There was no knowing what she might want it for, what mood she might be in. But she was actually in no hurry, and knew it. There were no more good-byes to say, outside of the Casa Pilár; she had the whole night in which to pack. Juanito was, as she had hoped, ignoring her departure. It was now a quarter-past five, and she had nothing to do until dinner at half-past nine but bear her heavy heart. Nothing on earth to do. No one to say good-bye to. Yet she could not risk she knew not what by consenting to waste those empty, hopeless hours with Agatha, glad as she would have been in a way of her companionship. She must be free—at the disposal of one chance in ten millions. He had said 'Hasta luego.' Oh, absurd, absurd.

"I had hoped you'd have a last cigarette at my window."

"I'm sorry, Agatha. I can't. Give my love to San Geronimo."

Agatha shrugged.

"I'm no good at that kind of thing," she said. They fell into silence again. Mary reflected that her train left at nine in the morning. She had therefore something less than sixteen hours still to spend in Altorno.

A very little time, a dull, dark stretch of night in which nothing could happen. Then she would be gone—and there would be nothing but a few half-clear memories, a sense of pain, and her confession—of the death and birth of love—to John. Nothing—not even her souvenir postcard. What a regrettable episode—from June to October. Eventful and fruitless—except in suffering.

"You'll have bullfights still," she said to Agatha.

"Yes. The train goes at nine?"

"Yes."

"I'll be there—if I may. To dry O'Toole's tears." Mary smiled.

"Pepe will want to do that," she said.

A Spanish lady who had been drinking chocolate got up and went out. The café was very quiet. Mary felt an urgent desire to leave it—to be on the streets or in the Casa Pilár, in case, in case—— But she was reluctant too to leave Agatha, and in general dreaded going out from this place for the last time. Another farewell disposed of, another bit of Spain chopped off. She laid the money for her chocolate on the table, but still sat, weary, heavy-hearted. There was nothing more she could say to Agatha—except good-bye, and that was now held over until to-morrow. She must get up and go back to Cabantes. He might have telephoned on a pretext. He might even have written by some device—ah no, he would never do that. There was nothing. It was over. She would be gone to-morrow. She must go and finish her packing.

The café door opened and shut. There was a gentle step on the tiles. Mary looked up. It was he, Juanito.

He stood by the little marble table where the engineers used to sit. He smiled at her, a gentle, questioning smile.

Mary rose. Agatha was looking from him to her.

"At the station to-morrow, Agatha," Mary said.

Then she went through the archway to Juanito.

THE GOOD BASQUE COUNTRY

Juanito opened the café door and they went out together and along the narrow street into the Alameda. They hurried through the dusk into a square where the black sports car was parked. They drove in it away from Altorno, at a great speed, out on to the road towards France. It was dark now, but the moon was up and brilliant. Mary caught sight of the sea here and there, and of little silver bays and fishing villages, as they zigzagged eastward. Soon the car climbed, took hairpin bends, passed through long woods, and by roaring waterfalls.

"This is my own country," said Juanito. "This is the good Basque country of my people."

"You seem to know it well."

"I know it well."

"I lost my postcard to-day. My postcard of the Holy Angels."

"I'll get you another. How did you lose it?"

"It blew out of my window."

He laughed.

"I was in despair, Juanito."

He drove more slowly over the stony track. Mary studied his gentle face.

"You're good at finding people," she said. "This is the third time."

"If you intend to find anyone in a given area, and have

302

an ounce of brain, you'll find her," he said, proudly. "Didn't you know I'd be looking for you to-day?"

"Juanito—how could I know?"

He pulled up. The track they had climbed ended here in an open, verdant shelf of a mountain range, which rose to their left in a dark cloud of forest. They got out of the car and stood looking down at what they had left behind them. Northward and far away, a thin silver line, lay the sea, and between it and them the land ascended richly, in pasture, orchard and woodland, all shadowy now, blue, grey and black under the moon. A few lights flickered from farmsteads; away to the north-west lay Altorno's chains of urban light, and furnace flares. There was no sound, not even the movement of a bird; in the hollow of the wide pastureland about them a few cows lay asleep; the air was full of the smell of pine and eucalyptus.

"It's quiet here," said Mary.

"I wish it were daylight. I used to come on picnics to this field when I was a kid. I wish the sun were out. I wish it were early morning."

"So do I."

Since their first words spoken in the car half an hour before neither had been able to keep a steady voice and each had forborne from touching the other, because of a trembling that made light contact impossible awhile. Now they found courage to look at each other with deliberation, and when Juanito spoke again, the febrile quiver was not in his voice.

"You are going to Ireland to-morrow?"

"Yes."

"I have much to say to you. Will you listen?"

She nodded.

"Come this way. There's a beech-tree I remember along this side."

He pulled rugs out of the car and they went upward along the slope towards the towering cloudy forest, until at its very edge they found the tree he remembered. He looked about in contentment.

"Yes," he said. "It doesn't change. Up here, playing 'torero,' eating strawberries, life was perfect."

He flung the rugs under the tree, but Mary did not sit down. She could bear her joy no longer.

"I love you! Juanito, I love you!"

She put her arms round him and pulled his head down for her kiss.

They embraced with rapture, with serious and fatal strength, with an adult acceptance and resignation that was both violent and very grave. If there was little hope in their kiss and no hint of peace, there was from both all that they possessed of vitality and courage. Moreover, there was love's pure, immense and central delight, which while it did not dim in either brain awareness of past and future, of guilt, and responsibility, desolation and shoddy embarrassment, of the meanness of their own situation and of the world which made it mean, yet held. There was everything else to be thought of before and after, there were the rights and wrongs of everyone else, there was to-morrow's parting, there were cowardice, loneliness and forgetfulness to reckon up, and life's million other chances, changes, cruelties and desires—but for this moment there was also, aware of all else and yet undaunted, this—their mouths and hearts, together, the foolish, young, incredible declaration of their two straining, beating bodies that they, let the world's heaped-up experience be what it might, belonged to each other, and, together or apart, would be lovers for ever.

Illusion! Yet woe to the sunless heart that has never been its dupe. It is at once life's falsest promise and most true fulfilment, as silly as it is deific, as irresistible as fatal to the courageous. Years and experience tear it harshly or amusedly to bits; knowledge, asceticism and sensuality agree in mocking it; convention shakes its head, theology frowns and science analyses the most extravagant attraction. But those who have endured the mighty lie of romantic passion remember usually, in spite of themselves, and would not have escaped it.

Mary took a decision while she kissed Juanito, and when he moved, and murmured uneasily into her hair, "We must talk," she answered, "No!"

He tilted her head back gently then and searched her face.

"Dear love—we must."

"No, no. We can talk afterwards—to-night or when we can. I'm going away to-morrow, Juanito, and I want you now. It isn't much to ask, although"—she laughed a little, moving away from him. "It's really a miracle."

"I—I don't know what you mean," he said unsteadily.

She dropped on her knees on the rug, and held her arms to him.

"Come here," she said.

He went on his knees beside her, but hesitatingly.

"Mary," he began, but she put her hand on his mouth.

"No, no. Listen. It's been fantastic, my time in Spain.

It's been a mad, impossible thing dropped into my ordinary life. To-morrow it will be over, and although it has changed all my plans, life will have to be ordinary again, in some way that I know nothing about yet. So, before it's over—finish it for me, Juanito. I can't see how I can ever care for anyone again—I love you so much. I suppose I will—when I'm old and ugly. But I want you to have me first—just for this one time, up here where you used to play when you were a little boy. Nothing else will content me, however long I live—if you refuse me this."

He was staring at her. His eyes shone, sweet and gold.

"But—there are things I must say——"

"No. All I want is now. I give you my word of honour I'll never trouble you again. I promise you that and I'll keep my promise."

"That's a dreadful thing to say."

"I don't think so. That day at the Hermitage we were afraid—and we said that we loved each other too much—that it would be hell. I see now it'll be hell anyhow, and that if it is, I'm ready for it. I swear it won't be hell for you. I'll see to that."

He still knelt motionless and without touching her. She had moved a little from him, and leant against the tree-trunk.

"Do you know that you're seducing me?" he asked her.

She leant forward, and pulled him down so that he lay with his head in her lap. "I can't go away until—until I've been your lover."

He turned in her lap and took her in his arms, drew her down until they lay together, face to face. Holding her

306

thus, very close to his breast, he spoke with urgent clarity, in the slow Spanish she always understood.

"I'm only twenty-five," he said, "and only two years married. I have always sneered at the vulgarity of infidelity. I have never given a snap for any other woman but Luisa. Now at the first test I am undone. Since my first sight of you I have lived in bitter unfaithfulness and coldness. You seem so terrifyingly beautiful, you're so artless and innocent and heavenly that I have fooled myself that you are the sort of myth that might ruin any man, however true, however virtuous! But is that so? Are you a fatal exception that makes splinters of everything normal? Or am I just vulgarly infatuated, and is this a showing-up? Are you my true love—or an illusion?"

She kissed him, very gently.

"I'm an illusion. So are you. But there's nothing to be afraid of in that."

"You're very young. Much younger than me. You know nothing about love."

"Only what it feels like."

"You don't know that."

"Oh, I know what you're thinking—but I'm not afraid. I know you'll hurt me, and that what I'm asking for will be painful and unhappy for me now. I know the risk too. I'm not a fool at all, Juanito. I've grown up very fast since meeting you. But if I think all that unimportant, so that no one else can ever have from me what I want you to have—oh, dear love!"

"Ah, darling! Darling!"

They clung together trembling. Juanito kissed her eyes and ears and throat and though Mary burned to kiss

him too, intuition told her to lie still awhile, to let him
love her. She lay under his hands and marvelled at her
peace. She thought of school and home, of John, of
God's law and of sin, and did not let herself discard such
thoughts. They existed, as real and true as ever, with all
their traditional claims on her—but this one claim was
his, and she would answer it, taking the consequences.
And as to John, she reflected with casuistic pity that what
she was about to do now would make things easier for
him. A moony story about being in love with a Spaniard
would render him prolongedly unhappy and half-
hopeful—but this other news, revolting him, would turn
his heart away from her, and cure it.

"Dear love, I love you," she whispered to Juanito's
whispers.

"I'm going to take you," he said. "I'm going to make
you my lover, but not, believe me, on your silly terms."
He smiled at her.

"Yes, on my terms."

"No, sweet. Love is not so easy as that. But we won't
talk now—we're lovers now."

He began to undress her, gently and kindly.

"Aphrodite!" he said, when she gleamed white and
shivered in the moonlight. "Ah, you're too beautiful!
You'll blind me! Mary, I love you, I love you!"

He took her quickly and bravely. The pain made her
cry out and writhe in shock, but he held her hard against
him and in great love compelled her to endure it. He felt
the sweat of pain break over all the silk of her body. He
looked at her face, flung back against the moss, saw her
set teeth and quivering nostrils, beating eyelids, flowing,

flowing tears. The curls were clammy on her forehead now, as on that day when she came into Luisa's drawing-room from the bullfight. She was no longer Aphrodite, but a broken, tortured Christian, a wounded Saint Sebastian. He held her still and murmured wild Spanish words of love. His heart hurt him as if it might in fact break. How grotesquely we are made, he thought, how terrible and insane are our delights and urgencies. I love her, love her, and yet I tear and break her for my pleasure, because I must, because I love her, because she loves me. Oh love, forgive me! Oh, forgive me, love!

She opened her eyes, and smiled a little at him.

"It's all right now," she said. "Oh, it's better now."

"No," he said, "you must have patience. Love takes a lot of learning."

She drew his head down to hers.

"Not such a terrible lot—honestly. I love you, I love you."

He kissed her then and let his own storm ride him, let her carry him, in her innocence and pain, along his journey of passion. Their eyes were open for each other as they went his road, and to each the near, white face of the other seemed now both deeply known and very strange. They searched their mutual experience while it stirred them; they were aware and clear-eyed, in spirit utterly each other's now, though in bodily sensation alone; they were in pain and at peace, triumphant, shaken and apprehensive; neither knew intellectually what the terrible storm was saying to the other—but grotesquely and harshly made one in the flesh by an urgency that wounded and overwhelmed, they were emotionally welded, not by their errant senses which might or might not play in unison, but by a brilliant light of sympathy which seemed both to arise from sensuality and to descend from elsewhere to assist and glorify it—so that Juanito, as his rapture mounted, shattered him and fell, leaving him sobbing on the girl's white breast, felt through all the liberating gust of it the hot burning of her pain, and Mary, more than forgetful of that pain, underwent in her spirit, through sheer love and without physical response, the essential rapture that she gave. So they were paradoxically together in that moment, as lovers, however well attuned, can seldom be. Together because, by great luck, they really loved each other from young and troubled hearts.

They came to rest. They were insanely happy. They clung and kissed. Juanito dried Mary's tears and drew the rugs about her. My shivering bird, my little wounded girl, oh, lovely goddess, oh my love, my rose! And Mary took his tender, stroking hands and kissed them. Dear love, dear love. Ah, Juanito, thank you. He laughed at that, and gathered her up and held her, white and languid, in the moonlight until she shivered, and he covered her again. In absolute surrender they rested and apologised and asked each other's blessing. They were content and oblivious to a depth which confounded their powers of expression, yet they found a million tendernesses now and flung them on each other in delirium.

"It's a dream; it's impossible—your beauty!"

But she must have his beauty too. They huddled together, two lost and white-limbed pagans, under their rug. They half-slept, soothed and lulled each other, kissing as they dreamt; they stroked each other's faces, searched and searched with wistful gaiety each into the other's tragically happy eyes. Until the storm of feeling broke and took them again. Juanito's tenderness was in this hour quite faultless, but he knew how to be a lover, and Mary's courage understood and followed him. Pain grew less as more and more her senses moved towards knowledge, and following her lover, she began to understand what love indeed might be. Then only did she let herself hear for a second to-morrow's tolling bell, and realise how true it is that 'love is not as easy as that' and 'takes a lot of learning.' She would not be here to learn—from her only master.

She groaned unwittingly.

"My heart, what is it? Are you hating me now?"

"I'm thinking of to-morrow."

"What of to-morrow?"

"Juanito! I'm going home to-morrow."

"Yes. You're going to Ireland—though I very much doubt——" he laughed at her, "if you'll be fit to travel!"

"Ah, sweet!"

"To-morrow is bad—but it isn't troubling me. This is for life. We will be lovers always."

"I'll be your lover always . . ."

"No fantasy. We have burnt our boats. So long as you live."

"Don't cheat, my darling. The terms were this one time."

"I didn't take them. If you go to Ireland to-morrow, I am not afraid. I trust you to do nothing savage. You will answer my letters, you will meet me again. I'm not afraid, any more than I was when they wrote and told me you were leaving."

"I thought you didn't care, that you wouldn't trouble to see me again."

"You see. You know nothing yet about love. You have a girl's extraordinary notions."

"You expect me to believe in miracles."

"No. Just in love. A mad thing to believe in too—but look how it can be."

Mary surrendered again. He was a dreamer. He believed even now when they stood at the brink of their really final parting, that his wilful, charming power of getting his own way still held. He believed that, married in Madrid, he might still have for lover a girl disappeared into Ireland. She laughed as she let him have the last word. She had got her way and would stick to her terms. No more groans to frighten him. Let him dream. She had given him all she had, the first and best of herself, and had taken the pain of love from him, from whom alone she wanted it. She had been his lover. She was content.

At last it was the last embrace, more lovely in its peace and weariness than the first.

"Good night, dear love. Good-bye."

"It is not good-bye. I will never say that to you."

This fairy-tale reassured her, in spite of her clear sense of realities. She took its comfort to help her to keep gay for this last half-hour with him. They dressed with reluctant languor, and gathered up the rugs. They looked about them at the sweet, moonlit field, then gently sought each other's eyes in gratitude.

Juanito lifted Mary in his arms and, walking as if asleep, went down the slope with her.

"I have half-killed you," he murmured, "I have hurt you horribly. And yet you seem to like me still, you seem quite happy."

"Yes, you hurt me terribly," she mused. "I feel half-dead. Oh, my love, I'm perfectly happy!"

As he drove, slowly and carelessly down the track, and through the long roads and round hairpin bends, she leant against his heart, too tired and peaceful to remember to-morrow or yesterday, or even with any vividness all the great happenings of the last hours. He murmured sleepily, often forgetting his words, "Come, live with me and be my love, and we will all the pleasures prove . . ."

As they approached Altorno she straightened up and began to remember and to feel to-morrow's long shadow. They drove through the Plaza San Martín, where crowds were dancing. They halted a minute under the trees to watch.

"I'd like to dance," said Mary.

He smiled at her with the most brotherly tenderness. "Oh, but we'll dance together soon."

She closed her eyes as he drove on.

"If you're really leaving to-morrow," he said, "there are things I have to say to you. All those things you would not let me say on the mountain. I shall arrange to talk with you to-night—or to-morrow."

"My train leaves at nine in the morning."

"Never mind. I shall talk with you. I shall get all those things said which you forbade me to say."

He gave her his gentle, boyish smile.

"Pull up here, Juanito. I must get a train."

But he drove past the station and all the way out to Cabantes, pulling up at the side-gate of his father's house exactly at half-past nine. As they walked dreamily through it, hearing its familiar bell, both still clung to the fantastic comfort of Juanito's notion that they had not now in earnest said good-bye. But as they looked towards the usually quiet-faced house, it took their attention from themselves. The hall door stood open, as usual, but the lights within it seemed more brilliant than was customary, and there were lights in many windows. The Casa Pilár wore, they both thought, an aspect of panic and excitement.

ANGUISH OF THE BREAST

DON PABLO sat and smoked on the stone bench of the terrace. He watched the fishermen fight with the market woman about the tunny fish and wondered how often he had watched them do so, how often again he might hope to. He had not felt well in these recent weeks, and knew that he was smoking considerably too much.

The afternoon had a vigorous air that pleased him. He liked the light movement of clouds in the clear sky and the crisp white curls that ran and vanished and ran again along the tops of the waves. The wind was comforting to his oppressed forehead. He considered whether he should one of these days find some gentle way of warning Consuelo—and Juanito—of the condition of his heart. Perhaps it was unnecessary. Perhaps when to-morrow was over, when she was gone with her strange, girlish trouble, whatever it was, when their responsibility had ceased and her enchanting face was no longer near to arouse idiotic, senile tenderness—perhaps then this sense of physical panic would be alleviated. If he could bring himself to stop smoking, and perhaps to lie still in bed for a week or more on any silly pretext—well, when she was gone he would be willing enough to do the latter. There would be no glimpses or chance meetings to look for then, and he would pull himself out of his folly by a long and honest meditation on his weakness of character, and the duties of his state and age. He would do that. And if thereafter his heart continued to alarm him and his fatigue and fear of excitement did not lessen, he might tell something of his condition to Consuelo. But he doubted whether there was any need to grieve and fret her with such news. His affairs were in order, and death when it came to him would strike neatly and quickly. An awful passage of pain—he remembered with a too clear accuracy the first attack in Madrid, and broke into a weak, uneasy sweat now, contemplating its return—and he would be gone. That shock would surely be easier for Consuelo than months, perhaps years, of fearing it for him? Better say nothing. Let her worry mildly, as she did now, about his growing weariness, not deeply and perpetually, as she would if she knew the truth. Juanito too—ah, the dear, beloved son! He would have liked to have seen him become 'one of Spain's great men.' But he left him happy at least, and fit and ready for that difficult and dangerous ambition. Poor Spain, her griefs were many and many more awaited her, but strength and individuality throbbed in her still, and she too was fit, if not ready, for difficulty and danger. He had wasted his life and left nothing behind him to his dear country save one son, a better and greater man than he, and three daughters who were not unlikely, in their different ways— he smiled—to add to life some little sum of happiness or good or decoration. Small gifts, his and theirs—but how small and painful each human span! How immense the view and tiny the spectator. Tiny, but greedy and egotistical much beyond his small capacity. He, for instance, how he had been for ever deflected from courage, from effort, from pity, from the service of Spain

and life, by amorousness and cowardice and final dislike
of everything but the languid life of the mind, and the
refuge of dreams. Well, dreams would be over soon, and
so would the pleasure his outward eye could take in
Consuelo's wifely comeliness, in his growing daughters,
in this sweet, undramatic view of sea and fishermen, in
Juanito's virile charm and goodness, in her so-soon-to-
be-departed face. Life was over. Life that had been so
lovely once, so disappointing later, and afterwards kindly
enough, as life goes. And into the end of it she had
broken to dazzle and shake him too much, to turn him
back in trouble to the poets, perhaps in all innocence
somewhat to hurry him to the end. Now she was to
vanish again, to leave him to die in peace in his own scene
as he had always known it. But she went away in trouble,
thinner and more grave of face than when he first beheld
her and with blue shadows always stressing now the blue
of her eyes. What was her trouble? What could a
stranger do, a dying man, to heal it? Spain had laid it on
her—he was sure of that. Estéban might joke as he
pleased, and she herself might weave uncertain fables, but
she was not hurrying back in homesick eagerness to her
eager lover. She was dragging herself home in pain,
because she was too much hurt to stay. It must be love,
of course. Love for whom? He smiled again at the
senile, angry excitement in his veins. Steady, steady! All
men with eyes must somewhat love her. When you are
dead some man will have immortal raptures of her. For
Heaven's sake don't agitate yourself. You are unfit now
for the smallest agitation. Love for whom? Someone
who picked her up in Madrid? But he had thought he saw

marks of dreamy sorrow on her before she went there—
indeed it was partly for that reason, thinking the trip
might help her, that he had urged Milagros to take her
beloved dueña to the capital. And had endured himself
the dullness of an absence now to be made permanent.
Still, he might have been wrong in that, because assuredly
since her return from Madrid her sadness had been much
more marked, indeed very nearly shameless. And within
a very few days of that return came her panicky request to
be allowed to return to Ireland. Who could it be? What
had he done to her? But steady, steady! That virginity
could not be lightly taken. She had in herself too pure a
strength for that, and the man who sought it would have
to be a savage not to see the consequence of such
bestowal. Some smiling Juan Tenorio of Altorno? Some
cad Manolo of Madrid? There was that curious trip to
Toledo. Like Pippa she had had one day, but she made
no songs of it. It was her own and no one was to know
of it. She had gone to Toledo—that seemed pretty sure—
but she had not seen it. He would swear to that. But must
he agitate himself like this? The girl's day off was her
affair, and even if someone had hurt her during or after it,
it was almost certain that he had done her no serious
wrong, or anything that she herself had not willed and
chosen. But why should so impossible a love as hers be
won without her having the prize and joy of reciprocity?
Why, why was she unhappy? No man that she could look
at in love, or at all, could surely deny her? Why, he had
even seen Juanito's eyes upon her in vast dreaminess
once, had even wondered—but that had been absurd.
The two had met perhaps three times since then. There

was certainly nothing in that notion. Had she met any of
the English in Altorno? But again he smiled. She was
hispanophile, and here in this country which had so
obviously taken some of her heart, the rest, if given at all,
would be most probably given to a Spaniard. Why, in
her emotional surrender to Spain, she even liked the bullfight. Ah, that old problem of barbaric beauty, indefensible, inexcusable art! Curious that the gentle child
had taken to it so hard and truly! She had said the other
day, in quite simple sadness, that she hated going away
from the bullfights. She hates going away from everything here, he thought, and, oh God, we hate her to go!
If we could keep her, or even send her home in happiness!
What could be done? What was the matter? He thought
of her packing in her room above him—Milagros had
said she was there. Thought of her and looked up
towards her balcony.

As he looked something fluttered from her window, a
piece of paper, a card. It circled downward slowly and
landed on the flagstones near him. He walked to it and
picked it up.

"Curious! The Holy Angels! I didn't know there were
postcards of it. Did she see the Ermita then? Who could
have told her of it?"

He turned the card idly in his hands, remembering the
glorious stone angels. He saw the inscription on the back,
in his son's beloved, unmistakable writing. '*Recuerdo
de hoy.* Juanito.' 'Souvenir of to-day.' He put the card
in the inside pocket of his coat, and slowly, leaning on his
stick, walked along the terrace and out of his garden
through the little gate with the clanging bell.

He went slowly down the sea-front towards the station until he came to the Café del Rio, where he had spent so many hours of his life in meditation or in friendly, jibing talk. The terrace was almost empty. He went to his usual table; the waiter brought him his usual manzanilla. He tried to sip it but replaced the glass quickly in the saucer, shocked by the drunken shaking of his hand.

He must take this thing slowly. He must keep hold of his outward, tranquil self, or he would never master, never survive the storm that was about to rise within when he understood, when he got things clear. Meanwhile, this circumstantial fluke, this fantastic postcard—there were a million possible explanations. Presently he would think of some of them. If he were not so ill just now, so foolishly tired. Those two, those two! How fatal, how inevitable, how natural! If it were true—but what a lengthy 'if'! Juanito, a very young married man in love with his beautiful wife; Juanito, so continent of nature, so temperate and honourable; Juanito, truthful, intelligent, ambitious, contemptuous always of his own personal wants and temptations and with his eyes fixed on the general human cause! And she, good, simple, without wile or coquetry, almost androgenous in her friendly detachment, she a stranger pledged to marry a man at home—but beautiful. Beautiful, my God, as few of Thy creatures can ever have been! Beautiful beyond endurance. Love then was naturally at its natural devil's tricks! These two whom he loved were the victims now. These two, his darlings. Victims without any hope at all —since, love as they might, their peace lay for each at last in his own breast, in his own nature, and in their natures, framed of a million accidents of teaching, nationality and intention, this love could find no enduring refuge. So they were doomed. Ah God! How natural, how obvious! Had he not seen on that night of their meeting how the untouched accident of beauty deposed and tarnished the lovely flower of culture? Why not then his quick-eyed son, in whom no virtue quenched objectivity. Juanito—whom else should she love, this creature from the songs of the Pléiade? Whom else but this intelligent, quick, pure boy, his son? His son! Not for him then, but for the son of his desire. Ah, his prophetic soul! She would be his since Juanito, so much loved and understood of him, was not only his flesh but spiritually him enhanced, corrected.

She would be his? What madness was he talking? There was nothing here in this discovery—if discovery it was!—but commonplace, juvenile grief. They had been lured by each other, had gone picnicking to the Holy Angels—he remembered how often he told Juanito to go and see that low-relief, and how he had said, 'Some day, some day—when I'm in angelic mood!' —Well, the mood had come. Now she was going home, in love with the impossible, and with blue shadows under her eyes. But she was twenty-three and he was twenty-five, and life was long. This was a juvenile passage of sorrow, without help in it—but the help of the years would come. They must face that dull assurance. There was no other. Both had duties and high morality; Juanito was completely committed to wife and child. Passion must accept the categorical denial.

Passion? He searched memory, searched his own recent memories of passion which her beauty had awakened. Categorical denial? Ah God! How glib the old were. And how especially glib was he! Did he grudge her to Juanito? And Juanito to her? Were his son free, could he have borne to see him go this glorious way? And could he have endured to give her, who had unwittingly taken so much from him, also his son, his dearest treasure? Was he jealous and going crazy? Was he inventing the whole thing? How could it be as he was madly thinking? How and where could they have been alone or learnt to know each other? Had the wretched card blown out of her window at all, or was that a trick his memory played him now? Had it not come from the window of Juanito's own room below, where so many of his treasures were lying about? Was that it? Was that the silly truth, and all this other the senile inventions of a dying man, a man half-crazed with fear of to-morrow's loss?

Yes. That was it. He was ill and much agitated, afraid of death and pain, afraid of life and over-indulgent of sick fantasies. This was one of them. Ah! how he trembled still. This threat in his breast—all his folly came from that. Sheer physical uneasiness, and over-smoking. He wiped his cold, wet forehead, lighted another cigarette somewhat fumblingly, and tried again to lift his wine-glass. This time, pleased with triumph, he got it to his lips. As he sipped he stared out at the quiet parade which led to the station. She went past running, her hat in her hand, her curls lifted on the wind. She did not see him. He smiled, watching her vanish into the station. No wonder, he thought, a sentimentalist goes mad and makes up crazy tragedies. She is lovely enough to explain the silliest notions.

He put down his glass. He thought he felt a little better. At least he had covered his immediate agitation, and had postponed examination of a terrible thing. A piteous thing. An improbability. Ah God in mercy, an improbability!

The man at the next table—he had not noticed that anyone had come to it—spoke to him. It was Don Jorge, the Andalucian priest whom he had dismissed from the post of music-master to his daughters.

"Forgive me, Don Pablo, I know your opinion of me— you expressed it somewhat vigorously in our last telephone conversation!" The priest smiled suavely. "But nevertheless I regret to see you look so ill. To see your hand shake so!"

The implication in the voice was half-sympathetic, half-jocose suggestion from one elderly man to another that he knew the kind of living that brings on such symptoms. Don Pablo looked at him in cold amazement, but made no answer. The Andalucian went serenely forward with his remarks.

"I see you still have your beautiful and—very virtuous-minded miss! She has just run past, most gracefully. Did you see her?"

There was no reply from Don Pablo, who was trying to gather energy to stand up and go home, but who felt most perilously weary.

"The Irish character is curious," the priest mused aloud. "They are reputed to be an open, talkative,

charming race. Charming—well yes! But open? They
have in fact great guile. Great guile. But I believe all
women have."

Don Pablo lifted his glass again. Perhaps the wine
would help him gather force to leave the café.

"Take your miss now. She reported me—perhaps
rightly—for light jokes, or what you will. That, I take it,
impressed you and Doña Consuelo and inspired confidence, as her great beauty might not have done. A
shrewd move. Not, of course, that there is any great
harm nowadays in a young lady dancing at night in the
Plaza San Martín! Why should she not?"

The priest paused and considered the closed white
mask of this proud man who had insulted him. He
remembered too the haughty prudery of the ridiculous
young miss. Yes, he would take his vengeance on them
both—such as it was—and then sleep easy, dismissing
them from his mind. He cleared his throat.

"What surprises me, however, is that your delightful
son, Juanito, should be so indiscreet as to dance with her
there."

There was no movement whatever in Don Pablo's
weary face. After a few seconds of silence, taking hold of
the iron table, he got to his feet, and leaning on his stick,
set off towards the pier and his own house.

He went indoors and to his library. He was in real fear
now of the threatening pain in his breast. Excitement and
panic were raging in his head. He must think. Think and
sit still. Work it out. What had happened to Juanito and
—and Maria? What had that filthy Andalucian said?
What was written on the postcard?

He sank into an armchair and, in spite of all his physical uneasiness, lighted another cigarette. I shall never know which is my last as I light it, he thought. He smoked, closing his eyes and trying to hold on to irrelevancies of thought. Whether this news was fact or fable, there was no help for it, nothing for the interferer or the fusser to do. All the external love on earth can do exactly nothing for two lovers. But ah, the shadows of her eyes, the eager, desolate pleading to go home! Such beauty hurt, such divine simplicity frustrated! By his son, who loved her. There is no proof. You are whipping yourself up again about an impossibility. Read, sleep, ring and ask where your wife is, ask her to sit and gossip with you here. Ask her to find a little flask of capsules that ought to be in your coat pocket, and must have been left in another coat. You are growing stupid in your weariness. You should never be without your precious pearls. Which coat did you have them in? Never mind. You don't want them. Sleep. Shut your eyes.

The telephone rang. It stood on the desk at his side. He took the receiver. It was Juanito speaking. He sounded very cheerful—almost nervously so, his father thought. Almost like a man trying a bluff—except that Juanito never bluffed.

"Ah, father! I hoped you'd be there beside it. How are you?"

"Pretty well, my son. A little tired."

"You sound tired. I'm on my way to Cabantes. I'll be at home some time to-night."

"Oh, that's good news. I had no hope at present. I thought you were busy."

"Two or three slack days. A good chance."

"Is Luisa with you, my son?"

"No, father. How are you all? How's mother?"

"Very well. The news that you are on your way home will delight her." Don Pablo drew a slow breath. "And the children too. It will help them. They are grief-stricken, you know!" He allowed himself a little laugh.

"Because Miss Maria leaves to-morrow, you mean?"

How decently he cheats, his father thought. No unnecessary falsehoods. So intelligently honest a man could be a genius in deceit.

"Exactly. We are all very unhappy."

"Does she go early? Is she packing now?"

Don Pablo paused.

"No. She has gone into Altorno for the evening, to say good-bye to some friends, I believe. Milagros is quite inconsolable——"

"Poor kid. You know, you sound extraordinarily tired, father. Are you sure you're all right?"

"Quite all right. I'm ageing, my son. That's all my trouble—an easy one."

"I hate you to talk like that. Don't age. Take a rest now. We'll talk to-night. I still think your voice is weary——"

"That's only the telephone, I expect. Where are you speaking from—Burgos?"

But they were cut off. Juanito was gone.

He leant back in his chair. He was amazed. Within one little hour, when he was at his most sick and inadequate, a whole undreamt-of story of his son's love, loss and woe were flung at him, in three quick jerks. And with it her story, whom he had learnt to care for so foolishly and tenderly. And with it the news that in sick humiliation he could come very near to hating his most fortunate, unfortunate son. Withal, half choked with pity, and broken by the knowledge of his own helplessness and life's obvious, natural working, and wild cruelty. He was amazed.

He staggered to his feet. He had no idea what to do or what he wanted to do. He wanted his flask of saving capsules, his little treasure of pearls. If now that pain returned that murmured, murmured at his breast, if now —oh Juanito, oh I know, I understand! Love is the folly of follies, visiting the dying too. Juanito, Juanito! God —I'll not see him again, or her. God, I'm dying. The pain will come any second now. Any second. I have no strength left. Consuelo, my dear wife! Consuelo!

He rang his bell with violence.

Someone came running, some maid whom he could hardly see. He clutched the edge of a table.

"My capsules!" he said. "Tell your mistress——"

She fled, leaving the door open. Dimly, he heard her shouting through the house. Then in the doorway and hurrying towards him, her arms outstretched, in her eyes the dear kindness of all their years together, his wife Consuelo. Ah, God was good, she was here. He fell against her breast, the mad pain drowning him.

"Consuelo!" he tried to say.

HASTA LUEGO

" . . . PER istam sanctam unctionem et suam piissimam misericordiam . . ."

It was over now, Juanito thought.

A dark-robed Augustinian bent above Don Pablo's narrow bed. The windows of the room were open and the swish of a choppy sea against the pier accompanied the prayers. All the lights were on. A doctor stood by a table where ether, brandy and hypodermic syringe lay discarded. They had failed.

Doña Consuelo knelt at the foot of the low bed; her eyes, tearless and compassionate, were fixed upon her husband's face. Jaime, the gardener, who had helped to carry his master upstairs and would not leave him afterwards, stood in a window, his eyes also immovably upon Don Pablo. Tears streamed down his cheeks and soaked his blouse.

Juanito thought that this celibate's bedroom, which he had hardly ever entered, might even please Luisa, so accidentally did it express personality. It was shabby, with white walls and only a few necessary pieces of furniture, brought long ago from the Areavaga house in Altorno and kept in use by this now dying Areavaga because of that origin, irrespective of whether or not they had beauty. Above the bed hung a photograph of Michael Angelo's statue of the Virgin and Child, and on a further wall another of the Burial of Count Orgaz. There were no family pictures, and no ornaments. A few books at the bedside. Juanito read the names of the authors wearily: Saint Augustine, Spinoza, Goethe, Aquinas, Cervantes, Saint John of the Cross, Bossuet, Pascal and Havelock Ellis; Mark Twain, Unamuno, Marx, Ronsard. How oddly he ranged! How little and much he believed!

There was no perceptible breathing. The hand Juanito held was clammy and cold.

"*Per sacrosancta humanæ reparationis mysteria remittat tibi omnipotens Deus . . .*" The Augustinian glanced towards the doctor, who came at once to Juanito's side, looked at the still figure in the bed and nodded.

"*Benedicat te omnipotens Deus; Pater et Filius et Spiritus Sanctus.* Amen."

There was silence. Juanito rose from his knees, still holding his father's hand. He bent and stared into the beloved, weary face, made a little strange now by the marks of recent agony. He smoothed back the damp, heavy hair from the forehead, and gently and without difficulty closed the dark, narrow eyes that never in his memory had cared to open wide on life. Then, laying the cold hand with its fellow, he turned to his mother, who still knelt at the foot of the bed. He raised her, holding her in his arms. She came with him and bent a second above her husband's face. "My dearest, my Pablo," Juanito heard her whisper, and then he led her away to her own room.

Mary did not leave Spain the next morning. She telegraphed to her father that she would stay in Cabantes until after Don Pablo's funeral. She could not leave the children in their first desperate grief. For they were overwhelmed;

Milagros wild and stricken. Mary had sat with them in the study on her return to the house until Juanito came to them, not forty minutes after his arrival home, to say that all was over. In that long-seeming span they had tried to tell her what they knew or could at present recall of the evening's terrible events. They had been idling here some time after five o'clock when the maid who had answered their father's bell came up with the news that he was very ill. They had rushed downstairs. He lay on the library sofa and their mother and the servants were doing all they could for him in frenzy, but no one knew what his appalling agony could be. The children broke down at this memory.

"Oh, such pain! such pain!" Milagros sobbed.

When the worst of it seemed over, they had carried him, the doctor and Jaime and strong Juliana, to his own bed. He said he wanted to be there. He said something too about Juanito having telephoned. He was not clear, but, "Keep me alive a little while," he said. "I'd like to see him again." At about eight o'clock he had asked for them, and they had gone into his room.

"He seemed much better then, Miss Maria," said Pilár unsteadily.

"He said something to us—'little daughters,' I think." But Nieves could hardly speak.

Milagros remained huddled in her chair with her face covered.

Mary could think of nothing to say that they would want to hear. She told them that Juanito was in the house and with their father. She sat, staring at Milagros' innocent, grief-bowed head, and felt her heart turn

330

leaden. "Keep me alive a little while . . ." They had been more than a little while under the beech-tree on the mountain, they had lived a whole life of pagan pleasure while he struggled here to hoard himself against their coming back. While he was dying they were recklessly and cruelly living. The pain and languor of that reckless-ness were still upon her, but he had fought another, colder languor in patient longing for a last sight of his son. Oh, had God in mercy granted it? Had he known Juanito at his eleventh hour? What had happened to him? Why, why should he be snatched from life in this savage way? He who was so gentle, so philosophic, so pitiful of pain and disdainful of violence. Mary thought of the first time she had seen him and of how his complicated face, closed and strange with narrow, dark eyes, had seemed somewhat alarming. It was difficult now to understand why she had thought so. He had grown into a friend. His wisdom and sweetness with his children; his detached, paternal benevolence towards herself; his slow, polite way of speaking to her; his grave, considering eyes; his eternal cigarette . . . ah, he would live! He must. This house, these children could not do without him.

"If they'd only come," said Pilár. "If they'd only tell us!"

And then Juanito had entered the room, and his face, Mary thought, might have been a white mask of his father's. He looked at her first, with piercing gentleness. She knew all that he sought to say of consolation and understanding and she tried to answer his eyes with courage. But she knew too what his message to his sisters was, and in this knowledge she felt herself become simultaneously a criminal, a stranger and a mourner.

The girls looked at Juanito imploringly. Milagros raised her head and waited.

"It's over now," he said very gently. "He's dead. He's at peace."

They were stunned and turned away from each other. They could not even cry out. Each had loved this father, in the measure of her character, as much as a parent could be loved, perhaps because he had never dreamt of such ideal exaction, perhaps too, in one of life's whimsical allowances of justice, because he deserved to be so loved. Each felt bereaved beyond her understanding, and Juanito, the bearer of the first heavy news of their lives to his little sisters, felt their own numbness creep on his, and was paralysed.

Mary turned away, went to the furthest window and leant out into the night. She would mourn him too, far more than they could guess, or she herself in this cold second apprehend. She too was undergoing heavy loss, but she was not his child and felt a useless alien now, cumbering the grief of his children. She leant out of the window, looked down at the little pier where he used to sit and smoke among the fishermen; she tried to pray for him.

After a minute she heard Juanito's voice again.

"Mother is in her room."

"Ah, mother!" said Nieves.

"It would help her to have you with her."

"Yes. We'll go down to mother," said Pilár.

Mary heard the study door open. She turned round. Pilár and Nieves were gone. But Milagros sat erect in her chair without moving, and Juanito stood looking at her sadly.

"Mila! Mila darling!" he said.

Her voice when she answered him was very childish and shaky.

"It's strange," she said. "I've thought out a million things about life, and I used to argue every possibility—with him. But I never thought once of this—that I might have to—do without him."

She huddled herself up again and her sobbing shook her with a pitiful violence. Mary could not bear the sight. She moved forward, conscious of helplessness, but unable to stand aside from the child's anguish. She touched the bowed head timidly.

"Mila! Mila!" she said.

The intervention seemed to reach the little girl. She groped for the stroking hand and clung to it.

"Oh, Miss Maria! Stay with me, please—I can't face downstairs and mother! Oh, let me stay here a little, please!"

"Ah, but of course!"

Mary drew nearer to her and looked for guidance to Juanito.

"Stay with her and help her," he said. "He'd be grateful. He could not have borne to see her sob like this."

His gold eyes, now heavy-lidded and dark-seeming, brightened suddenly with tears. Mary turned away, love and misery rending her. She bent above the little girl.

"I'll stay with you, Mila. I'm here."

"Thank you," said Juanito. "And you—don't grieve

too much. If you want to help me—don't torture
yourself."

He understood then—as always. And spoke fearlessly
out of the necessity to speak, even above his little sister's
head.

"Did he—know you were there?"

"Yes. He said 'Juanito' twice, and tried to press my
hand. He tried to smile too. He was at peace at the end.
He died only because the terrible attack of pain had taken
all the strength he had. But he did not die in pain."

"You're sure he knew you were there?"

"He knew. I'm going down to mother now. Remember, you must help me. Mila, don't sob like that.
It would have broken his heart!"

"But he shouldn't have died! Why did he do this to
us? There are doctors, aren't there? There are medicines!
He was young! Oh father, father, father!"

Mary dropped on her knees and put her arms about
the child. Juanito left the study.

The days of mourning and burial were a long, exhausting stretch of grief and ceremony. Don Pablo was,
though he had always refused the pomps of such position,
the head of an important and wealthy family, and he was
mourned and laid to rest with decorous ritual. The Casa
Pilár, shadowed by the funereal closing of its green
shutters, was filled and murmurous for two days and
nights with the grave comings and goings of many
relatives and friends. The long red dining-room was a
buffet where gentlemen in black ate smoked ham, drank
manzanilla and spoke with hushed reverence of the dead.
Doña Consuelo sat in the salon and, draped in rich black,

accepted the sibilant condolences of the ladies of Altorno. She had a stricken, aged look, as all these ladies remarked as they departed from her house in their Hispano-Suizas. For though she had never allowed herself fully to understand the passion of love, she had loved in many senses of the word the husband whom she had never understood, but whose gentleness and fidelity had been beyond all praise. She was desolate and in anguish, but she went through the formalities she respected with complete respect and with attention to all details. Pilár and Nieves crouched upstairs, teased by fittings for mourning clothes, alleviated sometimes by the kindly, graceful visitations of Luisa, who arrived from Madrid on the first possible train, and did all she could to ease Doña Consuelo's ceremonial burden in the salon. Milagros wandered between the study and Mary's room, unable to rest anywhere, bewildered and furious in grief. She had counted on her father. They all have loved his humour and gentleness, and deferred to his friendly wit, had trusted him absolutely. But she had grown on him, as a young peach-tree on a wall. She was his echo, he was her sounding-board. All her ideas rushed to him; all her ideals, all her knowledge came from him. She had loved him intellectually and friendlily, had dreamt of one day being a match for him and understanding him. She had counted intuitively on long borrowing of his wisdom for her years of immaturity. She was sick with shock and fear before her still immeasurable loss; her brain felt as if cleft and bled. And her childish kindliness had been outraged by sight of his pain as he lay livid on the library sofa, clutching at his breast. For all her life, she thought, she would see him thus distorted. Her distress was frantic, both for herself and him, and for whole hours Mary could do nothing but surrender her to it and let her sob herself into brief, broken sleeps which helped her somewhat.

Juanito had the heaviest load. Funeral arrangements, legal formalities, social and ceremonial obligations which fell on the only son of an important and respected man. His decorum was perfect. He attended to his duties as silently and swiftly as possible, listened or appeared to listen to the platitudes of Altorno, was observantly tender with his mother, sparing her all that he could of the great bourgeois ordeal of death. He knew her well and therefore knew that her sorrow now, though differing from that of a passionate woman who has lived in full concord with love, had a wintry bleakness of its own, arising from the cutting off of habits of unity and affection which have nothing to do with sensual love or with great penetrative understanding, and which would search her more harshly than marital love had done. He saw what the living, protective loyalty of her husband had meant to her unintelligent but spontaneous nature and how empty-handed she would be, deprived of an enigma she had never been asked to recognise. He pitied her deeply, but because she believed in the wearisome solemnities of the first days, he could not spare her much of them. At least they postponed a little the hollow, puzzled sadness that this bereavement had prepared for her.

Within himself Juanito held his waiting storms at bay. The fourteenth of October had brought him heavy and great gifts. There would be a reckoning. He would find time. But not yet. Not within this murmur, in this stuffy air of family grief. He was a realist, as he knew that his father had been. Grief anæsthetised awhile all urgencies, but they remained. For yesterday and to-morrow are as real as to-day to the realist, and life, while we live, is master of death. So though he grieved dumbly and simply for his father, as any son might, though he went through the secret extravagances of remorse and pity which sorrow brings, though he was overcome again and again by weak and weary tears and could not flog his brain to look awhile beyond the next thing to be done and then the next—yet his heart remembered and looked forward. Soberly, however, and with expectation of sobriety. For, to help that, he had found Mary's postcard—'*recuerdo de hoy*'—in his father's breast pocket, when charged with the task of setting his personal things in order in his room. He transferred it to his own, and considered the odd finding with gravity. It had blown out of her window on the afternoon of his death, and here it was in his pocket. He had died—as the doctors told Juanito now, causing him to marvel at his own blindness in not having perceived the symptoms more than a year ago—he had died of *angina pectoris*, seizures of which are induced by great emotional or physical excitement. He had himself rung up his father perhaps half an hour before his death, had idly and heedlessly thought his voice sounded strange, and had perhaps in his great desire betrayed to that quick intelligence the reason of his sudden coming to Cabantes. Then, while he made love in pagan frenzy a few miles away beneath the moon, his father, dying, held the relief of death at bay, in hope of seeing him once again. All that made weight in the heart and brain, and must be reckoned with. But none of it, any more than the essential grief it overloaded, deflected life's stream, still rushing past this frozen place, bringing to-morrow, carrying yesterday.

No one knew that better than his father, and as often as he could escape from the stress of officially mourning him, Juanito went alone to the shabby, monkish room where amid candles and flowers, in greenish shadow and hearing nothing now of the sweet, well-known swish of the sea, Don Pablo lay awaiting the mercy of burial.

At a quiet hour early in the afternoon of the second day of bereavement—the day on which at sunset he would be coffined and taken to the church—Juanito came to be alone with him awhile, and found Mary there, standing at the foot of the narrow, celibate's bed. He went and stood beside her.

Every time he had met her eyes in the last forty hours he had known that she was thinking, not hysterically, but in realistic pity and regret, of how his father had spent the hours of their stolen love in holding off death while he waited for his dallying son. He knew that she felt as he did the full weight of their love's fantastic, heavy anticlimax. Because of this and because he was a realist who insisted that what is done is done, he would never give her back now her postcard of the Holy Angels or tell her he had found it. He would keep it for them both, a sober pledge indeed—but love's reminder always, no matter who was dead. His father would agree with him that one day does not kill another, that grief's hour does not make the less of love's. She too, however her tired thoughts were trailing now, must know that anticlimax in its turn makes room again for climax, that what is true in us lives its full span, however many blows and sorrows batter it. He knew now, standing beside her, without a vestige of immediate desire, that nevertheless for good or ill he loved her fatally, and that all that he meant by that phrase would return soon to torture him, when she was gone. But so violent was his love and so vast his young sense of life's length and possibility that he was not afraid. They too would know each other—they were perfect together and fated. She would come to understand that.

She was looking at his father from whose face death's rigidity had now pressed out all trace of the last hours of anguish. Indeed, Mary thought, he is not Don Pablo now. Without the glint from the half-shut, sorrowful eyes, without the cavernous shadows from mouth to nose, without the dropping cigarette, this face was hard to recognise. She had come in to say good-bye, knowing all the family were resting and away from him—but there was no good-bye to say to this sad marble. She did not know him thus. For what she had done, for her great sin against his last hours she could ask no pardon of this stranger. To the true Don Pablo, she reflected now in weariness, to the Don Pablo of the terrace and the Café del Rio, what she had to say—not in justification but in pleading—could, and never would, have been spoken. He would actually have understood, she suddenly thought, the illicit thing that he could never have been told. He could have forgiven the unforgivable. But this lonely effigy was no longer he. This waxen thing in a brown robe, with rosary beads in its tobacco-stained fingers—there was no good-bye to say to that. Don Pablo was gone. Her hands twisted together suddenly and she gave a little sob.

Juanito laid a hand on her shoulder and turned her away to the open, shuttered window.

"You—you liked him?" he said gently.

"Oh, so much! I could never say. If only—oh, if it hadn't been that day!"

He looked at her mournfully, with deep understanding.

"I'm not trying to make things harder, Juanito; I don't want to be hysterical, but—it's unbearable!"

Juanito, taking her hand, looked back at his father's mask-like, unresponsive face.

"He is the only person I know who would have known what we will always feel about that."

"Yes. He would have known."

"He had a taste for irony."

"Ah, this past tense!"

"My darling!"

"Please!"

They stood and stared at each other helplessly, and yet strength came to both, painfully as with the evaporation of anæsthetic, from this look. For there was no use, their weary eyes said, in despair. Life's forces were mysterious and perhaps brutal, but life must answer them. Here, weary, crushed, at the edge of long parting after violent union, and alarmed by the harsh blow which Heaven had hurled on their stolen minutes of surrender, here hand-in-hand by the dead effigy of one whom they had both loved, they accepted, without energy to feel it, but only

with their understanding of each other and with a
strange, almost impartial appreciation each of the worn,
dim, grieving beauty of the other, that their love was
ruthless and would somehow stay between them and
prevail. Dreamily they apprehended this, without fore-
thought or plan—almost as if it were information spoken
to them incoherently by the stranger lying dead so near.
Something unproved, but which sounded as if it should
be true. Something there was no point in disputing.

The swish of the sea against the pier came up to them.

"I am going home the day after to-morrow," Mary
said.

"Ah!"

"I would like to say good-bye to you now. There
won't be another chance, with all you have to do these
days."

"It's not good-bye. You know that."

She smiled, not knowing what she knew.

"That hardly seems to matter now."

"But it will matter. Love is real. It returns. Griefs
like this don't kill it."

"Oh, I know. Love is real. I'll remember, Juanito.
I'll be faithful."

"More than that. You'll love me. There is no good-
bye for us now."

He had a little book and fountain pen in his hand. She
almost laughed at his ruthless common sense, by his
father's deathbed. But she gave him her address and he
wrote it with meticulous care. Then he wrote his on a
sheet of the book and gave it to her.

"But to there? To the Recoletos?"

"That is where I live," he said with the simplicity that so often baffled her. He certainly knew, as his father had thought, how to cheat honourably. She folded the piece of paper and felt strangely peaceful. They would do nothing savage to each other, he and she. They were indeed in love.

"It was heaven," she said. "I shall never forget."

His gold eyes filled with tears.

"*Hasta luego*," he said and broke into childish sobbing. Mary hurried away and left him to his father.

A MATADOR'S CAPE

THE train lurched through rain and wind to the Pyrenees. The sea on the north side, zigzagging into coves, was not silver to-day, as under the moon it had been a few nights ago. Southward the mountains rose heavily, but there was no way of identifying from here one beech-tree among many.

Altorno was an hour in the past. In two hours there would be the frontier—the end of Spain.

Mary sat in stupid reverie; memories from the last few days assaulted her without effect: Don Pablo's funeral, immense, amazing; Milagros' tears last night; Juanito all in black, his gold eyes seeking hers perpetually, in desolate entreaty.

She leant her head against the window glass and gazed out at the sea. Grey with white crests—just as it was all the week at Cabantes. Agatha had cried at the station— she never thought Agatha could cry. So had O'Toole and Pepe. "We're giving you a damp send-off, alannah!" All those *favoritos*—Ah, dear O'Toole. "I have nothing to give you," said Agatha. "I could think of nothing." Her face was desperately thin. Pepe's present. What was that? She was not to open the parcel until the train had moved. The train had been moving for an hour and she had not found energy yet. Until she was sure that she was past the beech-tree, she had not wanted to move or think.

She looked at the parcel on the opposite seat. She was alone in the carriage. She opened it. His processional cape. A matador's cape.

It was too much. It was the last straw. With a cry she gathered it up and buried her face in it. A matador's cape. She remembered her first bullfight and Pronceda going in to kill. She held her heart now as quiet to remember that as if again he took the journey. The moment of truth, it was called. Yes, like it or not, it was that. Milagros was right. There were truths that were indefensible, truths that changed and broke things, that exacted injustice and pain and savagery, truths that were sins and cruelties—but yet were true and had a value there was no use in defending. She was going home with a lame and hopeless story, a wicked story that would be agony to John, and had no explanation, no defence. And afterwards—she would take her god-mother's hundred pounds and go away. That was all. That was the fruit of her journey to Spain. Anguish and anger for everyone and only one little, fantastic, impossible hope. Yet there it was—a real story. As real as the bullfight—and, oh God, oh God, as beautiful.

Life was long; Juanito had a strange and cunning courage. His dreams—ah, they must be as they would be. The perfect thing had happened, the savage and inexplicable. She left Spain recklessly content and bitterly grieving. Don Pablo was dead and Milagros wild with sorrow; Agatha's eyes were full of tears; Juanito, dreaming, said "*Hasta luego!*" She was going home to her faithful lover with a brutal story.

Rain rattled on the window. As the train approached

San Sebastian she folded Pepe's cape and placed it in her suitcase. She had stained it with tears, and the heavy ornaments had hurt her face. As they slowed down for the station she read on a wall a last year's announcement that Pronceda would fight in the Plaza de Toros on Sunday. But the words swam before her in a new, wild mist of tears.

THE END